To Sense a Passion

AUDREY LYNDEN

PENSKE

For more information, contact: tricia@audreylynden.com

Cover Design: *Okay Creations* - Sarah Hansen
Editing: *All That Editing* - Lynne Pearson
Proofreading/Editing: *One Love Editing* - Sandra Dee
ISBN: 978-0-9973400-3-7 (paperback)
ISBN: 978-0-9973400-4-4 (ebook)

Published by Penske Publishing
audreylynden.com
triciaquinnies.com

Dedication

To my mom, Patsy Penske.
Thanks to you, I have a wonderful laugh, a fun appreciation for
Avon products, and a deep sense of family.
The best stuff in life.

Love

"It's such a happiness when good people get together."
—— JANE AUSTEN, *EMMA*

Chapter 1

DECEMBER

Lucy Maxwell's delicate nose twitched. The chow hall smelled of butter. A shockingly out-of-place scent, appropriate for the holiday, and much better than the air in the security entrance. She drummed her fingers on the dingy linoleum table while waiting for Julie to be frisked.

Earlier, when she'd surrendered her phone, hair bands from her braids, and a piece of jewelry into the basket before passing through the metal detector, her gag reflex got its usual workout. The small space always smelled so rancid. Because of the families, she sensed—with ragged and ruined emotions—coming through during visiting hours. They were filled with hopes and frayed nerves, desperate not to be turned away by the guards.

She had learned that lesson the hard way. Last fall, on the first trip to visit her incarcerated mom, she'd set off the metal detector with her underwire bra. An officer the size of a bulldozer escorted Lucy off the premises. At the time, she'd thought it absurd, but if she had been honest with herself, leaving the House of Corrections was an absolute relief. It was a horrible place for her mother to call home.

Since then, Lucy always wore the same outfit for visitations:

black leggings, a red sweatshirt, and all-cotton unmentionables. Before arriving, she sprayed her clothing with one of her lavender concoctions, and when stepping through the security corridor, she pinched her nose shut.

On several visits, she'd been tempted to try to sneak a vial of essential oil past security. Instead, she kept a collection of scents stashed in her truck. Really though, what could the guard do if a vial of her Soul-U-Tion broke and filled the tiny corridor with the aroma of oranges and cinnamon?

A young girl sat straight-backed at the table next to her, wearing trendy jeans with asymmetric rips. The girl's Uggs made a swishing noise as she swung her legs back and forth while sitting beside her father. Lucy assumed they were waiting for the mom. What a treat to be together with your parents for Christmas. Even inside a prison, Lucy felt a blissful sensation. She hadn't experienced *togetherness* since the day her dad had left them when she was ten years old.

The steel door inset with wire-insulated glass buzzed open, quieting the chatter. Inmates shuffled single file into the dining room. Their beige jumpsuits matched the color of the walls and tables. Lucy recognized inmate number 197241, because of her hair—matted, dull, and the color of dirty water. The knotty strings covered her scrawny shoulders. Julie's sunny highlights of gold had disappeared.

A swell of emotions passed through Lucy. How had a beautiful and successful artist found herself behind bars? As a sculptor, the woman wielded the flame of a blowtorch like a magician, creating incredible metal sculptures. Now, the only metal she looked at greeted her every morning when she woke up in a cage.

"Merry Christmas." She hugged her mom, making sure not to exceed the time limitation for bodily contact. "You look great."

"Don't lie." Her movements, usually calculated from welding, were slower. Sitting on the bench, she labored to adjust her knees under the table. "Why do you have to wear the same ratty sweat-shirt every time you're here?"

The high-pitched irritation in her question reminded Lucy that her mother possessed expectation levels that could never be achieved. Ever. She had been successful in the art world but never got enough attention. She'd sold her pieces on a regular basis but never to the highest bidder. Her savings account never added up to enough. So, when she'd collaborated with the world-famous sculptor Sinjin Reid, she coveted what he had—fame and fortune. Unfortunately for Julie, the sole way to get it was by trying to steal one of his most valuable sculptures. Her attempt had failed miserably.

"You love this sweatshirt. It's full of Christmas cheer." Lucy mustered up an optimistic tone. "We're together. And they brought the Ping-Pong table in from the yard. Wanna play a game after dinner?"

"At least we'll be eating food made for human consumption. If she can be trusted, my cellmate told me someone donated real turkeys for today, and a baker is here from the outside to make cookies."

"My nose detected butter, so your roomie must be telling the truth. What did you have to eat last Christmas?"

Julie inspected her yellow fingernails. "A year. I can't believe I've been in this hellhole for an entire trip around the sun. I don't deserve this shit."

Yes, you do.

Claire Beaumont jumped into Lucy's thoughts. She hoped her closest friend was healthy and sharing a romantic holiday dinner back home in Lake Bluff with her fiancé, Sinjin. Without suffering from the injuries that Julie had inflicted on her.

A little over a year ago, her own mom had stolen Sinjin's car (with his sculpture in the trunk) and attacked Claire, pushing her onto the sidewalk and hitting her with a handbag full of glass from smashed wine bottles. It landed Claire in the hospital. She suffered a concussion and deep cuts on her leg, requiring a lot of stitches. Yes, her mother deserved to be at the House of Corrections for three years.

Julie snorted. "I sat in my cell last Christmas. Since no one in my family bothered to show up, no reason to come out and eat."

"Understandable." Since Lucy was her only family in Wisconsin and probably in the world, she tried to remain neutral by maintaining a distant, cousin-Eddie-like relationship with her mom. The healthiest option for Lucy. *Her* life had been turned upside down the day of the attack, and she still struggled to turn it right side up.

A woman dressed in a black skirt and crisp white blouse stepped between tables. Black curls broke free of her headpiece as she placed a plate of cookies on each table and spoke briefly to the surrounding inmates and their families. Lucy appreciated the woman's smile and her sturdy orthopedic shoes.

"Sister Jan. She's a Sunday regular," Julie informed her, glancing toward the modern nun. "How are things going on the outside?"

"Great. I sold out of my Lust stock and—"

"Lust stock?" She grimaced. "My case. The latest updates?"

Lucy pinched her thigh to contain her exasperation. Would there ever be a day when Julie thought of anyone other than herself? "Same. Your lawyer is doing his job." And doling out one bill at a time.

"Wouldn't it be won'erful if my sentence got reduced to half? I could get back to my work by summer."

So subtle Lucy almost missed it, but it broke beyond the surface. *Won'erful.* The slip of a slur. She stared down at the beige table. How did an alcoholic in jail get her hands on booze? Cherries soaked in rubbing alcohol?

"Would you two like some cookies? Or, as they say in London, biscuits?" The nun sounded awkward. "Happy Christmas, Julie. Who is this?"

Lucy's heart melted into her snow boots. Hadn't Julie ever mentioned her daughter to this emissary of kindness and wannabe Mary Poppins?

"I'm Lucy, her daughter." She grabbed a Santa-shaped sugar cookie from the paper plate and bit off the head. "Her family. Are you British?"

"Oh, no." Sister Jan smiled. "I like to change up my message for folks and thought your mother had ties to England. She's spoken about a Sinjin, a very British name, I believe."

Julie giggled.

Holy fuck. Even if she were to get out early, there would be a lifetime of learning ahead of her and a lot of necessary sobriety to get past her obsession with Sinjin Reid.

"We're from Lake Bluff, Wisconsin." Lucy took in a deep cleansing breath and caught the vestiges of olive oil on Sister Jan. What a soothing smell. She used olive oil to make her candles, but now the aroma suggested something different when coming from a woman with religious faith. "Now though, I live up north in the cute tourist town of Baileys Harbor."

"I love Door County," Sister Jan said. "All those small, picturesque areas up and down the peninsula. It's like the Cape Cod of the Midwest."

"Lucy worked for Sinjin, but he was *my* protégé," her highness proclaimed.

Protégé? A dang lie. Julie had worked as Sinjin's apprentice. Lucy glared at her mother. Because of all her fucking legal drama, it was impossible for Lucy to live and thrive normally in Lake Bluff. She'd had to leave her home and start over.

"I'm an aromatherapist and started my business inside my mom's store. I mixed up scents and smoothies there. I created a skin balm for Sinjin," Lucy explained to Sister Jan. "He's a well-known sculptor and artist."

"Not as famous as his brother, Angus." Julie twisted a dull

clump of hair around her finger and giggled again. "He's an actor. Have you ever watched *Raven House*, Sister?"

"Why, yes." The nun sat beside Julie and gave her a beaded rosary. "It's an engaging television show. The mysteries are full of twists. I never would've known the actor was British. His accent isn't detectable as an American detective."

"The Reid brothers grew up in Wisconsin, so their accents have long disappeared." Lucy pulled another cookie off the plate, this time an angel, and gobbled down the frosted wing. "Mom, do you watch the show in the community room?"

"Every week, we fangirl over Angus Reid." She nibbled on a cookie shaped like a Christmas tree. "Have you seen any of the Reid men lately?"

"Not since last year." Lucy was unsure if knowing the Reids should be considered a blessing or a curse. However, George Reid, the family patriarch, had facilitated her move to Baileys Harbor, therefore she lovingly placed him in the boon column. "I've been super busy. Wicks & Balms will be opening in the new year."

Rubbing her temple, Julie left a smudge of green frosting on her dark roots. "Aren't you tending to my business?"

Lucy shuddered. How many times had she gone over the details? Over the phone and during visits. Julie pled not guilty, having no memory of the disastrous event. Since everything about prison came at a cost that needed to be covered, Lucy had sold the shop, Maxwell's, most of her sculptures, and the house where she'd lived in Lake Bluff.

"Mom, there have been a lot of changes. I'm not sure your lawyer will be able to have your sentence reduced." The idea made Lucy nervous. Where on earth would Julie go to live? "After all, you did hurt my good friend Claire."

"A fucking accident." Julie crossed her arms over her chest. "Why won't anyone believe me? She came after me, so I defended myself. That's why I hopped in the car and drove off."

"Even if your memory is fuzzy...the judge had the facts," Sister

Jan added with a sigh. "You injured another person, nearly ripping them apart from their soul. A dependency on alcohol isn't an excuse. Again, I ask, join the AA meetings I run on Tuesday nights."

Awestruck, Lucy gazed at Sister Jan. What a relief that the nun understood. Lucy's religious leanings weren't particularly defined, but after dealing with all of Mom's self-inflicted mishaps, she was dog-tired and would take any help she could get. "Thank you, Sister."

"Should we hire a new lawyer?" Julie's dull blue eyes widened. "I'm sure you can get one of the Reids to pay for it. Maybe Angus? You were close to him, weren't you?"

"Changing lawyers won't help. But changing your plea to guilty will." Lucy paused to navigate the chaotic line of questioning. Had Julie completely lost it? "The Reid family isn't a bank, and they're not exactly your biggest fans. And Angus? I met him once. He's an A-list celebrity who lives in LA. Why would you think I was close to him?"

"Because you two were mesmerized with each other at the gallery opening in Maxwell's."

Lucy squashed her frustration. Her mom hadn't remembered assaulting another human being, but she could recall the tiniest of interactions between her and Angus Reid.

"You're being totally absurd!" Lucy flustered.

Gus had been charming and funny, but the actor was in the midst of a torrid love affair with his gin and tonics. They'd spent time together at the opening of Claire's art exhibit. Lucy had simply helped him by mixing smoothies to aid with his hangovers. She did remember making small talk with him. Sadly, he'd worshipped his liquor, so she'd filed the memory and closed the drawer.

Another inmate dropped divided trays in front of the two of them. An unnatural smell accosted Lucy. The turkey looked like a gray meat roll-up. Maybe the cellmate couldn't be trusted because this wasn't anything close to a real gobbler. At least the cookies were authentic.

Sister Jan stood to leave. "Merry Christmas, ladies. Have a happy New Year. I'll pray for both of you. That you'll be free, Julie, and you two will celebrate together again next year. On the outside with a real tree and ornaments."

"Ho, ho, ho, Sister." Lucy blew her a kiss. "Merry Christmas. If possible, can we meet again?"

Sister Jan nodded. "I'll be in touch."

Lucy relaxed a smidge.

Julie plopped her head into her palms. "This is completely unfair. I didn't mean for any of this to happen."

"We can't change the past, Mom." Using her fork, Lucy played with the food on her tray. "At least the cranberry sauce is real. It's from a can and exactly how we love it."

She chuckled. "It's perfect."

"Did you know Wisconsin produces more than half of the cranberries in the US?" Lucy resorted to Wisconsin trivia to survive eating this single meal. "I went to the bogs while they were harvesting last season. The zillions of ruby-red balls floating in the water were beautiful."

When she didn't respond, Lucy focused on the plate of odious food and took a small piece of the slice of jellied cranberry. She chewed slowly to keep pace with the silence. Then Julie finally spoke.

"Sparks glimmered between you and Angus Reid. It's the gift."

"The gift?" Lucy dropped her fork, and it nearly bounced off the suspect meat. "You are hilarious. Are you talking about a wrapped box sitting under a Christmas tree?"

"It's intangible. No corners and impossible to wrap."

Lucy sniffed her mom's plastic cup of soda. "Have you been drinking woo-woo juice?"

"Ha, ha. Laugh all you want. You know what I mean. It's a spark of intuition. Like a breeze floating across your face on a humid summer day. Or a snowflake that lands on your nose, then melts. As silly as it seems, you can't ignore it. I've always been able to sense when couples were destined to be together."

"You don't have a new-age karma or Zen-like ability to match up couples, for goodness' sake." Lucy tried to adjust to this other side of her mom. "There is no such thing as a 'gift.' Maybe one time during a hippie convention...two people you met happened to fall in love. Or at one of your bartending gigs." Julie had lost many bar jobs from drinking while working. "You're not Emma Woodhouse. I'm guessing there were a lot of cocktails being doled out to the folks who bellied up to the bar. They mistakenly thought you were a love doctor."

"The gift is the one trait I've passed along to you. It will forever bond us. And even though I'm loath to admit it, you did connect Sinjin with Claire."

Already being bonded to her in every way had become exhausting.

"It's called science," Lucy argued. "I designed my essential oil, Lust, with pheromones. The scent is factually known to chemically induce or encourage physical attraction. There's no such thing as a DNA sequence for matchmaking."

"I've developed the *Anja* or third-eye chakra. It gives me the ability to observe the big picture and connect to my intuition. I know the truth about you and Angus."

"I appreciate your insight, thanks. My heart is good. For me, creating kismet is nothing more than business. I've survived because of science, lots of beakers, and no extra eyes." She gulped down a forkful of concrete-colored meat along with Julie's whacky ideas.

Any flicker between her and Angus Reid was pure nonsense.

Chapter 2

JANUARY

She couldn't afford to lose one drop of Lust, so Lucy clutched onto the beaker and waited for the wind outside the greenhouse to die down. Then, carefully, she poured her best-selling oil into the vials lined up on the potting table.

After dropping a pinch of lavender blossom into each small bottle and twisting on the roller caps, she placed them into the appropriately labeled storage box. Finally, she was caught up with the product since the Christmas rush. She turned off the fluorescent lights, took in a deep breath of rose-scented air, and closed the french doors.

In the main house, her bouquets of dried lavender hung from the ceiling beams over the kitchen table. Outside, stars streaked across the winter sky, and a layer of fresh snow blanketed Kangaroo Lake. Her new home, even though temporary, was idyllic. Perfect for a cold, crisp revival of her life. A great horned owl, one of her few friends since moving to town, stared at her with glowing yellow eyes from the top of the guest cabin in the backyard. Happily isolated, Lucy could have screamed at the top of her lungs without anyone on the peninsula hearing her.

Except, when the unmistakable sound of shattering glass

echoed through the great room, not a scream, shout, or squeak escaped Lucy's mouth. Only her heart pounded loud enough to be heard. With a trembling hand, she slapped the back pocket of her jeans to find her phone. Not there—she'd left it in the upstairs bathroom.

Stay calm. There has got to be an alarm system in this tripped-out house.

Just in case, she tiptoed to the fireplace and grabbed a couple of bags of ginseng roots. A few pounds of the knotty, rock-hard plants, strategically swung, could scare away a furry or feathered intruder...she hoped.

Gripping the heavy bags, she warily made her way down the darkened hallway and paused by the stairs. *Run up and call 9-1-1?*

Nope. Scary Movies 101—don't get trapped.

No alarm rang out as she neared the main foyer. Her trusty olfactory system kicked into gear. Nothing worse than the smell of her own fear.

Breathe. It's Baileys Harbor. It's safe. It's January. It's freezing.

"This house—" an angry baritone yelled from beyond the front door. "This is appalling." A stream of obscenities followed in a vaguely familiar voice.

She shuddered with a different kind of fear.

One of nine multi-colored windowpanes had been smashed open, and pieces of lime-green glass were scattered across the slate floor. A porch light glowed through the transom window, but her angle restricted her view. Lucy swung the ginseng bags back and forth like she was the next batter up.

An arm crashed through another pane. Red shards of stained glass landed near her garden clogs. She hopped back a step. "Stop, whoever you are. I'm calling 9-1-1!"

The arm flung up, hitting the jagged glass edge on the frame.

"Who the hell is in there?"

She aimed her ginseng toward the door. "I'm armed. Don't move. The cops are on the way."

"Good. Then I'll have them arrest you for breaking and entering!"

Breaking and entering?

She'd stuffed her lease, signed by George Reid, into a drawer. Although it wouldn't matter once she was murdered.

"Who are you?" she demanded, acutely aware of a haunting presence. "Tell me."

As fabric ripped across the ragged glass, she froze. A hand latched onto the door lever. It shifted lower and swung open. A beam of light poured in and spotted her vision. After blinking full force, the dots subsided. In front of her stood a beast wearing a long white jacket. A Yeti. A tall, furry-faced man with arms stretched out toward her. She held her breath and clubbed him on the shoulder with the weighty bags of roots.

"What the hell! My family owns this home. I'm Angus Reid."

Angus.

Shocked, she swung again, this time hitting him harder on the other arm.

As she stepped back, the bags of ginseng hit her thigh and stung.

She took in a gulp of air to slow her rushing adrenaline. Inhaling again, she detected Gus's scent. *Sweet. A fruit? Cherry.* After a couple of short sniffs, she also recognized the earthy smell of wet dog.

Cherries, wet dog, and Gus Reid.

Dang.

"Why are *you* here?" She tried to stay calm. "Don't you live in California?"

"Are you a squatter?"

Gus didn't remember her.

Lucy couldn't decide if she should be happy, sad, or utterly relieved.

"You're bleeding," she blurted as red-spotted feathers popped out from the torn sleeve of his puffy down jacket. She silently chastised herself for sounding concerned. The last thing she needed was for the wayward prophecy of Julie Maxwell to get rooted in her head.

But was it too late?

Gus had already been seared into her mind. At one of the lowest points of her life, the charismatic TV star had flirted with her, and although fleeting, she could never forget.

"Quite observant." He kicked the pieces of glass toward the floorboards. "You recognize blood. Now, tell me, who are you?"

Then, the FHW—Effing Hollywood Wanker, the nickname his brothers gave to Gus—grabbed his carry-on and slammed the door shut.

"Gus...I'm...Lucy."

"It's Angus," he declared disdainfully. "There has to be tape around here. My dear old dad barely moved from room to room without repairing something with duct tape. Hey, are you George's latest squeeze?"

Not an owl. Not a Yeti. Gus the lush.

"No, I'm not George's squeeze. How disgusting. Your dad is like a father to me. It's Lucy Maxwell from Lake Bluff. I'm friends with Sinjin? Oh my god, how many G&Ts have you had tonight?"

"Sober as a judge." He eyed her with suspicion, pulled out his phone, and held the light up toward her. "This house is usually vacant in the winter, and even though I despise it, I have to stay here for the night."

"Stay? Here?"

"Yes, darling. I grew up in this house full of fucked-up memories. However, I'm in a pinch. You'll have to deal with it."

Gus's sneering demeanor was outrageous; she wouldn't let him dismiss her. She'd started over, and no one, not even a Hollywood superstar, was going to derail her plans. "I'm not leaving. Again, my name is Lucy Maxwell. Not darling. If need be, I can get my lease to prove to you I'm not a squatter. I live here and have paid my rent through for the entire year." She avoided telling him that it was ten dollars a month. "I can call George to confirm."

"Not necessary, but who else knows you're staying in this house? I expected this place to be empty." After glancing out the front window, he closed every other shade. "For privacy," he explained while stomping to the hall closet. He rummaged around the top shelf and retrieved a cardboard box. "I need to cover up these broken windows. It's cold out."

"I'll get the dang tape." Marching down the hall and into the kitchen, she flicked on the lights. Gus Reid, why had he shown up here? What had she missed? Lucy dug out a roll of tape from the junk drawer. Grabbing it, she quietly cussed. *Angus Reid...People* magazine's *Sexiest Man Alive...*

"This house used to be a simple English cottage. Now it's on steroids. What are you doing in here?" He stood in the kitchen doorway and looked around.

She plunked the roll of tape into the palm of his hand. "Inventory for my shop."

"Thank you." He sounded somewhat civil. "That club thing of yours. It's one hell of a weapon. Is it part of your inventory?"

She thought a hint of a smile crossed his lips. Then Lucy blinked, and it evaporated.

"Ginseng roots." Irritated, she headed toward the broken door. "I'm starting over right at the moment, so I can't move out. Look, I know this is your family's house, but George assured me *his* vacation house was mine for the winter."

"This is plan B. My rental—near Cana Island, where I'm filming a show—there was a paparazzi van parked out front. I couldn't take any chances. So, my good friend brought me here," he said cryptically as he followed her.

"Filming a show? You mean *Raven House*?" She'd been sequestered and working a lot in the greenhouse. Still though, Angus Reid coming to town was big news, and she hadn't heard a thing. No one mentioned his name when she caught bits of town gossip while eating with Kat at the Beacon Bowl. "Here? In Baileys?"

"Yeah." Gus attempted to rip a piece of tape from the roll. "Plan A was to arrive without media hype, however, the fucking white van scratched it. On to plan B."

"Let me help." She grabbed the tape out of his hand. The cool touch of his fingertips reminded her that while Angus Reid may have been friendly toward her back in Lake Bluff, he was a superstar and obviously not on the same planet as her.

He laid his high-tech jacket on the leather sofa. Rubbing his immaculate ginger beard, he asked, "Shop?"

"Sorry?" She studied the wound on his forearm. The glass had cut straight through his sweater, and the jagged hole exposed a raw bloody gash.

"You mentioned you had a shop."

"Oh, right. Wicks & Balms on Main Street. I'm an aromatherapist and can fix your arm, however, I'm not sure about your sweater."

"It's cashmere." Sighing, he dropped onto the couch, idly tugged at the fabric around the cut, and stretched out his legs.

She bit back a nasty comment, ripped off a hunk of tape, slapped it on the cardboard, and covered one of the broken windows. "I have salves upstairs. They can clean out your cut." It took an effort for her to sound caring. "Might decrease the sting."

"Lucy Maxwell, are you on social media?" he asked, staring down at his phone.

"For Wicks."

He lifted one manicured eyebrow. "If you lived in Lake Bluff, why did you move here?"

She repeated herself, saying, "For Wicks."

How could Angus not remember her? They'd met in Lake Bluff, she'd fed him smoothies, and even her whacky mom, who was drunk as a skunk most of the time, had remembered their brief union. "Seriously, you have no idea who I am? Not even my Green

Gecko smoothies? They instantly cured your hangovers. Dang, that was only a little over a year ago." As she tapped the duct tape to make sure the window was secured, she kept him in sight. "I guess it doesn't make any difference."

He flinched. "I'm in the public eye every day and need to make sure you can keep my presence in Baileys Harbor on the down low."

"Yeah, sure." She understood Gus's nickname better—FHW—and fixed the other window with another piece of cardboard. "'Down low' is easy around here. It's winter, and generally," she added, giving him a stink eye, "pretty peaceful."

"That's what I'm counting on."

At least peace was the one thing they could agree on. Except this Gus, or Angus, was nothing like when they had met. Back then, he was gregarious and sort of silly. His attention, sloppy, inebriated jokes, and flirting made her feel better. For a short, glorious time, she hadn't worried about her mom.

Since middle school, Lucy had tried and failed to quell her mother's ever-worsening erratic behavior. Julie's creative soul was never satisfied without another cocktail down the hatch. Was this moment with Gus voodoo orchestrated from beyond her cell at the House of Corrections? Or her newly acclaimed *Anja*—the third-eye chakra?

Gus stood beside her. Way too close.

She inhaled his scent of cherry, stronger since he'd defrosted, and stepped away. She'd have to work to keep her unknown status next to the megastar. Gus's fairy-tale world of fun may have tempted her at one time, true. Nevertheless, she absolutely had to stay clearheaded around him. This do-over in Baileys Harbor needed her total attention.

"I'm filming at the lighthouse starting tomorrow, barring the weather." He sneezed. "Can you do something about the horrible smell? It reeks in here."

He probably expected her to pull all her plants down with a

bow and curtsy, but that "smell" was her entire livelihood. She changed the subject. "My herbs are in the bathroom. I can get you an ointment for the cut and lavender oil for your allergies."

"No allergies. The lack of real air on the plane gave me a headache. Or Sara's perfume," he said, following her up the stairs.

"She must have dropped you off because I detected a scent of..." He had forgotten her; why should she share another detail about herself? Her dang nose and passion for scents were her golden tickets.

"No, my friend Michael gave me a ride here." Shaking his head, he chuckled. "Sara's my publicist. We flew in from LA tonight, and she's sleeping tight at the Harbor B&B. The house that was rented for me wasn't supposed to be disclosed to the public. I know *ET*, *TMZ*, or *Access Hollywood* got wind of my arrival and are in town."

As an unknown, why was he sharing so much with her? "How do you know I won't call the local news station or announce your appearance on Instagram?"

"Gut feeling." Plopping on the teak bench next to the sauna in the bathroom, he brushed a fern dangling from a hanging pot away from his face. "Tell me, is there any room in this house free of leaves?"

"Probably not. I keep my *fronds* around me." She inhaled the ylang-ylang from her collection of Madly-in-Love candles arranged on the vanity for photos. Lucy retrieved her bear-shaped bottle of honey and two vials of oil from the medicine cabinet. "Maybe in the guest cabin. I haven't stepped foot in there."

"Fronds." Laughing under his breath, he took off his cashmere sweater and laid it on the wicker laundry basket next to him. "It's ruined."

Then he stripped off his last layer, a long-sleeved black Henley. *Whoa.*

His broad, bare chest and sculpted pecs made her tingly. She held her breath to stay rational while the bathroom turned into a steamy bathhouse. Opening and closing the vanity drawers, she looked for an unnecessary mortar and pestle to calm down.

"Nice," she muttered.

"My ruined sweater? Not really." He shook his head. "What are you mixing up?"

She forced her hand to keep steady and, with a baby dropper, placed two drops of eucalyptus oil and two drops of aloe onto a piece of cheesecloth. "It's a natural salve."

"Such hocus-pocus." He inspected the swollen gouge on the top of his forearm and then flexed his arm. "None of this will cause an ugly reaction, I hope."

"No." She flipped her braid from one shoulder to the other and discreetly took in his expansive upper body, bare and on full display. The intricate artwork of a raven scrolled across his bicep. It was incredible, but being fit and famous would never make this guy a keeper. Dang, how first impressions could be off the mark. "Nice tattoo."

"Only body art I allowed had to be done by a professional. Eddy Burk is the best tattoo artist in LA."

She wondered what the hell had happened to this man and then spotted a small disk hanging down his back on a tangled gold chain—an AA chip. Without booze, was he really a jerk?

Feigning ignorance, she asked, "Is that a poker chip? It's unique."

"It's a token for good luck," he replied coolly.

Angus Reid had been living in La-La Land—a world of make-believe where fake trumped real. How sad. Squeezing the bottle of honey, she soaked the cheesecloth and pressed it on Gus's cut—gently. "The aloe will decrease the swelling. The honey will reduce the soreness and expedite the healing. Keep it on overnight."

Gus tilted his head. "Aren't you familiar with Band-Aids and Neosporin?"

"If you don't want help, I'll leave you alone. I have to get up early." She unrolled a muslin bandage and wrapped it around the honey poultice, tempted to make it tight enough to cut off circulation. "You know, only an hour ago, I thought I had to defend myself against a home invasion."

"I'm sorry for scaring the hell out of you. When did you say we met?"

His smile appeared too picture perfect.

Fifteen months ago...a lifetime stolen away by my mom.

"I didn't." Grinding her teeth, she fought off his tempting charisma. She was unknown to him, forgotten, and Lucy had to face her reality. "How does the arm feel?"

"Sticky, but smarts less." He patted the bandage. "Will this thing stay on for the night?"

"It should," she replied, putting the vials on the glass shelf with her other apothecary jars. "I've been sleeping in the master bedroom, but since this is your family home...if the smells downstairs bug you, I can sleep in the smaller bedroom near the kitchen."

"Downstairs will be fine. What is the stuff hanging on the ceiling?"

"Mainly lavender. I have a variety of scents and make products for each one. I'm working on it here for the shop opening before Valentine's Day in the renovated schoolhouse across the street from the Beacon."

"The schoolhouse? It's a great old building. Prewar architecture." He put his T-shirt on, retrieved a towel from the bamboo armoire, and threw it over his shoulder. "When I see Sara, I'll ask her for publicity ideas for you. She's a genius, and she's made my career."

"Sure. Opening in the dead of winter is akin to business suicide."

They parted ways at the top of the staircase.

"You mentioned the lighthouse. Are you going there tomorrow?" She paused, deliberated if she'd gone gaga, and then asked, "I'm heading there. Want a ride?"

He studied her from the bottom of the stairs. "I'll take your offer since Michael left me without any wheels. Nice to meet you, Lucy."

The intensity in Angus Reid's leafy-green eyes and his somber expression captured her attention, and she trembled. Then it dawned on her—Gus's acting skills were his superpower. Rolling her eyes, she realized she was wearing the tattered red sweatshirt from her last prison visit on Christmas. Ho, ho, ho to her dang mom and her stupid *gift*.

Dropping into bed, she had to admit Gus's magnetism was tough to ignore. Dang though—his big Hollywood ego was intolerable. Good-luck token? Seriously? Anyone could tell an AA chip from a mile away. If only Mom had stayed sober long enough to earn one.

The last thing Lucy *needed* was to get tangled up with a famous alcoholic who had forgotten her, and the last thing she *wanted*...was for her mom to be right.

Chapter 3

Sitting up in the bottom bunk, Gus smacked his head on the timber slat above him. He'd probably been thirteen years old when he last slept on the bunk bed in the guest cabin. Last night, because of the strange smells, he couldn't sleep. At least, that's what he'd told himself. Even after many years, the fieldstone fireplace had elicited a visceral reaction in him. So, he'd relocated to the guest cabin.

He deliberated if he'd been more shocked by puncturing his arm or finding Lucy Maxwell in his childhood house. Under a homemade bandage, his skin felt tight and sticky. The sweet scent of honey had invaded his sleep, and he realized his crazy-real dream with Lucy wasn't a dream at all.

Regrettably, an overload of cocktails had blurred his memories from his recent past. He did remember encountering Lucy during his trip to Lake Bluff a little over a year ago, but the details were sketchy. It was a reckless, booze-filled week when his father and two brothers had written him off. Or, more accurately, when they'd tried to organize an intervention he'd avoided like the plague. His clearest memory was when he'd made it into rehab in

LA and learned his family had started calling him "FHW." An *Effing Hollywood Wanker.*

He didn't think he deserved such a callous nickname. However, since he'd gotten sober, he hadn't spoken to any of them. Who was he to judge? As a recovering alcoholic, he took one day at a time and owned up to the moniker. And he'd wholeheartedly agreed to film in Baileys—even if he preferred Door County cherry—because he needed to get home and devour a big slice of humble pie.

Semi-awake, he checked the lake out the window. The snow-covered slab of ice glistened in the early morning sun. He spotted the few ice shanties and doubted any of the paparazzi would go undercover as an ice fisherman.

Over toward the main house, he stared at his mother's beloved greenhouse. It looked as if plenty of plants were flourishing in it. His mum's favorite expression, *tickety-boo*, darted through his mind. It meant all was well. Unfortunately, she rarely used it after she'd divorced his father and moved him and his brothers to Baileys Harbor when they were kids.

A tall figure wearing black leggings and a long red down jacket tromped through the barren woods edging the greenhouse.

He grabbed his coat, wincing as it hit his sore arm, and shoved his bare feet into boots. Slapping open the wood-screened door, Gus ventured outside to make sure she was alone.

"Awfully early to be up." He scanned the barren trees and bushes as Lucy wound her way through them and came closer. As far as he could see over the fence, the home next door appeared vacant. "What are you doing?"

She flipped her hood down and pointed a garden trimmer at him.

"Careful," he scoffed. The last thing he needed before filming started was another wound for his makeup artist to cover. "I have to think about the close-ups."

"Of course, Angus. I'm collecting red dogwood because it's my signature color."

Her icy tone gave him the chills.

Loose strands of hair blew around her face, and when she swiped a gold one—one of the many shades of blonde—away from her mouth, he noticed Lucy's lips. They weren't glossy, stained, or oversized. They were soft, pink, and natural. His cloudy memories began to clear.

"Are you awake? You didn't lose a lot of blood from your cut." She crouched down and snipped off a branch. "When do you have to be at the lighthouse?"

"Not sure." When she didn't look up or respond, he swiped a fresh patch of snow from a branch and flung it at her. It landed on the top of her head, and the snow smattered down to her jacket collar.

"Seriously?" She scooped up snow and rose from her crouch in one motion, then nailed him in the shoulder with a well-aimed snowball.

"Whoa, did you play in the majors?" He rubbed his throbbing shoulder and held up his hands. "I give."

Shaking the snow from her hair, she swung a branch of dogwood and poked him in the chest. "You'd better. I'm working."

Rattled, Gus clutched the end of the branch. "Snipping trees?"

"I need loads of red in the shop for my opening. Remember?"

"Yes, it's called Wicks & Balms." He eyeballed the paltry amount of red branches she'd piled in the snow. There weren't many dogwood bushes around them. "You'll need to find more elsewhere. There aren't a lot in this yard. My mum loved dogwood...the flowers, sadly, they died out from the pine trees too easily."

He was pleasantly surprised at this recollection, still clear even though it was at least two decades old. The worst of his forgotten drinking debacles were recently procured from living in La-La Land. An unwanted by-product of his fame.

She grabbed hold of her bunch of sticks. "I've discovered lavender, morels, truffles, and ginseng up and down Door County peninsula since I moved here. I'm sure I can drum up dogwood. By the way, your phone buzzed this morning. You left it on the coffee table."

A knee-jerk reaction, Gus slapped his jacket pocket, the usual space for his lifeline.

"Thanks." As he strode toward the main house, he appreciated the fresh air and moment to get his act together. Tossing snow? Was he thirteen? *Idiotic bunk bed.*

Anxious to connect with his agent, Tristan, but obliged to contact Sara, once inside, Gus punched in his publicist's number first. While it rang, he looked around the kitchen in the cold light of day. He wouldn't have recognized it if he hadn't spent most of his time in the house as a kid. Baskets loaded with fruit and dried petals covered the countertops. Dried flowers hung like bats off every ceiling beam.

Sara's shrill voice pierced his eardrum. "I'm at the lighthouse. Cana Island is incredible. Where are you?"

He hit Speaker and set the phone on the counter next to a basket of oranges. His stomach growled. "The paparazzi found out where my rental place is, and I couldn't stay there. I'm at—" He picked up an orange, weirdly spiked with cloves, and hesitated. "I'm close by, staying at a friend's house. What time do I need to be at the set?"

"The cold temp is slowing the crew down. If you arrive this afternoon by two, Peter will shoot the scene before the sun sets. Then, you don't have to wait around and freeze. I'll talk to the rental property owner, see if she leaked your arrival in town."

Gus picked out the cloves and bit into the orange like an apple. Juice ran down his beard and chin. It smelled scrummy. "On my short list. I'm loving the cold. How does Lake Michigan look in this weather? Are there waves frozen over?"

"Waves? I don't see any. I can barely see the top of the light-house through the windshield."

"You're in a car?" Gus spit a chunk of peel in the bin and cut the orange into quarters.

"Yes, sweetie. I can't ruin my shoes in this snow. They're my favorite Choos. Leopard-print pumps."

He thought for a second about asking Sara to pick him up and then tossed the idea out. It would be best to keep his location under wraps. He needed space from his publicist, who was obsessed with his social media and had a habit of crashing boundaries while promoting him and *Raven House.*

This plan B was a stroke of luck. Only his oldest and most trusted friends knew about George and Rosamunde's lake house. Staying here, or rather in the guest cabin, he'd be out of Lucy's way, and for the first week or two of filming, he could stay under the radar long enough to focus on making amends with his brothers and father.

"I rented an Escalade this morning. Peter had a hissy, but it will second as an office. Plenty of room, and there's a bar. By the way, is Michael with you? Can you thank him for picking us up at the airport? Your fireman friend is gorgeous."

Hell no. There was no way he wanted his narcissistic publicist fixating on his good mate, who was, if he remembered correctly, in a relationship with Kat Orlov, the owner of the Beacon. And the reason why he wouldn't infringe on his best buddy's privacy by staying with him. He ignored her question. "Better mind your brother, as he's the show's director."

After ending the call, he sucked on the orange and wondered about Sara's shoes or if she'd already broken open a bottle of champagne. Either way, her first trip to Wisconsin would probably be her last because she was completely out of her element in the land of boots and beer.

The sliding glass doors opened, and Lucy came inside, her

jacket dusted with snow. She carried a meager bunch of red branches.

"Hello there," he mumbled through the pulp and smiled at her with a chunk of orange rind between his lips.

"How old are you?" she asked, smirking.

He took the rind out of his mouth and dropped it on a plate. "Mentally or physically?"

Snowflakes sprinkled about the yellow smiley face printed on the plastic rug as she stomped her boots on the doorway mat. She set the branches on the kitchen table and hung her coat on the wall hook. "Either. If you combine the two ages, I bet it won't close in on thirty."

"Too bad. I'm older than you think." He finished the orange. "This tastes great. Not as fresh as the ones in LA. I need to keep up my vitamin C while in Wisconsin."

She bent down to unlace her boots, and her hair tumbled over her shoulders. Gus was dumbstruck at the variety of colors—red, gold, and blonde—threading through her head of hair.

Standing, she gave him a quirky grin, showing off a pretty dimple.

He rubbed his jaw, relieved he just had to shave and not hoist it shut. What the hell was wrong with him? Less than twenty-four hours in his hometown, and he'd regressed into an awkward teen.

Lucy tossed a set of shears into a rubber tub, where he spotted more gardening equipment than he'd known existed. "If there's time, I can take you to a field where there might be dogwood."

"Really?" she asked, ducking into the fridge.

"If it's still around, we can go to the Coyote Roadhouse. There's a field on the property with a ton of dogwood. We'd go fishing and use the branches as spears to make the crayfish move in the streams." A picture of his younger brother, Rob, with his bright copper hair, flashed in his head. They'd often escaped to the Coyote to avoid their mum's drunken episodes. Of all the amends Gus had to make, Rob was the one he dreaded the most.

"The Coyote? Great hot chocolate." She closed the fridge and started pushing and searching the baskets of fruit sitting on the counter. "Okay...dang. I thought I had an orange set out to dry with cloves in it."

"What's wrong?" he asked, glad to be out of his head and back in the present. Then he realized his misstep. "Guilty. And delicious," he said sheepishly.

"You ate it?" Her eyes widened. "Oh my god."

"I'm...it was a really sweet orange."

Mumbling, she found another orange buried in a basket. "They're my pomanders to ward away bad spirits. I wanted to let them age for a stronger scent."

He wondered if there were enough pomanders around to purge the long-past and unforgotten smell from the fireplace that hit him from nowhere last night. "Well, I guess it didn't work because here I am," he said. "The cloves added a nice hint of flavor. Old family recipe?"

"Yeah, sure. It's a good thing I hadn't put the ribbons on them," she said, clearly irritated. "I want to hang them in Wicks because pomanders are supposed to bring good fortune."

He glanced around. "It reminds me of *Kiki's Delivery Service* in here."

"*Kiki's*? You know the movie?"

"Lover of anime."

"Well, I hadn't considered how it looks like a cartoon—"

"Not cartoon. Anime," he corrected her. "They're very different."

"Sure, thanks for the explanation," she said, with an evil eye. "Anyway, I do have to make a living, and if the image of *Kiki's* works, all the better. I need my candles, soaps, and oils to keep selling well. Especially my oils."

"The reason I slept outside in the guest cabin—" he said, needing to explain himself and struggling to sound rational. "The aromas were strong." As the corners of Lucy's mouth fell, he quickly added, "In a good way, and today, in here, it smells like fresh snow."

"Good to know." She grabbed her branches, arranged them with other boughs of pine in galvanized tubs on the hearth, and then rearranged them again. "You should be able to sleep in your family's house. If you're planning…if you need to stay, I can move into the guest cabin."

"No," he blurted out. The house he'd escaped and avoided after the demise of his mum was the last place he'd expected to be this morning. With his current state of mind, however, it may be the best space for him. "I was thinking of…hoping to have time with the bros on the down low. Trust me, I won't put you out. Just a week or two to stay on the QT from the media." Lucy was reviving a sense within him he found vaguely familiar. "I'm a lousy roommate. I tend to leave dirty socks around, so the cabin is best. I don't want to accidentally eat another orange and clove thingy."

"Okey-dokey," she said without any verve.

His phone pinged, alerting him to a new text from Tristan. He checked the message for an attachment. What he'd been waiting for, his updated contract, had come through. "Is there a printer here still? If I remember correctly, my mum kept one in her home office."

"Maybe? I've been spending most of my time in the greenhouse."

"Swell." He eagerly retreated back into his Nick Parker role and business. Lucy had thrown him off. "Is it all right if you take me to the lighthouse on Cana around two?"

"Should I wear a chauffeur's hat?" She followed behind him as he dashed to the old office. He suspected the fax machine was still on the desk.

"Not unless you want to," he said. "I'll have my baseball cap on though. Incognito."

She leaned against the doorframe. "Sure."

Until now, Gus hadn't known how a great deal of sarcasm could be packed into a one-syllable word.

Gus smelled a hint of lemony wood cleaner in the office, the kind his mum had always used on the bookshelves. A comfortable feeling penetrated him as he perused the framed photos of his family on the shelves behind the desk.

He chuckled when he spotted the photo of himself with Sinjin, Rob, and Maddie in front of the Beacon Bowl. Wearing baggy torn jeans and a snapback hat, he thought he was so gangsta back then. A hard look to pull off in a Midwest resort town.

Lucy sidled up beside him. "Oh, I recognize your brother Rob from last fall. He was at Claire and Sinjin's gallery opening. Is that his girlfriend?"

Rob and Maddie were holding hands in the photograph. He gulped down the guilt that had gnawed at him since leaving Baileys Harbor years ago and added Maddie to his list of those to make amends with.

"No, that's Maddie Logerquist," he replied. Just one of his true friendships he'd damaged due to his stubborn stupidity.

"Oh, that's what she looks like. Good to know for when we go to the lighthouse later. I need to pick up my Winterfest itinerary from her."

"Maddie and her family have a long history in Baileys. She's an ace influencer who recently moved back from New York. Her skills will give you a leg up with your store opening." His own history with Maddie was also long and complicated, something he needed to think about later, not now.

"It's more of a specialty boutique," Lucy said, looking at the printer. "Haven't seen one of these in forever. It's just like the model that was destroyed in *Office Space*."

He chuckled inwardly at the thought of the hilarious movie and punched the printer on.

What had happened between him, Rob, and Maddie was ancient history. It was a rough time; they had been reeling from his mother's death. On the upside, he'd made his way to sunny California. He rechecked his messages and printed the attachment from his agent—the updated contract for season four. This season had to be better.

Flipping through it, he scanned each of the six pages, looking for the addendum. On the last page, still, was the Single Status rider. He stared at the piece of paper and wanted to tear it up. He'd been an idiot, and it was his own fault.

Day one of season three, he'd shown up on set soused, and the tabloids exploded with photographic proof from the night before. His drinking and partying with one of the many stunning women who paraded around him in LA was splashed all over social media. Even *ET* got a hold of it. His fans, mostly women, became irate.

"How could the stalwart Nick Parker be such a douchebag?"

Peter had to postpone filming, and Sara had to reframe Gus's tattered reputation on social media. To save his career, he signed contracts for seasons three and four, agreeing to give up booze and drunken liaisons. His fans wanted Nick Parker back. And single. Consequently, Gus worked to resurrect his steadfast and noble character from the ashes of a social media dumpster fire.

"Everything okay?" Lucy asked from behind him. Her voice was filled with kindness. "You look like you want to kill someone."

He turned his frustration into a smoldering smile and hoped like hell she bought it.

"Peachy, as Nick Parker would say. Perfect." He kept the profanities in his mind from escaping. Gus had embraced a sober life for over a year, stayed solo for the past two years, and now he craved more.

"Great. For Nick," she said, sounding dubious.

He inhaled the lemony furniture polish to banish his disappointment and sent a quick text to his agent.

What gives mate? How come S-4 contract still cites the addendum?

A second later, Tristan's response came.

Peter and Sara insisted it stayed.

Gus caught a whiff of Lucy's perfume. It jarred another memory of her, and then it faded out before he could register it. The mystery of Lucy had to go unsolved. At the moment, he had two concerns: to make his amends and to nail the fourth season. Earning his life back was all that mattered.

Chapter 4

On Lucy's first visit to the lighthouse, golden and bronze leaves had scattered the winding road along Lake Michigan's rocky shore. No leaves today. Instead, angry, frothy waves escaped chunks of ice on the lake, crashed over boulders, and splashed onto the single-lane road.

"Did you know this lighthouse is one of the last remaining in the US and still functions?" Gus asked without looking up from his tablet. "This location is a brilliant place to find a dead body."

"Haven't you been here before?" A gust of wind shook the truck; she gripped the steering wheel and focused on her chauffeuring. This wouldn't become a near-death experience for her and the TV star wearing a baseball cap, Ray-Bans, and a Harry Potter scarf.

"Oh, yeah. Sinjin, Rob, and I partied with Maddie. There were plenty of all-nighters with more than enough Jäger shots."

"I've never been fond of that liqueur," she said. "The licorice is excessive, and there's not enough saffron."

"What's the difference? After a few shots, your tongue goes numb." When a torrent of water scraped across his window, he didn't flinch.

Since he had eaten her pomander, Gus had gotten on her nerves. It seemed as if he had no respect for her precious creations, and the pomander was a family recipe for good luck from her loving and delinquent mom. She tore off her scarf to cool down. "I'm looking forward to meeting Maddie—I heard she's been working her magic on tourism in Baileys."

"Her family has been integral in this town. They've provided funds for the lighthouse ever since I can remember," he said, his nose almost kissing the windshield. "The view from the top is amazing. You should climb up. The giant pines are dwarfed, and the lake is massive."

"No, thank you," she said, concentrating on the treacherous road. "Heights, treetop views, tall buildings...aren't my jam."

The lighthouse came into sight, and Gus thanked her for the lift. "Your driving is impeccable," he said kindly. "All tickety-boo, as my mum would say. I've forgotten about icy roads. Such a thrill to be in Wisconsin, where there are more trees than cars on the 405."

With relief, Lucy turned into the lot and parked. They would have to walk on the snow-covered causeway to get to the island. "Whoa, there are a lot of trucks around."

"Equipment deliveries," he said. "I wanted to finish another read-through of my lines for this scene. The writers have outdone themselves." He slipped his tablet into a leather messenger bag sitting at his feet.

"Can you film in this weather?" Lucy kept the engine running for her truck to stay warm. She turned off the headlights. "It's freezing outside."

He nodded. "The writers wanted an isolated backdrop with lots of snow. The storyline for this murder is reminiscent of *Smilla's Sense of Snow*. It's a mystery with an arctic backdrop. Have you ever seen it?"

"Yes." She was surprised at his mention of one of her favorite books and movies. "Does Private Investigator Nick Parker have a sixth sense for snowflakes?"

One side of his mouth turned up. "Nick has secret skills to solve the case. However, most are too painful to divulge to any other being." He added with a hoarse whisper, "Or he may have to kill them."

"Well, okay then... Does he talk to snow?"

"Not in the script, although I may try it out. We're filming near the lake. I find—I mean, rather, Nick—analyzes the victim's body near the lighthouse, where he determines the poor, dead soul had been dragged from the frozen, rocky shore of Lake Michigan: a Roaring Twenties and winter crime scene."

"I'm intrigued, *Nick*. Go on."

"You will have to watch season four unfold to find out." Gus gave her a charming smile. "Besides the outdoor shots, we're also filming inside the lighthouse. It'll be perfect for interior shots."

"How long until this season airs?" she asked casually. No need to go all fangirl on the *Sexiest Man Alive*. Dang, the hook at the end of season three had been a real nail-biter. "I mean, just asking for...for...my mom."

"Wait. I don't believe it. You've watched my show?" He leaned in close; they almost bumped noses. "Well?"

Unnerved by his proximity, she inhaled. Mistake. His scent today hinted at cherry with a touch of bergamot, and she couldn't resist. "Yes! Of course. I binge-watched season three a month ago. I love Nick Parker! Happy?"

"And your mum?" He waggled his perfectly shaped ginger eyebrows. "Is she a fan?"

"Huge," she said. *She gathers with her cellmates and Sister Jan at HOC in the community room.* "Your show has a following with her friends, too."

"Thank you. You've made my day. Let her and her mates know I appreciate them."

She hopped out of the truck and grabbed her backpack.

"It's cold out," he shouted, trudging a few feet ahead of her.

An icy wind slapped her cheeks, and she yanked up her hood and tightened her scarf. This was her first in-person meeting with Maddie since they'd only been able to talk briefly on the phone about the opening of Wicks, PR, and Winterfest.

A van, partially hidden behind a pickup truck, turned on its high beams. Temporarily blinded, Lucy shouted, "Buddy, turn them off." As she was about to give the driver the finger, Gus rushed to her side and grabbed her hand.

"I don't believe it," he growled furiously. "Somebody leaked it, and I just wanted one lousy week."

The side door of the van slid open with a loud pop.

She let go of Gus's hand. "What is happening?"

"The paparazzi have sussed me out."

Three men jogged toward them, carrying cameras with telescopic lenses. As Lucy tried to ascertain who or what they were doing, the door to another van to her left slid open. This time, a woman with a microphone waved at them, and a man with a video camera joined her.

All of a sudden, a satellite antenna rose from the top of an SUV. An older man with a comb-over hopped out behind his cameraman. As if a huge news story had broken, the reporter and cameraman stood across from one another and shouted, "Testing."

Then she realized Angus Reid was the breaking news. Except instead of a red carpet, swaying palm trees, and movie stars in tuxes and designer gowns, they were snapping pics of Gus among wintry pines on a snowy path and wearing a Gryffindor scarf.

"Why...is...this...happening?" Her teeth chattered. "Should we run back to my truck?"

"They've already seen us. If we, or just you, run back to the truck, the press will have a field day with speculations about you. And us. Not an option." He sounded truly apologetic. "I hope you can play along. I detest this part of my job, but it's a necessary evil. At least it's freezing outside. Otherwise, there would be triple the number of photographers around. This is such poppycock."

Lucy began trembling. She retrieved a vial of her scent Serenity from her coat pocket, twisted it open, and took a whiff of the lavender. "Poppycock?"

"My facial expression appears calmer with certain words. Can't say what I'm really thinking." He draped his arm over her shoulders. "It'll be okay, I promise."

To support her rubbery legs, she leaned against him. As flashes popped and buzzed, she squinted into a camera and then shaded her eyes with her hand to see who was behind the tripod. "Isn't he a guy from *TMZ*?"

"Yes. He's usually the last. My bet is that the local stations won the toss, so they'll head over first before the tabloids."

A woman, tall and slender, even though she wore a long, puffy down coat, strutted up to them. She pointed her phone at Gus. "Angus Reid. Welcome to Baileys Harbor. I'm Traci Berlin. WGBA from Green Bay. Can you tell us about your trip home?"

Gus displayed his superpower: glittery green eyes and a smoldering smile. "Kind of you to ask, Tracy. We're thrilled to film the fourth season of *Raven House* in this quaint resort town. It's a beautiful home, sadly not mine. I live in LA."

"How long will you be staying?" She sounded less professional and more personal.

"Depends on the director, Peter Boden. He's quite a perfectionist." Gus dropped his arm from Lucy's shoulders and then took hold of her hand. "My publicist has set up a press briefing next week for more talk."

Gus pulled her along, and they walked toward the next few people, close to ten, every one of them aiming cameras in their direction. Where had they come from? Were they hiding behind pine trees in the cold? It was surreal. Lucy wondered how long these people had been waiting, and didn't they have something better to do?

"Just smile," he whispered, tugging her close to him.

Gawd, such a 1950s ask. Instead, she wanted to practice her RBF—resting bitch face— until she caught sight of the bulging vein in Gus's temple. He wasn't as calm as she'd thought. Maybe he was unnerved—not as much as she was, but still a little though.

She smiled and waved hello to the cameras and struggled to keep up with his long-legged strides. After more waving and smiling and Gus's witty quips with most of the photographers, they made it to the *TMZ* guy. He shouted, "Angus Reid, what's keeping you warm these days in the tundra? Are you gonna meet up with your QB buddy?"

A Green Bay Packer?

"No, man. He's getting over the playoff loss," Gus said nonchalantly. "Doesn't have time for me. We'll get together in the spring at a golf tourney."

The *TMZ* reporter aimed the camera at Lucy. "And your story?"

"I...I'm, ah, I'm here. At the lighthouse," she sputtered. "With Gus."

"Oh, ho! Gus? You must be special." The guy gave his colleague a smarmy look. "What's your name?"

"Lucy Maxwell," she announced.

"Hey, Lucy. I'm Johnny. Tell me, how is it that you have the privilege to call Angus Reid 'Gus'?"

She froze.

Gus dropped her hand and put his phone to his ear. "She's my driver, Johnny. Nobody special. Don't let your imagination get the best of you."

Jerk.

"Hey, bro. I've got a Packer who wants to talk to you." Gus handed Johnny the phone, who chuckled and answered the QB's questions.

Lucy's brain churned. Was this the real Gus or a toxic side of Angus Reid? Or had Nick Parker made an appearance?

The camera lights flickered, and the clicks echoed around them.

"You are an FHW," she grumbled.

Glaring at her, he gave her a broad and toothy smile. "Yes."

"Props, bro," Johnny said, handing the phone back.

Gus shoved his phone in his pocket and waved at the paparazzi. "Looking forward to the press conference. Thanks for the warm Wisconsin welcome. Anyone have a cheesehead?"

A bright orange piece of Styrofoam molded into a wedge of cheese flew from the crowd and landed at Gus's feet. He picked it up and plopped it on her head. Laughing, he said quietly, "Walk like a rock star and go to your truck. Okay?"

She gave him a stiff nod.

"Thanks, all. Have to get to work," Gus shouted. "Don't want to hold up the crew."

He winked at her and strode toward the snowy causeway, the one road to the island.

Straightening her cheese hat, she strutted past the photographers and focused on not tripping or falling on the icy gravel. When she reached her truck, she hopped in, started it, and cranked up the heat. She wanted to scream, but a guy ran up to her window and snapped pictures with his phone.

Lucy pointed to her stupid-looking hat and smiled.

She backed out of the lot and away from the paparazzi. In her rearview mirror, she spotted Angus waving at the media folks milling about. "What a bunch of poppycock."

As soon as the madness was behind her, she tossed the cheese hat on the passenger seat and drove off slowly. The last twenty-four hours had been the strangest yet. She parked on Main Street and texted Maddie, telling her they needed to meet at another time.

A home-cooked meal and a visit with her friend Kat, the owner of the Beacon, might reveal intel on Gus's sudden arrival. Lucy didn't think she could take any more surprises.

Chapter 5

Sitting in the barber's chair and freezing, Gus rubbed his hands together and waited for his makeup artist. While Kayla mixed his foundation on her palette, he closed his eyes and let his mantra float in his mind. *Hari, Rama, Hari.*

The shouts and questions from the paparazzi had left a stubborn stain on his brain.

"Your jaw's clenched," Kayla said. "You need to relax, or your makeup will add on wrinkles instead of erasing them."

"It's fucking cold in here, that's why." Gus perused the dingy linoleum floor of the trailer for a space heater. "How come there's no heater in here?"

Hari Rama, Hari Rama.

"Chill out. They're coming. It's the first day on set." She began applying foundation on his cheek with a paintbrush. "Why are your undies in a bundle?"

"The local news and *TMZ*. They found out I'm in Baileys."

"So? Close your eyes."

He dropped his head back, allowing her to paint the makeup on his eyelids. "I wanted time to catch up with family before the press came for me."

"Open." She handed him a small bottle of eye drops. "Probably why your eyes are bloodshot. Drop them in. Then I'll dab. Didn't Sara devise an extravagant press conference for next week?"

"Yes," he said, dropping the liquid in his eyes. "Doing her job in her methodical way. I can't knock her for it."

Rolling her eyes, Kayla pulled out a trimmer from her apron pocket. "Whatever you say, boss."

He tried and failed to ignore the nagging question that had started when he'd seen the white van yesterday, then walked off from the *TMZ* crew to get to the lighthouse. Who had sold him out? It was a perfect match for Sara's MO.

As Kayla trimmed his beard, he held his phone above his face and scanned his Instagram feed. As far as he could tell, none of the pictures had landed yet in *Variety*, the *Post*, or *TMZ*. The frigid air must have slowed them down.

Gus let out a sigh of relief. However, as soon as his fans learned he was in town, the crowds would form everywhere he went. He'd have little privacy or time to think, which he absolutely wanted before he started groveling to his family and friends for forgiveness. He had owned up to being an FHW and hoped he could make it right. Even Lucy, who he'd forgotten, had called him a wanker.

Lucy? He wondered where she'd gone after their run-in with the paparazzi. He was fortunate that she'd played a fantastic chauffeur.

He googled Wicks & Balms, expecting a kitschy main page to pop up on his phone. But instead of flowers, oranges, and cloves, there was a polished and professional logo. Scrolling through, he was impressed with the website's design and discovered she'd sold several products online. "Do you know about a place called Wicks & Balms?"

"Absolutely, it's incredible. They sell this essential oil called Lust. I ordered it, and I'm waiting because it's on back order. Why?"

"They're opening a shop in town," he said, skimming over the website. He searched for a pic of Lucy and found an animated avatar showing off her dimple.

"When?" Kayla asked, excited.

"Around Valentine's Day?"

"Perfect, that's when my boo is flying in. I hope I can get my Lust in time."

The rickety metal door popped open, and Sara burst into the small trailer with her usual bullish flare. Her long red hair blew around her shoulders as frigid air followed her inside. "Why didn't you come see me first?"

"Shut the door," Gus barked. "I don't need to have Kayla add more makeup onto my red-tipped ears."

"Missing the balmy warmth of LA already?" Sara asked. "I know I am. This place is horrible. It's all North Pole cold without any cheer."

Gus glanced at Sara's wardrobe choices. A leopard-print sweater dress, no jacket, high heels, and bare legs. "This is Wisconsin. There will be a lot of snow, so you might want to pick up winter boots while we're here."

"Where? Stan's Hardware?" Sara snapped. "No way."

"Obnoxious?" Kayla muttered as she curled his lashes on one eye.

"Peter needs to talk to you, Angus." Sara bent over to slip off one of her shoes. She tapped it on the linoleum counter, letting the snow and sand spill out. After caressing the shoe, she put it back on her bare foot. "I guess I should have packed my Uggs instead of my Choos."

"Haven't you ever heard of frostbite?" Kayla curled the lashes on his other eye. "I have an extra pair of Uggs at the Harbor. Aren't we the same size? Eight?"

Kayla had been his personal makeup artist for over five years, frequently reminding him of life behind instead of in front of the cameras.

"Right, thanks. I'll meet you in the lobby of the lace and doily-covered B&B tonight," Sara said, staring at her phone. "Speaking of, Angus, where are you sleeping? The owner of the house we rented for you never returned my call. If I take the dolls off the sofa in my room, you may fit."

"You're good to go." Kayla slipped the eyelash-curling apparatus into her apron pocket and unsnapped the plastic cape sitting too snug against his neck. "The B&B isn't bad, Sara."

Gus stood, stretched, and cracked his knuckles. "Thanks. I'm settled in."

"Where?" Sara asked again with an edge he didn't appreciate. "I should know your living arrangements while we're on location. Don't you agree?"

A small ache crept up his neck, the familiar threat of an oncoming migraine triggered by Sara's demands. "I'm comfortable, no need to worry. I would prefer to stay where I'm at since the paparazzi found out about my arrival."

"Impossible! Did Michael rat you out?"

His oldest and closest friend would never do such a thing. Sara's audacious accusation pissed him off. He rubbed his temple. "Hell no."

Sara's phone pinged. As she looked at it, the color in her cheeks disappeared. "What the fuck is this about?"

She flashed her phone in front of his face, and there was a picture of him with Lucy, side by side, when they had spoken to Johnny from *TMZ*.

"I was forced to do my own media spinning. To get Johnny off my back, I connected him with my buddy on the Green Bay Packers."

"I could give a fuck about your furniture movers. I'm looking at the woman. *Who is she*? You're supposed to be single, remember?"

Staring at the picture, Gus recalled being so angry that he'd entirely missed Lucy's anxiousness. What had he gotten her into?

He had to make sure she was okay. "Nobody. An Uber driver caught up in the insanity."

The air in the small trailer seemed to evaporate. Kayla busied herself with organizing bottles of makeup in her cosmetic case.

"She sure as hell doesn't look like a chauffeur. She's beautiful, except for the awful-looking orange thing on her head." Sara swiped her phone, looking through a series of photos. "Here's another one." She pointed to the picture. "Whoever she is, she's all over you. And you have your arm around her shoulders, so don't tell me she's nobody. I'm going to discuss this with Peter. Your contract dictates that you have to be single."

A small gasp escaped Kayla.

The dull ache in Gus's neck crept closer to his ear.

"Don't bother. I'll explain it to Peter. Trust me, there's nothing to be concerned about. I'm fully aware of my contract."

"How could you do this to us?" Sara was on the verge of tears. "After everything we've been through? Three stellar seasons of *Raven House*, and you...you...have to destroy everything?"

Us? We? Is she delusional?

"I haven't botched up anything." Gus yanked his 1920s bomber jacket off the hanger, shoved it on, and flinched when the sleeve scraped his hidden, honey-coated cut. He tapped his chest to make sure his chip was still hanging around his neck. "Thanks, Kayla."

He punched the door and escaped the trailer. Outside, the falling snow twinkled under the beams of spotlights surrounding the lighthouse. Jumping over thick streams of electrical cords, he passed the generators, and his walkie-talkie emitted a loud screech.

"Snowmobile three is on its way to pick you up, Angus," his director howled. "We're ready for your beach shot."

"Ten-four, Peter," he shouted into the walkie-talkie.

When Gus reached the snow-covered boulders on the edge of Lake Michigan, he hiked toward the tent set up as a green room. Off his path, several dogwood bushes cropped up through the snow, reminding him of Lucy, and like a cold shot of tequila, he remembered the time in Lake Bluff when she'd cured his hangover with a horrible drink. Smiling, he yanked out a red branch, paused, then tossed it back into the snow. Anxious to solve another murder as federal investigator Nick Parker, he jogged over to the set.

Chapter 6

The lanes in the Beacon were usually dark and ominous, but this afternoon, they were lit up like a pinball machine. Instead of lavender, Lucy detected a faint whiff of leather. There were a lot of men bowling. Most of whom wore flannel shirts and reminded her of her grandpa. Thankfully, no cameras were around. Still jittery from her experience with Gus and the paparazzi, she rushed over to the dining counter, where a couple of other patrons sat.

"Hey, girl. Here's your onion soup." Kat raised her voice to be heard over the rolling balls and falling pins. "French-style, the way you like it, and I added a dash of your French herb concoction, too."

"Thanks for getting my order ready. What's up with the old dudes?" Lucy scanned the restaurant for cameras and inhaled the subtle scent of lavender in her steaming soup to keep calm. The bizarre brush with FHW fame had unnerved her. "I didn't think you used the lanes in winter."

"January day leagues for the fire department retirees." Kat filled her mug with coffee. "If you want to relax after working on your sundries, you might want to order takeout on Mondays."

"Nice rhyme." She scratched her spoon around the edge of the bowl and broke the thick layer of cheese free from the rim. The full-on aroma of her herbes de Provence blend happily hit her nose. "Actually, I wasn't at Wicks today. I went to—"

A crack followed by a burst of hollers grabbed their attention as it echoed from the vaulted ceilings over the bowling lanes.

She glanced toward the bowlers, where a Black guy with short dreadlocks pumped his fist in the air and then waved. He definitely looked a long way off from retiring.

When Lucy turned to Kat, her friend was blushing and appeared starstruck.

Intrigued by Kat's sudden glow, Lucy did a double take of the bowler. "If you're interested, I finished a fresh batch of my Lust oil. You might appreciate it; it's a great aphrodisiac."

"Now, why on earth would I need a love potion?" Kat blurted out as the shade of pink on her cheeks turned to fuchsia.

"I'm an aromatherapist, Kat. Not a witch. Lust is one of my top-selling scents. If you prefer, soon I'll have pillar candles of Madly in Love. They're full of ylang-ylang and vetiver. They set the mood perfectly on a first hookup, coffee date, or booty call. Whatever your preference is. I'm planning to introduce M-I-L for Valentine's Day. You two can have first dibs."

Mesmerized by the good-looking man, Kat murmured, "Who said anything about that fake holiday?"

"So, who is he?"

"He's the fire chief for Door County, and I have to notice him." Kat wiped the spotless counter vigorously. "I do not need him citing me for any kitchen violations." She arched a flawless black eyebrow. "Lust? Madly in Love? Your shop should be called Love Potion #9 instead of Wicks & Balms."

Lucy laughed. "I confess, I love that oldie. My nose for romance is my one superpower. It's my sixth sense. For sure, there's a connection between you and the fireman. I can smell it. I'm a wonk and gifted..." She paused. "Scientifically skillful in the ways of *Emma*."

"Emma who?" Kat asked. "You want more soup?"

"No, thanks." She finished without using a spoon, capturing every bit by drinking it from the bowl. "Emma Woodhouse. She's the matchmaker in the Jane Austen book. My favorite romance."

"Never read it. I'm a *P and P* girl, myself," Kat said. "Where were you today if you weren't at the shop? Weren't you supposed to pick up your Winterfest binder from Maddie? She's in PR, and with her help, your shop opening will be the bomb."

"Delayed today because of..." She vacillated. Did Kat know about Gus arriving in town? Lucy wondered what to say to her only friend in Baileys about her unexpected visitor last night. Even though, by now, the paparazzi had aired the video clips on the local news. "Well...um..."

"Hey, Kat. Do you have any beef stew left?"

Lucy swiveled around on the barstool as Kat's crush sat beside her.

"Of course there's more. It's my specialty," Kat said, seductively tucking one of her black waves of hair behind an ear. "Are you bowling another game?"

"All done." He held out his hand to Lucy. "Hi. Have we met? Michael Powell."

The Michael who dropped off Gus?

"Lucy Maxwell, the owner of the soon-to-be-opening aromatherapy shop, Wicks & Balms. Across the street and in the old schoolhouse."

Kat disappeared into the kitchen, returning with a basket of bread and a bowl of stew for Michael. She set them down in front of him. "Enjoy," she said and stayed put.

Locking eyes with Kat, Michael grabbed a slice of marble-rye bread and bit off a chunk. "Wicks & Balms is on my list. Thanks for saving that abandoned building."

"List?" Lucy asked, curious.

"I'm the fire chief and the safety inspector for Door County.

You can't open until after an inspection is completed and you pass."

"Dang, I've been stressed over boosting inventory for Winterfest, so I'm behind on my paperwork. Can I make an appointment with you now?"

"There aren't any other shops opening in the dead of winter. Brave as hell of you. You'll have to call the station to schedule the inspection." He handed her a business card. "Shouldn't be a problem."

"Don't sweat it," Kat said. "Michael grew up in Baileys. He knows every brick, piece of wood, and wire in your shop. And since his best friend is home, he's happier than usual."

"We're not supposed to talk about you-know-who." Michael shook his head, exasperated, and gave Lucy a sideways glance. "On the down low, remember, Kat?"

"Too late," Lucy said drolly. "You dropped off you-know-who at the house last night, and I live there. Renting it from Gus's dad."

"Okay then, that makes four of us who know Mr. Hollywood is here. Five, if we include his strange publicist." He wiped off the corner of his mouth with a napkin. "Getting Gus and Sara from the Green Bay airport was a cluster. It was a relief to get her out of my truck after she whined about the snow. Then I tried to get Gus to his rental house, and he freaked out over a white van parked a block away."

"Gus broke in and scared me half to death," Lucy said. "But he's been sold out. I chauffeured him to the lighthouse, and the paparazzi were waiting for the FHW."

"I wonder who tipped them off?" Michael frowned. "As much as he's a wanker…Gus deserves a week to himself."

Kat said, "Don't forget, he's *Angus*, not Gus."

"You know how his brothers call Angus the FHW?" Lucy asked, baffled.

Kat and Michael both nodded.

"And Maddie," Kat added. "Our stories with the Reids go back to middle school."

"My history with Gus is fleeting," Lucy said. "We met once, and it failed to make an impression. He forgot me." This caused her equal parts of dismay and relief. On one hand, it would have been nice if Gus had recalled one tiny thing about her, like—her hair. Or something. On the other hand, she could be sure a certain inmate wasn't mystically gazing at her and Gus with a goofy third eye.

Kat turned on the TV and landed on a local station. "We should see if there's anything on the news about Gus's arrival."

The newscaster announced another snowstorm and then rolled into a segment called *The Latest.* Lucy watched in horror as her face appeared on the big-screen TV above the bar.

Gus draped his arm over her shoulders, and she snuggled against him. She was all smiles and googly eyes. She squinted and stared at her mouth. There was no way she had so many teeth. Someone must have photoshopped in extra. And how come Gus didn't look angry or upset? She specifically remembered him being miffed.

Finally, the camera closed in on Gus, and the interview started.

A guy shouted, "Turn it up."

"It's true," a bowler yelled. "Angus Reid is in town."

Then, a few of the "greatest generation" guys stood around the counter to watch the paparazzi circus play out on TV.

Lifting up the edge of her scarf, Lucy tried to hide her gargantuan mouth.

Toward the end of the interview, the camera panned back, and Lucy, front and center, was in the shot and still smiling. "I have no idea why I look starstruck."

"More like a deer in the headlights," Michael helpfully added.

"Are you sure you and Gus don't have history?" Kat asked, staring at the TV. "You two have a hot Hollywood couple vibe."

"No, not in the least." Lucy struggled to cast off her mom's prediction. "The paparazzi terrified me. Too many cameras. And then Gus—I mean Angus—made sure to tell one guy I was his driver and a nobody."

"Aww, how sweet. Gus gave you a cheesehead hat!" Michael chuckled.

Frustrated over being a *nobody*, her cheeks sold her out. They grew hot and tingly.

Kat flicked the TV off, and the few gathered around Lucy dispersed.

"All right, the cat is out of the bag. A little earlier than planned," Kat said. "Gus will be great for business—the Fest and the whole town will receive long-overdue attention."

"True," Michael added. "Hell, if Gus needs alone time, we can go ice fishing."

Lucy contemplated her soft opening. With Gus in Baileys, the street traffic would increase. Although she couldn't open the doors early, her displays were ready. They were gorgeous signs with quotes about love for Valentine's Day. On the bottom of each sign, her website address was printed big enough to show window shoppers how to order items online. Lucy had to get them hung up in the windows ASAP.

"I'm heading out. Thanks a bunch, Kat." She paid her bill. "Talk soon, Michael."

Outside, the weatherman's forecast came to fruition. Big, wet snowflakes were falling from the sky and blowing around her. She strode across the street and headed to her treasured cherry-red truck. The only proof that she once had a dad was parked in front of Wicks & Balms.

A few people were looking in the windows of her shop as she approached, and she prepared a greeting and her standard Lust pitch. One guy made a quarter-turn, and Lucy spotted his camera. A paparazzi photographer.

She abruptly stopped. Before she could turn around, the guy

spotted her and jogged up. "Hey, you're the woman with Reid. Nice vintage truck. Can I talk to you?"

Lucy recognized the guy. He had taken her picture with the cheesehead hat on. She wanted to think he was interested in her shop but knew better. The jerk wanted her to lead him to Angus Reid.

Instead of turning to flee, she flipped up the hood of her jacket and kept walking. "Sorry, not sure what you're talking about," Lucy muttered as she passed him. Then she strode down the sidewalk without turning back and took refuge in the entryway of Stan's Hardware Store. She texted Kat.

Need a ride home. At Stans. You available? Cameras staked out in front of W&B.

Frustrated, Lucy scrolled her messages while waiting for Kat's response. It was ludicrous she couldn't get into her own truck or check on her own shop because of the FHW.

Her phone pinged. **Rescue coming.**

Opening Stan's heavy glass door, she groaned, then looked furtively from left to right. Her truck was parked down the street, and no one with a camera hovered around it. She jogged over and hopped in when a firetruck/plow pulled up to the curb.

"Hey, Michael. Thanks for the save."

"Not a problem, least I can do for you. Gus owes us *chauffeurs* big-time."

"I wholeheartedly agree." She layered on the snark. "I'm not a fan of being a superstar's little secret. Jeez. Harkens back to old Hollywood. Katherine Hepburn and Spencer Tracy."

"Will you be my partner on trivia night? Not many know Spencer Tracy's from Wisconsin. You're good." Michael gave her a high five.

"Sure. You have no idea the wealth of insignificant and old pop culture references and love stories filling my brain. Fair warning though, I suck at team sports."

Chapter 7

Lucy was essentially trapped in the house without a vehicle. Michael had convinced her to abandon her truck in front of Wicks so it wouldn't lead the press to the house and, therefore, to Gus. Even though she was a nobody to the star, Lucy assured Michael she wouldn't retrieve the truck until after the press conference, the FHW's big coming-out gala.

Her one day of celebrity chauffeuring had ended and been replaced with five days of house arrest. Fortunately, her isolation wasn't a big sacrifice. She'd processed back orders of Lust, distilled more lavender oil, and experienced a small miracle. Sister Jan had contacted her, and their conversation was brilliant.

Even though Lucy's worries hadn't disappeared, Sister Jan instilled a fresh sense of hope. Mom had attended an AA meeting. She didn't speak at all but stayed for the entire session and drank a cup of coffee afterward. Sister Jan, SJ, felt confident that she would show up at the next meeting—a few days away—and even say a word or two. When Lucy heard this, she'd happy-danced her way around the kitchen and called the attorney to tell him the good news.

If possible, with a nun on their side, the three of them could convince Julie to plead guilty. Instead of fighting a battle that wasn't worth winning, she could focus on getting healthy and winning the war against her addiction.

Sitting at her potting table, Lucy stared out at the frozen lake and then copped a glance at the guest cabin. She'd seen neither hide nor ginger hair of the FHW the past week. Only the early morning and late-evening sounds from Michael's snowplow alerted her to the TV star's comings and goings. It was as if, but not quite, her peaceful digs hadn't been obliterated by the celebrity house guest.

She opened the spreadsheet of online orders, and a sense of overwhelm seized her. It seemed as if she'd never catch up because sales of Lust were crushing it. To get a grip, she went to the yoga mat on the floor next to the yellow roses and started stretching. Sucking in a deep breath, she found the scent of the roses invigorating and focused on a cobra pose to open her lungs. Through the bottom half of the glass wall, she sighted a pair of hiking boots and jean-clad legs striding toward the greenhouse.

Her cobra pose flattened down on the mat.

At the door, which was decorated with strings of fairy lights, Gus peered through the fogged-up glass and tapped on it. "Lucy?"

"Knocking. Such a novel idea." After a couple of cleansing breaths, she stood and brushed the bits of flora from her tank and leggings and put on a robe. Feeling invincible wearing a kimono patterned with peacock feathers, she opened the door and smiled chaotically. "What's up? Need your cheese hat?"

In the morning sunshine, his green eyes glittered, and they were mesmerizing. How ridiculous. His muscular legs, clad in vintage Levi's, were steady and strong-looking. She cast out the thought of one steamy yoga pose she'd always wanted to try with a man.

"Morning." He glanced at her yoga mat. "I hope I'm not bothering you. I wanted to deliver this itinerary for the winter festival since, because of me, you didn't have a chance to get it."

His gaze swept over her face and landed on her lips. Her cheeks tingled.

"Thank you." She grabbed the canary-yellow binder and was surprised at the weight of it. "Wow, this is heavy."

"My binder is thicker." He entered her sanctuary. "Don't get jealous."

"Um. I was working...in the middle of work."

"You brought my mother's conservatory back to life." Ignoring her comment, he strolled around and stopped to rub a sage leaf between his fingers. "It's nice. I'm sure George never appreciated Mum's love of flowers. How many weeds did you pull to get this up and running?"

After setting the binder next to her open laptop, she glanced at the screensaver.

"Have enough courage to trust love one more time and always one more time."

She gently closed the cover on the Maya Angelou quote.

"A day-long affair. I threw out enough shards of broken pottery to fill at least six recycling bags. I had to make room for this baby."

She patted her copper distillery.

"It's beautiful." He touched the copper tubing jutting out of the still. "One of Sinjin's masterpieces?"

"Well, yes," she said warily. "Your brother was a good friend."

"Was?" Gus asked as he eyed the prop table where she took photos for her website.

Pissed at herself for letting "was" slip out, she wandered around in a feeble attempt to protect her plants which were her livelihood. After leaving Lake Bluff and her closest friends, it was all she had left. "Since moving to Baileys, I haven't spoken to your brother."

When he laid his eyes on her boxes of Lust vials, she wanted to growl like a protective lioness. "Please don't touch those. They're precious."

Gus held up his hands in retreat. "I want to say that the name Lust beats Lush."

Lucy's mouth dropped open. "You remember? Unbelievable."

The air of flora became stifling as she gawked at Gus.

He gifted her with a genuine smile. "It's a bit muddled, yes, though I recall a party or two in Lake Bluff. And an art exhibit, the opening of Claire's show. You and I were in your juice bar. Weren't you the bartender?"

Equally stunned and saddened, Lucy nodded. He remembered her juice bar, Lulu's, and she still ached over having to sell it along with the vintage shop, Maxwell's. "One of my many jobs when I lived in Lake Bluff. The good old days—bartending and serving hors d'oeuvres at Sinjin's art exhibitions."

"You mixed me several delicious gin and tonics," he said, tapping his chest. "Alas, I overindulged. Probably why my memory of meeting you was buried. My apologies."

She shuddered at his heartfelt apology. "Well, my expertise in mixing love potions isn't limited to essential oils. I had to start somewhere." She tossed the braid off her shoulder. "And you were a fantastic listener. It was a tough choice between Lush or Lust. I mean, the name for my signature scent had to reflect many elements."

"Understandable. Why did Lust win?" he asked while poking and prodding the rose bushes.

She stared at the copper oil distillery. "Lust won because of Sinjin and Claire, my best friends. Their connection became a true bond of love, and they've been inseparable since. A testament to the power of my lavender-based scents. True, the two of them are like yin and yang, meant to be together...but thanks to Lust, I became my own boss, and Wicks was born."

Gus gave her a quick smile. "My makeup artist, Kayla, is waiting for her order."

"What's her last name?" She leaned back against the table to protect her precious vials and found her phone. "Luckily, I'm trapped here. Easy to get caught up on my back orders."

"Quinn," he replied. "Michael mentioned the loss of your wheels. When we came upon the paparazzi, it was a surprise for me, and I'm sure a total shock for you. I'm sorry. I know *TMZ* and Johnny would have followed it and found me. I've been able to have a few days of anonymity. Which is huge, so thank you."

"I'm glad you've enjoyed being invisible. Can you give me an ETA on its return?"

"After the press conference."

She added, "Can you tell me, am I talking to Gus or Angus?"

He shrugged and smiled sheepishly. "It's Gus. May I?" He stepped over to the yoga mat and kicked off his boots. With hands in praying mode, he said, "Namaste."

He dropped into a downward dog pose and then folded his legs beneath his chest, letting his arms support his entire body.

"Impressive," she said, struggling to hide how awestruck she was at his stunning physique. "I'd break both arms if I tried a crow pose, dude. Really, extra."

As he came out of the pose, his AA chip slipped from his shirt.

She averted her eyes and stroked a rose. "These will be perfect for my bath sachets after I dry them."

"You are the one person who knows about my love for yoga. Actually, second, if you count my guru, Robert." Standing beside her, he pointed toward a spectacular yellow blossom. "You're right. It's a tea rose, and they're very fragrant. Named *Graham Thomas*. My mother grew them for my Uncle Graham."

"You're a rose lover? Am I playing second fiddle to Robert about that, too?"

"Can't say for sure. I suspect Robert may be a gardener between working on his flicks."

"Robert D. Jr. is your yogi master? Oh my god, I want to...I don't know...scream? Faint?"

"Go ahead and scream—no one's around. And if you faint, I'll make sure you don't hit the ground too hard." He winked.

"*The Iron Man!*"

Gus held out his arms to prepare to catch her in case she fainted.

She held herself upright and didn't need to drop into his arms, but she was curious. Instead, she plopped onto a green velvet settee. "I'm suffering from a permanent case of awe."

Chuckling, he sat beside her. "What? I don't do it for you?"

She sucked in a breath from his proximity. "It's just, you're holding my truck hostage, and RDJ...he's a Hollywood icon."

"He's also a survivor and a good friend. I want you to know it's true. I'm grateful to you for not letting anyone know I'm staying here." He patted his chest, hesitated, then spoke. "This is my AA chip, and I've been sober for over a year. Another *pose* Robert helped me with."

Gus's honesty sent shivers through her. "It's not a token for good luck?"

"About my tiny fib—well, I was on auto-defense. I'm learning, day by day, how to be honest. It's a skill I haven't used often, and it's frowned upon in Hollywood. Speaking of, by any chance, would you like to attend the press conference for *Raven House*?"

"I don't know. I mean...when you put the cheesehead hat on my head, I looked ridiculous." She pressed a finger on her upper lip and mumbled, "Also, those photographers freaked me out. I'm sure they air-brushed extra teeth into my mouth."

"You won't have to wear a cheesehead. And I'm certain there weren't teeth added in the pics. This will make up for what I put you through the other day. The stars of the show will be on the panel. You can sit front and center and, after, get a few selfies. And because you're the owner of Wicks & Balms, I think—no, *I know* —there are members of the production team who would love to meet you."

She pushed down a fear of becoming fodder for small-town

gossip. Her brick-and-mortar needed attention, love, and recognition. She'd do anything for Wicks. "I'll think about it. Where's it being held?"

"At the golf club, Maxwelton Braes, this Tuesday." He scrolled through his phone. "I'll introduce you to everyone."

"No, please, you don't have to do that. I just want my truck back."

"Okay, no to intros and yes to wheels." He held up his hands to surrender. "Whatever you want, Lucy."

She shrugged as if it were just another day when she'd meet a bunch of TV stars. Except...what would she wear? Or say? It had been a while since she'd gone anywhere alone and had to make small talk. She needed reinforcements. "Will Kat or Michael be there?"

"I reckon. When Michael picks me up, I'll make sure." With a cocky smile, he added, "And if Michael attends, Kat will, too."

Astonished at his goofy expression, she had to ask, "Why? I'm not trying to be nosy, ha." She pointed to her nose. "But I have a sense about Michael and Kat."

"Do you feel they're another Sinjin and Claire?"

"Exactly! They are meant to be together." Lucy relaxed. "I know those two are simpatico. I offered up Lust to Kat the other day, and she refused."

"Doesn't surprise me. Those two have been pulling daisy petals since we were in high school. *Does she love me, or does he not*? All talk and no action. Yada."

Lucy laughed. "So, you're an expert on love, too?"

"Well...I...don't..." His cheeks turned pink. "Michael and Kat are good people. True friends." He plucked a petal off one of the rose plants behind him. "Do you know what the yellow rose means?"

"I'm about the smells, I'm afraid." She clamped her lips closed to hide a silly grin. She appreciated how Gus—this *real* Gus—was speaking. Unaffected.

"As my mum's favorite son, I spent a lot of time in here with her. Her name? *Rosa*munde. I'm serious. *Rose*-a-munde. Anyway, in the Victorian days, yellow roses symbolized jealousy. Again, I want to emphasize that this knowledge is based on my very British mother with *British Rose*–DNA, who used expressions like tickety-boo."

Lucy sensed a note of sadness while he spoke. She picked up that he was being genuine and talking off-script. "Tickety-boo, I like it."

"However, now, the yellow roses represent joy and friendship and positivity because of their," he said, using air quotes, "sunny disposition."

One of her pervasive *Emma* thoughts flew out of her mouth. "Okay, it makes sense for me to add more dried rose petals into my sachets. Those two need a little love-nudging."

"Love-nudging? Is that a technical term in the aromatherapy dictionary? After 'love bunnies'?" He stared at her, reminding her of a cartoon hypnotist. "And most importantly, goo-goo eyes better be in your handbook."

A tingling heat spread through her cheeks, and she patted them, hoping to stave off the blush. "Kat is in love with Michael. I'm sure of it. Michael though? I just met him."

Crossing his arms over his chest, again, she was impressed by his pecs and how he'd achieved a crow pose in seconds.

"Michael's got it bad for Kat. I can confirm it for you. Or, should I say, Michael the fireman has been *carrying a torch* for Kat? Another term in your love glossary?"

"I'm glad you agree." She chuckled. I'll dig out a sachet, and you can give it to Michael to hang on the rearview mirror in his truck."

"Next to the fuzzy dice? Are you a love doctor from 1970?"

"Well, it's a thing. I love seeing people get together," she said, feeling awkward. "I just have a superpower similar to *Emma*, and I'm good with mixing pheromones."

Gus shook his head and laughed. "I love it. Emma Woodhouse. I'm on board with your love-nudging."

"You get it?"

"Hell, yes. *Emma* was one of Gwyneth's best performances."

"Right. I should have known you'd have the Hollywood insider info on the Goop queen." She grabbed her garden clogs off a bench and slipped them on. "Here's the real deal. Don't ever doubt the power of love. It's Mother Earth's best balm. The way of the world."

"I understand. How can I help," he asked, "before I take off for the lighthouse?"

She found a sachet and gave it a fresh spritz from an aerosol of Lust. "Kat, being the female, is more overt with her emotions. Michael, his emotions are probably stuffed down in an old shoebox in the back of his brain. When they gazed at each other—yes, gazed—I witnessed it. True and pure."

Gus swung the sachet of dried flowers on the tip of his finger. "Michael and Kat. Together. Forever. I've got it. Can I take the spray bottle, too? Michael's truck smells of Lewis, his dog."

"Sure." She handed him a brown glass bottle of Lust. "It's not as potent as the oil. However, it's completely worthy of our love-nudging objective. And"—she nodded—"it will subdue the smell in Michael's truck. I'm good, but not that good."

"I disagree." Gus looked around the greenhouse. "Okay, Ms. Emma. I'll be your sidekick. But...no tights," he chuckled. "Real men do not wear tights."

Before leaving, he tapped the yellow binder. "Make sure to connect with Maddie. There's a lot you can do for the shop during Winterfest."

"Thanks."

He strode out and put on his Ray-Bans.

Lucy was struck by a sense of awe and then pushed Gus out of her thoughts. No longer feeling overwhelmed, she opened her laptop and filled her orders for Lust.

Chapter 8

At the entrance of the banquet hall in Maxwelton Braes, Lucy slipped her phone into her vintage, pink quilted faux Chanel handbag.

"Name?" a security guard holding a tablet asked.

"Lucy Maxwell." She gawked at the paparazzi inside the room.

"Oh, here you are," the guard said, "on page ten."

She glanced at the list on his device. Her name was highlighted in yellow. "What's the color highlight about?"

He pointed into the crowded room. "You're seated at the table with the yellow cloth. Up front."

She followed the slim, open path around the perimeter. All the tables were occupied, each covered in a different-colored cloth. It created a festive atmosphere, and she had arrived last to the party. How could an Uber be so dang late in Baileys with a paltry population of a thousand?

I'm here for my truck. She flipped up the lapels of her furry black coat and passed the fireplace. The blazing fire in the mammoth fieldstone hearth made the huge room feel cozy. She inhaled the smell of toasting birch and pine cones. When she reached her table, she sat beside Kat.

"Hey," Kat said, "this is ace."

"Hi." She waved at Michael, who sat on the other side of Kat. "Any word on my truck?"

"Gus has your keys," he said. "He'll pass them to you after this shindig."

Across the table, a woman with sleek black hair stared down at her phone. She reminded her of Claire.

Looking up, the woman spotted Lucy and waved. "Cheers, I'm Maddie Logerquist."

Lucy blinked and cast off the small tug on her heart. She really missed her good friend. With all the changes and then the move from Lake Bluff, she'd lost touch with Claire. Now more settled, she would eventually have to respond to Claire's comments on the Wicks Instagram posts. The thought made her nervous as hell. After what her mother had put Claire through, Lucy felt guilty and found it easier to be friends with Lust than with other humans.

"Hey, Maddie, nice to finally meet you in person. I have the binder. Haven't had a chance to go through it though."

"Wicks & Balms is the star of this year's Winterfest. Please don't freak out when you see the list of activities I've included you and your shop in."

The overhead lights blinked off and on, so the two women exchanged contact info and waited for the press conference to begin.

Up front, two long tables were set on a stage with risers. Arranged for the TV stars, it looked ready to welcome a wedding party. Instead of champagne glasses, each spot had a microphone alongside the place cards. The card dead center belonged to Angus Reid.

As a few more latecomers arrived, Lucy glanced around the room and recognized the local news reporters and the dude from *TMZ*. Two tables over, Lucy saw the famous football player who was friends with Gus. To his right was a blonde who looked vaguely familiar. Maybe one of her followers on Instagram?

"Who is the woman next to the Green Bay Packer?" Lucy asked Kat.

"No idea. Don't do sports," she replied.

"It looks as if we've been color-coordinated." Maddie pointed at the purple tables. "Those are owners of Door County businesses. Not sure why their tables are draped in purple. I get green for the football players and red for the show's costume and makeup crew."

"How come I'm at the yellow table?" Lucy asked. "Because Wicks isn't open yet?"

"You're front and *yellow* to be with us. Gus's..." Maddie shook her head and then self-corrected. "*Angus's* friends in Baileys."

Lucy wasn't sure how to absorb this info since Gus had only recently remembered her. Acquaintance seemed more appropriate. "Who are the people at the orange table? Artisans?"

"Sort of," Kat said. "They're from the local theater group, the Peninsula Players. Where Gus started acting."

"News flash," Michael leaned around Kat to address Lucy. "Gus hung around the Peninsula Players, and I could only get him to leave to go ice fishing in the winter."

"And now he's famous," Kat added.

"I'm sure it's from his expertise in ice fishing," Michael joked.

The high-ceilinged room became stuffy; Lucy took off her coat and tugged up her knee-high boots. She regretted wearing her long red sweater because it was warm, and everyone else looked to be wearing black. She was committed to her business and branding, however, and red was her signature color. After pushing up her sleeves, she sat taller.

A hip-hop song blared, and the chatter faded. Lucy retrieved her phone. The light from the wagon-wheeled chandeliers dimmed, making it hard to find the quarterback's boo on Instagram. She pulled her vial of Lust from her purse and dabbed it on her wrists.

The music died down, and a tall, thin redhead with lips covered in thick matte lipstick strode onto the stage. Carrying a microphone, she waved at the room. The clicking of the camera shutters droned like cicadas in summer, ever-present and rarely noticed.

"Many thanks for your warm welcome for Angus Reid and the team from *Raven House*. We are happy to be here in Baileys Harbor. I'm Sara Boden, Mr. Reid's public relations specialist." She pointed to a standing microphone in the corner of the room. "We'll be taking questions from the audience. Please look under your chairs. If you find the *Raven House* postcard, you're the winner. You get to come up to the microphone as your table rep and ask our stars or any of the crew and, of course, Angus Reid anything. Except on a date," she tittered, "because Angus Reid's not available."

As people shifted about, feeling and looking under their chairs, Lucy wondered about Sara Boden's strange yet familiar demeanor. Kat tapped her on the shoulder. "Look under your chair, girlfriend."

Lucy reached below her seat, found the postcard, and considered ignoring it for a second. If it weren't for her tablemates staring at her, she might have tried to lie. She surrendered, pulled out the card, swallowed her obscenities, and groaned. "Hey, hey, I'm your question girl."

The chandeliers went dark, and multicolored spotlight beams bounced around the room and ceiling.

"Let me introduce you to our amazing cast, crew, and writers," Sara shouted. "First, the man who makes the magic, and I'm proud to say he is the best big brother I could have, Peter Boden, director of *Raven House*."

The audience applauded as a balding and good-looking,

middle-aged guy wearing an untucked dress shirt and jeans walked onstage and sat to the right of Angus's designated spot.

Next, Sara introduced the crew and the show's writers. They took their seats at the rear table. Then, she excitedly introduced the actors and actresses of the hit TV show. After each intro, there were pictures snapped and a short applause. She recognized the woman who played Nick Parker's assistant, an actress who had a small role in *Gilmore Girls*, the other show Lucy went fangirl over. Then, Sara introduced Gus's co-star, another actor she loved. He had played a bad boy in a soap opera she and Julie had regularly watched together.

"Are you ready for the star? The man? The delicious Hollywood A-lister?" Sara yelled, excited.

As the audience cheered, Lucy folded her arms across her chest.

Sara shushed the audience until the hooting and hollering died down.

"I'm pleased to introduce you to my one client, a brilliant actor and a fantastic performer." Her pitch evolved into a squeal. "Angus Reid!"

The crowd erupted in shouts and whistles.

Lucy covered her ears as a loud whistle came from Michael, and Kat shrieked. She glanced at her two latest love subjects, both rooting for Gus, and wondered about the rose sachet. Had Gus delivered it to the fledgling couple? They seemed comfortable next to one another, except they weren't acting lovey-dovey.

She yanked her attention back to the stage, where Gus stood, looking taller on the riser. He waved to the audience, draped his arm around Sara, and pulled her into his chest for a quick hug. When he sat, with the director on one side and his co-star on the other, they exchanged high fives and fist bumps. After Gus nodded to his fellow castmates and crew, he arranged the microphone and looked at the audience.

The conference proceeded with behind-the-scenes details of the show presented by the cast members. Several female actors praised the writers for creating twenty-first-century female roles with substantial lines in an early twentieth-century drama. Gus heartily applauded after every one of his colleagues spoke.

The publicist returned to the stage and called up the various press outlets. She moderated their questions by interrupting or rewording any personal questions. One reporter asked Gus about the length of his stay in Baileys, and Gus couldn't answer. Sara intercepted the question and rudely answered for him.

"LA is *our* home; Angus can't wait to get back there."

There were a few murmurs in the audience. Lucy wasn't alone in thinking that Sara's answer sounded condescending and disrespectful.

Johnny, the guy from *TMZ*, came up to the microphone. As it was stationed by the sports table, he waved at the players. Then, he said, "Thanks to all of you on *Raven House*. This is a great gig— I've never been to the Midwest. We'll be back. Especially to the lighthouse. I'm glad we were invited for a sneak peek." He waved and sat back down.

"Now it's time for our audience questions. When I call the color of your table, please have your rep come to the microphone," Sara said tersely, adjusting her lavalier mic.

Lucy asked her tablemates if they had any ideas. Kat came up with a personal one. "Who is Gus currently involved with?"

"No way," Lucy replied. "You can get up and ask that one, Kat. Sara will censor it, anyway."

Michael chuckled. "How about asking Gus if he'll go ice fishing with me?"

Facepalm.

Lucy figured Maddie cared nada about any questions because she was focused on her phone. And the rest of her tablemates didn't have any suggestions. They were too busy taking selfies with Gus in the background.

Questions sputtered and stalled in Lucy's mind as Sara announced the colors of the rainbow. When a little girl approached the microphone, she asked, "Mr. Reid? What's your favorite color?"

The audience cooed.

Gus said sincerely, "Yellow. The same as your dress."

Blushing, the little girl ran back to her table and jumped into her dad's lap.

After the green table was announced, a football player asked Gus about his favorite Packers matchup. Gus answered a game against the Bears.

When their table was called, Lucy took a short breath. She'd been in front of the cameras once, and she wanted to make sure she didn't smile again. At least this time, her hair looked great. She had wrapped a single braid around her head like a crown and let the rest hang loose. A style she saved for special occasions.

Striding to the microphone, she sensed all the eyes and cameras on her and overheard one guy, maybe Johnny, say, "That's her."

She brushed a strand of hair off her cheek and got a quick hit of Lust from her wrist. Being the center of attention wasn't her jam. Lucy glanced at her tablemates and was disappointed Michael and Kat had moved apart and let two chairs separate them. Then it occurred to her.

"If you're looking for a cheese hat," Sara said, "I'm afraid we don't have one."

A few folks, those who had seen the pictures, chuckled.

Exasperated, Lucy let out a long sigh. The microphone amplified her hot air through the room. "No. I know where the hat is. I'm wondering about the rose sachets. Where are they, Mr. Reid?" She gave a quick nod toward Kat and Michael. "They're really important."

The publicist sneered at her.

Lucy locked eyes with Gus, and the faintest of smiles crossed his lips.

Squinting, Gus rubbernecked the yellow table. Lucy could see his wheels turning. When he figured out her question, he sat back and chuckled. The audience laughed along as if they were in the know about their secret matchmaking goal.

"Thanks for asking. The sachet is safe. Promise." He crossed a finger over his heart.

She smiled and blushed. Several cameras clicked and buzzed around her as she strode back to the table. She asked Kat to move over two chairs to sit next to Michael again.

"What was up that woman's ass," Kat asked. "Have you met her?"

"Never." Lucy shook her head. "Totally bizarre though."

After the rest of the audience questions, Sara addressed the press in a condescending tone, warning them to stay away from Angus. She grabbed his hand, then left the stage with the others, and the conference came to a close.

As the paparazzi were shepherded out by security, Lucy stood to stretch and check messages. An unfamiliar woman from the red table approached her.

"You're Lucy Maxwell?" she asked. "I can't wait for Wicks & Balms to open."

"Thanks. You are?"

"Sorry, Kayla Quinn, Angus Reid's makeup artist."

"Oh! Shoot. I have your order of Lust. I haven't been able to ship it."

"Don't worry. Can I pick it up in the shop? I know it's not open, but..."

"Sure, not a problem. Tomorrow okay?"

"I'm dying to check out your other scents." Kayla laughed. "Is it true you'll be unveiling another aphrodisiac for in-store purchase?"

"Dang, how did you hear about it?" Lucy asked.

Before Kayla could respond, Sara interrupted. "Hello, ladies."

Lucy clutched the back of the chair as a terrible smell assailed her sensitive nose. The publicist wore the one perfume Lucy disliked—Fracas. She resisted frowning in disgust at the rude version of tuberose.

Kayla introduced them, and Sara gave her a mean-girl once-over. "You were the one in those pictures with Angus. You and your cheese hat caused him a lot of trouble," she said, glowering.

Lucy straightened her shoulders. "I hope it was good trouble."

"Chill out," Kayla said. "I know you're just as curious about Wicks as I am."

"Possibly." Sara turned away to address the others at the table. "Ladies and gents, Angus has invited you downstairs to the speakeasy. We'll be serving dinner."

As the angry publicist walked away, Lucy noticed the woman's dark red hair made her skin look sallow. She looked weathered and older than Lucy, yet they were around the same age.

"Finally, something I can get on board with," Michael groaned. "Food."

"I'm hungry, too." Kat followed Michael.

"Let's set up a time next week to talk about the Fest. Okay?" Maddie whispered, tapping her arm.

"Sounds good," Lucy said. "I'll have my truck back."

They followed the others down a carpeted corridor to a dead end with a brick wall lined with bookshelves. When someone pulled out a book, a shelf slid open and revealed a staircase. Maddie and Kayla were on either side of her as they went downstairs to a covert restaurant.

"What's the deal with Sara?" Maddie asked Kayla. "Is she Angus's SO? Partner? Boo?"

"No," Kayla answered, "but she'd love to be. Instead, she's his freakishly controlling publicist."

"Makes sense," Maddie said. "Sara has asked me several times to alter Gus's—I mean Angus's— appearances at the Fest."

Maddie pulled open a wood door using a bronze handle in the shape of a snake. The one-time speakeasy was aptly named the Snake Pit.

Lucy stepped in and sank into the plush forest-green carpeting. The rich mahogany bookshelves and Tiffany table lights created a sultry atmosphere, reminding her of the Gatsby era. "This is beautiful."

The décor vibe was vaguely mysterious, and the speakeasy's aroma made Lucy stop short. She inhaled the surrounding air appreciatively and let the scent tease her nose. A bouquet of cherries and oranges tickled her olfactory system. An earthy, lush base note and another fragrance evaded her senses and stymied her. She had to find out about the heavenly scent.

Chapter 9

Gus perused the room for Sara's whereabouts while talking about the upcoming Super Bowl with his football buddies. Thus far, he'd managed to stay calm after realizing how his publicist had sabotaged him.

Because of Sara and her magic with the press, his social media had been working for him steadily, and with her help, he'd forged his image as Nick Parker. Now, it was as if he'd made a deal with an exceptionally talented devil with a smartphone. Thanks to Johnny's slip of the tongue earlier, Gus confirmed it. She'd sold him out. Sara had revealed the location of his rental and the set to the paparazzi.

When Maddie, Kayla, and Lucy walked into the speakeasy, he excused himself from the group of men.

"Hey, ladies," Gus said, calmly trying not to stare at Lucy's full pink lips. "Thanks for coming."

"You need another beard trim," Kayla harrumphed, scrutinizing his jawline.

"Tomorrow, Kayla. It can wait," he said lightly.

"I have to check out that football player. His blue eyes are brighter than my boo's." Kayla headed toward the bar.

"Thanks for celebrating Baileys." Maddie gave him a quick hug. "Filming *inside* the lighthouse tomorrow?"

"Not sure." Maddie's hug was a good sign since she'd become the first person on his amends list. His tight schedule this past week had made it easy to procrastinate his commitment to making amends with his family. Starting with Maddie might make the others easier when he got around to them. At least, he hoped. "Peter and I have to check the lighting for the inside shoots."

"Any chance your publicist will be able to go over your Fest schedule with me tonight?"

"Probably, but not sure where she is," he said.

"I'll find her." Maddie took off.

Gus was relieved to have a second or two alone with Lucy.

"As my assistant," she said, adjusting her pink purse, "I might have to lower your grade. Michael's without a sachet, and Kat's without a bottle of Lust."

"Epic fail, I know. I'll get them the goods this week." Gus let his guard down. "I swear...on my mum's yellow roses."

"It's okay." She nodded toward the buffet stand. "They're huddling over the food, which is always a good sign."

Standing with Lucy, a yearning he'd almost forgotten came over him. *Camaraderie.* His mojo must have taken a beating. Here was a beautiful woman beside him, and he was at a loss for words. Chitchat and small talk had escaped him. Keeping up the appearance as *unattached* for the sake of his career was suddenly appalling and quite lonely.

"I have got to find out why this place smells incredible," she announced. "Wanna come with?"

"Smell?" Gus awkwardly asked her backside as he followed her.

Lucy was a scent detective extraordinaire. His character, Nick, might learn a new skill by observing her at work, so he tagged along as she wound from the bar, through the buffet, and into the kitchen, where he lost her. She followed a scent as he'd followed scripts and cues.

The staff in the kitchen gawked at him when he entered.

"Everything is delicious." His attaboy tone rang through. "Where did the woman in the red sweater go?"

One of the chefs pointed to the walk-in refrigerator.

"Thanks." He stepped into the cooler, where Lucy was holding an orange to her nose and inspecting the leaf.

"Oh my god. This is it. At least part of it...the heavenly scent," she said in a rush.

"Mr. Reid?" the manager asked nervously. "Can I get something for you?"

"Er...no, nothing. I wanted to find Ms. Maxwell. About the scent." He wanted both of the women at ease. He wasn't out to make any Hollywood demands. "Curious about how the owner of Wicks & Balms susses out her products."

Lucy bit off a piece of orange peel. "Orange joy!" She rubbed the leaf between her fingers. "I know I look goofy, but it's a Seville orange. I haven't worked with them, and neroli oil is an incredible scent."

"I'm out of my league here. Is that what you smelled?" Gus asked, confused and amazed.

"Yes, and with vanilla," she said, "but I'm going to use the tonka bean, vanilla's wicked stepsister. When I walked into the speakeasy, I smelled the oranges and cherries from the bar and the vanilla from the desserts. The mixture made a potent combo because we're in the lower level, and it's stuffy down here."

"Normally, we use Florida oranges. Luckily though, our head chef found these Sevilles at the Chelsea Market in New York and flew them in for tonight," the manager explained, looking relieved.

For numerous reasons, Gus was grateful for the simple Seville oranges. "Thank you."

Lucy hugged the woman. "Really, I'm not nuts. Sometimes my nose gets the best of me."

Rubbing her arms and rapidly exiting the cooler, she left Gus in the cold, trying to make small talk with the kitchen manager. He wanted to follow Lucy out of the refrigerator but couldn't. Even in a refrigerator, he had to maintain his image and ensure his social interactions with any potential fan were friendly and professional. When he returned to the speakeasy, Lucy was sitting at the bar with his friend, the QB, and his babe, Nina. The two women were head-to-head in conversation.

Though interested in joining them at the bar to have a mocktail, he had to cap his curiosity about Lucy and her enthralling persistence. He wasn't a cat, and he couldn't afford to be curious. His *one* life was still under contract.

Across the room, Gus spotted the actress playing Nick Parker's latest love interest. Alexandra was spectacularly gorgeous, like most of the women he'd worked with on set. When she waved him over, Gus groaned. At least his character had a good love life.

Posing for shots with his castmates absorbed his thoughts for the next hour. There was a selection of local photographers, and Gus was relieved Maddie was one of them. Per usual at these events, Sara had taken control of his every movement.

Peter came to his rescue and escorted him back to the bar. Gus finished the glass of water in one swig. "Thanks for the save, boss."

"No problem." Peter ordered a beer. "It's going well tonight, and I thought you could use a break."

His respite of peace was obliterated when Sara appeared and stood too close. Her perfume hit his nose like a sledgehammer, and he knew he'd be fighting a headache tonight.

"Angus, isn't she your driver?" Sara pointed at Lucy, morphing from a demanding photographer into a steely prosecutor.

"Yes." He clutched his cold glass of remaining ice cubes.

Peter tipped his glass toward his sister. "Nice job. Your first PR event in Baileys is a smash."

Sara blushed.

"Actually, second press conference." Gus chomped on an ice cube. "But who's counting?"

He glanced at Lucy. Maddie had joined her, and they were taking selfies with the trendy football couple.

"What did I miss? I thought tonight was our kickoff event for season four?" Peter sounded skeptical.

"It is." Sara patted her brother's shoulder. "Gus is confused."

"Confused?" His grip tightened on his glass. He'd embraced a sober life for over a year, and his sobriety had taught him to trust his own judgment. "You leaked my location to *TMZ*, Sara. Don't deny it."

"I did it as a favor for this forgettable town." She held up her phone. "Now there are more followers on the Baileys Harbor account. It's still paltry. A hundred is more than ten. This is part of my job."

Gus's whole body stiffened, and the threat of a headache turning into a migraine crept up his back.

"Are you out of your mind?" Peter glared at his sister. "Our team, this production crew, and this show—the success rests on the shoulders of Angus. How didn't you get the message? No publicity for a week?"

Peter's support reassured Gus.

Like a buzzing fly, Sara waved off her brother. "Don't get preachy on me. I organized every detail of this incredible party. You both should be thanking me."

Gus pushed his mantra to the front of his brain. *Hari Rama Hari*. Maddie caught his eye from the other end of the bar and signaled for him to join them. He held up a just-a-minute finger.

"Excuse me," he said to his publicist and director. "A few of my fans are looking for me. Are there any more photo ops I need to do tonight?"

"No. All done." Sara sneered at his friends. "And about the mix-up. Giving *TMZ* a hot tip wasn't supposed to blow up. Sorry."

Sorry, my ass.

He slapped Peter's back. "Inside shots? Tomorrow morning?"

"Yeah. Want your help with the lighting. Be at the lighthouse early, okay?"

"Sure, sure," Gus muttered, anxious to be free from his petty publicist. He wondered where the closest AA meetings were held around town. He needed to vent anonymously and get back into the driver's seat of his own life. The amends needed to be made.

* * *

Lucy finished the remainder of her delicious cocktail and ate the orange off its peel. The Door County cherries were too tempting. She had gobbled them up.

"Checking for cloves in a Seville?" Gus asked.

She snickered. "Not at all. There are no bad spirits in here tonight. Actually, the best kind of spirits because my old-fashioned was sweet with a top-rail brandy."

Could she mention anything related to booze with Gus? "Bad subject, sorry." She felt self-conscious. "Any chance you have the keys to my truck?"

"Talking about Wisconsin's signature cocktail is never off-limits, and the scent is still enjoyable, even more so these days." Gus pulled out her key chain from his pants pocket. A bright yellow disk that read *Reading is Sexy* dangled in front of her face.

She grabbed the keys to her truck and sang, "I'm reunited, and it feels good."

"Yes, but." He pointed to her lowball glass, empty except for a tiny bit of muddled cherries on the bottom. "Are you sure you should drive?"

"It's Nina's fault," Lucy said, relieved to be in possession of her truck. "The football guy's girlfriend is one of my clients, and she's a huge Lust fan. I had no idea she was seeing a famous quarterback. They're well-known, right? I'm not a sports person."

"Not even Travis or Tom? Never mind. Yes, most NFL players,

especially quarterbacks, have more fans than I do." Gus stared at her. "Have you eaten anything other than oranges and cherries?"

She wondered if her mascara had crumbled and smudged into raccoon status.

"I just had one cocktail." She'd been stoked about a new scent and, bonus, another Lust match to brag about on her Instagram account. "No, I forgot. I'll quickly grab a bite from the buffet."

"Erm, it's closed," Gus said, interrupted by his buddy and Nina saying goodbye.

"Text you tomorrow," Nina said, blowing a kiss in her direction. "I'm geeked. Amazing to meet you, Lucy. Or should I say, *Emma*?"

She waved goodbye and realized the crowd in the speakeasy had dissipated. She regretted not eating, but getting a testimonial from a famous football couple on her website would be tremendous for her opening.

"Okay." Lucy handed her keys back to Gus. "Your turn to play chauffeur."

"Whenever you're set, I'm ready." He twirled her key chain around his finger. "Where did Maddie go?"

"She left with Michael and Kat."

"I've had enough PR for one day," Gus said. "Let's get out of here."

"Are you sure you can ditch the celebrities for me? And what about your publicist? Don't you have to check in with her first?"

Shaking his head, Gus scoffed. "Fuck no."

Whatever land mine Lucy had triggered, she knew better and steered clear of it. She suspected Gus's emotional baggage was riddled with hidden bombs.

Once inside her sweet little truck, she sighed and caressed the ancient radio knobs on the dashboard. "Hello, darling. I've missed you. Did you know this truck was my dad's?"

"Makes sense," Gus grumbled about the oily steering wheel.

"Is his newer? Possibly made during the era of automatic windows?"

"Don't know and don't care," she snarked. "He's long gone, and I say good riddance." Either it was her one cocktail—or was it two?— or the stress about her brick-and-mortar opening, but her mouth had grown a mind of its own. "Just ignore me."

"Not possible." Gus pulled away from the golf club. When he drove over the causeway crossing Kangaroo Lake, she was nearly blinded by the bright headlights shining into her truck from an SUV behind them. "Dick."

Gus adjusted the rearview mirror and glanced back. "Here's the Coyote Roadhouse," he said, taking a hard right into the parking lot. "I wanna show you the field of dogwood that I told you about."

"Sure." She yawned.

Rubbing his jaw, Gus peered into the rearview mirror as the obnoxious car passed on the road behind them.

"You know," she told him, "this place uses my lavender herb seasoning in their kitchen."

"Wicks is more of a celebrity than I am." He turned toward the back window and frowned. "And you."

"Doubtful. Maybe another time on the sticks. I'm sort of tired. 'Kay?" It wasn't a lie. She was growing more fuzzy-headed by the second.

Gus pulled out of the lot, and as soon as they arrived at the house, she dropped her head back against the headrest. Her truck was back home. He parked in the garage, and she patted the dashboard. "Good night, sweetie."

"Good night," Gus responded with a grin.

She hopped out and took off for the house. "Thanks."

"Lucy, wait!" Gus jingled her key chain.

She grabbed the keys and strode to the front door. The cardboard still sealed the two broken panes of stained glass. Her hand trembled as she unlocked the door.

"One of these days, I'll fix those," he said, so close she felt his breath warm on her neck. "All right if I grab H_2O from the fridge? I ran out in the cabin."

Nodding, she walked into the house on jelly legs. One week ago, her main thought had been to open Wicks, and now she was anxious to create a new scent and had mingled with celebrities. A good thing for her business.

Lucy was tempted to hug Gus. Then she remembered he was Angus. She stumbled up the stairs to her bedroom and, before collapsing into bed, closed her curtains. The lights in the guest house below flickered on, and she wondered if this new Gus—Gus 2.0—might be better than the first version.

Chapter 10

Still half-asleep after last night's press conference, Gus barely heard Michael plowing the main house's driveway. He gulped down the last of his coffee, set his research reading aside, then packed his duffle with an extra hoody and threw in his tablet. He hurdled the drifts of snow in front of the cabin and hiked over to meet Michael at the snowplow.

"Thanks for the lift. I don't want to muck up the shoot schedule." Gus pulled out his phone and texted Peter. **Digging out of snow. Running late.**

"I thought I was finished as your chauffeur," Michael said, deftly maneuvering the plow on the driveway. "Where is Lucy's truck?"

"In the garage and hidden. I want to keep where I'm sleeping off the grid while I'm here." As the piles of snow grew higher, Gus contemplated his amends. He had to work fast, or all of this snow would melt away, and he'd be guilty of complete negligence. If Maddie was around Cana today though, he could get one apology completed.

Peter returned his text: **No problem. In lighthouse. Delayed cuz of lighting.**

The lighthouse meant Maddie, so he'd have his chance.

"Whatever." Michael yawned and drove away from the house. "This storm got me up at three. Jonesing to get lunch at Kat's after droppin' you off."

"Kat, yeah." Gus dug into his jacket pocket and discovered the sachet had taken a beating. The corner of the delicate baggy had torn, and many of the dried buds had dropped out and clung onto a loose piece of gum. He took it out of his pocket and carefully tied the silky drawstring around the rearview mirror. "This is a belated gift from Lucy."

Michael tapped the bag. "Better not be weed. You're a recovering alcoholic."

"No, absolutely not. It's dried lavender and rosebuds," Gus explained, finding it hard to keep a straight face with such a feminine-sounding line. "It's for you and Kat."

"Does it come with a pink diary?" Michael turned onto the causeway.

"Yes," Gus said, "and a heart-shaped lock. I have learned from an authority on love that you love Kat, and Kat loves you." He eyed the sad-looking sachet. "This will encourage you two."

"Lucy's a love doctor?" Michael stared at the snow-covered road ahead.

Gus adjusted his seat belt. "I guess. I know for sure Wicks will crush it in Baileys."

"Sounds like you and the *love doctor* have been gabbing." Michael snorted, giving him a quick look. "What else have you been chitchatting about?"

"Just business," Gus murmured. "Her shop."

"She is batshit crazy for opening a store in the middle of February." Michael flicked the sachet, sending a few more dried buds onto the dashboard. "There won't be many people waiting in the cold to go shopping for dried plants."

"You are dead-ass wrong. Even if it's thirty below, people will line up for the opening of her shop. Trust me."

Three cars ahead of them, a car had spun off the road and landed in a ditch full of snow. Michael slowed down and pulled into the snow-covered parking lot of the Coyote Roadhouse. He punched the address of the accident into the truck's emergency phone, called it into the station, and requested a tow truck.

Gus watched two other cars drive past the stranded motorist waving for help. "Bollocks. We need to help them."

"I thought you had to stay hidden." Michael put on his knit hat with the emblem of DCFD. "You can stay in here."

"No, *I* don't have to hide. I'm determined to keep my sleeping arrangements and the house on Kangaroo Lake hidden from Sara." He hopped out of the truck and tightened his striped scarf. "My publicist followed me and Lucy after the press conference last night."

Michael handed him a shovel. "You're being paranoid."

"Not at all. Sara sabotaged me, and I'm bloody pissed. She leaked my arrival to the paparazzi."

They trudged across the slippery, snow-packed road and toward the disabled car. Its front end had sunk into a snowbank. The marooned woman waved her arms above her head and shouted thank you.

Michael gave her a thumbs-up. "Sounds shady, man. Why would your publicist diss you? Isn't she supposed to make you famous?"

"Because of my contract, she's gone from a handler to a fixer. There's a clause in it saying I can't be seen partying or hanging out with women. It's for the show ratings since most of my fans are women. I need them to believe I'm available."

"What the actual fuck?" Michael's eyes bugged out.

"My fault—day one of season three." Gus wiped his cold and dripping nose with the back of his glove. "I showed up to the set completely shitfaced, and a beautiful fan posted my idiotic antics from the night before all over social media. I had to sign an amended contract and stay sober or get fired."

"Bad news, Gus. Are you bound to your female fans? How about the old guys? They love *Raven House*. Do you have to stay away from your uncle or grandpa?"

"Hadn't thought about it that way. Not a lot of elderly types on Instagram."

"Your loss." Michael sidestepped down the embankment. "Are you really Sara's only client?"

"Yeah..." Gus fell on his ass and slid into the ditch.

"She's scary." Michael grabbed his hand to help him up. "You better watch your back."

Gus brushed the snow off his jeans as his friend's words soaked in. Since his recovery and AA, his priority had become work, and he'd rediscovered his passion for acting. His days of partying and confusion were over, which caused his publicist's lifeline to be severed. Michael was right; he better watch his back...and his front...and his sides.

They approached the woman beside her vehicle, punting a snowdrift and rubbing her mittened hands together. "Alleluia, you guys are the best."

"Happy to help." Gus smiled, and his cold lips crackled.

"You take the left rear, and I'll take the right," Michael said. "Ma'am, the tow truck is on its way. We'll get your car better situated for it."

Gus strained to lift one shovel topped full of snow, gave up, and dumped half of it. "Shite, this stuff is heavy."

"When was the last time you shoveled?" Michael yelled. "And Malibu sand doesn't count."

Laughing, Gus finished freeing his first tire. His arms ached. It had been a long-ass time since he'd shoveled snow, and he wasn't about to admit it to his buddy.

The woman stared at him when he plodded to the front end of the car.

"Hey, you look familiar. Did we go to high school together?" she asked.

If Gus had a dollar for every time someone asked him about going to high school with him, he'd have a house in Malibu instead of an apartment. He shook his head. "No, I'm Angus Reid."

Her face fell as she recognized him. "Oh. Thank you. This is sick."

She gazed at him expectantly.

"Would you like a selfie with me?" Gus asked, feeling bolstered from the snow shoveling. "As long as you don't post it for a couple of months. You can go for it when I'm home in California." Sara would kill him if it showed up on social media.

"Hells bells, yes. You guys are saving my butt today. Do you know how many people drove past and just waved? We live in Wisconsin, for Pete's sake." She fumbled around in her purse and retrieved her phone. "Say *cheese.*"

He relaxed and smiled into the camera.

"A little help here?" Michael complained.

Gus spotted the flashing red lights of the tow truck approaching on the road above. "Yeah. Our reinforcements have arrived."

After they returned to the Coyote parking lot, Gus pointed toward the snow-covered patio. "Red dogwood. I know there's a ton of it behind the restaurant, and I want to get it for Lucy."

"Lucy, Lucy, Lucy." Michael opened the truck's storage compartment. "Are you sure your name isn't Ricky?"

"What are you talking about? Even if I could get involved, Lucy isn't my type. She's too..." Gus gladly returned the shovel to Michael and shook out his sore arms.

"Please do not say *complicated,*" Michael griped. "You're a TV star who lives a life of luxury."

"Lucy's smart and clever. You should have seen her on the trail of a new scent at the speakeasy. Like a dachshund digging for a squirrel. I mean that in the most positive way as a dog lover. But, let's face it, she's intelligent and genuine. I'd bore her to death." Lucy's brain wasn't hot-wired and on overdrive like his. When he'd paged through one of her plant books, he appreciated the glorious pictures more than the words. She was way out of his league.

"You're selling yourself too short, buddy. True, books or math isn't your forte..." He held his hands up like he wanted to wring his neck. "But you're a hands-on kind of guy. You learn from jumping into the frying pan."

A few colorful shanties dotted the frozen lake in the distance. The ice fishermen, or women, were prepped. Gus sighted an early morning bonfire. "The ice is perfect," Gus yelled. "Any of those sheds yours?"

Michael scoffed. "Don't change the subject."

"They don't call me the FHW for nothing," Gus joked.

They hurdled and sank into the mounds of snow to reach the scattered brush and bushes on the edge of the lake. When they stopped to catch a breath, Michael pointed his exceptionally large trimmer toward the eastern edge of the frozen lake. "My shack is over there, closer to your place because I wanted to make it more convenient for you. No complications."

Gus cleared his way through the snow and barren brush, stopping at the dogwood.

Michael hopped over and downed a dozen or more red branches in one fell swoop with his enormous scissors.

"Geez, are you using the Jaws of Life?"

"Not quite. I'm on duty and can't mishandle the equipment. It's a hedge trimmer, stored in the truck. Just for this occasion... and Lucy," he teased, dropping branches at his feet. "Something I want to shoot by you."

"Sounds serious." Gus sawed at one branch with his tiny pocketknife. "Spill."

"When did you quit drinking?"

He tapped his chest, where his chip stayed under layers of winter clothing. "It's been over a year. About fifteen months, and there were a couple of times in the beginning when I stumbled."

He brushed off the lingering guilt from his last trip to Lake Bluff. "Why?"

"In Wisconsin, drinking is a national pastime. After Kat quit, I had a tough time dealing."

"It's bad in LA, too." Gus gave up and just tore the branch out of the ground. "I get it. Is it why you two were barely speaking during the presser at the Snake Pit?"

"Probably. I'm an idiot," Michael said. "It's been a little rocky and why we aren't...together."

"According to Lucy, you two are a match made in heaven."

"Kat is..." Michael's voice faded. "...an incredible person and fine-looking. It's tough changing though. Giving up beer for her...I don't want to do it. Does it make me a d-bag?"

"You're such a romantic." Gus chuckled. "Has Kat asked you to give up beer?"

"No, but around her, I'm worried I'll accidentally cause her to fall off the wagon."

Gus collected the branches, unraveled his scarf, and wrapped it around them. Speaking with Michael—blue-lipped, freezing, and traipsing through snow—brought their friendship back into focus. "Sorry I've been out of touch. I hadn't a clue about Kat. Don't bother worrying though; you're wishing for something bad to happen. And she's in a good place. I hope I can follow her lead. If she's a twelve-stepper—in AA—you two will be golden."

"Yeah," he said, "been with the group the past four years."

"Go to a meeting with her and see what it's about. Then, if you want, hit up Al-Anon to talk to others who are in your boat—in love with a person who fights a bad habit daily and has to win." Gus followed his buddy as they trekked back to the truck. "It's a good way to see firsthand what Kat deals with. You might learn how having a beer around her is the least of her challenges."

"See...you are *smart*." Michael scoffed as he hopped into the truck. "It's been a while since you've been back. Really great to have you here, man."

"You're just buttering me up to go ice fishing with you," Gus joked, realizing he'd inadvertently made amends. He pulled off his gloves and splayed his fingers in front of the blast of warmth coming from the dashboard.

"Is it working?"

"Hell yeah." Gus stared at the red branches in his lap and felt a flash of Lucy. Her signature reds: the coat, her sweater, and even the sad, red sachet hanging off Michael's rearview mirror warranted a closer look. As they drove into town, Gus tried to toss out the notion of a simpler life, but the red branches wouldn't let him. How long did he have to be attached to a contract and live with the cluster and complication?

"Hey, there's Lucy's truck," Michael pointed out as he slowed down on Main Street. "Wanna stop and drop off the branches for her?"

Gus glanced at his beard in the side-view mirror. "Absolutely."

Chapter 11

"This one..." Maddie picked up a candle and sniffed, then took another deep breath of the purple pillar. "This reminds me of Chanel No. 5."

"Like No. 5, it's loaded with ylang-ylang. Madly in Love is my latest scent in the aphrodisiac line." Lucy rescued the ferns from the cold draft by the front door. The delivery man had set her greenery on the top box of the shipment. "Better be careful. M-I-L is pretty potent. You might fall in love."

"I already fell in love." Maddie swung a cute Swedish backpack off her shoulder. "And he dumped me."

"I'm sorry." She set the ferns on the cash wrap and sorted through her display crates of soap next to it. She handed a yellow flower-shaped bath bomb to Maddie. "Here's my Love Stinks. It doesn't take away the sting, however, a nice long soak in a tub with the scent of lemon and cinnamon is restorative."

"Thanks." Maddie dropped it into her backpack and pulled out a manila envelope. "Here are the updates for the Winterfest schedule. I wanted to give you a heads-up. There's been a major change. Gus's publicist reorganized his schedule, and he won't be stopping here."

"So?" Lucy replied, regretting she hadn't bothered to open her yellow binder. "I didn't realize, sorry. I already have promos organized for the weekend and just invited the football dude and his fiancée. They're coming for my soft opening."

"Fantastic." Maddie prayed to the ceiling. "Angus won't be missed. But still…"

Lucy pushed the boxes away from the door when there was a knock. "Kayla's here. She and her boo, I hope, will also do a testimonial for Wicks during the Fest."

"Testimonial?" Maddie asked.

"Yeah." Lucy flung the door open. "It's when…oh, hey. Hi."

"Speak of the devil," Maddie said. "It's Angus, and he's in Wicks."

"I thought you were Kayla." She stepped aside for Gus to enter while carrying an awkward bundle of sticks. "Is she with you?"

"No, on my way to work." He glanced at Maddie. "I expected to find you at the lighthouse."

"Were your ears ringing?" Lucy said. "Maddie popped by to talk about you…I mean…you in regard to the Fest."

He scrambled to unroll his Gryffindor scarf and handed her an armload of sticks.

"We were on the causeway by the Coyote and spotted the dogwood. I thought you might want some." He strolled around the maze of unpacked boxes and empty displays.

"Dang, you scored big. These are incredible, thanks." She hugged the sticks against her chest and caught a whiff of Gus's cherry scent. This time, there was a hint of fresh snow. She almost let a soft moan escape, so rushed around the shop and hunted for one of the tall, galvanized steel vases she used for flower displays.

"I'm kind of pissed, Gus," Maddie declared. "The opening of Wicks is the biggest thing to happen to Baileys in a long time besides you and your show. But the shop is here to stay, and you'll be heading back to LA. Why can't you give Wicks a shout-out during the Fest?"

"What are you talking about? I'm scheduled to stop at every business on Main Street in between each planned event." Gus gazed at the chandelier. "It looks as if the lights are pieces of licorice."

Maddie glanced at it. "You're right. Twizzlers."

Unable to find a tall vase, Lucy dropped the dogwood sticks in a vintage coal bucket. "Red Vines, actually. My mom made it. She used recycled aluminum for the candle-like lights. And metal piping makes the circular base."

Gus must have entirely forgotten about Lake Bluff, including her, because the chandelier was the star of the exhibit in Maxwell's. If this was good or bad, she couldn't decide.

"Wow. It's beautiful." Maddie gawked. "She's incredibly talented. Does she sell her work?"

"Not at the moment." Lucy stared at the piece and quashed her mom's sixth-fucking-sense and hoped to hell Gus had also failed to remember Julie. "Hey, look, Gus, about your appearances. It's no biggie you can't make it here. I'm stoked to have couples coming by and giving their testimonials. I'll be recording and loading them on Instagram. I've collected several love stories already. Couples answering me on how Lust swayed their swoony moments or influenced their love lives or the first moment they fell in love."

"Oh! Testimonials. Now I understand. Lucy, you're brilliant, but..." Maddie gave Gus the stink eye. "You're a Hollywood superstar. How come your publicist pulled you from Wicks and is making you judge the chili contest? I thought you hated chili?"

All the color drained from Gus's face.

"I'm not sure about any eating contest with chili," he said stiffly. "I'll have to speak with Sara. While filming, I usually stick to lean proteins."

"You despise chili. I remember. In every form. Meat, veggie, and vegan."

"It's just chili," Gus said, strolling around the shop and

looking into empty glass cases. "I'm sure there's a reasonable explanation."

"Bull crap." Maddie stood with both hands on her hips.

Lucy wondered if Gus had been the one to break her heart.

He chuckled. "I'd forgotten how you ignore the filters between your mind and mouth."

"She's straightforward." Lucy gave Maddie a high five.

A suspicious *Emma* vibe crept into Lucy's thoughts. The sparks between these two were sizzling. If Gus and Maddie were to reunite? It would be another fantastic testimonial for Lust and Wicks. And the bonus? Proof showing that Julie's love omen was dead wrong.

"You are in Wisconsin, not in La-La Land." Maddie added, "People here are down-to-earth, and we can smell *bull* from miles away."

"It's two against one, ladies," he said. "I'm on board and all in for Baileys. Yes, I hate chili. I will manage judging the contest, though, because it will be great for the Beacon. As for Wicks..."

Gus displayed one of his superpower gazes, and Maddie jutted out her chin.

"I'm single, hopeless, and lovelorn," he said, looking at Lucy. "So, instead of me, wouldn't it be in your best interest to get a testimonial from Sinjin and Claire? They are the *it* couple and started everything."

"Oh, no, they're not around." Lucy's stomach plummeted. "How about you and Maddie? You know me and my *Emma* thing. You two remind me a lot of Sinjin and Claire."

"Hell to the *no!*" Maddie turned beet red. "Not in a million years."

Gus shook his head, mouth wide open, clearly horrified at the prospect of hooking up with Maddie.

Lucy had stepped onto another one of Gus's weird land mines. When her phone rang, she grabbed it off the cash wrap and pressed it against her chest. "Be right back. I need to take this in the office for better reception."

Dang.

After escaping, she closed the door and looked at the caller ID. *Shit.*

"Yes. I'll accept the charges." She enunciated each word. "Julie. Maxwell. Number. One. Nine. Seven. Three. Four. One."

Listening to the regulations from the House of Corrections, she twisted the drawstring of her red hoodie.

"Lucy, can you hear me?" her mom shouted.

Calls coming from the prison were almost impossible to hear. Background voices bounced off the concrete room housing the phone banks. In-person visits, as rough as they could be, were often better than the phone.

"What's up?" she yelled, pleased her office was soundproof. "How are you?" *Sober?* She hoped the first AA meeting had made a small dent.

"Tired and still behind bars," she griped but sounded stone-cold sober.

There was a din of women cackling and swearing in the background.

Their last visit on Christmas still lingered for too many reasons: no ornaments, too many cookies, in jail, and one suspicious *gift*. However, meeting Sister Jan was worth it. Especially since her new-age mother had been soused.

"I talked with James," Julie yelled. "He seems ready."

"Yes, he's prepared for the upcoming hearing." Lucy plucked a key out of the top desk drawer and unlocked the desk's filing cabinet. "It's what I pay your lawyer for."

"Well, I know, but...he asked about you. Are you ready?"

"Working on it." She pulled her planner from the cabinet, dropped it next to the stacks of shoeboxes arranged on the edge of her desk, and opened it to February—two weeks away. "Just doing the final touches on my statement."

After lying, she set the phone down and rubbed her temples. Lucy wasn't prepared in the least, and the prospect of her alcohol-dependent mother being released with nowhere to go terrified her. What was she going to say in the courtroom?

Well, Your Honor, my mother became obsessed with fame and fortune. She tried to swindle and cheat Sinjin Reid. She tried to steal one of his most valuable sculptures and struck his girlfriend, Claire. Or, Julie Maxwell, my mother, turned from a relatively sane woman into a bizarre and unhinged person. Better yet, Mom claimed her actions were in the name of love, but really, they were caused by one too many bottles of wine that became a toxic deliverance from her pain.

"It'll be fine." Lucy struggled to muster up a confident tone. "You sound good."

"I'm sorry about Christmas," Julie said, barely audible. "It was a fluke. I didn't know there was booze in the fruit punch." A moment of dead air filled the office until she continued. "I'm being transferred to the Kohler jail a day before the hearing. If you can get there, then we can talk."

"It isn't a great time, Mom. There's a lot to do for my opening next month." She added to clarify, "The opening of my shop, Wicks & Balms."

"I know what Wicks & Balms is," Julie snapped. "Just an extra day? For me. It's been difficult, but Sister Jan and I have spoken."

"Mom, I don't have a place to stay. Remember I had to sell your house? And I can't afford the time or money for a hotel in Kohler."

"Can't you stay at Sinjin's?"

"Sinjin and Claire aren't speaking to me." She spoke loud and clear to make sure she understood every word. "Thanks to you."

She paced about her office. What a clusterfuck.

"Oh right, I forgot," Julie shouted, sounding remorseful. "Can't we put that to rest? It's a long time ago."

"For you." Lucy let out a rush of air. "But they still suffer from the happenings that day. Not to mention my own bouts of anxiety. I'm alone and have a lot to deal with. My shop takes priority."

"I...I...understand." Her voice faded off; more dead air followed. An automated operator announced a ten-second warning.

"See you soon, Lulu. Please think about it."

Lulu? She hadn't heard the nickname her dad had given her in a long-ass time. "Please try to go to one of those AA meetings with Sister Jan."

"I will, I promise. My chakra has been working overtime. Any chance you and Angus Reid have met up?"

Lucy was accustomed to worrying about Julie's liver; now, she worried about her mind. How much alcohol could a person's brain absorb until it turned to mush? "I have to meet up with a vendor in Kohler to check on my inventory in their store, so call me again next week. By then, I'll have a better sense of my schedule. Okay?"

"Perfect. Thank you. Have a good week, Lulu."

The phone call expired.

Lucy highlighted Thursday, February 1 in blue, scribbled **Final Court** in red, drew a big circle around Wednesday, and scribbled in **Kohler?** Flipping back through the pages for November and December, she read more of her nervous scribbles. She noted the weekly meetings with Julie's legal entourage. The attorney, the parole agent, and several experts on alcohol dependency. Dealing with the painfully slow wheels of an archaic judicial system had been exhausting.

She flipped the calendar back to January and jotted herself a note for tomorrow: **Call Sister Jan**. Lucy needed another convo with her. The next two weeks were going to be stressful, and just hearing the lovely nun's voice would keep her calm. Then, a big wish broke into her thoughts. Would the kind Sister join her in the courthouse?

She closed the planner. It shifted under her fist and bumped into the stack of shoeboxes. As she straightened them out, the top one fell and tipped open. The contents spilled over her desk.

Exasperated, she plopped the planner into her backpack and picked up the strewn-about hotel and motel soaps. The collection of old soaps was a constant reminder of her dad, who had given them to her...to *Lulu*. She tossed them into the Vans box, closed it, and returned to the shop.

While Gus and Maddie were conversing quietly, her *Emma* vibe kicked into gear. "You two are full of it. I can tell there is a spark between you."

"Okay, Ms. Matchmaker," Maddie laughed. "Busted."

"But your sachets are crossed," Gus said, "or should I say your cosmic love streams?"

Maddie elbowed him in the ribs. "Gus and I, we were best friends in high school, but..." Maddie coughed. "It's Rob, his brother, who is, or was, *the guy*. You know, the one for me and the guy who got away."

"Great." Lucy wanted to cheer and gag at the same time. Rob Reid. Lawyer extraordinaire and the man who would be prosecuting Julie. "Love it. Take as many Madly in Love candles as you want. I insist. You never know."

Maddie dropped a purple pillar in her backpack and gave her a quick hug. "I've gotta get to the lighthouse. Call me later, okay?"

"Sure, of course." Lucy let her out the door.

"What's your *Emma* solution for pining?" Gus looked serious. "Maddie and Rob. They need to be together like Michael and Kat."

She tilted her head in question. "I'm an aromatherapist. Really. They'll find a way to reconnect if it's meant to work."

"Not what I expected to hear from a woman who always wears rose-colored glasses."

"I have a sturdy pair of safety goggles back in the greenhouse," she said.

"*Where there is love, there is life* by Mahatma Gandhi." Gus said, reading the quote from one of her framed photos. "Good news. I have a love story update for you. Kat and Michael are on track and may be a solid testimonial. But why not Sinjin and Claire? And how come you're *meh* about Maddie and Rob. And you, Lucy? Always a bridesmaid and never a bride?"

"Are you Nick Parker-ing me?" she asked, trying to ignore his captivating smile. "Let's just say when it comes to *pairings*, my scents do the work, and I'm more than okay with being the love nudger." *It's safer.*

His inquisitive expression turned into one of his smoldering Hollywood gazes, and a prickly sensation climbed up her spine. Then, a thunderous engine rumbled outside. "The paparazzi has arrived. Do you want to use the back door?"

"It's probably Michael. He's been patiently waiting for me at the Beacon with Kat." He winked and jogged out the back. "Off to the lighthouse on Cana Island. I'll see you later."

The tingling sensation subsided, however, it never completely disappeared. Gus Reid was the type of man who made women's heads spin. At least she owned a lot of winter hats and turtlenecks to help keep her head on straight.

The glow of fluorescent lights cast an eerie light over the backyard as Gus hiked through the snow. Passing the greenhouse, he spotted Lucy working at her distillery. A vague sense of guilt tugged at his conscience, and he ended up pounding on the door, even though it was past midnight.

With safety goggles and earplugs attached, Lucy's head popped up, and she frowned.

He waved and gave her a weak smile.

She jogged to the door, opened it, and jogged back to the potters' table. A cloud of steam escaped after she took the top off the copper distillery.

Inside, the balmy rose-scented air cocooned him. "Can I do anything to help?"

She pulled off the goggles and yanked out the earplugs. "No, thanks. I'm just frustrated. The scent from the Snake Pit has been keeping me up tonight. I really want to use parts of the orange for the oil, but it may be too heavy for the tonka bean."

"Whoa, I'm lost. Sure you're not a mad scientist? Trying to take over the world and letting love rule?"

"Maybe." She gave him a mischievous grin. "If I did, you'd be a perfect ally."

"Didn't mean to interrupt you. I wanted..." He hesitated. How could he frame this situation without disappointing her? "Your shop, it's lovely. Regrettably, I can't switch any of my scheduled appearances during the Fest. My publicist explained," he said, grinding his teeth, "the Beacon is more in line with my brand and perfect for PR reasons. It's a Prohibition-era bowling alley. I won't be able to stop by Wicks."

"Don't worry, it's okay." Lucy tossed her apron on the table. "Want a cup of hot cocoa?"

"Absolutely," Gus said, sounding a bit too gleeful. "Michael was in a fine mood this morning when I left your shop. Couldn't stop chatting about Kat when we drove to the lighthouse."

"Did you give him the sachet?" Lucy flicked off the lights. "I'm sure it helped."

"Indeed, I did. It's dangling from the mirror in his snowplow."

"Good job, Mr. Assistant who won't wear tights."

The fluorescent tubes sizzled and cracked, and then his mum's rehabilitated greenhouse plummeted into darkness. The moon shone through the glass ceiling and brightened the roses. He spotted the bench where he'd spent more time digging for worms in the pots of dirt instead of, at his mum's request, reading.

Following Lucy into the house, he had to fight to keep a stupid grin off his face. Almost everything about this day had been brilliant, yet the shine faded compared to ending it with Lucy.

In the kitchen, she pulled out two pots and two mugs from the cupboard. "Did Nick Parker catch any crooks today?"

"Still sussing it out, doll," he replied, dropping his gear on the counter. "Nick's closing in on the murderer though. The coppers had a big breakthrough in the investigation."

Scrolling through messages on his phone, he stole glances at Lucy. Her hips swayed as she broke off chunks from a bar of chocolate. Dropping them into the double boiler, she hummed, and he couldn't drag his eyes away from her fabulous ass. Was it the scent of chocolate making his mouth water? Heat surged through him and almost powered up his dick. He crossed his legs.

"It's good news about the sachet," he said. "And Kat and Michael?"

"It's awesome." She twisted two slices of orange and hung them on the lip of each mug. "You are on top of it."

Yes, on top.

"Michael and Kat are gaga for one another. I'm smelling another one of your *Emma* matches in the air."

After mixing the hot chocolate, she set a full mug on the counter in front of him. Gus lifted it to his nose and inhaled the luscious aroma. "Scrummy."

"I'm still thinking about you and Maddie," she said. "My vibe was strong this afternoon."

Shocked, he almost slurped the chocolate gold. He had to get it out there with this love nudger and nip any plans Lucy might concoct within her budding sachets.

"Maddie and I were friends during high school," he said bluntly. "But it wasn't anything." Making amends with Maddie this morning reassured him that their friendship had a future. When Lucy left them alone in her shop, he couldn't believe his luck and grabbed the chance to apologize.

"I thought you two were close?" She assessed him over her mug of hot cocoa. Her amber-brown gaze intensified, and he felt as if he was under the hot lamp in an interrogation room.

"Yes, just friends," he said, sounding inexplicably defensive. "She was part of our posse. Her, Rob, Sinjin, even Michael and Kat. We'd go to the lighthouse, party, and have a good time. It's part of my past I want to keep buried."

"Sounds bad," his interrogator said, taking an innocent-looking mouthful of hot cocoa.

"Well, you remember those reckless, carefree times? Right?"

She shook her head. "Not really."

He realized Lucy's high school days were probably more consumed with test tubes and beakers than shot glasses and beer bottles. "I was with Maddie and Rob one night after way too many shots of Jägermeister. After—" He cleared his throat. "—my mum had died."

"I'm sorry. It sucks losing a parent." Lucy foraged around the fridge and came out with a can of whipped cream. "Want a shot?"

"Sure, thank you." The distraction was welcome. "Are your parents still around? The chandelier in W&B was made by your mum, right?"

"Yeah, she's still breathing." Lucy squirted a mountain of cream on top of his hot chocolate. "My dad. He's gone. Cancer killed him a while ago."

Gus was taken aback by her cool objectivity until the realization hit him. He sounded a lot colder when he spoke of his family. "Earlier, while you were in your office, we talked. I hadn't seen Maddie since..." He was elated about making amends with Maddie and hesitant to go back in time.

"When?" Lucy nudged him to continue.

"Since I left for LA and she moved to New York. Today, you witnessed two old friends catching up. Your *Emma* thing missed the mark."

"No. My *Emma* mojo doesn't fail."

Gus stared at his mug. Completing his first amends since coming to Baileys had gone smoothly. Maddie was the only one under the heading, *Sorry for When a Lethal Combination of Booze and Puppy Love Turned Me into a Raging Asshole*. He could officially cross her off his list. "Here's the deal." He tapped his chip. "Remember I told you about my sobriety?"

She nodded.

"Is there any chance your *Emma* mojo could have different classifications? I'm not into science. I mean, what happened with Maddie today is called amends, and I made my first amends with her. In the AA dictionary, this is when we own up to past actions.

Mostly the actions that have hurt our friends and families. So, Emma, what you sensed or witnessed was the start of a new story for Maddie and me."

"Kingdom, phylum, class, order, family, genus, species." She counted them off on her fingers. "I totally get it, and better than you think. It's about reconnecting on all levels, and family is the toughest."

Gus had been just eighteen and foolishly thought shots would erase the picture of his mum, dead on the floor in a pool of blood. He barely remembered catching Maddie and Rob in bed together, except his embarrassment had settled into his bones like concrete.

"My brothers are my worst critics. Rob's turn is next. Or Sinjin. Not ready to deal with my dad." He gave her one of his celebrity smiles, oozing with warmth and goodwill.

She narrowed her eyes and pointed at him. "That gaze of yours —your super-powerful smile—it's a shield, isn't it?"

"Your shop, when is the official opening?" He avoided her question with one of his own, returning to his more comfortable role as the interrogator. "Why don't you invite the Lust power couple, Sinjin and Claire?"

She plunked the old metal pots into the dishwasher. "My *Emma* vibe, it's science with a lot of luck, so you're probably right. Baileys and Lake Bluff are both small towns and very different. Claire and Sinjin—" Her voice cracked. "—are in Lake Bluff, and I don't want to do anything to screw up my debut love match."

"If you have an *Emma* registry like Santa Claus, I know for sure you could move Maddie and Rob from the Out-of-Love to the In-Love column."

His heart skipped a beat when she laughed.

"I have no doubt Maddie's in love with Rob. She has *always* been in love with my little brother." He finished the last sip of hot chocolate and gathered up his gear. "It's late, and I have another long day starting in a few hours."

"Good night," she said softly. "Sleep well."

"You, too." He stopped in the three-season porch and stared at the multitude of boxes stacked up to the ceiling. "Is this your inventory?"

"Yeah. It's ready to transfer."

"There's a lot." He scanned the box labels. Each one was a different quote, a romantic quote about love. "Need a hand?"

Rubbing her forearms, she stood in the doorway. "If you want. I don't want to bug you."

"This weekend okay?" Gus was about to give her his *smile.* Instead, he laughed inwardly and tapped a box. "I need a good workout, and these should do it."

"Sure, thanks."

Back in the guest cabin, Gus calculated how to avoid the paparazzi and his publicist in order to help Lucy. If he had to jump through multiple hoops, so be it.

Instead of just grabbing a pair of sweats for the night, he decided that after almost two weeks, it was time to unpack. He hung his T-shirts and hoodies in the antique armoire in the bedroom, next to his dad's collection of flannel shirts. His MVPs —the Tupac sweatshirt, the three Green Bay Packers T-shirts, and his plaid flannel shirt with ripped-out elbows—kept him sane.

He kicked off his jeans, put on his sweatpants, and threw on the Tupac sweatshirt. Completely faded and worn-out, it had served him well while in rehab. A huge comfort to him while drying out was music...and Tupac's rap made him think.

He had been nuts the night he confronted Maddie and Rob. Being drunk wasn't an excuse, only a miserable fact. Most days since sobering up, he would resist clearing this foggy memory. He'd sucker punched Rob while Maddie yelled obscenities at him. It was a horrible role in a terrible scene that he never wanted to reenact again.

Making amends with Maddie was a new beginning, and it had inspired him.

They'd been tight senior year and talked a lot about escaping

Baileys for good, but Gus had no clue about her deep feelings for his younger brother. Gus's lack of experience—or lack of confidence—had misled him. He believed their friendship was akin to a romance, and he was dead-ass wrong.

When he spoke to Maddie this morning, with the help of his mantra, he could focus on his words. Each claimed accountability for his past actions. He'd reassured her that while his maturity had often matched that of an angsty teen, he'd grown older and somewhat wiser in rehab. Through the years, he'd come to learn the difference between friend and lover relationships but hadn't yet mastered the art of romance. His tormented teen phase had long ago passed, and he told Maddie that he had no intention of ever acting like a dickhead again unless, of course, scripted for Nick Parker.

Maddie responded with an enthusiastic hug and accepted his amends. She did have one request: to call him by his real name, Gus. He had to stop and think before acquiescing to her demand, but the realization smacked him in the face when he did. He had to become Gus again to get his life—a sober one—back.

Gus shoved on his headphones and sank into the Cadillac of mattresses on the bottom bunk. Tupac's *Dear Mama* eased him. His family kept bickering and nagging in his mind though. And there wasn't even a scrumptious meal at his imaginary holiday table.

Gus still owed amends to Rob, Sinjin, and even Claire, whom he barely remembered. And his father, George. Face-to-face worked best for amends, so he had to plan who would come next and how.

As a famous sculptor, his older brother, Sinjin, was an artistic perfectionist and never into drama or legal squabbles. His younger brother, Rob, took on any legal malaise for the Reid family.

Lucy and her *Emma* juju seeped into his brain. Sinjin and Claire were synonymous with Lust. It was madness that she hadn't invited the King and Queen of Lake Bluff to the opening of Wicks.

Gus found his phone and looked up the Wicks Instagram account. He scrolled through the pics of couples and groaned at the sweet smiles. Obviously absent were Sinjin and Claire. Had Lucy's first love match soured? Bugger, he needed to buy a pair of tights.

When Tupac's "California Love" ended, he pulled up his calendar. After repeating his mantra a few times, he rang Sinjin.

Chapter 13

Lucy settled into the cushioned green-pepper-colored bar chair and watched the crowd grow in the dining area. The Beacon was hopping. "Have I crashed a private party?"

"Not at all. You're on the"—Kat used air quotes—"*list*. It's lunchtime for the *Raven House* crew."

Lucy recognized a few of the show's stars. The guy from the soap opera and the actors from *Gilmore Girls*. "Does Maddie have a backstage pass? We're supposed to meet here."

"Yeah." Kat pulled out a red binder she'd stashed between mason jars of hot cocoa mix. "Where's yours? This Festival is Maddie's Olympic moment."

Lucy yanked out her still-unread yellow binder, unable to cool off after the bad news. Her Packers super couple, Mr. QB and Nina, had to cancel and wouldn't make it to the opening. Lucy clenched her jaw. How could a football award be more important than a testimony of love?

"Gus reserved my entire place all weekend for the cast and crew. This is a huge boon for business. Usually, until the Fest starts, it comes in small spurts." Kat eyed her imploringly. "Hey, are you willing to try a new dish? My special is oxtail soup with cardamom."

She was starving and couldn't resist Kat's excitement, so ordered the cardamom soup as well as a bowl of onion soup. Lucy slapped the binder open and gawked at the Hollywood players around her. She copped a few glances at Adam...what was his last name? *Dang.* He was a hot beta with dark hair and geeky glasses. Totally her type. She tried seeing if Kayla, the makeup artist, had shown up, but no luck.

Kat set a steaming bowl of brown liquid with little texture in front of her. The cardamom fragrance made her mouth water—an earthy, rich scent with a hint of lemon. Thankful, she clutched Kat's hand. "This smells heavenly."

"You haven't even tried it!" Kat laughed. "Eat first, talk later."

The liquid gold bobbled about in the spoon. Without losing a drop, she slurped the contents of the tablespoon. She let the soup rest on the front and back of her tongue before swallowing. "I can tell you added the cardamom last, Kat. The heat of the broth popped out the flavor from the seed. Outstanding."

"I bet you say that to all your foodie friends," Kat said.

"Yes, Chef, but these days, you're my only friend."

"Nonsense! You've got Maddie and Michael, too."

"Speaking of Michael. How are you two doing?" Lucy asked casually, hoping and praying she'd have a replacement couple. *Who even cares about football?* "I mean, I know you two have been sort of friendly? Right?"

"I haven't seen Michael for a couple of days," Kat said. "This snow and his buddy Gus have sucked up his time."

Frustrated, Lucy plucked at the pages of the binder and skimmed the events happening during the three and a half days of Winterfest.

The ice-sculpting winners would be announced on the night of the kickoff. Each of the following three days included a large-scale race: the 5K run on Friday morning; on Saturday morning, snowmobiles would race on designated trails through Baileys Harbor; the sleigh bed race commenced Saturday afternoon on Kangaroo Lake. The chili cook-off was scheduled for late Sunday afternoon, and the judging occurred that night.

Angus Reid was the King of the Fest. He would participate in every event and make stops at each business on Main Street during the festival.

Except for Wicks & Balms.

"Here you go." Kat set down her other bowl of soup. "Do you eat anything else?"

Crow?

Maddie came up and plopped a cardboard box down on the counter. "Sorry I'm late. My morning has been pure hell at the lighthouse. The LA bigwigs were arguing about lighting. I couldn't get out of there fast enough. What a cluster."

"You want to try my oxtail soup?" Kat asked Maddie. "It's my new masterpiece."

"Veggie chili, please," Maddie replied in a rush. "The director, Gus, and his publicist were arguing. Now I get the true meaning of drama queens."

"Why the hell did Sara drop Gus from Wicks?" Lucy let the words fly out of her mouth. "She's following me on Instagram. I know she's a Lust lover."

"That's another mess," Maddie said. "Possibly, it has more to do with Gus and you than your shop. If the gossip is true from one of the cameramen, Sara is even more fixated on Gus than before... especially since seeing the two of you together in those *TMZ* pictures."

"I was his *nobody* driver," Lucy barked. "And I was in shock, a frozen deer in the headlights. Remember?"

"According to my source, instead of staying in her trailer, Sara's right on set watching Gus's every move. Also, she's forcing him into judging the chili contest, even though he's on a special diet. Gus was livid earlier. I've never seen him so angry."

"Sara comes off pretty controlling, true," Lucy said, "but isn't manipulating a Hollywood thing? Cutthroat publicity?"

Kat shrugged.

Maddie tapped her lip and pondered. "However, even his makeup artist mentioned how Sara has a *monumental* thing for Gus."

"When will the ice blocks be delivered?" Kat asked, staring at Maddie.

"Ice blocks?" Lucy dragged her mind back to the conversation. Thinking about the muck of Hollywood gossip was not helpful.

"For the carving contest," Maddie explained. "The ice will arrive at Stan's a few days before the kickoff party. It'll give the sculptors plenty of time to carve to their delight. Every business on the main drag will have a sculpture in front of their front door for the opening night of the festival."

"An ice sculpture, great. I'll take anything since Mr. Hollywood is a no-show for the Fest."

"I thought the Packer and his girlfriend were your stars for the opening?"

"Canceled." Lucy gave a thumbs-down.

Maddie set her phone beside her binder, and Lucy wondered which was more important: the phone or the binder.

"I assume Gus will be judging the ice sculptures and the chili?" Kat poured herself a cup of coffee. "If he's dieting, I may talk to him and offer my culinary suggestions."

"Good idea." Maddie paged through her binder. "The sculpture contest will be interesting. One of the contestants is Sinjin."

Sinjin means Sinjin and Claire. Could this day get any worse?

"Speak of the Hollywood hunk," Kat announced. "He's in a sorry state."

All three women groaned as Gus lumbered into the restaurant, with Peter following a step behind. Both men looked pale, tired, and scruffy. Then Sara strutted over to their table. Immediately, she started taking pics of Gus.

"You need to rescue him. He needs a wake-up call, bad," Maddie said.

"Me? Why me?" Lucy protested. "Aren't you two besties?"

Maddie pointed to her backpack. "You're the one with the smelly stuff."

"Kat has a fantastic aroma to wake him up." Lucy folded her arms across her chest. "It's called coffee."

"I can brew a fresh pot," Kat offered.

"No, Gus needs Lucy to intervene." Maddie's insistence was intimidating. Lucy could tell she'd lived a good part of her life in New York.

Mumbling obscenities, Lucy rifled through her backpack and found a vial of Revive, a scent with lots of peppermint. She set it on the counter in front of Maddie. "Here, this may help him. It's a stress-reducing fragrance."

Maddie pushed the vial back in front of her. "Baileys is lucky to have you and Wicks. I may recommend honoring you with a key to the town."

Lucy gritted her teeth. "Made of soap, please, since I'm doing the dirty work."

"You *are* the one who sells the stuff." Maddie grinned. "And Gus looks more like he's on the skids than on a walk of fame. I sort of feel for him. He needs one of your famous concoctions."

She grabbed the peppermint oil and her yellow binder.

"You go, girlfriend," Maddie and Kat cheered.

Playing the part of an Avon lady, Lucy approached the table. "Hi. I'm the owner of Wicks & Balms. I thought I could..."

"How are you?" Gus's voice sounded raspy.

"Good. I couldn't help noticing, though, you look a little tired." She tried to contain the feelies spreading inside her and focused on Peter. "Both of you look exhausted. I don't want to be presumptuous, but sleep deprivation can really affect your health."

Yawning, Peter waved. "Nice to meet you, Lucy. You're right, working out in the cold has been grueling."

She handed the Revive to Gus. "Put this oil on your neck and wrists. It's peppermint and lavender. Good for relaxing." She swallowed a lump in her throat. "And one other suggestion. Chamomile tea before bed. It'll help you sleep better."

"Angus doesn't need any of your healing scents," Sara said dismissively. "He may get an allergic reaction from them. And he doesn't need you dictating anything about his sleep or bed."

"The fragrance of Revive is subtle and very therapeutic. Allergic reactions are minimal to nonexistent." Lucy pointed to Sara's phone. "Gus looks anemic. I would think you'd want him to appear a lot healthier for your camera."

"Your little backwoods leafy antidotes are cute and unnecessary," Sara said. "Angus has the best doctors in LA to keep him healthy."

"Shite. I am bloody beat. Physically and mentally drained. And worse, I feel the oncoming of a migraine." Gus opened the vial, rolled it over his neck and wrists, and took a whiff. "It smells nice, and it's already giving me a boost. Ta, Lucy."

"Revive is good for headaches, too." Then she ripped out a page from her binder and handed it to Sara. "There's been a mistake. W&B isn't listed on Angus Reid's Fest schedule."

In a frenzy, Sara grabbed the paper from Lucy's hand, crushed it into a ball, and tossed it into her oversized designer purse. "It's an old version. I'll have to get the update to you. I apologize."

Lucy wasn't sure who Sara's performance was meant for and found it unworthy of any award. The publicist's deceit was unsettling and reminded Lucy of her mom—chaotic, disingenuous, and desperate.

"Now you're able to find time for Wicks?" Gus glowered at his publicist; his laser-like stare could have shredded Sara into slivers. "Why are you dicking around with my time? It stops. Immediately."

"It's not that, Angus...your schedule is tight. I'm trying to accommodate everyone in Baileys and all over Door County." Sara was frantic.

"The peninsula isn't big." Gus stood abruptly. "I'm not hungry. I need fresh air and a behind-the-scenes tour of Wicks & Balms to prep for my stop during the Fest. All right, Lucy?"

"Of course." She shoved the binder in her bag. "And thanks, Sara."

Frowning, Sara looked down at her menu.

As she walked out, the butterflies in her stomach kept fluttering. "Won't the paparazzi be around to bother you?"

"No, I bought them lunch at the Lure. It's a restaurant ten miles north of here in Sister Bay, so no cameras will be on Main for at least another two hours."

When they reached the front foyer, Maddie ran up to them carrying a strange cardboard box. "Oh no, you don't..." she said, pushing it toward Gus. "Don't forget this thing."

"Thanks." Gus grabbed the box and shoved it under one arm.

Maddie blew kisses and waved them off. "Later, you two."

It was fresh-snow quiet and void of vans, cars, or cameras on the street.

"A gift from Maddie?" Lucy shoved on her mittens.

"It's for you," he said softly. "I bought the candles she was selling in the lighthouse souvenir shop. They're old and dusty, but they say Seville on the label. Thought you could use them to help with the scent you're working on...the one from the Snake Pit."

"How sweet. And thoughtful." Lucy's heart flipped. She'd been rescued from a terrible day by the one person she should probably stay clear of...but who made it impossible to resist. "Thank you."

Chapter 14

"Are you sure you want to do this today? You do look exhausted." Lucy looked at him, concern clear in her gaze. She added, "I mean, in a good way. A tough Hollywood way."

"Shite, no." Irritated, Gus knew his temper could have flared at any moment inside the Beacon because of his fanatical publicist. Sara had been looking over his shoulder nonstop for the past week. Gus wanted to be nowhere near the self-absorbed woman.

"Sorry about the cancelation," he said to change the subject.

"You heard? I am pissed. They canceled for a stupid football trophy."

"MVP of the year is sort of a big deal in the NFL." Gus laughed and let the cold air blowing around wake him up. "The Packers' QB deserves the award. And I'm hyped for him."

"Careful, there's a lot of drifting snow on the sidewalk, and it might be hiding ice patches," she said. "I do not want you to fall on your butt and hit your head. I'll get blamed for it. I can see it now on *TMZ*: RH Postponed! Star in Coma! Desperate Toothy Driver at Fault!"

"How about," he said, looping his arm around her elbow. "If I slip, I'll take you down with me. We'll go together."

"No, thanks." She squeezed his arm tighter. "Dang, it's cold."

Bumping against one another while shifting between patches of snow and slippery spots, Gus tried to guide her footing. Snug against him, Lucy fit perfectly.

They stopped at the crosswalk to wait for the one car on the wintery road to pass. The snow swirled across the deserted street, and Gus felt like one tiny, insignificant snowflake in a glittery snow globe, courtesy of Baileys. Even if he'd had a hand in maneuvering the production team to the Beacon and the paparazzi to the Lure, this moment of anonymity was blissful.

"I parked in the back alley," she said as they crossed the street. "There are crates of stock in my truck. Still okay with helping me unload?"

"Sure, hold on." He grabbed his phone, snapped a picture of the red brick schoolhouse, and got the white cupola in the frame. "This building is beautiful."

"You've been here already." She unlocked the three locks on the cherry-red front door. "Didn't you notice the other day?"

"I was in a rush and barely saw anything." *Except you.*

Gus looked up and down Main. Where two taverns were once located on the street, gourmet restaurants had taken over. His favorite ice cream shop was still operating, and across the street, a cream brick building had been turned into offices and retail shops.

"My claw-foot tub arrived this morning. I'm excited to fill it with rubber ducks when they're delivered. I finished my lighting, and the ferns were hung. Things are coming along."

He admired the beautiful gold-scrolled decal with the name *Wicks & Balms* adhered to the display windows. "Your logo is outstanding," he said truthfully.

"Thanks, I designed it. The font is a pain. It took me forever to get the swirls to cooperate in the circular pattern in the heart shape."

Gus followed her inside, noticing there were fewer shipment

boxes than last time. The floors creaked like a pirate ship as Lucy walked to the back of the shop to get the lights.

A warm glow showered over him. Paper Chinese lanterns hung from the ceiling's exposed pipes and illuminated the shop. Interspersed between the soft lights were strands of twinkling Christmas tree lights. The comfort of the light and the space awed him. "Fantastic lighting. I'm impressed."

She hung her coat on a wrought iron coat rack, and he set the box of Seville candles on the counter. A second later, the licorice chandelier lit up, and it was spectacular. The black metal spiraled up like a round staircase and was hooked onto an exposed water pipe. The tall red candlestick lights stood in line along the circular frame.

"Pretty nice, hey?" Her voice held a big dollop of pride. "The lights look better when they're on and twinkling."

"I'll say it again...this chandelier is beautiful." He stared at it, amazed by the artistry, this time fully appreciating the talent of Julie Maxwell. Although he knew little about Lucy's mom, he did remember she'd been one of his brother's best welding students. "They do remind me of Twizzlers though. Not Red Vines."

"Two separate worlds," she argued.

"Red Vines? What licorice lover advocates Red Vines?"

"Those of us licorice connoisseurs who know real licorice, that's who. Besides, one can't use a Twizzler as a straw. Haven't you ever tried to drink soda through a Red Vine? It turns it into a fizzy lifting potion."

Relaxed, he leaned against the cash wrap. "Are you quoting Willy Wonka?"

She climbed up a step stool and rummaged around the top shelf of an antique apothecary cabinet. "Yes, I guess."

Her red shirt rose when she reached up, exposing a swathe of smooth flesh. The sight of her bare-skinned waist made Gus stand up straight. He couldn't help but stare at her figure as her braid rocked against her back. Her movements enthralled him.

"Here it is," she shouted, hopping off the step ladder.

He averted his eyes and gave her a real smile.

"Checking me out?"

He tilted his head left to right. "You're so...efficient." Blood rushed up and stained his cheeks. He scratched his jaw to stop the bloody tingling. "It's warm in here. Mind if I head out back to start unloading the truck?"

"Efficient? That's a new one." Her dimples blossomed. "The patio has to be covered in snow."

"Is there a shovel?" He needed physical activity for his blood flow to return to a less primal state.

She nodded as he made a beeline out the back door.

The patio was indeed covered with snow, and Gus chuckled. Could he replace cold showers with snow shoveling? The hazy winter sky charged him, and he filled his lungs with ice-cold air. He was invigorated by each toss of snow. Pitch by pitch, he created a mountain on the far side of the fence.

The top of the Dutch-style door opened. "You okay out here?"

"Yeah, it's nice. Come out with me," he invited her.

Outside, she wrapped her arms around her waist. "With so much to do until the opening, the patio is low priority. This is great."

He pitched his shovel into the mountain of snow. "I'm pretty good at being a handyman."

"Sounds promising. First though, this will give you another boost." She stood in front of him.

She was fantastically close, the cold outdoor air dissipated, yet she still shivered. Compelled, he draped his arms across her shoulders. Instantly, her hip bones grazed against his, and before he could register the comfort, she gently dabbed an oily substance on his throat. Within seconds, he was transported back to a sick bed with his chest covered with Vicks VapoRub.

Nothing like a dose of medicine soaked in teen torment to

prevent any of his thoughts from going into the delightful gutter of sin.

"Whoa. Strong medicine." He rubbed it into his neck.

Instead of taking a step away from him, she stayed close. Her breath warmed him, and one of the many knots in his shoulders loosened.

"The eucalyptus can be a lot, but this is combined with chamomile. A little different from the peppermint. Like it?"

"Oh, I'm relaxed. I've been oiled up a lot today—I could probably slide down a fireman's pole in less than a second."

"Fireman!" She stepped back, tripped, and almost fell into a mound of snow. "Oh dang, I forgot."

"What?"

"To call Michael. He's the fire and safety inspector." She jogged inside. "I have to schedule my inspection."

Gus followed her. "He's my best mate. I'm sure you're good to go."

Already, Lucy had her phone propped at her ear. She shrugged. "I can't afford—literally afford—anything to go wrong. The business I attract during the Fest could be better than the glut of vacationers coming in next summer. And with you here..."

In the office, he sat on the desk next to her—close enough to hear the ringing phone.

"Michael Powell, please," she said shakily.

"Put it on speaker," he told her.

She hesitated, then set the phone on the desk between them and tapped the speaker icon.

Picking up the call, Michael answered knowing her. She fanned herself. "Whew! I thought you'd forgotten me; it's been hectic. Especially since Gus arrived."

"That asshole doesn't get me off my game. I know my job probably better than the Peninsula Player. I've got my schedule in front of me."

"Back at you," Gus shouted. "And don't knock my days as an extra for the Players. They made me what I am today."

Michael guffawed. "Should have known you two would be together."

"I'm lending moral support to Lucy," Gus said. "Wicks & Balms will put Baileys on the map. This shop is beautiful, and I'll do anything to make it number one on a Google search. So, you better not make her life difficult."

"Yeah, whatever you say. I'm ready to get over to the shop for the inspection. The first open day available is February one."

"You're kidding!" Her cheeks turned ghostly. "Seriously? The soonest day?"

"Breathe," Gus mouthed.

Her eyes glossed over, and he was at a loss. Crying over a safety inspection?

"Yeah," Michael continued, "but the inspection takes less than two hours. Once we complete the checklist, your part is done. You'll have confirmation by the end of the day."

"You're certain there are no sooner days? I mean, it's cutting it close to the opening."

"With a passing grade, you'll have plenty of time."

She sniffled. "I know...but...the problem. It's the day. I can't be here in the store because I have commitments in Lake Bluff and Kohler."

Gus scratched his head and paced. The old floorboards creaked, and he stopped. Trying to comfort her, he laid his hand on her shoulder. He wished he had gotten more information when he'd spoken to Sinjin. His brother changed the subject and became rather curt when Gus attempted chitchatting about Lucy or Wicks & Balms. Fortunately, he managed to apologize to Sinjin. Although these amends wouldn't be officially complete until he saw Sinjin's face and they talked more in-depth.

Looking directly at Lucy, he asked, "Hey, Michael, I know I'm not the owner, but can I be Lucy's proxy for the inspection?" She inhaled sharply like it was the last thing she expected from him.

At first, there was radio silence. Then Michael began shuffling papers. "If you're certain the date can't be changed, I promise I will follow Lucy's instructions to the letter. Hell, I'll wear one of her sweatshirts and a braided wig. You won't know the difference. My performance as *Lucy Maxwell* will be Oscar-winning," he said, winking at her.

Fortunately, her eyes were no longer glistening.

"You are one sorry asshole," Michael said. "Okay, you're in. Don't let it go to your fat-headed ego. I'm doing this for Lucy, only Lucy."

"Thanks much, Michael." The gratitude in her voice filled Gus with relief.

She tapped off the phone after saying their goodbyes.

"I'll be here before sunrise on the first of February. Nothing will keep me away. Not even the Abominable Snowman."

"Thanks. Whatever I can do. For you. To help...help you." Her voice cracked.

"You've already been a source of aid." He pushed up his sleeve and thrust his forearm toward her. "Your healing powers have proved trustworthy. I'm cured!"

Gazing down at his arm, she lightly stroked the faded outline of his cut. Her touch quickened his pulse. He brushed his lips over her cheek and dropped a kiss on one freckle. Lucy's fingers froze.

Had he gone too far?

Chapter 15

His tender, peppermint-scented kiss lured Lucy closer. With a trembling finger, she traced the last bit of his wound. Her blood rushed, then stilled. Before a thought or worry escaped, she covered his mouth with hers and erased the distance between them.

An urgent ache took hold of her. She had to explore every curve of his luscious lips. It was an absolute must.

Kiss. Gus. Immediately.

Lucy wrapped her arms around his shoulders to steady her racing heart and darted her tongue across his lower lip. Gus pressed her against his chest, let out a soft moan, and playfully swirled his tongue with hers. Their first kiss turned from innocent to passionate.

Her breath shortened, and every one of her nerve endings sizzled and snapped. Gus's kiss swept away her senses. Ending this kiss? Completely out of the question. The kiss quenched an indescribable thirst.

"I'm feeling groggy. All the scents in here have me in a haze," he murmured.

Her cheeks burned. She had to be glowing brighter than one of her Lust candles. As she fluttered her eyes open, his long ginger lashes danced before opening.

"You're beautiful," he whispered.

Pressing her cheek against his rough beard, she let the little sparks of friction warm her. "It's the power of Lust."

Reality knocked her back to her senses as soon as the words left her mouth. Gus or Angus Reid? It didn't matter. Both were too risky; she needed to avoid any *groggy, foggy, or boggy* type of situation.

The shop. Lust. Her nose. They weren't minor dalliances. They meant surviving.

Dang Lust.

The front doorbell rang.

"Another delivery. I hope it's the rubber ducks," she stammered and stepped back.

"You'll have to explain the duck thing to me." His voice sounded low and gritty.

As she walked through the shop, Lucy smoothed down her sweater. She was acutely aware of leaving Gus behind and positively sure he was eyeing her ass.

Expecting the FedEx guy, she swung the door open. A maniacal-looking redhead burst into her shop and stormed toward Gus. When Sara bumped into her chalkboard sandwich board and almost tipped it over, Lucy lost it. "What the hell are you doing?"

"Working," Sara yelled.

She imagined fumes coming from Sara's nostrils as she stood nose-to-chest with Gus.

He crossed his arms over his rock-hard pecs.

Readjusting her sandwich sign, Lucy wondered if she could drop-kick and pin the publicist to the ground. It would probably be bad for business though, so she ambled closer to the dueling divas.

"What's going on?" Gus demanded.

"Johnny is coming back any minute. Wherever you sent the

paparazzi for lunch, they served fast." Sara pointed at her. "You two can't be seen together. Remember?"

"We're not *together*," Lucy said. "This is my business, and your client is endorsing it. I'm sure you can appreciate professional success. Girl power?"

"Your asks are draining Angus, and he needs to be in prime condition for filming," Sara said, exasperated.

"I'm not your property." The vein in his temple vibrated.

When Maddie and Peter entered, Lucy wanted to hug them both.

Peter rushed toward the toxic couple and Lucy went up to Maddie as she tapped the cowbell hanging above the door. "Get ready for more drama because it's heading our way. And because it's for our sweet town of Baileys, it's worth every single penny."

Shaking her head, Lucy whispered, "Sara has major issues."

"I have to tell you the deets." Maddie grabbed Lucy's hand and tugged. "Now is the perfect opportunity to show me your office."

They strode past the trio in the midst of a heated discussion.

When they were safely out of earshot, Maddie let out a long sigh. "She is a cuckoo bird."

"Why is the woman in such a tizzy? I've been with Gus less than an hour."

Maddie sat in her desk chair and twirled around. "After you left, I joined them to go over the Fest schedule. And not gonna lie, Peter is sort of hot. He reminds me of one of the guys I worked with back in New York."

"He has a Jason Statham look with his bald head and all-day five-o'clock shadow." Lucy wanted to ask more about her life in New York but didn't get a chance. Maddie kept talking.

"Right? Anyway, Sara complained a lot about how Angus needed to be part of the conversation. Even Peter gave me a wild-eyed look while she carried on. Then, her phone started pinging."

"I'm an aromatherapist, not a psychotherapist. I do think her personality is intense and borderline stalker-ish. She may be obsessed with Gus."

Lucy didn't bother to add how Sara reminded her of Julie.

"It's sad. Actually pathetic. Why does Gus put up with her?"

Lucy squashed her refusal of pain. She'd never been able to interpret the constant hurt into words, and yet, she'd repeatedly shown up to defend her mom. "Tough to say. What do you think they're talking about?"

"Probably lighting. They didn't figure it out at the lighthouse this morning." Maddie pointed at her shoeboxes. "Love Vans."

Lucy kicked up her foot to show off her winter high-tops. "Wearing them. Those boxes are filled with ancient bars of soap."

Maddie gawked at the boxes. "Can I see?"

"Sure, nothing too exciting. Just my collection."

"You collect soap?"

"Whenever my dad traveled, he'd bring back a soap from the hotel he stayed at. When I was ten, he ran off and left my mom." *And left me to take care of her.*

Maddie lifted off the top of the box. "This is a lot of hotel-motel soaps."

Lucy pointed toward the other boxes she'd stored on the shelf. "There are the rest."

"So, you've had a lifelong crush on scented stuff?"

"I suppose you're right." Lucy counted, and there were a dozen shoeboxes filled with soaps wrapped in thinning paper and stamped with Holiday Inn or the Hyatt. "He was a sales rep and on the road. Long after he took off, I'd get packages of soaps in the mail from him. Last I heard, he'd died."

"I'm sorry."

"Don't be. I can barely recall his face." But she'd always remember his scent—Polo. Lucy arranged and rearranged the boxes of soaps. "Can I ask you a personal question?"

"Sure."

"Are you and Gus good?" Lucy loved how he had introduced

her to the idea of amends. It was more powerful and versatile than any candle she'd ever created.

"Completely. We've known one another and have gone through hell and back. A lot happened after Rosamunde died, which was a sudden tragedy. Gus found her on the floor of the house, lying in a pool of blood. Apparently, she'd had cirrhosis, and no one knew it except for his dad, George. Although Gus would never believe—"

"Gus found Rosamunde in the house? The place I've been staying? That house?"

"Yes. I'm shocked Gus is sleeping in there."

"He's not, actually. He's been staying in the guest cabin." Lucy called to mind how Gus had made a point of coming into the greenhouse but didn't stay long in the great room or adjoining kitchen. "What about his dad?"

"Poor Gus...not really, because he's a stubborn ass, but he always blamed George for not being around for his mom."

The passing of one's love was heartbreaking. Lucy suspected that her Philos, Eros, and Agape vibes, like the *Ghostbusters*, had crossed streams and had been muddling up her *Emma* sense. Suddenly, things cleared up for her.

A chilly thought raced in and out of Lucy's brain. Was jail a better place for *her* mom? Or would she die alone, another soul lost to alcoholism.

Maddie looked at her phone. "It's been five minutes, and I don't hear any high-pitched complaining. Should we go and save Gus?"

Lucy pressed her ear against the rippled glass inset on the office door. The wood floors squeaked, and the conversation had quieted to a lull. "I hope he's okay. We need to go on a rescue mission."

Once in the shop, no one had to be saved. Gus and Peter were hunting around, inspecting the windows, and staring at Lucy's paper lanterns. Sara had disappeared.

"What's going on?" Lucy asked.

Gus turned toward her, squared off his fingers, and framed her within the box. "There she is. The star of the hour."

She squinted. "Are you okay? Where's Sara?"

"You ready for your debut?" Peter circled around her and scanned her from head to toe. "Wicks & Balms is tremendous. The lighting is beautiful."

"What is going on," she repeated, getting jumpy and wondering about Sara. Had Nick Parker snuffed her out? She walked over to the front windows and looked around. No paparazzi and no Sara.

"My publicist left to go and update my Fest schedule," Gus said.

"Oh. Right." *Doubtful.*

"The lighting in your shop, with these lanterns, is perfect for *Raven*'s indoor scenes," Gus explained. "It's brighter than in the interior of the lighthouse. Is that okay, Maddie?"

Maddie shrugged. "You're making money for our humble town, so more exposure for Wicks? Be my guest."

"Whoa! Wait a minute!" Lucy interrupted. "This is...is...my life. This shop. Using it in a TV show? What...how..." She clutched onto the edge of her cash wrap. "I have a ton to do to prepare for opening. There are still boxes in my truck for you to unload."

"We'd do everything," Gus said calmly. "Every bar of soap will be rearranged or moved like a Steinway. Nothing will get damaged. If you want, you'll be able to keep the props."

She hadn't even gone into labor with this baby, and she was already concentrating on her breathing.

"The natural lighting in here is ideal," Peter added. "You have fantastic transoms. And your lighting design? It's better than some I've seen on other set productions. You would be doing *Raven House* a huge favor."

"More light than in a lighthouse? Sounds like an oxymoron."

Lucy feebly attempted to make a joke. She glanced at her claw-foot tub, still waiting for the ducks. "I don't..."

"I know this is terrifying." Gus gently grasped her shoulders. "Will you trust me?"

Her palms started sweating, and she wiped them off on her jeans. "I..."

"You can be an extra if you want," Peter cajoled. "Wardrobe would love to dress you."

"No, I...thank you." She shook her head. "I don't know."

"Of course, you'll be compensated for your..." Peter strolled around the shop's perimeter, scanning the windows, walls, and floor. "...beautiful contribution to *Raven House*. You'll receive a daily stipend. Will a grand per day work?"

Lucy hadn't fainted over Robert Downey. However, this news couldn't be more swoon-worthy.

"This is incredible." Maddie picked up a bath bomb and tossed it to her. "Do you know the kind of recognition this will bring to Wicks? And the product placement for Lust?"

Catching the bomb, Lucy sniffed it like smelling salts to stay alert. Depositing a thousand dollars per day would pad her dwindling bank accounts. "You three are ganging up on me."

"I don't mean to pressure you, but this *is* beautiful in here." Gus pointed at the ceiling. "Those are original copper plates. Indicative of Art Deco. The building was built in 1920. It's a perfect setting for Nick Parker and can be turned into an incredible speakeasy."

She lifted her eyebrow. "You've done your homework, haven't you?"

"Hey, I'm not just a pretty face."

"Can I have the studio process the paperwork?" Peter gave her a roguish Statham smile. "I can drop it off in person. For your signature?"

"Can I oversee things?" Lucy asked. "Make sure nothing gets damaged?"

Peter nodded. "Every minute we're in here, you should be, too. I'll get you a director's chair with 'Maxwell' printed on the back."

Gus jotted down something on a slip of paper and handed it to Peter. "Here's where I'm staying. Have the studio email the paperwork to me. I can print it off at my mum's house and go over the legalese with Lucy. Please, mate...keep this address between us. All right?"

"No problem. Lucy, you are a lifesaver, thank you." Peter replied.

"I haven't agreed to anything yet," she teased.

His bald head turned pink around the edges of his director's cap.

"Kidding. I'm okay since Lust will be one of the stars."

Maddie hugged her. "OMG, this will be fantastic for you. For Baileys! I have to take off. Let's talk soon. I have ideas. Do you want to use my photography expertise?"

"Sure," Lucy said, "but first, let me get a handle on this and reconfigure my schedule."

After Peter and Maddie left, she faced Gus. Alone.

Steady, girl. Breathe.

"Thank you for filling in for me. For the inspection." She flicked a toggle to dim her Red Vine chandelier. "Can this piece be used in the filming?"

"Yes. And I meant it...you can trust me. I won't let anything happen to your baby."

She filled her lungs with air, blew it out, and relaxed. "Today's a strange one. If you had told me back when I decided on Lust over Lush that you, the inebriated Hollywood megastar, would be my proxy for a safety inspection...I would have laughed all the way to the bank when I got my loan."

Gus licked his lower lip. "Different time. And now?"

"You get onstage, pour out your heart, and fearlessly face a silent audience. If you can do it every day, I know I can do it. Once. For Wicks. Even though you're an *actor*...I believe you." She held up a finger like a teacher. "But don't get cocky on me. And the smoldering smile doesn't work."

However, your luscious kiss...

"You will be in your shop, on my set, every day. I fully expect you to watch over and keep me in line." Gus grabbed the box of Seville candles. "Filming here will be an adventure."

A mix of exhilaration and terror stirred inside her. This was a big deal and an incredible opportunity. Lust becoming an A-list celebrity and her shop on TV. As long as it went according to plan. Dang, she hated to think it...when was the last time plans had gone smoothly? Of late, *best-laid plans* felt riskier than ever.

Chapter 16

Lucy's routine had been turned upside down since last Friday. Morning yoga was replaced with pre-dawn office hours to make sure her baby was in good hands as *Raven House* renovated W&B into a film set. Now, her apothecary was transformed into a secret reading room that seconded as a hidden speakeasy, and the cast and crew of the show had taken over her shop.

She called Stan's Hardware from her desk to make sure he'd opened. It was barely six, but she needed to pick up her lavender to adjust her Serenity scent. She wanted to make sure there were enough soaps and lotions for when she went to visit Julie in one week...only six or seven days away. She still hadn't decided whether to go to Lake Bluff/Kohler a day early. This terrible sense of foreboding was lingering in Lucy's mind. Even with all the action happening in the shop with *Raven House* and her own personal collection of de-stressing oils, Lucy was a jumble of nerves.

Waiting for Stan to answer, she stared at Gus's signature newsboy cap hanging on her office door and wondered. *Did he remember the kiss?* Her lips still tingled after an entire week had passed. Since filming began though, it felt as if their fiery kiss never happened.

Gus barely looked her way.

When Stan answered, she rubbed her cheeks, still burning from thoughts of Gus. Since the hardware store was prepping for the next snowstorm—"a doozy," Stan had called it—Lucy put on her winter gear and trudged out the back door. The best way to avoid the early morning paparazzi shift.

Behind the shop, the trailers were lined up end-to-nose, and the alley had been sectioned off from traffic. Equipment trucks clustered around the fence enclosing the back patio, and camera umbrellas sprouted above it.

Within the next hour, the set techs, camera operators, makeup, and wardrobe artists would start to arrive. Peter and Sara usually came together, and only the stars in the day's scene would come and linger about the tent that doubled as a green room and cafeteria. A few photographers, part of the crew, straggled around the rear of her building. Lucy spotted Kayla and waved.

The walk to the hardware store was short and treacherous. Lucy kept slipping because of the pretty fluffy snowflakes falling around her. They were a lethal prelude to tonight's storm.

Stan greeted her at the door. "How is it in your shop?"

"Really cool and a little unnerving," she confessed. "A lot is going on. I hope this is helping your biz."

"Oh yeah, a couple of the stars have come in. They're nice folks except for one of them. There's a gal who's way too fancy for Baileys. And techs have bought equipment from me. I've had to special order a couple of items, but they've found what they are looking for in-house. I haven't met Angus Reid though."

"This is why I love your store," she said, feeling lucky to know Stan. "It's a flea market and bazaar on steroids."

Stan handed her two big bags filled with dried lavender. "Any chance you can get me an autograph from Angus Reid?"

"It's the least I can do since you've given me great deals on my packaging and wrapping supplies," she said, paying for her purchase. "Can you add on a bag of salt? I almost slipped and fell on the way over."

"No prob." He added, "Hey, it's quiet. I can salt up the sidewalk for you."

"Oh, no, Stan. I don't want to bother you."

"This is Baileys. I can give you a hand." He grabbed his buffalo plaid jacket from behind the counter and called for an employee to come up to the register. "Any chance I'll catch a glimpse of Angus?"

"At this time, you'll get a good look at the paparazzi. They're camped in front of the shop most of the day." She tucked her braid under her Stetson as they left the hardware store. When they closed the four-block distance and neared the paparazzi, she lowered her hat over her forehead.

She spotted a lone van on the street. When they walked by it, no one was in it. Johnny from *TMZ* was smoking a cigarette and hanging with the lighting guys.

Stan waved. "Hey, Jack. Hiya, Kenny. How are the ladders working out?"

Lucy waved the smell of stale tobacco away from her nose.

One guy called over, "Good. Thanks, Stan."

"Sounds like you know plenty of the crew already," she said.

"It's all because of Detective Nick Parker." He followed her into the shop. "This place looks incredible."

Wicks had been turned into a Prohibition-era reading room that also converted into a speakeasy. The cash wrap and chandelier served as the centerpiece for the set. Floor-to-ceiling bookshelves with Art Deco carvings across the top shelves hid a cocktail bar. Like the Snake Pit, the set designers incorporated a mechanism for moving the bookshelves and exposing a back-lit mirrored bar with a neon sign.

There were tufted leather chairs placed around mahogany tables. Vintage Tiffany lamps and vases of fresh gardenias were centered on each table. The white gardenias were Lucy's idea since they represented Billie Holiday, an icon around the same time period.

Technicians clamored about, and Lucy pointed at her chair. "That's where I usually sit. I'll ask the director to get another chair if you want to stay and watch."

"Love to," Stan said, dropping the bag of salt by the door.

Sitting in one of the library-style wooden chairs, Gus spun around, leaped out, and strode toward them.

"Morning." Gus held out his hand for Stan. "And who's this?"

"Um, Stan." Lucy felt invisible as he looked right past her.

She reminded herself that the world Gus lived in was an escape for her, and one steamy kiss wasn't strong enough to bridge the gap between their real lives.

"I'm Stan Reeves, owner of the hardware store. Lucy invited me to watch. Hope it's hunky-dory."

"Fantastic to have you. Let me get you a chair," Gus offered. "Are you a fan of the show, Stan? Ever watch it?"

"Hell, yes. My poker buddies, too."

She tried to make eye contact with Gus without any success. He was too busy googly-eyeing Stan.

"Good to know." Gus sounded like one of the guys. "Do you like the set? How does it look? Authentic to the era?"

"Is it 1928?" Stan gawked around. "Your costume, the classic spats, bomber jacket, and trousers make Nick Parker look better than Eliot Ness."

Lucy was impressed with Stan's attention and knowledge about men's fashion during prohibition. Seemed strange until he went on.

"And the guns, man. They are incredible. Can I see the props? Any tommy guns?"

Gus laughed. "Oh yeah. Let me show you the prop trailer."

Feeling snubbed, Lucy held tight to her bags of lavender and settled into her chair behind the monitors. Waiting for another long day of shooting to begin, she pulled out her phone and reviewed her photos. She'd taken pics to show the transformation from apothecary to speakeasy to use on Instagram.

Lucy learned how creating a magical escape back in time for TV was tedious to watch and occasionally downright boring. All of the actors' movements had to be calibrated for the camera. A lot of time was spent deliberating over minute details. There were moments when she almost dozed off and had to adjust her position in the chair so the wood frame jabbed her back and kept her awake.

The activity and bustle escalated in the 1920s reading room. Peter gave her a wave and sat behind the monitor two seats away. Three of the guys who'd been outside were settling in behind their individual cameras; the rest took control of spotlights on top of sticks by climbing up the ladders behind the lights.

Stan returned carrying his own chair, spoke to a cameraman, and bounded over toward her. "This will be great for your business," he said, pointing at the recycled wine bottles on the back of the bar. "Aren't those the ones you bought at my store?"

"Good eye, Stan. I filled them with colored water and put on labels. Instead of booze types, I used my scent names. What a long day. The set designers spent hours arranging them on the glass shelf so the name Lust wouldn't stick out. They decided to use the seven deadly sins instead of just one to make it work."

One of the men, grasping both handles on opposite sides of the spotlight, turned the light toward her and Stan. They both shouted hellos. In the intense heat of the huge light, she laughed.

Stan said, "It's great what Gus is doing. He'll be stopping in the hardware store during the Fest. For the ice-carving contest."

Lucy frowned and experienced a twinge of jealousy over Stan-Stan, the Hardware Man.

Sara came onto the set elbow-connected to Alexandra. The gorgeous woman looked amazing in her costumes, even though she wasn't a very good actress. Today, she wore a shimmery, pine-green satin evening dress. The floor-length gown matched the green waistband that hung lower than her actual waist. Lucy adored Kayla's choice of lipstick shade for her, a deep tangerine, but the dress looked a bit hinky.

"Cripes." Stan slapped his knee. "She is one looker. A real beauty."

Lucy held her tongue. According to Peter, Alexandra was the reason it had taken five days to finish a scene that typically took one day tops. The slow process became slower, and Alexandra kept flubbing her lines. Lucy had wondered if she'd been taking nips of hooch in her trailer between shots.

Silence descended in the room.

Sara slipped free from the beauty, gave Lucy another one of her hourly icy glares, and leaned against the brick wall.

Peter shouted, "Ready. And...action."

Beauty strolled to the bookshelves, tapped the wood shelf, pulled out a book, and the shelves slid closed and hid the bar. Then, she pulled out a compact and adjusted her coifed hair.

Gus stepped onto the set.

A boom mic descended from the tallest ladder placed behind the cameras.

Whenever Lucy watched Gus turn into Nick Parker, she was mesmerized. As he questioned the beauty, she never tired of his facial expressions. The subtle quirk of his lips, the flick of his eyes, and broody stares portrayed his character along with the dialogue.

On the other hand, Alexandra, who played the owner of the speakeasy, was awkward.

Today, she delivered her line with "Nick Parker," and it came out sounding as "Nick Porker."

"Jesus Christ," Peter shouted. "Cut!"

The lights faded.

Gus marched into the office, and Alexandra came up to Peter.

"What the hell is wrong with you this week?" Peter demanded, shaking his head. "In the other shots at the lighthouse, you were fabulous."

To appear as if she wasn't listening to every single syllable, Lucy lowered her Stetson.

"I'm good. It's okay. My mouth feels dry from the cold air," Alexandra said.

Lucy couldn't stop tapping the foot rail of the director's chair.

"You are slowing us down. If you can't nail this scene today, we're tipping into budget trouble," Peter warned.

"Let me get a drink of water," Alexandra said, sounding a little tipsy, and then she scurried out the back door.

"Take five," Peter yelled.

The tension in the room was at its all-time worst.

"Can I help?" Lucy asked Peter. "I've got lemon oil for Alexandra. It might clear her head and her lines."

"At this point, I'll try anything," Peter said, sounding disgusted.

Lucy went behind the bar, her onetime cash wrap. Underneath, she'd stored her vials of oil, previously located in the apothecary cases before it had been turned into a speakeasy. She retrieved a vial from the basket labeled Lemon and went outside to Alexandra's trailer.

"You okay?" she called, knocking.

The door slammed open. "No. I totally suck."

Although she'd only talked to Alexandra in passing, the young actress was usually pretty chill. Unfortunately, Sara hovered around her as she did with Gus, so Lucy tended to stay clear of the Hollywood drama.

"Here's my lemon scent," Lucy said, stepping inside, then added, "If you're hungover..."

"How did you know! I'm so mad I let Sara talk me into drinking champagne last night. Those bubbles are the worst."

"Roll this under your nose." Lucy handed her the vial. "Then pinch one nostril closed, inhale, and then switch nostrils. Do it three or four times."

"Kayla's gonna be pissed. She'll have to redo my makeup," Alexandra said, "but what the hell."

Lucy texted Kayla. **Don't freak. Get over to Alex ASAP**.

After a lot of sniffing, Alexandra sighed. "It's working. My head feels clearer. Thanks, Lucy."

Stepping out of the trailer, Kayla came up to her. "How is she?"

"Better. Her upper lip is super oily. You'll have to powder her up."

Kayla laughed. "No problem."

"Did I miss anything?" Lucy asked Stan when she slipped back into her chair.

"The PR gal, she's a piece of work. She's the one who came into my store and was a pain in the ass. Excuse my French. Even here, she's rude to everyone, especially Gus."

Lucy blew raspberries. "Just a normal day of filming a blockbuster drama."

"And we are rolling, people," Peter yelled, ratcheting up the set's already tense atmosphere. "Take two."

When Alexandra came out, she didn't appear to be stiff.

Peter shouted, "Action."

The scene unfolded the same as the first take, however, this time, the two co-stars quickly gelled into their roles—Nick Parker, the detective, and Pauline Morton, the speakeasy owner and suspected killer.

Lucy was riveted by the scene. Stan must have been immersed in the story, too. She barely heard his raspy breathing.

Nick took off his signature newsboy cap and lowered his head. "I've got to take you in, baby."

"Buzz off, Parker." Pauline strode past him. "I've got a business to run. And I didn't kill no one."

He grabbed her arm and dangled the handcuffs in her face.

She stumbled into him. "Oh, Nick, please? Can't you let me

go? My kid, think about her?" Pauline touched his cheek, leaned in, and kissed Nick.

Lucy opened her mouth a smidge as Gus and Alexandra kissed. The two actors locked lips so tight she wondered if they had melted into one person. The silence on the set was as stifling as the heat from the spotlights.

Nick Parker grabbed Pauline's shoulders and pushed her away from him. "I'm feeling a bit groggy from your ruse, but it won't work. You don't have any kid." And with that, Nick Parker spun her around and slapped the handcuffs on Pauline's wrists.

Peter screamed, "Cut!"

The floodlights dimmed, and the crew let out whoops and cheers.

Stan leaned over to her. "What did you give the beauty? She made Gus look like *her* co-star, hey?"

Lucy was thrilled, and not for Alexandra.

Nick felt a bit groggy. Gus felt a bit groggy.

She clutched the handles of her chair.

"You nailed it!" Peter shouted at Gus.

"I did nail it, didn't I?" All smiles, Gus shook Peter's hand.

When Gus caught her eye, he winked. A ridiculous giddiness filled her. He had remembered their passionate kiss.

Chapter 17

The strain in his shoulders pinched, and Gus slowly came out of his crow pose. He grabbed a towel, wiped the sweat off his neck, and checked his timer. Three minutes. Good, not great, but a solid way to start off a bona fide snow day. The latest snowstorm blew through Baileys last night and shut it down for the weekend.

While waiting for the shower to heat up, Gus scanned his messages. He brushed his hand across the water, still cold. When he turned the faucet, instead of warming up, the water became icier. Was the water tank filled with snow?

He gave up, threw on his sweats and hoodie, grabbed his gear, and trudged outside. Once over the mounds of snow, he rang the bell to the main house. Lucy had to be inside; she had also gotten word about the snow day. He rang the doorbell again. Unless... Gus pounded on the back door. He sincerely hoped Lucy hadn't driven to Wicks. The roads were treacherous in this weather.

"Lucy?" He hiked away from the house and sank into a bank of snow. Blue light from a TV bounced around the upstairs bedroom. "Are you in there?"

He made a snowball and threw it at the second floor. It cleared the guardrail and hit the french doors. It was a winning shot, and after a few more three-pointer snowballs, she finally came out onto the balcony. Gus looked skyward and prayed *thanks.*

She folded her arms over a fluffy pink robe. Matching pink headphones were around her neck. "Doesn't Nick Parker get a snow day?"

"Yeah, of course. My shower's busted. Can I use...come in and use yours? I'll be quick. In and out." Gus cringed at his choice of words. "I mean. It won't take long. Promise."

Even worse.

A faint aroma of buttery popcorn made his mouth water when she opened the back door. He kicked off his boots and followed his nose to the stovetop, where a tall stainless-steel pot sat on the burner. Inside the pot, remnants of salt and butter covered a few lone kernels.

"It's a snow day. I'm binge-watching *Gilmore Girls* upstairs," she said.

"What season are you on?"

Her cheeks turned pink, matching with her robe, headphones, and slippers.

"Only the first. I had to hit pause on the Donna Reed episode when snow splattered all over the balcony doors."

"Donna Reed? The episode when Rory and Dean have their first fight?"

"Dang! You're a *GG* fan?" She wiped out the bottom of the popcorn pot. "I'm impressed. It's a total chick show."

"As you've experienced this week, filming a show can be tedious. A lot of downtime. While I was working on season three, I watched *GG* during takes to prep for Adam and Liza. Both had solid credentials from working in it and were hired for *R-H.*"

"It's good. Isn't it?" she asked. "It's not completely void of testosterone elements."

Gus chuckled. "It's a great drama, and the writing is excellent. I was also watching for research, so not sure I'm a typical viewer. I suspect most guys would prefer a good football game. I feel lucky to have Adam and Liza on *Raven* though."

"There are a lot of good twists and turns. It's fun. And I love the pop culture references. The Lorelai and Rory story though," she said. "A classic mother-daughter drama is a total escape for me."

Gus gazed at her like a lovesick puppy. Every minute filming in the shop, he'd been severely focused on avoiding her. His mantra had gotten a workout as he forced his mind to block out their kiss. He couldn't risk getting caught. Not one look, glance, grin, or, god forbid, a smile in Lucy's direction or Sara would have a reason to accuse him of violating his contract.

Glancing out at the snow-covered yard, he'd lucked out. This snow day had turned into a much-needed reprieve. He was safe and could unwind. No paparazzi. No looky-loos. And no PR assistant watching his every move or holding a camera in his face.

"Want company?" Gus stretched out his arms and loosened up his shoulders.

"Surprising," she said. "I mean, don't take this the wrong way, you've been sort of...standoffish. I thought you were pissed."

"Not in the least. On set, there's a lot going on, and it can be stressful. I'm sorry."

"Well, at least you and Stan hit it off."

"He's a good guy. Thanks for bringing him around yesterday. It was..." He let out a long breath. "A good feeling. Almost liberating to meet a guy who watches the show. I tend to assume all the fans are women."

"Will it be men or women who faint when yesterday's kiss scene airs?" She gave him a sexy smile. "It was smokin' hot. I'm glad I gave Alexandra my lemon essential."

"Lemon what?" he asked, ignoring a wake-up call coming from under his sweats.

"Before the second take of the scene, I gave it to your co-star to rub under her nose and give her a boost for her hangover. I thought it could help."

"She was drinking? Or hungover? If so, it's grounds for getting censured or even axed. Are you sure?"

"Dang. Did I just get her in trouble? I wasn't positive and only suspected when she slurred her line. I went into her trailer, and she told me she'd been drinking champagne with Sara the night before. She was miserable." Lucy straightened her shoulders. "It's not my business, but your co-star is totally stressed out because of Sara. Is the microscopic scrutiny from your PR woman a normal Hollywood thing? Because it's extremely toxic."

Understatement of the year. Alexandra would have been removed from the set if she'd drank champagne with anyone other than Sara. Gus realized Sara had started to use the same tactics on Alexandra as she'd used on him when they'd started filming *Raven House.* The show wasn't his first gig, but it was a far cry from his role in the vampire series. He was anxious and jumpy and wanted to impress Peter, therefore fell into Sara's routine of champagne drinking to steel his nerves and focus.

"She really wanted to relax," Lucy said.

"Do you believe..." He paused. "...she'd been drinking all week? I don't want to put you on the spot. I'm simply baffled. Alexandra was performing well when we were at the lighthouse. And trust me, if you were sleeping while we filmed, I won't hold it against you."

"Your job is kind of tedious. I did catch a few z's in the office once in a while. She just appeared awkward, and I thought she wasn't a great actress."

Alexandra was green, but she'd been a professional since filming began. The champagne drinking had Sara written all over it. "So, how did the lemon help her?"

"It's a blend I created for hangovers."

"I didn't smell any lemon," he said. "But whatever it was, it worked. Thanks to you, the scene rocked. Peter wants to send the episode into the Emmys."

"Seriously?" Lucy gave him a high five. "You are going to get an Emmy Award. Props to you. This is big." She grabbed the pot. "This calls for a celebration. Up for some popcorn? It's my mom's recipe. I make it with coconut oil and dust it with cheese powder. As long as it's okay for your diet and all."

"Hell yes to the popcorn. I'm starving. But hold up on the celebration." He sat at the kitchen island. "This party is between us. It's a long road to an Emmy Award and a tough gig. There are a ton of talented actors and brilliant shows in TV Land. It is still a thrill to be tossed into the ring."

She scooped out a chunk of coconut oil and dropped it in the pot. "Wait a sec. Are you sure you didn't smell lemon on Alexandra? She had to have her makeup redone by Kayla. There was an oil slick around her upper lip."

Gus couldn't keep it to himself any longer. "The kiss nailed the scene because of you, Lucy. As soon as Alexandra came on set the second time and the cameras rolled, the scent of Lust made me think of you."

* * *

Lucy was ecstatic. Lust, the kiss, and the scene had come together and burst into fireworks.

"I must have grabbed the Lust vial by mistake," she said coolly, struggling to contain her nerves and keep the butterflies from fluttering. "Shows how potent my signature scent is."

"Right! Which is why I don't understand. Sinjin and Claire should be included in your love campaign." He went to the fireplace and opened the flue. "I'll get a blazing fire going for our marathon."

"They're way too busy," Lucy said warily. "I don't want to bother them."

"Don't know about that. When I called Sinjin, he mentioned he'd be in Baileys for the Fest and the ice sculpting."

"Oh, really." She found an old maid in the bottom of the pot and bit into it. "I'm sure Claire is working on an art exhibit. We've been barely able to talk."

"Maybe we can get together at the Fest." He poked at the fire until the flames multiplied. "This looks good. I'm in need of a shower. All right if I go upstairs? I'll make it quick. I promise not to keep Rory and Dean on hold too long."

After he left, Lucy took over popcorn duty. The slow process pushed out thoughts of Claire and Sinjin. She had to stay calm, or she'd burn it. When the oil sizzled, she dropped in one kernel. It popped, so she poured the rest of the kernels into the pot and stirred them. Eventually, they popped, and she kept stirring until fluffy white corn puffed up to the brim.

"Almost perfection."

After dumping in melted butter, she added a fair amount of salt, yeast, and cheese powder, stirred with her fingers, and transferred it into the copper bowl. "Perfect."

Lucy found her phone and scanned through her Instagram feed. Again, Claire had commented on one of her posts. She'd written **Beautiful** by a pic of Wicks as a speakeasy. Lucy nibbled on the corner of her mouth. She tapped out **Thanks** and then deleted it.

What the heck was wrong with her? Claire was her closest friend.

She clutched her phone, tapped out **Thanks** again, and posted it this time.

She found the show on the huge TV in the great room and paused it at the beginning. Even if she'd enjoyed the time spent in her pink robe, with Gus in the house, she wanted more layers. She jogged upstairs to change. What did one wear while watching *Gilmore Girls* with a mega-hot celebrity? She shrugged and put on black leggings, a T-shirt, and her long red cardigan.

Back downstairs, she found extra blankets and pillows in a cupboard and tossed them on the two overstuffed couches. Then, she set the bowl of popcorn on the coffee table between them.

"Smells delicious," he said, jogging down the stairs. "Not sure what's wrong with the shower in my place. All right if I use this one for a few days?"

Lucy caught the scent of bergamot. "You used one of my soaps?"

"Of course. How could I pass up a soap named *All the Young Dudes*?" Gus rubbed his hands together. "Ready for the marathon?"

"It's my jam. And we have plenty of time. The snow is still coming down."

"Let's hope we don't lose electricity," he said, wrapping a blanket around his shoulders. "It doesn't take much with the abundance of pine trees. During the summer, there used to be one big rainstorm knocking out the lights for a day."

"At least there are enough candles in the house." She grabbed a handful of popcorn and stuffed it in her mouth. His Henley tee stretched tight across his chest, and the last of three buttons was doing most of the work.

Dropping his phone on the coffee table, he plopped on the other couch and stretched out.

She fluffed the throw pillows around her, trying to get comfortable and appear cool and casual as if there was nothing out of the ordinary going on. Except when his sweats fell a smidge, Lucy caught a glimpse of his happy trail.

She blinked, stared at the TV, and hummed along to the theme song.

"Any Kleenex around?" he asked.

"It hasn't even started yet." She tossed a box of tissue at him. "Are you telling me you're a crying type?"

"It's the theme song. Come on, it's sappy. A real tear-jerker," he teased. "I want to be prepared."

"Carole King makes you cry?" Lucy chewed on her popcorn, and the sound made her cringe. Was she always this dang loud when she ate? "Is that how you get the tears going during a scene? Thinking about sad songs?"

"Fortunately, Nick Parker doesn't shed many tears. In acting classes, I used to envision a dying puppy."

"How awful." Lucy huffed. "Did it work?"

"Hells yes. I love dogs, so if a scene needs a tear or two, it works like a charm."

"Do you have a dog?"

"Yep. Two. A big retriever and a small one. A corgi. They get on well." He grabbed his phone and showed her pictures. "Humphrey is the retriever, and Bogart is the corgi."

"They're beautiful." She crunched on one piece of popcorn at a time so she wouldn't disturb the neighbors across the lake. "Who's taking care of them in LA?"

"A dog sitter who stays at my place in Malibu while I'm on location."

As the show opened, Lucy tried to contain her mixed-up nerves. This whole scenario seemed impossible. To confirm, she kept glancing at Gus. His eyes, the color of a lush green forest, sparkled. Was she imagining it? And their kiss. Would there be another? Probably not. *Keep it in your brain, girlfriend. He lives in LA, and your mom is whackadoodle.*

"I'm going to ask you one question. Don't answer right away though. Who do you consider to be the best guy for Rory? Dean, Jess, or Logan?"

"I'll let you know at the end of this season," Gus said. "But Dean, he's a solid choice."

"No, he isn't," she bellowed. "He's wishy-washy. Rory needs a strong, intense type like—"

Gus threw a pillow at her. "Oh no, can't tell yet."

Lucy put the pillow under her head and watched the show. A few episodes into the small-town drama, she started roasting from the heat of the roaring fire and pulled off her sweater. She stretched out on the couch. Relaxed enough to almost, but not quite, forget that Angus Reid was on a couch a few feet away.

"Beautiful tattoo. Is it a flower for inspiration?" Gus gazed at her arm.

She folded her arm over her chest. Relaxed, she'd forgotten about the ink. "It's a wood violet. Wisconsin's state flower. It's not really anything or beautiful."

He paused the TV and sat on the coffee table. "May I?"

She'd look like an idiot if she hid her arm under a blanket. "It's nothing."

To get a closer look, he lifted her arm onto his knee. The touch of his fingers set off a storm of feelies.

"The colors...the purple in the flower...is superb. Who created it?"

"No one as famous as your tattoo artist. We had him design it, too." Lucy's heart raced.

"We?"

"It's one of two tattoos. My mother has the same one on her arm." She tapped on the lettering below the flower. "This is my birthday, and this is hers. I must have been nuts to have my arm inked like my mother's. Matching mother-daughter tattoos. Ugh."

"It's quite pretty and well done. If you want it removed, I can make a recommendation. My guy will fly here from LA if I ask."

"Not necessary. I can't afford a removal. And it's prettier now than what would remain after it's *erased*. As if. Besides, both dates are embedded in my head. It would be silly to think removing a tattoo would remove it from my mind. It's a generous offer though. Thanks."

Gus read aloud the two dates beneath the purple-violet design. "April 1, 1972, obviously your mom, and your birthday is March 21. April Fools and the first day of spring."

"I know. It's either a really bad joke or a seriously clever plan."

"Your birthday's coming up. Do you have any plans?"

"I'll be at the shop. Just another workday, and it's more than okay with me."

"It's a couple months from now, plenty of time to change your mind. I'd be happy to throw you a bash. We could have it in LA."

"Thanks, but...you're so generous. I'm not a West Coast sort of girl." She glanced out the snow-frosted window. "But a break from the ice, snow, and salt sounds heavenly. Salt on the rim of a margarita instead of the sidewalk? What a treat, but I don't know."

"There's nothing wrong with sunshine, ocean, and spring break."

"I've made friends in Baileys, good friends. I'm pretty sure they aren't interested in babysitting Wicks for me while I'm off surfing. And remember my, uh, resistance to heights? Planes aren't my jam either."

"If I can babysit for the inspection, I'm sure Michael or Maddie, or Kat? They would do it for you. As to your 'resistance to heights,' we could take a train."

She was gob-smacked at his utter kindness. Who did things like this? "Let me get through my opening first." She gathered her hair together and pulled it to one side. The generous offer was one she'd never expected to hear from Angus Reid. "I'll put a Malibu vacation with a question mark in my planner."

The lights flickered off, and her breath stuck to the back of her throat.

In the dark with Gus?

Miraculously, they flickered back on a second later. Sighing, she put on her sweater. "Let's roll the tape, Mr. Hollywood, before we go into blackout mode."

Chapter 18

Gus had tried to stay awake last night to watch *GG*, but he was exhausted and fell asleep on the couch around the beginning of season three. Blankets and pillows were strewn about the other couch. When had Lucy gone upstairs to bed?

He stood, stretched, and needed a cup of tea. From the china cabinet, he found one of his mum's teapots and a box of Earl Grey tea. Glancing toward the fireplace, he froze. Last night, he'd started a blazing fire without flinching. He'd stood near the space where his mum had died and hadn't given it a second thought.

Waiting for the water to boil, he kept glancing at the hearth between checking messages. There was one from Peter confirming a second snow day and sending a small script change. Nothing major.

He opened the drapes and gazed at a winter wonderland. The snowfall and today's sun turned the lake into a dazzling ice rink.

A knock at the back door startled him, and he stepped away from the window. Had the paparazzi found him?

"Lucy, you up?" Michael shouted. "Checking in."

Relieved, Gus opened the door. "You scared me. Kinda early? Where's your truck?"

"Next door. Neighbors lost power." Michael came inside. "Wanted to make sure you and Lucy were okay."

Lewis, Michael's Bernese mountain dog, lumbered into the house. After shaking off the snow from his tri-colored fur, he came up to Gus and nuzzled against his leg, asking for a pet.

"Good morning, Lewis."

Michael brushed off his jacket. "It's almost noon. I've been plowing the lake since this morning. Didn't you hear me?"

Shivering, Gus moved away from the door and closer to the radiator. "Exhausted, man. Slept in. I'm pumped about this snow. Wanna cup of tea?"

"Any coffee?" Michael lifted his eyebrow in suspicion.

Gus went into the kitchen. "Yeah, yeah. I'll make a cup of joe for you. And Lewis? How about a bowl of fresh water?"

"Where is Lucy?"

"Upstairs sleeping."

"Not anymore," she said, plodding down the stairs in her fluffy pink slippers. "You two are louder than bulls in a china shop with your clomping about."

"It's Lewis's fault," Michael said, gazing at Lucy and Gus from head to toe. "Ope, sorry. Didn't mean to interrupt you two."

Lewis bounded over to the bottom of the stairs and greeted Lucy. His huge, wagging tail threw pellets of snow around the floor.

"Meet Lewis. My Berner," Michael said.

"Nothing to interrupt," she echoed, scratching the dog's neck. "So nice to meet you, Lewis."

Gus handed Michael a cup of Keurig-made coffee. "We've been watching a marathon of *Gilmore Girls*. If you want, you can join us."

"I'll take a hard pass. Besides, Kat's been wanting me for a long time to watch that show with her." Michael made himself comfortable at the kitchen table. "Not sure, but skipping over her might be rude or against binge etiquette."

"What a good..." Lucy coughed. "Friend."

"The ice fishermen are accumulating." Gus squinted outside at the bright sky and ice. "A lot of shanties on the lake."

"They're nuts," she said, making a cup of coffee.

"Ice fishing is the best sport in the world." Michael scoffed. "And Gus promised he'd gear up and get out on the ice with me while he's here."

"Boohoo, bro. It's been a busy time." Gus glanced at Lucy's long, ruffled hair and the sheet marks still embedded on her soft cheeks. "I made a promise, and I plan to keep it. Just not at this point in time."

Michael smacked him on his shoulder. "Then when?"

Lewis sat by Gus, tilted his huge furry head, and gave him the look...pleading brown eyes of sadness. "You two are ganging up on me."

"Do you actually catch anything?" Lucy leaned against the kitchen counter, gazing down into her coffee cup. "It sounds cold and boring."

"Boring!" The two men were aghast. Even Lewis whined.

"Not at all. It's a first-rate endurance test. Like acting." Gus scratched Lewis behind the ears. "Ice fishing is survival of the fittest."

"I'm not a fan of fish. They stink." Her face puckered.

He shook his head. "Not really."

"Yeah," Michael said defensively. "Maybe you should take your nostrils out and about. Sniff the fresh air, perch, and walleye."

"Or blue gill bass." Gus sounded like a twelve-year-old defending his favorite Packer player. "Haven't you ever been fishing?"

"Not once. Never. Jeez, you two."

Gus gave Michael a furtive glance. Fresh air and ice fishing were in order for the day, with Lucy giving it a try. "You shouldn't knock something before you've tried it."

"Yeah, Lucy. Think about the new smells you'll be able to sniff out on the frozen lake," Michael added.

"Is this a dare?" she asked with a smirk.

Lewis barked.

"I reckon Lewis makes it a triple *dog* dare," Gus teased.

"Lewis knows where my tip-ups are located out on the lake. The flags are bright red," Michael explained. "All you have to do is, if you two wouldn't mind, check them out. Jiggle them about. Pull up the hook and see if I caught anything. Of course, if you want to go fishing on your own, the auger and plenty of wax worms are stored in my shanty."

She looked confused and then smiled. "I have no idea what you're saying, but I can't back down from a triple dog dare."

"Hey, I thought you wanted to go with me?" Gus asked Michael.

"This is more interesting." Michael checked his watch. "I've been out on the ice this morning. Time for me to check in with the station."

"If Lewis is coming with," she said, heading toward the greenhouse, "I'm in."

Gus listened until the scuff from Lucy's slippers disappeared. "Mate, are you trying to be a matchmaker?"

"Back at you, brother. Just returning the favor." Michael handed him a leash. "Don't worry. I won't be far if you need any help. Still know how to use the auger to chisel a hole?"

"Sure. How wide of a hole again?"

"Go with eight to ten inches. There are big walleyes in the lake. Caught one the other day and made it for dinner."

"Sounds delicious."

"What sounds yummy?" Lucy asked, returning to the kitchen. "I'm getting hungry. The popcorn didn't fill me up."

"I'll let Gus fill you in," Michael said, "I've gotta head out. I'll be back later to pick up Lewis, thanks."

Michael stroked Lewis's head and took off.

"So, you're an ice fisherman?" Lucy asked the dog.

"Apparently," Gus said.

"Hey, is there any way you can guarantee I won't break my neck out on the ice? My boots are not so amazing out in the snow. I mean, it's slippery."

He opened his mouth to ask her if she knew how to ice-skate, then clamped it shut. He already knew the answer. Outdoors and winter weren't everyone's cup of tea. "Sure. I'll dig around the garage and find the ice cleats."

When she sighed, Gus relaxed. "Promise, if you fall, I'll catch you."

After they'd layered themselves until they could barely move their arms in their coats, Gus, Lucy, and Lewis on a leash stepped on the glittery ice of Kangaroo Lake.

"Can I hold the leash?" she asked. "He's sweet."

"And good trouble. He's named after John Lewis. And trouble can lead to pain for you if he sees a rabbit, squirrel, or any other critter. He'll take off, chase it, and leave you with a broken arm or butt."

"Okay. You get to hold on to Lewis, so I will hold on to you." She clutched onto his elbow as they carefully walked farther out onto the ice. "These cleats are great."

He tightened his arm around Lucy's, and then they followed behind their frozen breaths. Stopping at Michael's shanty, he retrieved a bucket of minnows.

Fishermen were sitting on wooden crates out on the ice while others had brought living room chairs. One man had a grill set up.

A long-lost sense of awe came over Gus. The cold air was peppered with the scent of evergreens, and he appreciated the quiet and sense of privacy. His mind was clear and focused. All his thoughts lined up like dominoes and fell in place as if he were on set. Even the house had become less threatening. After completing his amends with Maddie and getting to the halfway mark with Sinjin, he felt propped up to face George. Gus recalled spending a lot of time with his father on this lake. The man had the patience of a saint. Most weekends in the summer and winter, George came to Baileys and took him out fishing, and Gus complained his way through it. Rob would tag along, but not often. It could have been because of Gus's chronic angsty whining or because his younger brother was a car geek and preferred to be at a race track with Uncle Graham.

"Is this ice thick enough?" Lucy asked, tightening their elbow lock.

"It has to be close to twenty inches thick." He nodded toward a truck in the distance. "Otherwise, that guy would be breaking off and sinking in."

He spotted one of Michael's tip-ups. The red flag lay flat against the placeholder in the ice. Lewis tugged on the leash, and Gus jogged up to the fishing hole with Lucy bumping against him.

"Catch anything?" she asked.

He handed the leash to her. "No luck. The flag will pop up if a catch takes hold of the hook. I want to check the bait and make sure the minnow isn't frozen."

She knelt beside him. Between them, Lewis panted and drooled on their shoulders.

"This dog needs a Tic-Tac." She fanned her nose.

Chuckling, he lifted the line and shoved off the Frisbee-shaped placeholder. The line was long. Must have gone down deep into the water. When he pulled up the minnow, it was solid as a rock.

"Gives a whole new look to frozen fish sticks," she said through chattering teeth.

Gus pulled the fish off the hook and dropped it in the hole. From the bucket, he scooped up a flailing minnow, speared the hook into its gullet, and let it wiggle around on the end of the line. "Bring it on."

"Can't you count this as a catch?" Lucy joked. "It is a fish."

"Catching bigger fish is more fun. You never know what will come up on the other end of a line." Gus set the placeholder into the hole and laid the line and flag flat against the ice. "Always a good mystery."

They traversed the lake arm in arm and scoped out Michael's lines. The crisp air descended into his lungs and cleared his mind. He spotted an old wooden ice shanty standing out from the high-tech, brightly colored tents. It reminded him of his father's and drew him back into a past memory he could never forget—the book.

One freezing day out on the lake, his father brought a nondescript book and the fishing equipment. When they'd been warming up in the shanty, George had handed it to him and said, "Here are the basics for your tools."

At that moment, Gus had no idea what his father, an engineer, was handing over to him. A book about fishing equipment? Lines and lures? Then he paged through the small, hard-covered "manual" and realized it was about sex. He froze when landing on a page with a numbered illustration of a man's reproductive "tools."

"I'm sure you've been noticing a lot of changes in your body's mechanics," his dad stated.

Gus had stared down at the fishing hole. He wanted to dive into the icy water and swim away with the fish. Instead, he slammed the book closed, and after a deathly silence, he stuffed it into his backpack. "Thanks, Dad. I'm pretty good with my piston."

The big "talk" was interrupted, to Gus's relief, by the line splashing in the hole. The two men worked together to get the big walleye out of the water. "Good work, Gus," his dad said. "Just try to remember, before jumping into the sack with someone, to suss things out and decide about the endgame."

Gus hadn't taken his father's advice that day or since. Now, he was committed to it. An idea struck him about how he would make his amends to his father.

With only the crackling of the ice underfoot and Lucy's

warmth, he returned to savor this moment. "What do you smell, Ms. Emma?"

With their elbows locked, she dropped her head against his shoulder. "Fresh air. A lot of pine. And a bit of dog. Which explains a whole lot."

"How's that?" he muttered since his cold lips trembled. "A couple more fishing holes to check. All right?"

"Peachy," she said. "The scent of Lewis is what I smelled on you the night you broke into the house. I smelled a combination of cherry and wet dog, and both scents threw me off."

Crouching by the next tip-up, he pulled up the line. The minnow still wiggled on the lure, and he dropped it back down.

"The cherry," he said, shivering, "is from my favorite mocktail. A Shirley Temple. And Lewis was in the truck when Michael dropped me off."

She tucked the flaps of her hunting hat under the collar of her jacket. Her cheeks were pink from the cold air, and bits of dew adhered to her eyelashes, making them sparkle. "Liking ice fishing so far?"

"Yep. And loving the fresh air," she said. "Baileys is really magical."

"As good as Stars Hollow?"

She stopped, took the dog leash with two hands, and blinked at him. "I don't know. Baileys is idyllic and charming. It can be too close for comfort and at the same time isolating."

"Do you mean you're lonely?"

"Maybe more alone. Not a big family, and I'm a bit of a wonk. And everyone knows everyone in a small town. I'm reliving high school. Desperate for an invitation to sit at the popular table, giving up, and then escaping to the library."

"But like Stars Hollow," he countered, "in a small town, everyone has your back. Not an option in LA. Talk about lonely."

She wiped a drip of icy dew off the tip of her nose with the back of her glove. "Here's the thing. The show exemplifies togetherness. And the bonus is that, unlike reality, it won't sour."

"In Stars Hollow, you get the best of both worlds. Togetherness and autonomy." Gus had a strong hunch Lucy missed one or the other. Or both.

Having his friends in Baileys—a posse supporting him—had made him feel stronger. They would do anything for him. Even though Michael, Maddie, and Kat hadn't known Lucy for as long, he knew they would do the same for her.

"Fun fact," he said, "there was a lot of tension on the set of *GG*."

"What kind?" She started walking.

"Usual stuff. Clashing egos, opposing personalities, script disagreements."

"How can they work together if they don't get along?"

"Because the actors are given lines and words that are meant to pull at the heartstrings of viewers. Mostly, we mere humans have to think through our feelings, and then there aren't a lot of words to describe them. Writers do the heavy lifting and make acting easy. People prefer silence because putting our feelings into words, then saying them out loud is difficult." He closed his mouth and watched her.

She peeked up at him through thick lashes, then down at her feet, but said nothing.

Chapter 19

"You're a smart guy," Lucy announced. Then she yelled as Lewis took off and ran to the next tip-up. She held on to the dog's leash and pounded her cleats into the ice. Falling on her ass and injuring herself because of a mountain dog would not fit into her schedule. "Heel, Lewis, heeeel, please."

Gus skipped in front of her, held tight to the leash, and tugged. Lewis stopped running, sat down on the ice by the tip-up, and whined. "Good boy."

For the first time while on this icy trek, the red flag attached to the neon plate thingy was standing straight up. Icy air trickled down Lucy's throat.

When Gus went to check the fishing hole, she blocked him with her arm. "Let me."

"Have at it." He stepped back and waved her on.

She handed him Lewis's leash. "Don't sound surprised. You don't get to have all the fun."

She took off her gloves and held them between her teeth. Rubbing her hands together, she crouched down. Carefully lifting off the tip-up cover, she held on to the fishing pole that looked like a fat, wooden knitting needle. When she clutched the pole and pulled, it tugged back. Her heart skipped, and she spit the gloves onto the ice. "Dang."

Pulling on the line, she dug her cleats into the ice to maintain her footing. The strength in her arms was tested each time she yanked the pole and clutched onto the reel. Her fingers grew numb from the cold, but she managed to squeeze and turn the reel. "This is hard. My arms are aching. I need to do more push-ups."

"There's a big fish down there. Want me to take over?"

"Hells, no," she yelled.

"Keep it tight. Straight as possible." Gus knelt next to Lewis.

"Am I catching the Loch Ness Monster?"

Silver streaks thrashed in the black water a foot below the ice. "I see something fishy."

Excited, Lucy smiled and exerted all her energy to get the slippery little thing out of the water. She jerked the line harder and swiveled her hips to dance. "I'm appealing to its scaly nature."

Gus laughed. "It doesn't have feet."

"Ha. Ha." After spooling the line around the reel again and again, each time, it grew tauter and tauter. Finally, water splashed over the ice.

The silver-and-gray fish flailed in the black water. Why couldn't all fish be like Dory? Way easier to see. Lucy stepped back from the hole and jumped, twitching and screaming. "Get your wiggly ass over here."

Dory's ugly stepbrother popped out of the hole.

It slid near her feet. "Oh my god! It's huge."

Lewis barked with excitement.

On top of the ice, the fish wiggled closer to the hole.

"Oh no, you don't." She yanked the pole, and the fish skated across the ice. "You're not going anywhere. Now what?"

"Walleye for dinner sound okay?"

"Won't Michael want it?" she croaked and took in an extra gasp of air. "Isn't it his?"

"Michael's out of luck." Gus picked the fish up and tugged the lure out of its mouth. "This walleye is big. Must weigh a few pounds. Nice job."

She curtsied and took a bow. "Thank you. Thank you, kindly."

With a dog leash in one hand and a fish in another, Gus kissed her cheek.

She immediately warmed up. "We have to take a selfie with Nessie."

"Let me take it. Give me your phone," he said, handing her the fish.

Lucy made the trade and was disappointed. Why wouldn't Gus be in the pic with her? Too toothy and not enough interest from *TMZ*?

When the fish thrashed with a vengeance, she laughed. Gus stepped back and took pics of her trying to contain Nessie. Then Lewis barked and ran around her. With a flailing fish and a mountain-sized dog begging for her attention, Lucy instantly felt invincible.

They strolled to the house. She held Lewis, and Gus swung the bucket with their fish dinner back and forth.

"Up for more *GG* tonight?" he asked. "I confess I fell asleep and don't recall much of season three."

"I don't know if I'll be able to sit still. This fishing thing is exciting. Can you give me more dirt on the stars who quarreled on set?"

"This is my livelihood. Not sure if I should be sharing too many Hollywood secrets. I'll do it for you though. Liza had mentioned a behind-the-scenes drama going on. Nothing ugly or disparaging, more a clash of creative titans. The opinions about single mothers and mother-daughter relationships became fodder for a lot of heady discussions."

"Fascinating." She remembered all the times she'd watched the show and how she ached for her and Julie to have a relationship as cool as Lorelai and Rory's.

Gus stopped and set the tip-up and flag on the chair inside the shanty. "The discussions, not necessarily bickering, added a lot of good tension on the set. Scenes between mother and daughter were charged with emotion. It's a writer's dream to have two actors disagree off set and then say their lines on set with plentiful emotion."

"Aargh. You are the worst gossiper."

"Hey, it's a job with a lot of boring parts, and gossip is a real downer. Scripts can't create characters alone; good actors do."

"I really hope you don't throw Alexandra under the bus," she said when they reached the house. "I feel responsible."

"It's not her fault. So, no. Besides, if this Emmy nomination goes forward, she'll have to be at my side for every promo."

Back on land, she tapped the totem pole. "I love this thing."

"Here long before we came. I'm not sure about the tribe or the images represented."

"I'm clueless as to its origins, but it's a family. I named the faces when I moved in." She listed the names she'd given the totem pole last October. "George, Jane, Harriet, and Frank."

"And naturally, you're Emma. Careful taking off the cleats. They're sharp."

"I feel like the fish whisperer," she said. "I wrangled in a big fish, and I've never held a fishing pole in my life."

"Beginner's luck. Usually, you have to freeze your ass out on the ice a lot longer." He pulled her prize out of the white bucket. "Now comes the fun part. You get to gut and clean it."

She stared into the black, dead eyes of the silver fish, looking at the red spots dripping off its gills. "Yuck."

"Your loss," he teased.

"Okay, wait." She held up her hand. "I've only chopped up a lot of green stuff. This is a new one. I'm not bailing on the triple dog dare. Just that it's slippery."

"You won't have to do it alone. I promise."

Her phone pinged as Lucy scanned the knives on the fish table set up at the back of the house. The timing of Sister Jan's call couldn't have been better. She'd started to feel a bit queasy at the prospect of filleting her catch.

"I have to take this call." Lucy waved her phone toward Gus, who gave her a dubious look. She heard him bawk like a chicken as she headed to the stairs.

With court looming, a week away, she'd successfully avoided thinking about it while playing host to *Raven*. As soon as she heard SJ's voice, Lucy felt calm and able to deal with this next phase for Julie. They spoke briefly because Sister Jan's suggestion was spot-on, and her plan reassured Lucy.

She bounced down the stairs to go back to Gus. If she could face her mother, she could do just about anything, even fillet a walleye, because she wasn't alone anymore.

Chapter 20

Gus met Peter for lunch at the Beacon to discuss the final shots, however, he had more pressing matters weighing on him. Since arriving in Baileys, his work had been impeccable, and Sara's toxicity had become unbearable.

The two men sank into one of the leather couches behind the ball return. The alleyways would be a perfect setting for the season's final fight scene. While waiting for his food, Gus spotted Stan bowling with a group of older men and waved.

"Good-looking extras, hey?" Peter boasted.

"The owner of the hardware store is an extra?"

Peter pointed to a hipster couple with two kids bowling. "No, the family. Won't the kids be perfect in knickers and newsboy hats? We need kids to play the pinsetters."

"Right. Where'd you find them?" Gus looked at the end of the alleys and admired the display of neon bowling pins.

"The Peninsula Players Theater. They put out a casting call."

"I worked for the PPT stage crew through middle and high school. Fantastic organization. A lot of talent." It was life-saving for him. PPT gave him his start when he discovered school wasn't his jam. "And the older gents playing on the first lane. Are they extras?"

"No, they aren't, but they would make great bowlers in the background for the scene. Most of them look to be in their seventies," Peter said.

"I know Stan is a huge fan. And probably the other guys he's bowling with. They'd love a walk-on part or a bowling part. Not all of the show's fans are young and female."

The waitress set their food on the vintage score table in front of them.

Peter took a swig of his beer. "You're right. Baileys has opened my eyes. These folks are incredibly generous with their home and the accolades. Mostly because of you, Gus."

"Has a nice ring coming from you, Peter." He had to get back to basics, and Gus knew this was a brilliant starting point. "Makes me want to change my stage name to Gus."

"Why don't you? It's more fitting to the Nick Parker character, anyway. We can spin it for the show." Peter nodded toward the older bowlers. "They'll love it."

"Nice. I don't have to be *just a pretty face* any longer." He sighed. "And I can show off my acting talent?"

"Hate to break it to you, but it's your talent that brought us this far. I'm already planning seasons five, six, and seven." Peter stared at the *extras* who were still bowling. He gave a thumbs-up to the casting director and turned back to Gus. "Your work as Nick Parker has excelled since day one. Have Tristan process the paperwork. First name is Gus. Done. Now, what's really on your mind?"

Gus pushed his costume's chronically too-tight suspenders off his shoulders to face the bowl of chili, his food nemesis.

"Wait, don't tell me," Peter said before taking a bite of a delicious-looking cheeseburger. "It's my sister."

He tapped the chip hidden under his shirt. "I've been sober for over a year. I owe you and your sister many thanks for taking a chance on a guy starring in mac-and-cheese commercials. I know her job isn't easy since every person in Hollywood wants to get famous, and the bandwidth on social media is limited. But she's crossed too far over the line. First, she leaked my arrival to paparazzi, followed me home, and recently, I found out she's been filling Alexandra with champagne before shoots."

"You and Alexandra have been brilliant this past week. Has she been drinking on set?"

Gus shook his head. "No, I reckon Alexandra's been 'brilliant' because she's been using Lucy's oils and avoiding Sara. Your sister has, for whatever reason, become overprotective of Alexandra, the whole crew, and me. It's obnoxious. We'll be better off if we can film without Sara on or around the set."

"I know my sister, so I'll talk to her and make a deal. Let's say she's only on Fest duty. And tomorrow, make sure she does promo shots of you and Alexandra in the shop. I'm sending in three episodes to the Emmys. Once we start filming here at the Beacon, Sara can go back to LA."

Gus glanced toward the restaurant. Lucy hadn't shown up yet. Instead, Liza's rhinestone flapper headband glittered as she walked in for lunch with Adam. "It's going to be a rough conversation."

Peter rubbed the top of his bald head like a magic genie. "I'll deal. Here's the not-so-great news. We have to reshoot the opening scene at the lighthouse. The lighting wasn't as suitable as I had hoped. It's not up to par, and now you're on a roll. We may be in Baileys longer than planned."

"No problem, more opportunities to use my star power to help out here." Gus ate a spoonful of chili. "Not bad."

"I requested the veggie version for you to prep for the contest." Peter pointed to the bowling lanes. "Eat up. You have to brush up on your bowling skills while wearing suspenders before we head back to Wicks."

Again, Gus scanned the restaurant for Lucy. They'd planned to meet and talk about the inspection. He wanted to be near her, even just in the same air zone. They'd been like work colleagues the past five days. The snowstorm had been a blessing and a curse. He'd had one-on-one time with Lucy for two days last weekend, but since then, the cast and crew had to work around the clock to make up for the lost days. He hadn't had a second of alone time with Lucy at the house or shop.

When Sara and Alexandra strolled into the restaurant, the hairs on the back of his neck stood up. "See what I mean?"

"Oh shit," Peter said. "Can't delay the convo. It has to be now."

"Good luck." Gus watched Kat to make sure she didn't crack open a bottle of fun juice for his co-star and publicist. "At least we've finished filming in Wicks with only the promo shoots left."

Gus forced himself to finish the chili, guzzled down a glass of water, and headed over to Stan. One quick game while in his suspenders would make his director and the Baileys' old-timers happy.

He waved goodbye to Peter before leaving the Beacon. Sara, Alexandra, and Kat were gathered at the counter and hadn't noticed him, which was a relief. However, Lucy's failure to arrive before he had to get back to work was quite disappointing.

When she walked into the Beacon, Lucy couldn't stop staring at Adam and Liza. Their costumes were incredible. Liza's 1920s dress reminded Lucy of her kimono with its satin shimmer and bright floral pattern. Adam wore a wool three-piece pinstripe suit that fit the period beautifully.

She was tempted to introduce herself and vetoed the idea. They were seated at a table with Alexandra and Sara. Because Alexandra waved her over, she made her way to the star-studded table.

Alexandra greeted her with a hug. "Lucy! You are a genius. Your lemon essential oil has been miraculous. My concentration is better."

As Alexandra continued to heap praises on Lucy, Sara ignored them and dug around her purse.

"I've been hearing a lot about your oils," Liza said. "Any chance I can buy one from you?"

Adam shook her hand. "Great to talk to you. Your shop has been the best setting yet for the show. Many thanks."

Talking to Adam and Liza left Lucy feeling a little lightheaded. She felt like she was in an episode of *Gilmore Girls*. Until now, she'd only watched them from her director's chair or seen them come and go from the shop.

"Thanks, Adam. Sure, Liza. Actually, Alexandra, the oil you're using isn't lemon. I accidentally gave you a vial of Lust. If it's working for your focus, all the better. It's good to know it has more uses than just a love concoction."

"Makes perfect sense. It's easier working with Angus," Alexandra said. "Our on-screen chemistry is sizzling."

"That's the stupidest thing I've ever heard," Sara snapped. "You should be thanking Angus or me, not Lucy. You're too fucking green to know anything. I'm sure the champagne made a difference and relaxed you."

"You're wrong, bitch," Alexandra snapped back. "The champagne gave me a headache. Thanks to you, I could have been pulled from the set. It was definitely Lemon. Or Lust."

"I have to talk to Kat," Lucy said, backing away from the table as Adam and Liza stared angrily at Sara. Three against one, and Sara had lost. "Nice catching up with you all."

"Where's Gus?" she asked Kat, glad to be sitting at the counter and away from the publicist's lethal snark. "He was going to meet me here."

"Too late. He went back to Wicks. Didn't you see him?"

"Dang, we must have just missed each other. I have to go over the list for the inspection. Oh well." She pulled out a vial of Lust from her backpack. "Before I forget, I want you to have this. I confess, Gus and I have been doing a little matchmaking. Gently *nudging* to make sure you and Michael bond and stay close."

In between laughing, Kat snorted. "Must be the reason why I have a crumpled sachet in my car. *And* Gus gave Michael a huge box of candles. I bet he snuck them out of your shop."

"You're kidding. What color are they?"

"Dark purple. Like eggplant."

"My sidekick is rocking it. He gave you Madly in Love candles loaded with vetiver and ylang-ylang. The mightiest of mighty aphrodisiacs. Whew, I know all will be fine while I'm out of town."

"Where are you going?" Kat sniffed the Lust. "Your opening is right around the corner."

"Lake Bluff. Only a day or two at the most."

"Is everything okay?"

Lucy hedged her answer. "I have to take care of my mom. She's not in great shape. I'm hoping she'll be in a better place after I get back."

"Is she sick? Need anything?"

"I suppose you could call it a sickness." Seeing Kat's genuine concern allowed Lucy to open up. "Thanks, but at this point, the best help for my mother needs to come *from* my mother. She's addicted to alcohol."

Kat pushed her harlequin-printed apron aside and retrieved something from her pants pocket. Then she dangled a chain with poker chips hanging off it. "Four. Read 'em and weep. Sober for over four years."

"You are incredible, girlfriend!" Instantly, Lucy appreciated how lucky she was to have befriended Kat. She genuinely felt as close to her as she was to Claire. "Kudos!"

Kat gave her a high five. "I won't lie, it's been a bitch to get to this point."

"Does Michael know?"

Kat nodded. "Although there were dark times. I'm still shocked he stayed my friend. I was the sloppiest drunk this side of the Mississippi. My love of vodka must have been passed down to me from the Russian side of the fam."

"Unreal, but Michael is about loyalty and generosity," Lucy said, awestruck. Alcohol addiction disintegrated the most solid of relationships, and they'd managed to stick it out. "Did you have to make amends with him?"

"Hardest thing I ever did," Kat groaned. "After my first year of sobriety, I had to come to terms with how I'd treated him. As if he'd been put on this earth to clean up my messes. I'd abused our friendship and constantly dissed him."

Lucy understood how Michael had felt. She had been picking up one mess after another for Julie. Now though, seeing how these two stellar people had fought to stay close, blocking the corrosive effects of addiction, she was fortified with a fresh sense of hope.

"And then he made me go ice fishing with him." Kat rolled her eyes. "I'm not sure which was worse—the amends or fishing in subzero temperatures. But showing Michael I'd freeze my ass off for him may have solidified my apology."

"I guess there are a host of psychological benefits to ice fishing. I just caught my first walleye." After they chuckled, Lucy took on a serious tone. "Do you think...can you keep this stuff about my mom between us? I don't want anyone knowing. Especially Gus."

Too complicated.

"No problem. If it's any consolation, according to Michael, you have nothing to worry about when it comes to Gus."

As she tried to decipher Kat's comment, her phone rang. She grabbed her stuff as soon as the caller ID lit up her screen. "Perfect timing—this is my mother calling. Gotta take this someplace quiet. It's hard to hear...with the bowling."

"Good luck," Kat said cheerfully.

She huddled in the foyer's vestibule, accepted the collect call, and answered the correctional facility questions. The *TMZ* van was parked out on the street. *Doesn't Johnny ever leave Gus alone?*

"Lulu," she screamed, "will you be here before court?"

"Yes," Lucy answered, letting out a long-held breath and silently thanking Sister Jan. If not for her call last weekend, Lucy wouldn't have been able to respond with such a level head. "I'm not sure about the visitation times in the Lake Bluff jail though."

"Thank you for coming, Lulu. My baby will be with me before and after I get out."

Lucy rubbed her neck. "Please don't get your hopes up, Mom. You don't know for sure if you'll be released after the hearing. You're barely at the halfway mark of your sentence."

"I'm sure they'll let me go once they hear the truth. Then I can get back to work. I have loads of design ideas I'm anxious to create. Another chandelier and wall sconces. Copper pipes this time."

Truth? Julie had mastered the art of lying, and there were serious mental health issues she'd have to address.

"I'll be close in spirit and have lavender-scented soaps for you. I call it Serenity. I thought you could use them. I know there are restrictions since you're—"

"Behind bars? I won't be. I'll be free to go and use them in my own shower." She let out a long sigh. "And then I can sleep in my own lavender-scented bed."

Pacing, Lucy concentrated on her breaths. No matter what she told her, it always went in one ear and out the other. Important information was forgotten or mixed in with boozy delusions. "Be cool," Sister Jan had said, sounding like a seventies sitcom character.

"You'll love Serenity," Lucy added optimistically. "It also has jasmine in it."

"Sounds nice," Julie said, meaning, "*Whatever.*"

Thank goodness she and Sister Jan had come up with a plan.

Not only was Julie in a holding cell, but she was also in a holding pattern. There was no shower or bed for her to come home to because Lucy had to sell it to pay for fees, damages, and lawyers. She'd told Julie this critical piece of information every time they spoke, and it never stuck in her brain. She'd become a broken record. Lucy needed to push the needle.

"Have you gone to another AA meeting with Sister Jan?" She held her breath, hoping for the truth.

"I went last Tuesday," Julie shouted.

Lucy felt giddy. "Fantastic, Mom. I have several friends who have been able to stay sober because of fellow AAers."

When the operator interrupted with the ten-second warning, Lucy couldn't stop smiling. She patiently listened to Julie's list of complaints. With one second left, Lucy spoke up. "Take care, Mom. I'll see you soon."

Lucy ended the call.

Cutting Julie off had been SJ's advice. They both hoped this would get her out of a cycle of negativity.

Sister Jan had assured Lucy that Julie was considering entering a guilty plea. If this were the case, the rest of her sentence would be waived, and Julie could be released. So the hopeful nun and the hopeless daughter concocted a plan.

Lucy had reserved a room for the two of them at the American Club, a luxurious resort hotel and spa in Kohler, near Lake Bluff. With the money coming in from *Raven House*, Lucy could pay for it. If Julie gained her newfound freedom, they would have one night to talk it out. Face-to-face.

An hour-long Swedish massage was scheduled for them, a room service meal, and an upbeat playlist. Lucy had cued up Carole King, Aretha Franklin, and yes, she added in "I Want It That Way" by the Backstreet Boys. Sister Jan had requested Adele, but Lucy nixed it. The last thing she needed was for Julie to hear sad and lovelorn songs after being released from prison. Their room, she planned, would have an abundance of Serenity-scented products because nothing promoted calm more than lavender.

Then, Julie Maxwell would be in a tranquil state when Lucy had to break the news. The only new home she could go to the next day—a rehab facility recommended by Sister Jan and the Department of Corrections.

Chapter 21

Gus found his dad's snowshoes, prepped for the cold, and headed outside to hike to Wicks. Since ice fishing with Lucy, the shanties on the lake had doubled. Gus was relieved...no paparazzi. Almost a whole month, and no one had discovered the house. The frigid air clung to his lips and cheeks. Covering his mouth with a scarf, he started his trek across the ice of Kangaroo Lake.

When reaching the causeway, he sighted the parking lot for the Coyote Roadhouse. Almost noon on a Sunday and nearly full. The businesses around town thrived through the coldest part of the year because of the Fest. A sense of pride filled Gus. This year, his appearances at almost every event, even the terrible chili cook-off, would assist in the survival of his hometown. Whatever he could do for it, he would. Baileys had invigorated him and his career.

He put on his Ray-Bans and trudged onward. Once the causeway turned into the golf course at Maxwelton Braes, he tracked north on the side of the quiet snow-covered road. Gus wasn't in the mood to be spotted by *TMZ*. Johnny always had him in his sights. He edged down into the ditch. When a horn blared from the road above, his heart pounded. He'd been discovered, but it wasn't a media van. It was a white Prius with Maddie behind the wheel.

"How did you see me?"

"You're the one thing moving in a sea of white," she yelled through the open passenger window. "Caught my eye. Where are you going?"

"Wicks. Promo shots and inspection prep. The list Lucy texted me is long."

"She sent you a honey-do list? Me, too. You want a ride?"

Given the time, Gus realized he wouldn't get much done after his hike, so he capitulated to Maddie's offer. Besides, he'd worked off a lot of tension, enough to be in the same room at the looming meeting with his publicist.

"I'll bet my list is longer than yours," Maddie said. "Lucy asked me to take photos of everything inside and around her shop. The building, façade, and display windows for her website. Hop in. Throw the snowshoes in the trunk."

He stared at the small car. "This thing actually has a trunk?"

"Ha-ha. Yes. No need to go all car aficionado on me."

"Why? Do I sound like Rob?" Gus squeezed into the passenger seat.

Maddie glared.

"What did I say?"

She shrugged. "I loved when you made your amends with me, but there are times when you can really be an FHW."

"You're right. I confess to being a total asshat. I wholeheartedly believe you and Rob belong together." He gazed at the snow-covered pine trees on the frozen edge of Lake Michigan. "I've learned a lot from Lucy and her *Emma* mojo."

"I bet you have," she said. "Where is Lucy?"

"In Lake Bluff for a business meeting. I'll be working with Michael during the inspection tomorrow. I want to make sure the crew didn't break anything when they moved out the equipment."

On Main Street, Maddie slowed down.

"Can you go around the block and park in the alley? There's the *TMZ* van. I'll deal with the paparazzi after I finish the promo pics."

"Sure. Do you know when she'll be back? I have more ideas for her opening—cross-marketing with the lighthouse."

"In a day or two." He grabbed his duffle.

Maddie got out of the car. "I'm glad you're here for Baileys."

"Happy to help. I'm using my charm when possible. I talked to the director of the Peninsula Players. I may end up collaborating on projects to raise funds for the group."

"Speaking on behalf of the Logerquist family and my mother... thanks. If she were still around, she'd be pinching your cheeks for taking on her beloved town. The tough one is the lighthouse. It's in shambles, and I can barely keep my car running."

"I can help with the lighthouse, but the car? If you want to call it that. I half want to ring Rob and laugh about it together." It struck him how car talk would be a good way to initiate his amends with Rob.

"Yeah, yeah. Rob collects vintage cars and races them. La de da! I happen to love my stealthy little Prius. I'm sure it's easier to fix than Rob's Jaguar."

"I completely forgot about that old thing. I wonder if he still has it?"

"He does," she said quietly.

"You have significant insight on Rob." Gus opened the shop door for her. "I bet you know where he is as we speak."

"Yes. I invited him to the opening of the Fest to be with Sinjin for the ice sculpture contest, and he declined. Said he was working a case in Kohler and wasn't sure if he'd have time to come."

They made their way into the shop, and Gus dropped his snowshoes in the office. "You know he's avoiding me?" He flicked on the light switch for the chandelier. "I was such an ass to you two. Thanks for giving me a pass. I won't get as lucky with Rob."

He stopped in his tracks, and Maddie bumped into him.

"Watch out," she said.

"Are you sure Rob's in Kohler? Not prosecuting a case in Chicago?"

"Yes." She circled around the empty claw-foot tub in the center of the shop and pushed around the boxes to read the labels. "This is such a clever idea. I love it. One job on my list is to unpack the rubber ducks, fill the tub, and take pics."

Either his character, Nick Parker, had taken over his mind, or he was losing it. It could not be a coincidence Lucy, Rob, Sinjin, and his dad were all in Kohler on the same day. He glanced at the chandelier and thought of Lucy's mom. Something was up in Kohler and its sister town, Lake Bluff.

Sara rushed into the shop. "Alexandra's getting into her costume."

"I'm running behind," he said, jogging to the back door. Instead of opening it, he shook his head and strode back. "We'll have to cancel this shoot. There should already be plenty of photos to use. If not, we can pull stills from the film."

Sara scowled. "No fucking way. This is the last chance I can take shots of you and Alexandra. We need these pictures for the Emmys."

"There will be a ton of photo ops for the two stars at the Fest." Maddie suggested. "And then they'll be filming in the bowling alley at the Beacon."

He appreciated how Maddie had come to his defense.

"I've been kicked out of Baileys. After the Fest, I'm going back to LA. I couldn't care less though. This place is the worst." Sara huffed. "I can't believe you survived living here, Angus. Let's get this done today."

After a torrent of obscenities left his brain, he spoke. "There's business I need to take care of with my family. You can take the photos when I return."

"I'm not waiting around for you. I don't have time for this

bullshit." Sara tossed her hair and stormed out in a dramatic diva move.

"Wow, she is pissed," Maddie said. "What about the inspection?"

"Any chance you can cover for me? I'll get Rob to come in for the Fest. If I need to, I'll rope Sinjin into helping me," Gus said, "but I have to leave for Kohler right away."

"Of course." Maddie grabbed his wrist and dropped her car key into his hand. "I'll take care of Wicks. Trust me, this town needs it as much as Nick Parker."

"Great. Ring Michael and tell him you'll be here instead of me. I'll make calls on the way," he said, grabbing his gear. "Peter will make sure any leftover equipment is out of here."

"Just hustle."

"Thanks," he shouted, rushing out to the car.

Before hitting the road, he texted Sinjin.

I'll be at your house in an hour. FHW

Chapter 22

Since checking in to the ultra-posh American Club, Lucy had been sorting through a mix of emotions. The transfer process hadn't happened when she tried to meet Julie at the jail yesterday. Inmate 197241 would be escorted directly to the courthouse this morning.

As soon as she tiptoed into the courtroom, the pesky nagging feeling of *something forgotten* crashed into her.

Dang.

Julie wore a garish orange jumpsuit. Her court clothes, a navy skirt and white blouse, were hanging in the closet back in Baileys.

As she slid onto the front bench in the gallery, the faint scent of waxy lemon accosted her. The silence was as heavy as the dark wood paneling. Beyond the opaque bulletproof shield and seated at the Parsons table were the backsides of Julie and her attorney, James Hartford.

James whispered in her ear, covered by tangled knots of dishwater-brown hair. Her brassy blonde dye job had grown out and disappeared completely.

Sinjin and his brother Rob, seated on the prosecution side, stared ahead toward the judge's bench. The postures of *client* and *attorney* were ramrod straight. Their profiles were remarkably similar. The contours of their jawlines mimicked one another. If Gus sat beside them, they would be triplicated. Thankfully, Gus was taking care of her shop, none the wiser about this embarrassing situation with her mom and convoluted relationship with his brothers.

When Julie's vacuous gaze fell on her, Lucy mouthed, "Sorry."

Her mother shrugged, and a wave of sympathy and anger washed over her.

James nodded.

When Rob and Sinjin glanced over, Lucy froze. Their looks of pity were ten times worse than any outright anger.

"All rise," the bailiff announced.

The mahogany door behind the judge's bench opened, and the Honorable Kathy Johnson appeared in her robes. "Morning all." She took her post and struck the sound block with her gavel.

As usual, a chill ran up Lucy's spine.

"Please be seated," the judge instructed. "Hello, Julie, nice to see you."

In a courtroom laden with layers upon layers of old furniture polish, Judge Johnson's kindness always sliced through and made it less intimidating. Luckily enough, she'd been overseeing the case from the beginning.

Judge Johnson added, "Good morning, Mr. Reid and Mr. Reid."

"Good morning, Your Honor," the brothers responded.

"Will you be speaking today, Lucy?" Judge Johnson asked.

"Yes, Your Honor." She glanced down at her journal. It had turned into a tome through the past year and a half. "Of course."

Judge Johnson shuffled and inspected the papers hidden away on her bench. Julie Maxwell's court appearances had all mimicked one another. Lucy was accustomed to the usual whispers and directives given by the judge and the clicks coming from the court reporter.

At each of the proceedings, the outcome never surprised Lucy.

Her mother had pleaded not guilty to aggravated battery. It was an ugly crime of passion, and Julie refused to confess because she couldn't remember any of the details. Unfortunately, once again, she pled not guilty.

Sister Jan took a seat next to Lucy and gave her a hug.

Lucy's heart lifted. "Thanks for being here," she whispered, "but no go on the plea change."

Sister Jan took hold of her hand and squeezed it. "There's always hope."

Judge Johnson began by addressing Julie and James with the customary list of mandatory legal questions.

While holding tight to SJ's hand, Lucy studied her notes.

Her mom was almost halfway through her sentence, and with good behavior, Judge Johnson could waive the rest of the sentence, but a guilty plea would have been life-changing.

Lucy was conflicted about her testimony. Julie had paid a small debt to society, yet she wasn't remorseful for her actions. A dependency on alcohol had created too many rifts in the matter of truth. Her mother needed a way to purge her demons without the use of chemicals and alcohol.

Lucy had searched long and hard to find someone or something to help. There weren't many options without a big fat checking account. Hazelden in Minnesota cost a fortune. And the only affordable rehab option probably wouldn't get Julie to tell the truth. Alcohol had stolen her moral compass.

"The justice system is unjust," she whispered.

Sister Jan draped her arm over her shoulders, and she took in a deep breath of olive oil.

When Claire entered the courtroom, Lucy gave up processing any pain and willed away the tears. Oh, how she had missed her best friend.

Judge Johnson called Sinjin to the witness stand.

As planned, he chronicled the events fifteen months ago. How Julie Maxwell had attempted to steal his sculpture from the trunk of a car and then physically assaulted his girlfriend, Claire Beaumont—by pushing her to the ground, attacking her with a purse full of heavy sharp objects, and landing her in the hospital with a concussion and in need of stitches.

Lucy squelched the urge to go to her soul sister and apologize for the millionth time. Instead, she stared down at her journal and clutched her pink purse tighter. An ancient gift from Claire.

James stood and asked Sinjin one question. After he answered, Rob took the floor and clarified the timeline of events. Rob Reid was a prosecutor with a reputation for being a shark. Thankfully, in this case, he took a softer approach.

When Judge Johnson called Lucy to the witness stand, her body went on autopilot. She grabbed her journal and gave SJ a weak smile. After pushing the gate open, she counted the ten steps to the witness box. The counting slowed her mind down and kept the nerves in control.

After agreeing to tell the truth with the bailiff and the Bible, she came face-to-face with her mom. It had been a little over a month since she'd seen her last. Lucy blinked hard to stop staring at what was left of her mother. Her frame had deteriorated to a shell. Her hair was mostly made up of strands and knotted threads. Her formally full breasts had shrunk to the point that they appeared to retreat behind her shoulders. And her eyes. Julie's voluminous blue eyes were cast deeper in a sea of morning-pee yellow.

Lucy wanted to cry.

Even if she were to be released from prison, she wasn't free at all. The demons had jailed her for eternity. Jaundice signaled the imminent arrival of liver failure.

James approached her. "Thank you. Please state your name."

She couldn't recall it.

"Please state your name," he repeated, "for the court."

She tossed her braid behind her shoulder. "Lucy Maxwell."

"And your relationship to the defendant?"

She scanned the faces in front of her one at a time. Sinjin's brotherly demeanor, Rob's angry mouth set in a straight line, and Claire. Her violet eyes were filled with sympathy.

"She's my mother." *An empty vessel, but still my mom.*

"Thank you, Ms. Maxwell. Let the court know the witness is testifying on behalf of her mother's future pertaining to Julie Maxwell's incarceration."

"Go ahead, Lucy," Judge Johnson stated.

Lucy swallowed hard and opened her notebook. She wanted to read it, but after seeing her mother's eyes, her words would be fatal. She had wanted to pitch the idea of her mother staying at Corrections instead of another rehab center. It was her one hope. It offered a routine, a bed, and a meal. Seeing her mother's deteriorated condition made her certain. If the court upheld her request, her mom would die in prison.

"I don't know," she whispered.

James leaned into the witness box and whispered, "What's the matter? We agreed. Julie needs to stay where she is. She refused to change her plea."

"I know, but..." She looked at Judge Johnson. "Your Honor, my mother. She's ill. I'm conflicted."

"Follow through on your original testimony. We have the morning for discussion," Judge Johnson's empathetic response nearly brought Lucy to tears.

Instead, she let out a long breath and began reading out loud her evaluation of her mother's condition since she'd been imprisoned. It wasn't the best living situation, yet it offered her a glimpse into a normal routine without alcohol. There were several bouts of hallucinations after she'd gotten her hands on rubbing alcohol, but for the most part, she functioned better within the barbed-wire walls. At one point, Julie had started teaching an art class to fellow inmates.

After finishing, the silence weighed her shoulders down, and she craved a long bath with a hefty dose of Serenity. The stenographer's clicks and clacks on the keyboard and a few sighs filtered into the quiet.

Lucy stared at her distraught and angry mom. She'd propped her head in her palms and covered her face. Julie Maxwell was shattered, not broken.

On the other side of the opaque bulletproof glass, which made the gallery feel far off and in a different era, the pair of mammoth six-paneled doors split open, and Gus entered the courtroom.

He gave her a curt nod and a quick smile. He took a seat in the back of the gallery on her family's side.

"Ms. Maxwell," James said, "is there anything else you want to add on your mother's behalf?"

She sighed. "I wish there were another option. It's not my intent to keep my mother incarcerated. But if she has any chance of surviving longer than her liver may allow, an environment with a routine might be best."

"Thank you, Lucy." James smiled.

The judge added, "You may step down."

"Wait, can I add one more thought?" She pulled out a letter from her journal that George Reid had written to her.

James and the judge nodded.

Trying to keep her voice steady, she read:

"*Always remember alcohol addiction is a disease and not a choice. When the addiction takes hold of a person, it tries daily to lock them up and throw out the key. Just as often, it fails.*"

"Not a choice, I know. Yet it's judged as if it were a conscious decision." Lucy held the letter to her heart and stared at Julie. "Occasionally, we need a little help and a do-over to get by."

Judge Johnson said quietly, "We'll take a fifteen-minute recess. When we reconvene, we will discuss the arrangements to be made for Julie Maxwell."

Chapter 23

Seven, eight...

Lucy paused beside the defendant's table. "Love you, Mom."

Julie turned her back on her.

Nine, ten...

With a heavy heart, she pushed the gate open to the barricade and stepped into the gallery. It was for the best, for her mother, for her...and overwhelming. She'd decided ages ago Julie was incapable of telling the truth. Liquor had reduced her to a conniving liar...on her good days.

Lucy kept her focus on Gus.

Eleven, twelve, thirteen...

Gus met her in the aisle, wrapped his arms around her, and whispered, "How are you doing?"

"Aren't you supposed to be with Michael? My inspection?" She tried to sound irritated, but her voice became muffled as she melted against him. She couldn't help it. Seeing Gus lifted her spirits.

"Why the hell didn't you tell me about my brothers going after your mother?"

Lucy inhaled his scent of bergamot and smiled. "You haven't

exactly shown any brotherly love toward Rob or Sinjin. How did you even find me?"

"Maddie."

"But...how...?"

"And Rob." Gus nodded toward the prosecution table. "And Sinjin."

Confused, she stared at him with an open mouth.

"You have another job to do, Emma. Get Maddie and Rob together. I don't have my tights on, but I started the ball rolling for you."

"Who *is* at Wicks?"

"Maddie. Thanks to her love for my brother, she knew he was here. I drove in her tin can of a car. She's taking care of the inspection this afternoon."

"When did you get here?"

"Last night, I slept at Sinjin's house." He tucked his arm around hers. "We need to talk. Let's go into the hallway."

She sat on the hall bench made of the hardest wood. The marble floors and walls reflected the austerity of the courthouse—grand and suffocating at the same time.

Gus handed her a paper cup of water and sat next to her. "What happens now?"

"It's up to the judge. My mom is sick. Alcohol has stripped her of everything. She refuses to plead guilty, and prison is the only place where she's relatively safe from herself. Still, I'm terrified that if she's not released soon, she's going to die."

When Gus hugged her, she whispered thanks into his ear.

"Seems as if your lawyer is doing a good job. He's managed to keep Rob in control."

"I suppose so."

"I'm sensing a but coming." He lifted one of his ginger eyebrows.

"No 'but.' It's a slam dunk. Her lawyer has cost a fortune. It's been financially debilitating. Between the court system's costs and the lawyer's fees, they've sucked every penny from her. Not to mention the stints in rehab before this debacle started." She took a gulp of water. "And now it's me. I can't even afford to talk to her on the phone. Her collect calls cost three dollars a minute. Luckily, at this point, there's not a whole lot to say."

"She's at rock bottom. It's not a joy, however, it helps when you can only look up."

"Easy for you to say, Mr. Hollywood. Your smooth moves make everything easy."

The intensity of his gaze sent icy shivers through her.

"Nothing's ever easy. After my mum died, liquor made for a wonderful treat. The numbing effects are outstanding." Gus's voice took on a deadly calm. "I fled to LA, and I was a mess. No smooth moves and no Mr. Hollywood. And zero dollars in the bank."

She squeezed the paper cup and tossed it in the bin.

"Your mother will get better," he assured her. There's always hope."

"Thanks," she sighed.

"I'm one of the lucky ones. Alcohol tries to lure me into its grip on a daily basis, and I have to constantly fight it off." He stared at her. "Your mum needs another chance. Look, I'm a confident actor with talent in a sea of actors with a lot more talent and more confidence. My ego would love a hug from a nice gin and tonic more than I'd like to admit. There's the rub. It offers a shot of courage, and a few of us don't have the strength to say *no*. It's not a character flaw. It's an easy button we can't stop pressing."

Lucy nodded. "But what she did to Claire was horrific. And Sinjin."

"Claire—" He hesitated. "—and Sinjin are tough. They're surviving. And because of you, they are together."

"My ears are ringing, bro." Sinjin stepped into the hallway, with Claire and Rob following close behind.

Lucy's palms started sweating, and a lump swelled in her throat as the trio circled her and Gus. All she could manage was a stiff nod.

"Morning, all," Gus said cheerily. "We're playing catch-up."

"Your testimony was riveting," Rob ignored his brother and spoke directly to her. "Your words describing your mother's situation are accurate and fair. This system is challenging when it comes to mental health issues."

Lucy stood and cleared her throat. Gus held her hand.

"Thanks for being so kind. You've been more of a dolphin than a shark." Tears threatening to break free, she dared not look toward Sinjin and Claire. "And your dad. George is a lifesaver."

"Yeah, thanks," Gus added. "Appreciate it."

"I'm not always an asshole, Gus," Rob said. "I do have a heart. You should find your own."

Her grip on Gus's hand tightened.

"Enough. Both of you. Not the time or the place to air your nasty history." Sinjin glowered at his two younger brothers. "This has to stop. Pronto."

While the three men were in a stand-off, she bit her lower lip and ventured a quick peek at Claire. She had cut her purple-black hair into a short pixie style. It set off her purple eyes and heart-shaped face. Lucy glanced back at Rob to avoid looking at Claire's leg. It always made her cry, even though nothing looked out of the ordinary.

"After this is over, is there any chance you can get to Baileys?" Gus let go of her hand and patted Rob's shoulder. "Winterfest is coming up."

"I'm in the ice sculpture contest," Sinjin said. "Claire and I are going. I could use an extra pair of hands with my chainsaw and block of ice."

"We would love for you to come." Lucy's *Emma* vibe took on a whole new groove as she tried to alleviate the tension between Gus and Rob.

"I...I'm...not sure." Rob's jaw clenched as he pulled his phone from his suit coat. "I have to check the calendar. There's a case coming up in Chicago."

Gus crossed his arms over his chest. "I was wrong about you and Maddie. I was a total wanker. I'm sorry."

"You punched the shit out of me," Rob protested. "And Maddie? She was a wreck. I don't remember how many, but it took days before I could leave her alone. She couldn't stop crying and blaming herself, as if she was at fault and had led you on."

"Rob, I'm here because I made peace with Maddie," Gus said, sounding bleak. "We were never together. My wicked imagination, I know. She was a good friend and still is, mate. What the hell can I do to make it up to you?"

"You broke us up. Maddie and me," Rob said. "It's too late."

"No such thing!" Claire shouted. "Haven't you ever seen *Frozen*? Let. It. Go. I love you, Rob, but guess what? You're the one who's acting like a wanker."

Lucy held back an obnoxious snort-laugh.

"You three are total douches. We are here for Lucy. Remember?" Glaring at each of the brothers, Claire came to her side, wrapping an arm over her shoulders. "My best friend needs your support, not a bunch of bickering."

"Claire...I'm...so sorry. I didn't know what to say to you."

Claire hugged her. "None of this is your fault, sista. Please let me be here for you." She tapped her thigh. "I'm good. Stronger than ever. I'm running in the 5K at the Fest."

"Dang, that's fantastic," Lucy sputtered.

James poked his head around the courtroom door. "Sorry to interrupt. Judge Johnson is back in court."

"Jesus," Rob said. "Now you two boneheads are going to get me disbarred."

Rob straightened his tie and opened the door. Claire gave her another quick hug and followed Sinjin inside.

Air clung to the back of her throat.

"It'll be okay, Lucy," Rob said with professional calm.

Arms wrapped around one another, she and Gus ambled back into the courtroom. She introduced him to Sister Jan as they sat down. Julie's posture was the same, as though she hadn't moved a muscle. Lucy smelled defeat.

Shuffling papers, the judge looked up and scanned the gallery. When she smacked the wood block with her gavel, Lucy flinched.

"For the ease of the parties involved, this court will promptly discuss the matter of Julie L. Maxwell. Informally and on record." Judge Johnson folded her arms across her chest and stared at Lucy's mom. "Both the defense and prosecution want to help you, Julie. As we are limited in this system of justice to make reparations for the needs classified as mental health, your case has taken a winding course. It requires a unique disciplinary measure. You will be released from your remaining time at the House of Corrections and placed under the supervision of a newly established halfway house for women located in Green Bay, Wisconsin. It will allow for the routine your daughter, Lucy, has requested. You will report to a Department of Corrections officer working within the Alcoholics Anonymous chapter weekly for one year, at which time you'll return to my courtroom for an assessment. As well, you will begin treatment with an FDA-approved medication to help you combat your dependency on alcohol, and you will be required to wear an ankle monitor."

She let Julie's fate sink in. Could it be so organized, almost simple? Halfway house, AA meetings, a few pills, and a bracelet? There was *always hope*. Lucy wanted to clutch onto this last straw, but it could also be the straw breaking the dang camel's back and not a lifeline.

The judge continued. "Will this be satisfactory to counsel?"

James and Rob both nodded and said yes.

"Lucy?" Judge Johnson's eyes widened. "Do you have anything further to add?"

After clearing her throat, Lucy raised her voice. "I'll remain hopeful, Judge Johnson. Do you have any information pertaining to the costs of this new halfway house? I've missed it in my research."

"The halfway house is a privately funded facility."

Her blood stilled, and a pounding in her head grew louder. She clutched onto the bench in front of her to control her breathing. "Your Honor, I can't...I don't know how to take care of...I mean, pay for this type of living situation. My mother's funds are tapped out, and my funds are—"

"This living situation has been paid for in full by an anonymous donor, Lucy."

A swoosh of air left her lungs. Then Gus squeezed her knee. A heady lightness took hold of her. "Was it you?"

Gus nodded. "And Claire. And Sinjin. They were like a couple of kids in a candy shop after I told them about this place in Title-town for your mom. They wanted to be part of it. And my dad. He's on your side."

Claire, seated on the prosecution side, winked at her.

Lucy was stunned.

The judge continued. "Julie Maxwell, you will be remanded into custody at the Lake Bluff police station for the night and transported to the halfway house in the morning. Court is adjourned."

Judge Johnson made one quick pound with her gavel and slipped back into the judge's chambers.

Julie turned around. "Love you, honey," she mouthed, staring at her and Gus. Then she pointed to her eye, smiled, and blew her a kiss. Two of them.

"Love you." Lucy, like her mom, spoke the truth.

Chapter 24

The prison journey had ended, except uncertainty followed Julie Maxwell everywhere. In the hallway, Lucy willed the torrent of tears to stay dammed. She fiercely hugged each of her friends. They had to pull free from her. She needed a moment or two or three to process this strange turn of events. After saying goodbye to Sister Jan, promising the Reid family to meet up later, and finally kissing Gus, Lucy escaped the courthouse still in a state of disbelief. She wouldn't crumple into a ball and cry like a baby in front of them.

Getting back to work was the best way to unscramble her thoughts. Still in a blur, she stepped into Sweet Tomato, a high-end boutique in Lake Bluff and a Lust vendor. She inhaled her bestselling oil and felt energized.

She focused on the front table displaying cherry-red cashmere sweaters featured for Valentine's Day. The red color screamed her brand. She brushed her fingers over the baby-soft wool and found a size small for Julie. Digging into the pile of black sweaters, she found a large one for Sister Jan. Lucy set them on the cash wrap and plodded to the shelving units dedicated to Wicks' products.

Every one of her muscles was taut, and her exhaustion had worn her down. She kept a tight lid on her emotions by concentrating on one business detail at a time. Splish-splashing around were her feelings for Gus. She still couldn't believe he'd shown up at the courthouse for her and was paying for Julie's rehab.

A question crept into her overloaded mind. *Why is Gus paying for rehab? Or is it Angus Reid paying for it?* It had been a taxing day, so she tried to shake off the snaking doubt, but it stubbornly lingered.

The Green Bay facility had to cost a fortune. Why would Gus generously open up his wallet to her mother? And did he expect something in return? She tapped her temple with an oil vial. She'd never been good at receiving gifts, always looking for the catch.

There were ten vials of Lust left. She opened and broke the seals on them and rolled each over her wrist to check the viscosity. Still fresh. She unzipped her carrying case and slipped out the red container holding new labels made for the holiday. She tore off the old labels, wiped the glass vials, and resealed each with the new label design—a red heart surrounding a cupid.

Cupid. Lucy wondered why she'd developed such a bond with this dude. He was the original "love nudger." Who was she to suppose she could do a better job than the mischievous bowman? Playing with that kind of control, if she thought too hard about it, made Lucy nervous.

"Lucy? I thought you weren't coming until later?" Jill asked, holding a sub sandwich. "Want to have lunch with me?"

"Thank you, I can't," she said, relieved to get back to work. "I'm running behind and have two more appointments to get to."

"Not at any of my competitors." Jill glanced at another client coming in the door, hid her sandwich, said hello, and then refocused on Lucy.

"Not in the least," Lucy said. "I'm staying at the American Club tonight and booked a massage this afternoon." She hesitated, then added, "Big day for my mom. She's getting out of prison."

"Fantastic news," Jill said without a hint of judgment. "How are things going in Door County? We're all missing you and your mom at the yoga studio."

"I've missed you, too, and hopefully, one of these days, Julie will be able to get back into yoga." She rearranged the bars of soap on the display. "Baileys has been wonderful though. I've kept up with my stretches. Do you have enough product for the holiday?"

"I'll take all that you can give," Jill said, giving her a half hug. "Then you need to shop for yourself. You look shattered."

"My opening is around the corner, and I could use a dose of retail therapy." She grabbed her tablet and pulled up Sweet Tomato's inventory log. She tracked the sold items and entered the new stock. "Any chance you want to try something different? I have a new scent called Serenity. It's a lot of lavender with jasmine. Good for relaxing."

Jill finished a bite of her sub before answering. "Honestly, it's the first of the month, and I'm beyond ready to move past Valentine's Day and get into spring. I can't wait to show off my pastels. This place will be getting a major overhaul and Serenity sounds as if it will fit right in with my ideas."

Lucy scrolled to her log for the Serenity line of body products and marked off sugar scrub, lotion, and massage oil. Then, she retrieved ten of each from her inventory case and gave them to Jill. "I'm still working on the sachets. I'll come back and drop them off before you reset the shop."

Jill popped open the lotion and inhaled. "Another winner, hon."

"Goes nice with salami." Chuckling, Lucy tucked tissue around the remaining Serenity products and closed the case. She hoped they would be able to go to the new rehab facility with Julie.

"I have the perfect dress for you to wear at your opening." Jill tugged her from the apothecary display.

Lucy shivered thinking about wearing a dress in the icy temps, but the opening of Wicks deserved a new look, and her over-the-knee boots would keep her legs warm.

Jill swung a gorgeous red dress in front of Lucy's face.

"Is this a real Diane von Furstenberg?" She eyed the tag in disbelief. "I mean, it has the signature wrap, but...the waist is rucked. It's so sleek."

"A classic DVF," Jill said, laughing. "We've had it for over a month. I've been wanting to sell it to the right person and make sure it goes to a happy home. It's ideal for you."

"Can I try it on?"

"Of course." Jill cradled the dress and carried it off. "How about a cup of chamomile tea?"

"Please." Lucy went into the fitting room. The velvet settee, marble-top table, gold-framed mirrors, and crystal chandelier lured her in and whispered *relax*. Nothing wrong with a little luxury.

"I'll be right back." Jill closed the door. "Take your time."

Tired, Lucy undressed slowly and gazed at the shimmery red fabric of the dress. When did she last wear a dress? Or, for that matter, when was her last opportunity to dress up?

Please...please...fit.

Carefully, she slipped the soft fabric over her head, and as if angels had blessed her, it was a perfect fit. Sister Jan must have put a good word in for her. She pinched her cheeks to get color back into her face. Other than feeling exhausted and hungry, Lucy loved how she looked. "Perfect."

"Lucy? There's someone here asking for you. "What should I say?"

"Hold on," she said, opening the door for Jill. "I need—"

* * *

Gus shoved his hands in his pants pockets as he gazed at Lucy in a stunning cherry-red dress. "Hey."

"What are you doing here?" she asked. "I thought you were going out with your family?"

"You ran out of the courthouse." Gus maintained eye contact. The low-cut dress exposed a lot of creamy skin and hugged Lucy's incredible curves.

"I've been looking for you. Maddie texted, and Wicks passed the inspection."

Her face paled. "Good news, but..."

"Here's your tea," Jill said, gawking at Gus. "Would you like some, sir? Angus? I brought two cups, Mr. Reid?"

"Gus is fine. Yes, please," he said, stepping into the spacious fitting room. "Please, don't let the other clients know I'm here. If you wouldn't mind."

"No, I won't say a word." Jill set a tea tray on the settee. "I assume you'll be taking the dress?"

Lucy nodded. "Thanks, Yes. I'll take it off in a few."

Focus.

After Jill left him alone with Lucy, he closed the door, moved the tea tray, and sat beside her.

"What's the matter?"

"I can't believe it. I forgot about the inspection. How can I call myself a businesswoman?"

Gus tried to avert his gaze as she crossed one long leg over the other and arranged the red fabric to cover her bare thighs. He failed miserably. "Cut yourself some slack. You've been through a lot this morning. The inspection is good. Maddie loves being in charge of Wicks, and I knew for sure Michael wouldn't give you a hard time."

"You're right, I am sort of tired. How'd you find me?"

"Your brilliant red truck."

"Right." She held his hand. "What you did? I don't know if I'll ever be able to thank you enough. I know my mom could have died if she stayed in prison, but the rehabs I looked into were either full or too expensive."

"Lucy, I..." He swallowed hard. He'd already lost his own mother to alcoholism, and as much as he'd wanted to help Lucy, this was also a way for him to make amends with Rosamunde. "It's the least I could do for you. I've had inside experience with rehab centers, so I only had to make a few phone calls."

She tilted her head back and forth. "Oh dang, you're paying for it all, aren't you? I don't know how I'll be able to pay you back."

"Stop. You don't owe me a penny. The truth is, Lucy, when I lost my mother, it was horrific. I didn't even know she was suffering from cirrhosis. I couldn't have done anything to change the outcome, but I still struggle. Maybe if George had been around for her..." He dropped his head in his hands to erase the horrendous picture. Blood was smeared over the fieldstones, blood pooled on the floor in front of the fireplace, and blood had soaked into his mum's yellow T-shirt. Her skin was cold as he closed her eyes. "I know your mother will survive because you stuck with her. Personally, I don't want to ever lose another loved one to alcoholism."

"You're going to make me ugly cry," she murmured.

When her shoulders started shaking, Gus wrapped his arms around her. "Never...ugly."

She fell against him, and his fingers ached to trace the curve of her neck and back.

"I don't," she sniffed, "want to ruin your suit coat."

"Go ahead, it's not mine. It's Sinjin's."

Chuckling, she nestled into his shoulder and cried it out for several minutes.

Gus held her tight, listening to her breathing until it became steady. "Do you want to go outside?"

"Are you sure? What's the situation with *TMZ*? That guy is a stalker."

"I drove Maddie's Prius, no one followed me, and I've stayed off the paparazzi radar."

As soon as she moved from him, Gus regretted suggesting

fresh air. A few more minutes alone in a fitting room with Lucy was a better choice. "When did you last eat?"

"Yesterday. Maybe."

"Let's go get a bite."

She shook her head. "I can't. I have to get to the jail in Lake Bluff. I want to talk to my mom before she's transferred to Green Bay."

"Are you staying here tonight?" Gus tried to sound casual as lusty images of Lucy without any red dress floated through his mind.

"I am." She stood and shook out the dress. "I had expected to be with my mom at the American Club. To figure out her next steps."

"Okay, can I make a reservation for dinner, then? At the Immigrant Room. For us. I know the head chef."

"It will have to be later. I won't be back from my massage until seven."

Red dress, massage, Lucy. Gus struggled to rein it in. All he wanted to do was slide his hands under the silky dress and all over Lucy's gorgeous curves. "I can hold off until then. Let's say eight? Meet you at the restaurant."

"Can I wear this?" Lucy flipped about the hem of the dress. "It feels fantastic to dress up and forego my jeans."

With blood rushing to his groin, he could barely disguise his desire. Wearing the dress or jeans didn't matter; Lucy was...he couldn't find the right word. Yes, *beautiful*, but not superficial. A profound beauty.

"Well?"

He dragged his mind back from the murky pool of lusty feelings. "Jacket and tie for me. The dress will be great." *Absolutely stunning.*

"Really?" She flicked her tongue across her lower lip. "I get to be your arm candy tonight?"

"Yes." He cleared his increasingly dry throat.

And then I desperately want to unwrap the dress and slowly peel it off you.

Outside in the parking lot, Gus sucked in cold air to clear his head and get a hold of himself. He'd been rushing around since he'd arrived in Lake Bluff and needed a break to gather his thoughts. As he drove back to Sinjin's house, he went over the events of the past twenty-four hours.

Once he saw Sinjin in person, they fell back into the brotherly camaraderie from their younger years. The good old times before Mum had passed away. After Gus made his amends with him, he called Claire and apologized.

The two brothers worked side by side all evening researching rehab facilities for Julie. Gus suspected Sinjin felt the same way as he did. They both had a deep need to take action and make sure another beautiful soul wouldn't succumb to alcohol poisoning.

Gus slowed as he wound through Peace Park in Lake Bluff. His encounter with Rob earlier had gone haywire. He had to figure out how to get the guy up to Baileys so they could talk.

When he arrived at Sinjin's palatial estate, Gus parked and tried to stretch out his legs in the tiny car. He watched the clouds float across the blue sky and was unusually calm. He was about to fall asleep when Sinjin pounded on the window. "You all right, mate?"

"Better than ever," he responded as he exited the cramped car.

"Come inside." Sinjin pushed him ahead. "I found that ridiculous sex book you were looking for in the guest room."

"Brilliant." Gus had three amends in the bag, but the two last apologies would be the hardest. At least he had dinner with Lucy to look forward to and could make sure it was a spectacular evening for her after everything she'd been through that morning.

Lucy tried to read the plaques posted by the photographs lining the hallway leading to the Immigrant Room, but the history of the Kohler Company would have to wait. She couldn't keep her eyes off Gus.

He looked down at the ornate carpeting while speaking on the phone and pacing by the restaurant entrance. His navy suit fit across his shoulders immaculately. A Rolex peeked out from the cuff of his white dress shirt. And the red tie matched her dress. Gus looked deliciously handsome.

After seeing her in the hall, he hesitated and ended his call. Slipping the phone in his pocket, he strode toward her. Gus said hello, but his eyes spoke more. Gazing at her, he took in every detail of her face and held her hand. "How are you feeling?"

"Wonderful, thanks to a stellar massage. I had an acupuncture treatment, too. Very cool."

"I'm jealous," he said with a quick smile. "The chef here is outstanding and you'll love the food."

Lucy fanned her face as her cheeks grew warm. "Don't get me wrong, I adore Kat's cooking, but eating a meal using a linen napkin will be nice."

As soon as they walked into the four-star restaurant, there were hushed whispers. She adjusted her dress to make sure the deep opening of her DVF didn't slip and show off her matching red lace bralette. "Don't you ever get tired of being the center of attention?"

"Oh, no. They aren't bothering to look at me. I'm *your* arm candy." Gus ironed over the three-point kerchief in his suit jacket pocket. "You're the rock star tonight. You look gorgeous in that dress."

"We've prepared the English room for you two this evening," the maître d' said in greeting.

"English room?" Lucy inquired after they sat at a quiet corner table. Small and tasteful Union Jack emblems were embroidered on the corners of the napkins. "English, I understand. And the other nationalities?"

"French and Dutch," Gus paused in thought. "German, Danish, and Normandy."

"And you had to pick the least desirable culinary experience?" Lucy teased. "I mean, let's face it, the Brits' food compared to the French? We both know the winner."

Gus chuckled. "True, but this table is the most discreet."

Lucy fidgeted. In less than a second, she'd gone from tepid to boiling. To cool down, she took a sip of water and sucked on a piece of ice.

"It's been a long day for you. How did it go with your mum at the jail?"

"The good news is that the security at the Lake Bluff jail was minimal, and I had no need to worry about the bra I was wearing."

He looked confused, but she continued without explaining.

"But mostly terrible. She hated the sweater I bought for her, complained about the ankle monitor, and again, forgot that she no longer owned a home in Lake Bluff," she said, feeling mortified. "She's been very unappreciative. Even Sister Jan was frustrated. It's embarrassing."

"There's nothing to be embarrassed about," Gus said. "After she's in treatment and recovering, her anger will diminish."

It was clear to her that he spoke from firsthand experience. "Having you with me today was a giant relief. Thank you. It's hard to talk about this. There's such a stigma attached to mental health and incarceration. It seems as if women in particular are branded as nutcases or menaces to society, and *polite society* wants nothing to do with women suffering from alcohol dependency."

"Screw *polite society*. As a lone wolf, I've learned—since being an actor—it's best to avoid critics. Every one of them." He leaned forward and swiped a loose tear off her cheek with his thumb. "Today though...you, Lucy Maxwell...you're my hero."

"Stop!" She cleared her throat and looked around for the waiter.

"I mean it. In court, with your words, not even the best scriptwriter could have composed such a beautiful and loving tribute. You saved your mother's life."

"I hope she's okay tonight. And comfortable," she said.

"This time tomorrow, she'll be in her new home. A rehab facility without barbed-wire fencing, watch towers, or metal bars clanking 24/7. She'll be comfortable in a new bed. The house in Green Bay is similar to a picturesque cottage in the Cotswolds."

The waiter stood tableside. "Good evening, miss. And Mr. Reid, thank you for joining us this evening. I hope there haven't been too many looky-loos tonight."

"Greetings, Chuck," Gus said. "Tonight, all the attention from the 'looky-loos' is on this brave woman, Lucy Maxwell."

"Oh, please," she said without one iota of bravery.

"What would you like?" the waiter asked. "The kitchen will prepare whatever you desire."

"I, if it's possible...I'm craving a melt-in-your-mouth steak."

"Certainly. We have a beef Wellington. Will that be satisfactory?"

"Wonderful." She realized how hungry she'd become. Or was she simply feeling empty? "I'm starving."

"I'll have the short rib with the mushrooms." Gus ordered and the waiter left.

"I should have figured out how to eat...or spend the night with my mom."

Gus locked her in a lush, grass-green gaze. "No. Because of your behind-the-scenes work, your mother has a second chance."

The truth of his words settled into her. She'd been in lockstep with her mother for over a year, and if any proof was needed, she had a planner splattered with her many dates with the criminal justice system. And tonight, wearing a silky wrap dress and sitting with Gus, it was a *date* she could actually enjoy.

"Don't fret. As my own mum would say, everything will be *tickety-boo*. I'm certain that in the near future, Julie's food will be just as delicious as tonight's."

She let herself relax. "So? You're having the ribs with *shrooms*?"

"Yes, why?"

"You're just as I thought. A *fun-guy*." She smiled. "Mushrooms? Fungi? Get it?"

"Hey, right. And people really *lichen* me."

"Here are your two Shirley Temples, with extra Door County cherries as requested." The waiter set the drinks on the table.

Gus winked at her. "Our mocktails."

Charming, devilish, and sweet.

"Aren't we a little too old for Shirley Temples?"

"Maybe. Nonetheless, what's not to like about cherry juice and sweet soda pop? Named after a brilliant actress."

"Shirley Temple. A patron of the performing arts," she added, "and your dream girl?"

"A survivor and courageous like you." He lifted his glass for a toast. "Lucy. I'm stoked to celebrate the opening of Wicks with you. And I can't wait for *you* and your superstar, Lust, to outshine me."

She tipped her glass to his. "Here's to Wicks & Balms."

After the most incredible dinner that she'd eaten in a long time, Lucy wanted a sweet. "I have to try one of the desserts."

"I've got it covered." Gus waved Chuck over to their table. "I'm apologizing in advance, but I wanted to celebrate your daring and bravery today."

"Hey, I caught a huge walleye...remember? I'm pretty tough."

"Ready?" Chuck asked.

"Yes." Gus got up and stretched.

As if on cue, the few remaining diners around them also stood and stared at her.

She shook her head to control the incoming flood of emotions.

Gus grabbed her hand and gently tugged her from the table. "In a way, today is your birthday. I know it's not until March, but...it's not necessarily about the time you came into the world. It can be about a day, like today, when you stood up and fought. For your mum and you."

Lucy swayed against Gus's shoulder. His incredible sentiments blew her away.

He kissed her cheek.

"You are going to win an Emmy," she whispered in his ear.

"Don't care," he said. "You smell heavenly."

"Neroli. Left on after my massage," she whispered.

The others sang "Happy Birthday" as a server brought out a chocolate cake with a popping sparkler on top of it.

"Happy birthday." He held her waist and dipped her.

Safe in Gus's arms, she fell backward.

As close to a Hollywood smacker as she'd imagined, Gus entwined his fingers in her hair and gave her a long, sensuous kiss, a Tinseltown smooch worthy of all the pictures being snapped. Her knees almost buckled from the over-the-top feeling of joy coursing through her.

Everyone applauded.

With a sweeping hand, Gus introduced her. "This is Lucy

Maxwell, folks. Owner of Wicks & Balms. I'm sure you know about the fragrance Lust?"

"Thank you." She took a bow and then curtsied.

Two women came up to their table and asked about ordering Lust. Still giddy, she grabbed her phone from the pocket of her fantastic dress and entered emails into her mailing list. "Thanks. This is head-spinning."

After the commotion of her starry night had calmed down, she caught Gus staring at her. "You can't get enough of me, can you?"

He took a bite of cake and swallowed. "Not by a long shot."

"Are you staying at Sinjin's tonight?" She slowly licked off a crumb of chocolate ganache from her fork.

"Yes, can't wait to get out of this suit of his."

"If you want..." She tugged her lower lip between her teeth, found a key card, and slid it across the table. "I'd love to help you take it off. In my room. 202."

A slow smile spread across his face.

As they left the restaurant, Lucy walked ahead of him, swaying her hips. She let the dress dance across her legs.

By the time she reached her room, her cheeks burned, and her fingers ached. An urgent need hummed through her. Before opening the door, she scanned the hall to see if he'd followed. *No.* A sliver of doubt crossed her mind, and she squashed it.

His lusty looks, even in the fitting room, had revealed the truth. Gus desired her. And Lucy wanted him.

Chapter 26

Gus swiped the key card too fast and then too slow. The red and green lights taunted him as he tried to gain entry into her room. He swore under his breath and shook his head to clear his lust-driven thoughts. For Lucy, he had to slow the heat thundering through him.

Looking around the dimly lit room, he loosened his tie.

"Lucy?" He knocked on the bedroom door and glanced at her laptop on the marble-top coffee table. Next to the velvet couch, her tall black boots were splayed on the carpeted floor. "All right if I come in?"

When she opened the door, Gus forced his mouth to stay closed. His eyes were glued to the low neckline of her sexy red dress. It hugged her curves and, lucky for him, showed off most of her long, bare legs. If he'd never known until now that he was a leg man, the tightness in his pants proved it.

"Hey." She tucked a loose strand of hair behind her ear. "How are you?"

"Uh. Good." He almost tripped on the plush carpeting. A faint citrus aroma muddled his thoughts. With his back, he pushed the door closed behind him. "Lovely evening."

Her hair draped over a bare shoulder.

He coughed for no reason and realized that most of his thoughts were coming from below his waist.

She came close to him, untied his tie, and pulled it from around his neck. "Better?"

"Much," he whispered, dipping down and kissing the succulent spot of soft skin between her shoulders and neck. He needed to kiss her everywhere and had to start right here. "I've been wanting to do this all day."

"Even in the fitting room?"

"I won't lie, it did cross my mind." He ran his finger around the curve of each breast and let out a ragged breath. "Good thing the owner kept checking on us."

"Do I look like that kind of woman?" She pushed his suit coat off his shoulders. After untucking his shirt, she kissed his chest each time she undid a button. "A woman who would screw in a public place?"

Groaning, Gus pulled her tight against him and tangled his hands in her hair. He dragged a kiss across her forehead. With his cock against her hips, Lucy wrapped her leg around his waist, and they dropped back against the door.

"No." With heat burning through his veins, he pushed the hem of her dress over her hips, caressed her thigh, then clutched her ass and lifted her up and onto him. The sultry feel of her bare skin in his palms ignited his cock.

"Another time," Lucy growled and folded her arms around him. "Finally. I feel like I'm going to scream or explode. I want you bad."

"How bad?" He held her tight and blew in her ear. "Tell me."

"I'm on fire," she gasped. "Please. Only your kisses will cool me down."

He crushed his lips against hers. Desperate to soothe her longing, he turned one kiss into a long and passionate one. When she moaned and fell into him, he burrowed into her neck and felt a deep connection, as if she and he were one. And complete.

He slid his hand around her breast and glided his thumb across the silky fabric of her dress, from one nipple to the other until they budded.

"Feels wonderful," she gasped.

"Just returning the favor." He peeled off the dress and took a nipple between his lips. Playfully, he circled his tongue around until it hardened. An urgent need pulsed through him. As he kissed her breasts and stroked her bare waist, her skin tingled under his touch. Gus held her tight as they made their way to the end of the bed, where he let her down.

Looking up at him, she unzipped and tugged off his pants. "These have to go, babe."

He kicked his trousers away and sat next to her. Pushing him back onto the bed, she kissed his hip bone and slid a finger under the waistband of his boxer briefs. Gus grabbed her hand. "You, first."

With a hard-on barely in check, he pulled off the bedding and piled the pillows against the headboard. "Relax. Lean back against the pillows."

"Sure." She slowly pushed her dress down and off.

He grew harder at the sight of her breasts.

She lay against the pile of pillows and patted the bed in front of her open thighs. "Come here."

On his haunches, Gus crawled over, and she draped her gorgeous legs over his shoulders. Slipping his fingers under her bum, he gently squeezed, brushed his beard against her smooth inner thighs, and greedily kissed her delicious center.

* * *

Lucy bit her lip, trying to contain the bolts of heat surging through her. "Gus. Come. Play. Please."

With her legs straddled over his shoulders, he kissed her thighs and massaged her hips. She dug her fingertips into the pillows. When he slipped his tongue inside her, she moaned and wanted to play harder.

"Your underwear has to go," she hissed. His skin sweeping against hers was the only heat source she ever wanted again.

She reluctantly broke free from his tantalizing kisses and pulled her legs off his shoulders.

"My thoughts exactly," he moaned.

She pulled his briefs down, and a wild burst of desire shot through her. "Wow."

Gus laughed. "Why, thank you."

"I didn't mean to say that out loud," she teased.

"Right." Gus gently pinched her nipples, and more sparks of friction traveled south.

A fiery, frantic desire took over her thoughts.

She closed her eyes and sank back against the mound of pillows. Her breath shortened as Gus's lips brushed over her curves. She let out a groan when he tenderly bit her nipples. Arching her back, she wrapped her legs around his waist.

Gus cradled and tightened her against him. His cock was rock-hard against her hip bone, and she caressed the base.

"Not yet," he moaned.

He moved down and kissed her belly button. Dancing his lips around her clit, he traced her folds with his tongue. Rolling and shaking sensations overtook her.

"Like this?" he asked.

"Mm." Her mind swirled in and out of coherent thought.

As Gus explored her folds with his tongue, she grabbed onto his shoulders to stay steady from the building pressure. Her thighs trembled. The effort to hold on to the increasing waves of passion rolling through her stole her breath. As her hips writhed, she delayed and demanded a release. *But when? Does it matter?*

Kissing her breasts, Gus made her ache. When a cool breeze swept between them, she wanted to smack him.

"Where did you go?" Her question came out in a grouchy demand.

Gus handed her a condom. "Here. This is for you."

Carefully, she slipped lower into the bed. She kissed his rod, playfully licked him, and rolled the condom down his length. With every sense in a haze, she kissed his stomach and trailed her tongue across his chest and then his neck.

Gus became a need she hadn't thought she needed or wanted. And her gift for scents was useless. A yearning for Gus had taken over as he kissed her.

When he tickled the inside of her thigh with his tip, she stretched her legs apart to welcome him to join her. Lucy hugged his shoulders, held them tight, and explored the tattoo on his shoulder with her lips.

"More kisses, just for you," Gus growled, slipping deep inside her. She swayed along with each of Gus's ever-multiplying and thrusting *kisses*, each one deeper and more gratifying than the next. Lucy rocked her hips to keep up with the growing pleasure. She wanted to scream out. Release all the delicious passion building within her. Instead, she relished the sense of bliss coursing through her until Gus moaned...softly.

They climaxed together, and Gus dropped his full weight on her. She straddled his hips with her legs and guided him onto his back.

Staring down at him in all his naked glory, she grinned. "This is fun," she said. "All right?"

"Fantastic." He pressed up to give her a quick peck on the cheek. "Ready for another ride?"

She rocked her pelvis against his until he let out a low, devilish chuckle. "Oh yeah," she said, then kissed him luxuriously.

The bed banged against the wall the second time...or was it the third?

After Gus had satisfied her yearnings and she eagerly subdued his cravings, they spooned under the covers and slept. *Peace.*

Chapter 27

"Lucy?" he murmured, rubbing her bare back. "Sorry to wake you. I have to get going."

She was still swoony after last night's lovemaking and thought she'd imagined it until she saw Gus. It was all real. "Morning."

Waking up, smiling, she checked her phone for the time. Pulling the sheet around her, she was acutely aware of the tenderness between her thighs. "It's only nine. Do you have time for breakfast?"

"No, sorry." Fully dressed, Gus looked at the mirror, adjusting his collar and straightening his tie.

In the reflection, she caught a shadow of worry cross over his face. "You okay?"

"Yeah. I'll ring you." His lips tightened as he scrolled through his messages. "Drive safe."

"Sure thing," she said resignedly. As he walked out of her room without a goodbye kiss, she had the miserable feeling he was running from her. "Ciao."

Gus rushed back into the bedroom and kissed her, a slow and passionate smooch. "See you later. Promise. I know it's not as risky as a dressing room, but have you ever done it on a bunk bed?"

"Top or bottom?"

He laughed and kissed her forehead. "Ring me when you get back home."

"Home. I like the sound of that," she said. "Will do."

She went into the shower to make sense of her mix of thoughts and feelings for Gus. Without question, last night had been in her top five of life's best events. The dinner, the romance, and the sex. Except watching him walk out the door rattled her. Lucy washed her face and hair and shook off the ridiculous unease. It had been a long time since she'd felt capricious, impulsive, and even risqué. Gus had renewed her sense of adventure, and it made her feel famous. Even if temporary, she was going to enjoy it. No, scratch that—she planned to revel in it and give her sensible wonk side a long-deserved break.

She checked out of the hotel, stopped in the spa, and purchased every neroli scented product available. Again, for her *Emma* research, but for the first time, her matchmaking vibe was making her heart pound wildly. It was hollering at her. *Think about yourself, your heart, your happiness.* Forget about Angus and take a chance with Gus.

Before walking to her truck, she made sure there weren't any white vans or photographers hiding around. She drove past the Lake Bluff jail and waved goodbye. Inmate 197241 had been transferred this morning and was probably already at the new house in Green Bay. Lucy chuckled. Her mom was more than likely reveling in the fact that her chakra had been right about her and Gus.

Sitting at the stoplight, she quickly texted Sister Jan to say thanks. Even though there was another mountain to climb, Lucy was fortunate because SJ had volunteered to be her AA sponsor.

When she arrived home and headed down Main Street, an icy-cold fear crawled up her spine. Michael's firetruck was parked in front of Wicks. Her large signs with love quotes were still displayed as she passed the front windows.

Good.

Pulling into the back alley, she passed the production trailers and gagged. Bright yellow tape was swinging off the rear entrance. She parked around the corner and wiped a loose tear from her cheek. Her legs turned into rubber as she entered her shop. She almost threw up when she inhaled a putrid stench like charred cooking oil instead of the usual flowery smell.

"Michael?" She shook her head and hissed. "This can't be...happening."

"I'm sorry," Maddie said, jogging over and giving her a hug. "Yesterday, you passed the inspection, and the shop was fine."

Michael looked up from his phone with a frown. "We got a call this morning from, of all people...a news guy. One of the paparazzi saw the water pouring into your shop from the ceiling."

"What the hell happened?" Lucy forced her feet to move forward as her cortisol levels spun out of control. "This isn't right."

Michael's flashlight flickered and bounced around the darkened shop. The mirrored bar and every bottle used by *Raven House* were smeared with condensation. Water dripped off the Art Deco shelves and streaked down the brick walls. Her prize licorice chandelier hung half-cocked from the ceiling. She picked up one of the Red Vine candlesticks from a puddle on the floor.

"I have to examine the pipes to check for anomalies and write up a report," Michael said. "The wiring throughout the shop might be defective. The sprinklers were activated with zero flames, little heat, and not enough smoke."

"It looked amazing in here yesterday." Maddie squeaked a rubber duck. "At least we know your sprinkler system works. And your display tub helped. It captured a ton of water; only a few ducks went overboard."

Lucy picked up one of the dozen or so yellow ducks and

squeezed. Water squirted out of its tail. "This is un-fucking-believable."

Michael pointed at the utility closet. "The origin is in there. The electrical panel is burned out. The only thing with smoke damage."

Rolled woolen Oriental carpets in perfect condition leaned against the inside wall. Not a smidge of water had leaked into the closet. A distinct aroma stunned her overworked olfactory system. A fresh waft of Sara's perfume, Fracas, hit her nose. It smelled as if she'd just been inside the utility closet.

Nothing was amiss in her office. Her desk and shelves weren't damaged. She quickly unlocked her desk to make sure her files were intact. All there. And again, she caught a fainter whiff of Gus's PR person's awful perfume. Probably left from a couple of days ago. Why would Sara do such a horrendous thing to her?

"This is my fault," Maddie moaned, coming in. "I should have checked the utility room before I left yesterday."

"Not in the least," Lucy said. "You can be one hundred percent certain that you have no part in this disaster. Sara did it."

Maddie shook her head in disbelief. "How? Why?"

"Not sure. I can smell her perfume though. It's everywhere. Please don't say anything. I want Michael to figure it all out."

But Lucy was absolutely certain Sara was responsible. She may have forgotten after drinking loads of chardonnay—whoops, not chardonnay but champagne. Sara, like her mom, had lost control. When Lucy first saw Sara and her sallow, yellow-looking skin, she'd suspected Sara was as untethered as Julie had been two years ago. Just as Julie had condemned Sinjin and Claire for all that was broken in her life, Sara blamed her and Gus.

Maddie hugged her again, and they went back to the utility closet.

Michael flipped the electrical box open with a gloved hand. "When I got here, the panel was exposed. The wiring is dated but up to code. It's the sealant. It took a beating and gave out. And it's cold outside. Maybe a frozen pipe bursting."

"This is one of the original buildings in Baileys," Maddie said. "Thankfully, it's brick."

"What do you mean, 'a beating'?" Lucy asked.

"A heavy amount of wear and tear, I suppose." Michael aimed his flashlight into the panel. "This isn't my specialty. I'm going to have to call in a fire detective."

"Didn't the alarm go off?"

Michael climbed on a chair, aimed his flashlight at the smoke detector on the office ceiling, and pushed the test button. Immediately, it emitted a high-pitched squeal, and then he shut it off. "It's working, but there probably wasn't enough smoke to activate it. This is an old building, so the sprinkler system isn't as high-tech. There might have been a leak, or the heat from the fuse box may have triggered it. Hard to know. We'll have to look at the water source on the outside."

"Insurance should pay, right?" Lucy tempered her anger with concern. "What about the filming? The show? Could it have caused this?"

"As long as we can get to the cause and prove this was an accident, insurance will pay." He closed the panel. "I called Gus and haven't heard back. He and his director buddy should get over here."

"Wonder if it wasn't an accident?" Lucy voiced her suspicion.

Michael peered at her. "Well, then, if and only if that's the case, we'll have to find out who's responsible. And they'll be liable."

"For now though, we can clean this up, air it out," Maddie said, "and it'll be good to go by the Fest."

"Not right away," Michael said. "We have to investigate. Everything must stay put until the team has had time to check it out. The wiring and the sprinkler systems may need to be replaced." He pointed up and aimed his flashlight toward the ceiling. "See those black streaks? It's where the copper tiles fell off and indicates an anomaly in the wiring. An overload possibly, and the heat source made the sprinklers go off."

She stared up at the disfigured chandelier, and water dripped on her head. "Cameras and lights?"

"Yeah, maybe." Michael aimed his flashlight toward the outlets. "Strange. Not any disfiguration around the connectors."

"Where is Gus?" Maddie asked. "He should be here."

Lucy bit the inside of her cheek to stop the tears. The last thing she needed was more water in her shop. She tried to look at the soggy mess around her as another adventure. Opening a brick-and-mortar was a gamble from the start, but she'd found a new home because of it and wouldn't let the town of Baileys down.

Michael clamped his hand on her shoulder. "We don't know anything for sure."

Carrying a roll of paper toweling to the front end, Maddie wiped off the bay windows. "Your love signs are perfect. We'll figure it out. FYI, I have a ton of photos for your website. May be helpful."

She meant well but Lucy couldn't get excited about marketing right away.

"I know things look dire... I'll do everything in my power to get to the bottom of this," Michael promised. "We'll fast-track the investigation to get you open."

"Gus should be able to help," Maddie said, "and the studio. It has to have insurance."

Lucy scooped up a handful of bath bombs that had exploded and melted into one lump of soap. "At least we have plenty of cleaning products. Thanks, you two."

Gus sighted Lucy, and all the pleasure from last night flooded into his mind. He wanted to hug her, hold her tight, and kiss the tiny, erogenous spot by her ear. Unfortunately, with Peter standing next to him, he had to be Nick Parker, single and available. He shoved his fists into his coat pockets.

"What happened?" His jaw ached from clenching it. For Lucy's sake, he kept his temper from flaring. She, however, looked resolute and determined, even though the shop was a dreadful sight.

"Finally," Maddie said. "Where the hell have you been?"

"Publicity meeting with Sara." *Explaining one fucking picture of him with Lucy.* "Sorry for being late."

Lucy crossed her arms over her chest and glowered at him. He couldn't explain anything yet. He'd abruptly left Lucy in Kohler and raced to explain, essentially nothing, to his publicist. A blurry photo had shown up on social media, taken while he was in Lake Bluff, and Sara had skewered him for it.

He thought she'd bought his explanation—he'd gone to Sinjin's and made amends, which was true, and then he'd run into Lucy, truer—but looking around the shop, he'd been utterly mistaken. Gus wanted to kick himself. He'd been caught in another one of Sara's traps. Her hounding in the name of publicity for Nick Parker had become stalking and controlling him.

"Do you know the cause?" he asked Michael, even though he'd already identified the culprit. Sara. This was the last straw.

"Just starting the investigation." Michael gave Gus a half hug, then twisted it into a headlock. He muttered, "You are in deep shit, bro. This is bad."

"I know." Gus freed himself from Michael's elbow.

"Here's the name of the studio's insurance agent," Peter said, sending a text to Michael. "Get a rep out here. We need answers fast."

"I have a quicker way," Lucy snapped. "Go ask Sara where she was this morning."

"I get you're angry." Peter cocked his head. "But there's no way Sara would ever do this. It's not in our DNA."

Gus believed Lucy, except he had to tread lightly in front of his director. "I'm sure this is an accident from the camera equipment. It might have affected your wiring. Once we get the info, we'll pay for damages."

She threw her hands in the air and shouted, "I don't want any more of your money. I can't open my business."

"Can we talk? In your office?" Peter asked apologetically.

"No, thanks, Peter. I can't afford the time," she said, deflated. "Look at this place. It's destroyed, and I have to figure out a new plan."

Rubbing his jaw, Gus scanned the damage in the shop. Two days earlier, it had been in immaculate condition, ready to stock and open. "Michael, do you have a guess about what time this happened?"

"Morning," Michael answered, "around eight thirty or nine?"

Gus had met Sara at the B&B at eleven. She'd had plenty of time to fuck up Wicks. His nails bit into his palms. Sara had played him like a fiddle.

"This isn't what you want to hear, Peter," Gus said, flexing his hand, "but you should talk to your sister. DNA or not, Lucy's right. Sara's to blame."

Peter shook his head. "Michael, when you get the facts, can you pass them my way? I don't want to make any accusations without correct information."

"Will do," Michael said.

"You'll have to figure out how to replace Wicks' lost business." Maddie stood next to Lucy.

"No, thanks." Lucy threw her backpack over her shoulder. "I don't want any of Gus's celebrity solutions. I've already made it far with Wicks before I had any walls to take care of."

Gus was completely hollowed out. If he wanted any kind of a future, he had to get out of the draconian contract Sara kept yanking his chain with. "Peter. We aren't filming in the Beacon until after the Fest. And Lucy's store is all about lovey-dovey stuff."

Michael chuckled.

"I'm aware of my contract and the stipulations. However, for the sake of Wicks..." Gus paused to choose his words carefully. "I need to..."

Maddie squealed.

Gus looked at Lucy. "I need to focus any and all of *Gus Reid's* social media on Lucy...um, Wicks. Whatever she needs from me to regain lost dollars from the damage. Especially if we discover your sister caused this catastrophe."

Lucy's face went pale.

Peter shuffled around the puddles on the floor. Picking up a wet bottle, he wiped it on his expensive designer coat. "Gus, you're the star of *R-H*. We wouldn't be anywhere without you. Regardless of the contract, go ahead and do what you want to. For Lucy."

Gus wanted to make sure he'd understood. "Can I contact Tristan and get my contract revised? Officially letting me off the hook as a single Nick Parker?"

"And me?" Maddie said, offering Peter a high five. "Do I get some love?"

Nodding, Peter slapped Maddie's hand. "Whatever you and your amiable town needs, it's yours. And Gus, call Tristan ASAP and let him know you're back on the market."

"I don't know who will get the key to Baileys. Will it be Gus? Or Lucy?" Maddie took Lucy's hand and tugged her along as she approached Gus. Then Maddie, standing between them, grabbed his hand. "Hey, guess who will be the unofficial royal couple for Winterfest?"

"Maddie, you are incorrigible." Gus kept his eyes on Lucy, relieved the color had returned to her face.

"Oh my gosh," Maddie giggled. "You two will be together on the sleigh bed race."

"Hold up." Lucy stepped away from them. "I have a lot of stock to replenish. I don't know if I can participate in any of the events during the Fest."

"W&B will be the sponsor for the bed. Go for it. Make it all about your shop for any other event you choose to participate in. Ask me for any help," Maddie entreated.

Gus's heart pounded as Lucy paced around the claw-foot tub. He flinched when a rubber duck she stepped on squeaked. "I'm good with this, but give me a day or two to reorder my thought process."

She hadn't thrown him out with the bathwater, but he still had some swimming to do. At least he'd maintained his position in her *genus* and *family*. Getting back into her *kingdom* would take serious work.

Michael headed out. "Lucy, I'll call you later with news."

"It's ugly in here." Lucy picked up a duck and threw it in the tub.

"Tomorrow afternoon, I'll make sure the investigators do their thing beforehand so you can clean up," Michael said before leaving.

"I'll get going on studio insurance detail." Peter followed Michael out.

"Okay, Ms. Emma," Maddie said, "We'll start with pics for your Instagram account. You and Gus in front of W&B. Let's go."

"I look terrible." Lucy smoothed down her hair. "And the paparazzi, they're out there."

"Nonsense," Maddie said, "you're glowing. And your boots look fab with the long red sweater."

"I agree." Gus ached. He wanted to feel Lucy's hair between his fingers. "If you want...we can talk to Johnny and give *TMZ* an exclusive?"

She gave him a considering look before digging out a red beret from her backpack. "This hat will make me look jauntier. Red is my signature color for the shop."

Gus loved her strength and resiliency. "Take pics with your phone, then you can decide how to use them." He opened the door to the paparazzi gathered out front. "Or not. We have a photo op at your doorstep." Once in a while, timing was on his side.

"Curiosity killed the cat, right?" Lucy muttered.

Maddie scoffed. "Not when the cat looks like Angus Reid."

"Ready?" he asked.

Lucy nodded. "Sure, Nick."

He stepped out and waved at the photographers. "Hey, all. How are things going?"

Johnny ran up to him. "Is it true? Are you up for an Emmy?"

"A little too early to tell. As soon as I know the details, I'll find you, Johnny."

Maddie and Lucy came out and stood on either side of him. He dropped his arms around his two favorite women. "Are you ready for Winterfest?"

The photographers shouted, hooted, and snapped pictures. Then Gus found his phone and took selfies, a lot of them with Lucy at his side. The pressure of the day dissipated. He didn't have to walk away from Lucy anymore but wasn't sure if she would run away screaming because of his obsessed publicist.

"Hey, what about me?" Maddie elbowed him in the ribs. "I'm all in for Baileys."

Gus aimed his phone and took pictures with Maddie. Then, when Lucy pulled out her phone, he made sure only the two of them were in her shots.

For *#Lust, #W&B and #Lucy #Baileys.*

Chapter 29

"Hey there, Lucy," Stan said, strolling down the aisle with a chainsaw in his hand. "Anything you need, grab it. Don't worry about the bill. It's a shame about your shop."

"Thanks a bunch." She mustered up a smile for his generosity, even though the rest of her body ached. Pulling out another bag of dried lavender, Lucy sniffed it and dropped it back on the shelf. "I'm happy for you. It's busy here this morning. Don't people rest on Sundays anymore?"

Stan waved the chainsaw. "It's ice-carving time. The sculptors are coming in to get their blocks of ice. They'll be carving and showing 'em on Main Street the next three days."

"Better not go near my shop. Their blocks will probably melt." She sniffed another bag of dried lavender buds. "When did you get these flowers? They smell stale."

After setting the scary tool on the floor, he inspected the plastic bag. "Says here it's good for another month."

She scanned the sell-by date. "A year ago. Do you have anything fresher?"

"Sorry, no. I special order it for you from up on Washington Island," he said. "How are things going at Wicks?"

"Terrible. I won't be able to open Thursday night. I'm pissed." She tried to keep the anger out of her voice. "I'm not sure why I agreed to Maddie's absurd idea. Who is even going to pay attention to a sleigh bed decorated with lavender?"

Stan hesitantly wrapped his arms around her and gave her a cosmic-sized fatherly hug. "It's rough being a retail owner. I've been in business for over thirty years," he said, "and it's changed entirely. I wonder when the day will come. Eventually, I'll be replaced by my computer."

Inhaling his clove-scented aftershave, she relished Stan's kindness, and a lousy tear dropped onto his sweatshirt. "At least you've had thirty years. I can't even get to day one, and worse, I haven't been able to step foot in the shop. It's been deemed a hazard zone."

Before more dang tears fell, she stepped back. "My opening is completely dependent on an electrician because the whole store has to be rewired."

"Who did you hire?" He retrieved his phone from one of the pockets on his leather utility apron.

"Shocked Monkey," she replied. "The guy has not returned any of my calls."

"Bad business, then," he said, tapping his phone. "You need my guy. The best. He's out of Sister Bay and magical with wires."

While Stan called and spoke to the electrician, she dug around her pink purse for a tissue. The past few days, she'd been stretching on her yoga mat in the greenhouse, listening to Adele, stuffing down tears, and avoiding Gus. Her head told her that he'd had nothing to do with the flooding, yet her heart kept aching. With the loss of her shop, she'd lost her mojo. How had she missed Sara's obsession with Gus? If love connections were her bread and butter, she should have been able to detect the sour combos as well as the sweet ones.

"My buddy is laid up with gout and can't get to work until after the Fest. Can he come in on the fourteenth?"

She nodded forcefully, even though she wasn't sure of the date. More meetings were coming up with investigators and insurance reps. But Valentine's Day seemed totally appropriate. Why not celebrate the most romantic day with an electrician? Her business *was* all about making sparks fly.

Stan ended the call. "Sorry about the lavender. What is Maddie's cockamamie idea?"

"During the Fest, I'm sponsoring a sleigh bed for the race, and she thinks decorating it with lavender will scream aromatherapy." Lucy tossed the year-old bags of dried purple buds into her basket. "She's been incredibly supportive. I'm just not creative in that way. Artsy. You know what I mean?"

"Follow me." Stan picked up his chainsaw and led her into the paper products aisle. "I'm a boomer, but I've been learning a lot from you millennials on Instagram. Your shots of Wicks are fantastic."

He plucked off anything the color purple and tossed it into her cart. A ream of purple paper, big pieces of purple cardboard, plates, napkins, jute, and ribbon. "I'll have Bob go downstairs in the stockroom and pull out anything purple for you."

"I have no idea what I can do with it all, but it's nice to have," she said. "Too bad I can't light candles for the bed race."

Stan grabbed the front end of her cart and yanked it. She followed him into the lightbulb aisle. From left to right, he scanned the shelves and pulled down a box. "Huzzah. Here are some fake and flameless candles. I could paint over the white with purple if you want."

Lucy was agog at Stan's ingenuity.

"I was an art major," he said before she could ask, "with an MFA."

She pushed the cart next to him, and he set the box in it. Then, he reached into the shelf's nether land, retrieved five more boxes, and stacked them into her cart.

"What size is your bed for the race?"

"Full. You're amazing. Thanks, Stan."

"Around fifty pillars should be enough. If not, I probably have more around here."

"I'm all good. Still want to figure out how to decorate this bed."

"Stan," Bob yelled from the end of the aisle, "get to the delivery dock. The truck's pulling up with da blocks."

"The ice truck hath cometh." Stan grabbed the chainsaw and jogged down the aisle. "Go into lawn and garden. There might be fake lavender or purple pots."

In Aisle 13, she spotted florists' buckets with foot-long sprigs of artificial lavender. Lucy dumped a bucket over and let the fake purple plants fill between the boxes of fake candles. These would work for a bed sliding across the ice of Kangaroo Lake. She dug around the buckets and pulled out every purple plant she could find.

"Lucy?" Claire called, poking around the corner by the watering cans. "Hey."

"You're in Baileys." She stayed calm, even though she wanted to jump for joy at the sight of her best friend. "I didn't think I'd see you until the Fest kickoff on Thursday."

"Not quite," Claire said. "It's about the ice sculpting."

"There you are." Sinjin kissed Claire's cheek. "Hey, I'm on a mission. I need my ice block."

Claire rolled her eyes. "You're an evil overlord trying to take over the world with an ice sculpture. Way too enthusiastic."

"Yes, because I'll have a chainsaw in my hands." Sinjin let out a devious laugh.

"This is a lot of purple stuff." Claire snooped around the cart. "Celebrating the artist formally known as Prince?"

Sinjin sang the chorus for "Purple Rain."

Seeing Claire and Sinjin together, Lucy realized how they

made an amazing match. They had a lovey-dovey vibe. Her suffering mojo took a turn for the better. "It's lavender stuff for the sleigh bed race. Not sure if you know, Wicks won't be open for Winterfest."

"Yeah, we heard about it." Sinjin gave Claire a sideways glance.

"It's awful," Claire said. "So sorry. Please let us know if there's anything we can do."

"Anything," Sinjin added.

"Well, I am attempting to keep Wicks on the radar by sponsoring a bed." Lucy pointed to the contents of her cart. "I'm clueless at this point. Something else to figure out."

"If you want, I can design it." Claire smiled hesitantly.

"Great, but...what would be terrific is if you and Sinjin made a testimonial of love since you two were my first *Emma* match made with the help of Lust."

Claire grinned at Sinjin. "What do you think, babe? Wanna go on record? Share our love story with everyone for Wicks and Balms?"

"As long as it's not a kiss-and-tell situation, I'm on board." Sinjin arched his eyebrow. "Only wanna share the G-rated parts."

"Those are the most important." Lucy was hopeful for the first time in days. "I won't take you away from any of the Fest events. I have to decide on where and when to film, so I'll text you."

Claire hugged her. "Let us know. We have plenty of time for you."

Stan's Wisconsin twang boomed over the intercom. "All you block boys. Get to the loading dock. Aye? Bob will be delivering you and your ice to your location on the street."

"Sinjin, where are you?" Gus's voice boomed louder than the ice announcements. He appeared at the end of the aisle, looked up from his phone, and stared at her. Lucy felt like she did the other night in the Immigrant Room: a celebrity, a star, and a luminary. Then, she immediately extinguished the thought.

* * *

"Look who we found?" Sinjin waved a purple branch in his face. "In the plants."

Gus swatted it away and cleared his throat. "Hey. How are you?"

He couldn't stop staring at Lucy. She hadn't returned his texts, and after he'd politely pounded on the back door of the house, she hadn't answered. They'd only made eye contact when she was in the greenhouse. Wearing a pink robe, pink slippers, and pink headphones, she just waved and dropped down on her yoga mat.

"Pretty dang bad." She frowned.

Sinjin slapped him hard on the shoulder. Gus felt the sting through his thick down coat.

"Ow, what the hell?"

"I have ice to conquer," Sinjin said. "We are at the Harbor B&B. You two should come by for dinner tonight. The four of us?"

"Please?" Claire folded Lucy into a bear hug. "I'll draw sketches for the Wicks bed, and we can talk lavender."

Lucy shoved another purple stick into her cart. "I, um, have..."

"Great." Sinjin yanked Claire out of the aisle. "We'll see you around eight."

Gus shook his head at his brother's lack of finesse. He should know Lucy was the matchmaking expert. When they were alone in the garden aisle, he noticed Lucy's hair. The braid crowned the top of her head, styled like when she'd stood boldly at the press conference and had asked him about the sachet.

"Lucy. I'm miserable and sorry about your shop."

Stan started to come up to them, gawked, pivoted, and left.

"Why? It's not your fault. It's Sara's."

"Which makes me responsible," he said, brushing his fingers through sprigs of a fake plant. "I have a difficult situation with my job. And the others who work to support me."

"Cry me a river. At least you have a job." She picked up a white candle. "This is it. I'm reduced to fake plastic candles. You know what's worse? You don't believe your publicist destroyed my shop. When I said it, you looked at me like I was bonkers. Oh my god, I can't believe I...we..." Shuddering, she dropped her head and whispered, "Never mind. Best to forget about the other night's shenanigans."

Impossible.

"Lucy, there's a lot more we need to talk about. Yes, I know Sara is guilty, but I have to figure out the details." He kept his voice steady, even though his heart pounded hard.

Stan popped around the corner again. "Sorry to interrupt you two. I had another idea. How about building an arch over the headboard with purple balloons?"

Lucy chuckled, and Gus was relieved.

"Thanks." Ignoring him, she pushed her cart toward the front of the store. "I've gotta get going. Can you check me out, Stan?"

Stan ran ahead, and Gus followed them.

"You can't avoid me forever," he said to her back.

"I don't have anything to say." She shrugged. "To you. I can't trust your smoldering smile, and I'm not one of Nick Parker's femme fatales."

There was plenty more he needed to say to her, but the hardware store was not the place. Too many eyes and phones around. This wasn't the kind of attention Lucy and Wicks needed.

In order to stay near her without looking like a loiterer, he went up to the three men already in line and took out his phone. "Hey, guys, what are you all making with your ice and new chainsaw?"

One guy laughed. "Angus Reid, the megastar of *Raven House.* Cool to meet you, dude. My buddies and me are combining three blocks and cutting it into the White House."

"Wow," Gus said, impressed. "Hey, I've got to see it when you're done."

Even Lucy appeared to be fascinated.

"Selfie?" Gus asked.

They all high-fived him, and he snapped the pic. Stan photo-bombed it.

"Stan, I'm tagging Baileys Hardware and *R-H* in the pic." He put Lucy's boxes of fake candles on the counter. "It will build up your Instagram account before the shoot."

"You don't need to help," she said, trying to discourage him.

He wouldn't leave her alone.

"Ace news, Stan. You and your poker buddies will have roles as bowling extras."

"I know." Stan tapped his tablet. "Peter called me."

"Here's a copy of your purchase, Lucy. You can write it off as a business expense."

She tried to give him her credit card. "Can't I pay you for any of it?"

"Nope. We're both shop owners and need to watch each other's backs."

When she nodded, her head dropped, and Gus saw tears glistening in her amber eyes. She really wasn't used to people wanting to help her.

"See you in the Beacon when filming starts," Gus said.

"In two weeks." Stan looked over his readers. "Can't wait."

"How did you know the date?" Since the destruction of Wicks, Gus hadn't had a chance to get any filming details from Peter. Unfortunately, discussing Gus's break from Sara had taken up most of their time.

"The beauty told me," Stan replied.

"Who?" Gus asked.

"Alexandra." Lucy zipped up her jacket. "Your co-star."

Stan shook his head. "Not that beauty. The other one. The one who has a pole stuck up her you-know-what. I don't mean any disrespect, but she's come in here often and never bothers to say hello or thank you."

"Sara? She's been coming into the hardware store? For what?" Gus's surprise turned into shock. "Are you sure? Sara Boden? Dark red lips?"

Shaking her head, Lucy rolled her eyes.

"Yeah. She bought long underwear we sell for the guys and flannel shirts. A couple times, she had keys made. When she first came, she was looking for boots, but none of them were pretty enough for her."

Long underwear and flannel shirts were too practical and unfashionable for Sara. Since they had arrived in Wisconsin, she'd refused to dress for the weather. Suspicious in itself, but having keys made cemented her guilt in Gus's mind. Now, he wanted to prove it to Peter and the studio. Sara should be responsible for every cost necessary to get Wicks up and running again.

"Thanks, Stan, we'll talk later." Gus followed Lucy out the door. "Let me help you load this stuff in your truck."

"Thanks." She unsnapped the tonneau cover. "Listen, opening during the Fest was key to my annual budget, and the loss of the shop sucks." She tossed the fake flowers in the flatbed. "But I haven't heard a word from my mom, and I'm worried. Since you found this rehab place, do you know about anything going on with her?"

Gus placed the boxes of plastic candles next to the flowers. "No, I haven't received any updates because she doesn't have a phone," he said. "At the facility, they don't allow them. It's part of the treatment."

Johnny from *TMZ* started walking toward them and snapped a few pictures.

"Lucy, I need to talk to you. Meet me at the Harbor tonight. I'll be there by seven. Please? And I'll try and call the rehab to find out about your mom."

"I'll think about it. Okay?" She hopped in her truck.

After she drove off, he ducked back into Stan's before Johnny made it over to him. Gus did not want to explain another photo of him and Lucy. At least this time, if it landed on social media, he couldn't care less. The only upside to the destruction of Lucy's shop...he no longer had to worry about his contract.

Chapter 30

Lucy checked her Instagram account while waiting for the others to show up at the Harbor restaurant. Her followers for Wicks had jumped up to over ten thousand. When she'd looked yesterday, there were only eight thousand. *What the hell?*

Gus must have pulled his celebrity strings. That nagging feeling bit her ass again. Why was this man going to such lengths for her? Actually, paying for addiction treatment wasn't a "length" but a dang trip around the world.

She looked through her photos to decide what she should post. The recent pics she had taken were for the insurance agents. Every angle of her gutted shop.

"Can I get you a drink?" the white-mustached bartender asked as he wiped off a glass. "It's happy hour."

"Perfect timing, yes. Do you know how to make a proper old-fashioned?"

"Lots of muddled cherries, an orange slice, and only the best brandy," he said, lifting a bushy gray eyebrow. "Unless you would prefer whiskey?"

"Brandy...I'm a purist. And extra cherries, please. And thank you." She jotted ideas on her phone for an info campaign to update her followers about the shop's status. Everyone loves a good phoenix-rising-from-the-ashes story. Even Dumbledore used it for Harry.

She spun her stool around, looking for Gus. No sign of him, and the dining room tables were filling up. As soon as phones were aimed at the entrance, she would know.

"Here you go, miss."

She jerked back around toward the bar.

The bartender set her cocktail down on a coaster, and cherries toppled over the edge of the cut crystal glass. "Extra Door County cherries, as you requested."

"Thanks. I deserve a little *happy* today." She plucked off a cherry, dropped it in her mouth, and stared at the orange slice hitched onto the glass.

Gus had made multiple attempts to talk to her while she'd shut out the world and bonded with Adele, but after their night of steamy shenanigans, he'd sprinted out of the hotel room.

Nibbling on the orange, she scrolled through her new Instagram followers. The crew and stars from *R-H*, all of the Chrises... Hemsworth, Pine, and Evans, Robert D. Jr., the stars from the *Gilmore Girls*, and even a couple of sports dudes, like the Packers' QB.

"Hey, Bob," Gus said, sliding onto the empty barstool to her left. "Hi, Lucy."

She stifled a sigh that would have surely come out sounding like a moan. Gus wore a navy suit with a navy shirt. His unbuttoned collar displayed the interior pinstripe detail on the shirt, a hint of his raven tattoo, his AA chain, and a mouthwatering teaser of his incredible chest.

"Good to see you, sir," the bartender said. "The usual?"

When Gus's thigh grazed hers, she sipped her drink to cool down. "Where are Sinjin and Claire?"

Gus rubbed his immaculate beard. "They aren't coming.

We've been *Emma'd*, Emma. By Sinjin and Claire, couldn't you tell?"

Lucy shook her head. "I wasn't in a great mood and missed it. Is Claire still planning to create the sleigh bed?"

"Yes, she's designing a bed of lavender as we speak. I'm stoked they'll be taking their place of honor for Wicks. They are your prototype, Ms. Emma. Can't get any more lovesick than those two."

"Here's your Temple, Gus," the bartender said. "Lucy, need another one?"

"Wait. Are you Bob from Stan's Hardware?"

"The one and only," he said. "Jack-of-all-trades. Handyman by day and bartender at night."

"And one of *Raven*'s newest extras." Gus sipped his Shirley Temple. "Thanks for gathering the guys together to support the show."

Bob whipped his phone from his breast pocket. "Another selfie? Same tag?"

Gus draped his arm over her shoulders. "Say cheese."

Bob turned his back on them to take a selfie.

After he left to serve others, she couldn't seem to move away from Gus. Inhaling the scent of his bergamot-and-orange aftershave, she kept glancing at the sweet spot on his neck. She recalled kissing the luscious morsel the other night. "The hometown superstar knows everyone."

"You're a celebrity, too," he said, toying with the cherry-laden toothpick in his mocktail. "I sincerely hope you're doing okay." He coughed. "I need to explain something to you."

"Oh, I'm fine, thanks to all the cherries in this sweet drink. By the way, thanks for talking up Lust. A lot of your Hollywood friends are following Wicks on Instagram."

"Good."

"About the other morning. I didn't mean to be in such a rush. I wanted to"—he gazed at her seductively—"go to breakfast. Or the yoga studio. It crossed my mind to take in a shower or a massage. Then, a photo cropped up on the show's Instagram account of us together at that Tomato shop and sent me into a panic."

"The two of us photographed together made you panic? Am I embarrassing?"

He winced. "No! It's my...*was* my contract for the show. I had to be single in the eyes of the fans. No pics could be posted of me with women. It's ridiculous, I know, but two years ago, it saved my career."

"So how could you take all those pictures at the Immigrant? You were camera-happy after dinner."

"All the diners signed NDA agreements for me, but the next morning, I flew into damage control. After Sara texted me about the pic, I assumed there were other shots. I rushed back to Baileys and found out there was one blurry shot with us in the background while we were by the fitting room. A customer had taken a selfie."

"Sara has a lot of control, doesn't she?" Lucy couldn't stem her irritation. Oh, how she wanted to drop-kick his nasty publicist across Lake Michigan.

"An abundance, which is why I haven't spoken to her. I'm sick of being beholden to her mania. She's leaving for LA after the Fest. And now, after her abhorrent actions...it's clear she's in a black hole. Because of me, she destroyed your shop."

"It's because of *us*. Or me, but not you alone." She bit off the last section of her orange slice. "I'm baffled at what to say. Or how to act. It's how Claire must have felt after my mother... Most clearly, I know your publicist needs serious help."

"I'm not ready to feel sorry for her," Gus declared. "There are a lot of reparations she needs to make for you and the shop. I never doubted you. My publicist is to blame, however, I know she didn't do it alone. You don't need to be my femme fatale, but I'm going to use my Nick Parker skills."

"Interesting."

"Another?" Bob asked Lucy.

"No, thanks. I'll be walking home." The brandy had warmed her up nicely. "You make a great cocktail."

Bob smiled his thanks and wandered off.

"It isn't only my friends in Hollywood who now follow Wicks," Gus said. "A few of your new fans are from the Immigrant Room from that night. I contacted them and told them to go nuts. Post to their delight. Tag the 'birthday' pics with my name, your name, and both our businesses: *R-H* and W&B."

She scanned her followers. "You're right. I remember that woman, wait." She found her tablet and looked up her online orders for Lust. They had tripled in two days. "This is great. Dang, I may need to get more lavender. The real stuff, not Stan's."

"Slow down," he said, interrupting her rambling ideas. "You'll find your orders, organize, and get it done. Don't worry, I'm the one with the attention span of a squirrel."

Gus took her hand. "Another thing. I connected with the rehab center and spoke to the facilitator."

She let out a long breath. "How is my mom?"

"Good. She's adjusting."

Lucy perked up. "Translated, that means she hasn't been cussing everyone out, maybe only one or two people."

He tipped his head side to side. "And the group facilitator mentioned a bit of 'salty language,'" he said, using air quotes, "but also said your mum has been sleeping better."

"Did she say how many hours? With the clanging noise in prison, not to mention cold, hard fear, my mom never slept more than an hour at a time."

Gus pulled a small leather notebook from his suit jacket. "I took notes so I wouldn't forget."

"Is that a *Nick Parker* prop?"

"Hey, you have your ways, and I have mine. I enjoy notebooks, pens, and books. Do you want to know what I wrote down?"

"Of course." Gus's generosity was like a dang heat lamp. His genuine caring made her feel warm and comfortable.

"Your mom's bedroom looks out over the house's victory garden. She sat up all night when she arrived and stared out the window. Eating every one of her meals. Last night, she fell asleep around midnight. And according to the night nurse, she slept until four in the morning without waking when the nurse made her hourly checks."

"Four whole hours is an incredible achievement."

"She's in a good place," he said, "and she will get better. Oh, and apparently, she's been talking a lot about her *chakra*?"

"That's because we were together at the courthouse. I'll explain it all on another day. Did the facilitator mention anything about the scent of the place?"

"I don't recall." He gave her a smirk and flipped through his notebook's pages. "No, nothing, but my guess is that it's more medicinal."

"I can't wait to fill in Sister Jan on this news. Lavender. My mom and the other residents absolutely need it." She looked at her tablet to check her orders for Serenity. They weren't as high as Lust, though she had just introduced it. Then she spotted a message from Sweet Tomato, ordering a lot more of it. "I have to make a trip to Washington Island for lavender. Dang."

"What's the problem?"

"It's an hour's drive north from here, followed up with a treacherous ferry ride over a body of water called Death's Door." She added, "On my last visit to the island, during normal weather, the ferry ride had been rough. I puked off the side of the boat."

"Never been up there. I can go along and hold back your hair for you."

"You're very sweet. I'm sure, though, you have better things to do for the Fest."

"Look, as your sidekick, I don't want my grade to drop below a B."

"You're already earning an A+++."

Suddenly, a rotten smell assaulted her. She covered her mouth and nose as Sara strode toward them, with Peter following. Sara looked bleak. Lucy tried to be concerned, but her anger had washed away any empathy. She only hoped that Peter was okay.

"Erm, this is bad." Gus shook his head.

She didn't think it would be *bad* for Peter but knew it was worse for Sara. The woman had wigged out and lost it. And since she'd destroyed Wicks, Lucy had zero sympathy to offer.

* * *

"Have you lost your phone?" Sara asked acerbically. "I sent confirmation times to you for the photo shoot with Alexandra. I rescheduled it at the Snake Pit."

"There's been a lot going on. I'm sure you know about the destruction of Wicks," Gus replied, staring at Peter. "My priority is Lucy and her shop."

"Unfortunate." Sara fired eye-daggers at Lucy. "But we're behind on the press pics for the Emmys."

"There will be time," Peter said. "There's no rush."

"Oh right, *no rush* says the douche who booked my flight on Valentine's Day." Sara dropped her bag on the back of the barstool and fisted her hands on her hips. "The crowd in here is thanks to me."

Gus clenched his jaw while Lucy ordered another old-fashioned.

"Kenny, Jack, and Cody gave me your location, so I posted a pic with the Winterfest handle." Sara tried handing her phone over for him to look. He declined to take it.

"Hey, folks. Welcome," Bob said. "What'll you have?"

"Any rosé? Whispering Angel?" Sara asked.

"How ironic," Lucy said, under a cough.

Bob huffed. "Yes, we have the rosé for you, ma'am."

Ignoring the bartender, Sara glared at Gus. "I'm pissed as hell I won't be here when you film in the bowling alley, but since the place reeks of Bengay, I won't be missing anything."

"The last scenes will include my new extras to attract a different demographic." Gus gritted his teeth. "There are *Raven House* fans you haven't tapped into. A lot of older men watch."

"Is that why you're kicking me out of town? I haven't paid enough attention to the geezers?"

Threads of frustration tickled the base of Gus's neck. Up until today, he'd managed to avoid a full-blown migraine. Could he make it to Valentine's Day?

Sara's shoulders slumped as she grabbed the glass of wine. Instead of emptying it with one swig, she stared at the swirling blush-colored liquid, then set it down. "I can't wait until we're back home in sunny LA."

Gus almost winced at the idea of returning to LA. The 405 traffic, the smog, the tumultuous parties, and the constant grabs for his attention. His brain had been on overdrive every day while living there, and Baileys had given him peace. He hadn't succumbed to one migraine, and his thoughts were clearer. "Filming in the Beacon won't start until after V-Day. For the time being, I'm staying put."

"I can't wait to get back and take a road trip on the PCH in your Porsche."

Dredging up the onetime thing he'd completely forgotten about was off the wall. To make sure Lucy understood how little Sara's memory meant to him, he glanced her way and rolled his eyes.

Lucy gave him a slight nod, stirred her cocktail, and returned to staring at her tablet.

Addressing Sara, he added, "I'll be making changes—"

Peter interrupted. "He'll be going by Gus Reid instead of Angus starting with season five."

From the corner of his eye, Gus caught Lucy's quick smile.

Sara picked at the thin fabric of her dress. It dove down low and nearly exposed her breasts. He wondered where her purchase at Stan's—the flannel shirts and long underwear—had gone.

"You'll be known as Gus? Are you a parking attendant at a cheap hotel? Was it her idea?" She jutted her chin toward Lucy. "She knows nothing about brand or marketing."

Gus grasped the leather edge of the bar as blood rushed into his head. The vein on his left temple was vibrating. "As I said, I'm making changes." His jaw started to ache. "First, I'll be hiring a new publicist, and your services won't be needed any longer. In fact, you need to give me all my social media accounts and passwords as soon as possible. And delete me from your contacts. Someone else will take over."

One corner of Sara's mouth tugged down, and her lips puckered. "You need me. I'm a huge part of your life."

Peter jumped to his sister's side.

For a fleeting second, Gus thought he'd stepped into a pile of horseshit.

"Sara, Gus will be working on other projects *after* Winterfest. When we get back, we'll have a top-line conversation." Peter said calmly, then glanced at him, looking for support. "Okay?"

"Right. After Baileys and the Fest, we'll talk," Gus said without choking on his words.

As much as he'd wanted to be finished with Sara, there were too many loose ends. He couldn't fire her yet. For one thing, he had to prove she'd destroyed Wicks.

Lucy looked at him, her expression full of concern. Gus was sure she would be massaging an essential oil on his temples and then his neck by the end of the evening. He hoped.

Sara took a sip of her rosé. "Don't be so condescending, Peter."

Gus's blood was pumping too hard. He tried to call on his mantra to move his mind into a calmer place. But his *Hari* and *Rama* had run off and escaped his brain. "I have to get to the lighthouse."

"For what?" Sara demanded.

Peace.

"I'm working on different ideas for Friday night of the Fest."

Sara grabbed her purse. "I should come along."

Hell no.

"Not necessary. We're working on a Wicks promo." He handed Lucy her coat. "Ready?"

At his mention of Wicks & Balms, Sara waved him off.

"Here." Lucy dropped her truck keys into his hand. "I could use the fresh air, too."

Gus nodded bye to Bob and the siblings and draped his arm over Lucy's shoulders. As they left the Harbor, he sucked in some air. When exhaling, he counted to five to keep his aggravation at bay. He hoped that the lighthouse would calm him down...as well as time with Lucy.

Chapter 31

Lucy played with the radio to find a song for Gus as he drove north on County Q to the lighthouse. She wanted him to relax. His jaw clicked and flexed as he fixated on the road. Since leaving the Harbor, he hadn't said a word. She tried to find a mellow tune like one of Carole King's and wound up with Taylor Swift singing "Shake It Off."

A small grin crossed his lips. "Trying to tell me something?"

"No, not at all." She couldn't shake off anything, and it was lucky that she hadn't lunged at the vile publicist. Although Lucy wasn't a violent type, it had crossed her mind to pull Sara's perfect hair. Fortunately, she was more concerned about Gus.

"We'll have the lighthouse to ourselves." He turned down the radio volume. "I had to get away from Sara to think. My publicist came to town and fucked up your shop. I have to figure out how."

They drove over the frozen access road leading to Cana Island and parked. Unlike her last visit, when they'd been stopped by the paparazzi, the island was accessible. Walking to the lighthouse, she marveled at the statuesque beauty of the rare maritime building for a moment and then panicked. It jutted way high up into the sky. Did Gus expect her to hike up it with him?

She slipped a vial of Serenity out of her backpack. Before emptying the bottle on herself, she offered it to Gus. "I know you may not want any, but this will help you to chill."

"I was hoping you'd offer me one of your concoctions." When he pocketed the vial, she was pleasantly surprised.

"Thanks. What's this one called?" He walked ahead to open the outbuilding.

"Serenity." Inside, she stomped her boots on the stone floor. When the screen door slammed shut, she recoiled. "Tell me what you think when you get a chance."

Off to the right, a dark and deserted antique kitchen was divided from the entrance with a velvet rope hanging between two chrome stanchions. The temperature inside was the same as outside. Shivering, Lucy adjusted her eyes to the dimly lit space. A few battered and beaten wood steps led up to the souvenir shop. Lights flickered on, and Gus met her on the top step.

Rubbing her hands together to keep warm, she followed him into the musty-smelling gift shop. There were mostly empty shelves with a few knick-knacks. A collection of incredible black-and-white photos hung on the crumbling walls and stood out from the damp and dreary surroundings.

Gus wiped a layer of dust off a shelf with his hand. "It's the saddest-looking shop, right? Not a whole lot of memory-making gifts."

"I love the photos. Maddie's view of New York City?"

Nodding, Gus rotated his shoulders, unhinging them from his neck. "Have you ever been to the top of the lighthouse?"

"Never. No. I'm not sure it's my cup of tea." She glanced around the sad shop. "But you go, I'll stay on the ground. I like it in here, and I can do a little product placement."

"It's a spectacular sky tonight—clear and cold, and loads of stars." Gus browsed through a rack of sweatshirts, handed one to her, and kept one for himself. "Throw this on. It's easier than your coat. Less bulky."

She shuddered as they passed through a velvet-curtained doorway. Musty and damp air surrounded them. The white-washed brick of the lighthouse encased a circular iron staircase that rose, rose, rose way above them and to the top. Lucy swayed back and forth as she looked up. And her mouth began to water. She took off her coat, set it on a rickety table with her backpack, and put on the sweatshirt with Door County scrolled across the chest.

When Gus took off his suit coat and slung it on the cupboard door, she expected him to put on the sweatshirt. Instead, he took off his shirt, stripped down to his Henley T-shirt, and tied the sweatshirt over his shoulders.

Lucy's fingers twitched to slide under the Henley. Their one night at the American Club had made a lasting imprint. Maybe she could seduce him to skip this hike up into another ozone layer.

"This lighthouse has always been able to get my mind back to a good place." He pulled his foot up behind his butt and stretched. "There's history here, but it's in dire need of some TLC."

Nope. Can't seduce him. "Kind of scary, too," she said, looking around and pretending not to wobble. "If you need time alone, I can hang back."

"Not at all. I love this thing. Every lighthouse has a legend attached to it. Easy to find a story about love, pain, and loss. Light-houses not only light the way for ships. They're a good guide for the lonely. They're sort of magical. Beacons of hope to save lost souls." Gus handed her a flashlight.

Absorbing his words, she turned it on and lit up the interior of the lighthouse.

"There are ninety-seven steps, and each one is worth the hike."

"Ninety-seven, seriously? It's a lot of dang steps."

"Yep. Up and then down." Gus hopped on the bottom step. "I'm good with steps. The Twelve Steps with AA made me a pro."

Lucy aimed the flashlight at him. "You're funny."

"I'll stop at the control room. There are landings by the portholes where you can stand and look out of when you need to catch your breath," he said. "Ready? I'll start up. Stay close."

Getting and staying close to Gus was all she could think about. "The control room?"

"The computers. The tracking system to operate the lantern."

Lucy cautiously began ascending the spiral staircase. Her boots scratched each decorated wrought iron step. To stay calm, she focused on Gus's hips and ass as he slowly walked up. If he could do it, she could. It was one step after another. She could just close her eyes at the top.

Her heart pumped hard, her nostrils absorbing the cold, crisp scents of stone and water. At the first window, she spied the moonlit lake. Ice caps sculptured the shoreline. She made it to what she hoped was the halfway point without fainting.

"We're almost to the bulkhead," he yelled. "Watch your head. It's a low entry."

At the last of the portholes, she forced her eyes from Gus and glanced outside. The tips of the pine trees leveled up with her sight line. When she reached the bulkhead, she half climbed and half crawled onto a stamped metal floor.

"You okay?" He offered her his hand. "How are your legs feeling? It's a lot of steps."

"Good," she shouted to be heard over the crashing water and gusting wind. She clutched onto his hand. When she made it onto the watch deck, the freezing air slid into her lungs. Swallowing, she closed her eyes and listened to the unsettling roar of Lake Michigan below.

Gus pulled her against his chest. "Oh, Lucy. I fucking forgot... you're not good with heights. I'm sorry."

"It's...it's okay. I'll just keep my eyes closed." She nestled into his chest and relished his heat. "Are you okay? Feeling better? I'm sure it's a gorgeous view."

"It is." He held her tight. "I'll tell you about it. The sky is blue swaths of indigo with ribbons of purple, and it's speckled with stars. To translate for you, the ribbons would be scented with patchouli and a hint of clove, and the stars are scented like snowflakes."

She laughed and held him tighter. "Now I have to see it. Don't move though. I've never been up this high." Lucy gradually opened her eyes and took in the stars. She dared not look down and held fast to Gus's hand. "Okay, you're right. Worth the view."

"And a great workout. My trainer in LA would love these stairs, but I like the Malibu sand. The beach is easier and warmer."

His home.

"What's your favorite part of the lighthouse? The history? You know a lot about it." Lucy leaned close to the wall for safety and stared straight ahead. "The snow is glittering."

"The calm, the reprieve, and the silence. And you?"

"I'm sure you could guess." She closed her eyes and inhaled deeply. "Nothing better than the fresh scent of pine."

He agreed. "Look at that star."

She peeked out of one eye. "Which one? There are a lot. It's like sprinkles of gold dust all over the sky."

"The brightest star," he whispered, pointing at the sky. "See the Big Dipper? Follow it to the top of the handle, and above it is the North Star. The best part of Baileys Harbor...a small town with fewer people means a gob-smacking number of stars."

"Glad to hear you're keen on Baileys," she said, staring at the North Star to avoid getting dizzy. "Do you know when you'll be leaving?"

The wind swirled around them; she tightened the hood of her sweatshirt.

"A date hasn't been determined; it depends on the reshoots. My guess is by the end of February after we finish filming at the Beacon."

Lucy couldn't ignore the sad reality. Hollywood was Gus's home, and he would be exiting Baileys soon.

She kept watch over the twinkling North Star. "Now I know

how to conquer the turbulent ferry ride. Find and focus on the North Star when I go to Washington Island."

"You're leaving?" He sounded surprised. "When?"

"Tomorrow," she said, deciding instantaneously. "On a quest for lavender. Remember?"

"Right, sorry. Are you sure you don't want my company? I'm pretty good with roses. I may be of help with lavender."

"Not necessary, thanks. This lighthouse needs you," she added, "and Baileys can't get enough of you." Lucy rubbed her arms. "Ready to go down?"

Gus wrapped his arms around her and was about to pull her in for a kiss.

An awful sense of light-headedness took over. "Can we get going?"

"Sure, fine."

It was far from fine. The last thing she needed was to kiss Gus. He had taken up considerable space in her head, and after he left, she'd be empty.

Love was a chancy racket, and it had always proven safer for her to use her matchmaking skills for others. She'd learned to live with alone, but lonely? That put her in the same desperate spot as her mom, and she couldn't risk it. She wanted to get down, go home, be alone, and escape to Stars Hollow.

Chapter 32

After three days of cold showers and a lot of shoveling, Gus plonked the shovel into a pile of snow and stared at the main house. He missed Lucy. She had only responded to a couple of his texts, but service on Washington Island was sketchy at best. When he caught the fluorescent lights flickering on in the greenhouse, he hopped over the piles of snow to greet her. His heart sank as he stormed into the conservatory and Sinjin was standing over the copper distillery, inspecting it.

"Hey, bro." He took out a wrench from the toolbox. "Thought you would be in town. Don't you have to be at the Fest?"

Gus tried rubbing, then picked off the tiny clumps of snow that had frozen onto his jeans. "Taking a few days to rest before the kickoff tonight. What are you doing here?"

"Lucy asked me to come by to look at this." He pointed to the copper still. "Apparently, she'll be coming back with a lot of lavender and wanted to make sure this is in perfect working order."

A twinge of envy hit Gus, and he wasn't sure if it was caused by the lavender or his brother. "Makes sense."

As Sinjin went about the business of tinkering with the still, Gus wandered around the greenhouse, hoping to grasp a bit of Lucy's aura. He adjusted her beakers and made sure they lined up straight, like soldiers at the ready for another battle in the name of love. "How is the bed coming? For Saturday's race," he said, fiddling with a set of pots on the workbench.

"Bed?" Sinjin set down his wrench.

Gus brushed out the debris from the pots, then went to the case of tiny empty vials used for her oils. "For the bed race on Saturday. Isn't Claire decorating it for Lucy?"

As he lifted a vial to his eye to check for dirt, Sinjin came over to him, took the vial from his hand, and returned it to the case. "I'm hurt. No interest in my ice sculpture?"

Gus tucked his hands in his pockets. "Sure, is it done?"

"Cut the crap." Sinjin inspected his face. "You look terrible. When was the last time you shaved? Lucy's been gone—" He lifted his hand and counted his fingers. "—one, two, three days?" Then Sinjin took in a long sniff. "And what have you been showering in? Dad's ancient Old Spice?"

He scoffed. "I've been training and getting ready for the 5K tomorrow morning by doing a lot of cardio. And shoveling. A lot of shoveling." Gus neglected to tell him that showering in the guest cabin was closer to a quick wipe-down in an outhouse. "A slight stench hovering around Nick Parker may give me space."

"At least a mile or two." Sinjin laughed. "Seriously, what gives, man. You're jumpy. I haven't seen this side of you since you were a kid. Why don't you go upstairs and take a long, hot shower? If I remember, Dad had the bathroom in this house remodeled with a lot of bells and whistles."

The idea was stellar, but as pathetic as it sounded, Gus was chicken to go into the main house alone. He'd looked at it every day since Lucy had left, and it felt just as it had been the last time he lived in it...cold and inhospitable. It was Lucy, with her greenery and *Kiki* energy, who made him comfortable inside and made him get near the fireplace.

"Wait a second," his brother said, clasping his shoulder. "Have you talked to Dad since you've been in Wisconsin?"

"No." He gritted his teeth and tasted peppermint. At least he was sure his breath was fresh. "Not yet."

"Don't you have to make amends with him, too?"

"Yes, however, Maddie, you, and Rob have taken priority," he said, still frustrated about how he hadn't connected with Rob. "I have a plan for Dad. He's the toughest because I feel gutted about Mum. He should have been here for her, don't you think?"

Sinjin dropped his screwdriver into the box and slammed it shut. "Dude, I'm good with the AA amends thing, but you need a reality check." He opened the french doors leading into the great room. "Get in here."

Kicking the snow off his boots and feeling unwelcome on the welcome mat, Gus scanned the darkened kitchen and glanced at the fireplace. The center of his mum's world and where her life had ended. "Hey, look, Sinjin. I'm good. There's no need to get big-brotherly on me."

"This is the perfect time to knock a heap of sense into you. You've been living in Baileys for over a month, and"—he pointed to the floor near the fireplace—"we're in this house together. Even though I wasn't here when she died, I miss Mum, too. And here's a news flash: so does Dad."

Gus crossed his arms over his chest to contain the ache threatening to gut him. "Dad was in Lake Bluff. He'd left Mum alone. And she had me...the worst kid ever. A Tasmanian devil."

Sinjin sat on the leather couch, inches away from where his mother had lain lifeless. "Get over here and sit your arse down."

Gus followed his older brother's orders. As he sank into the couch across from him, the cushions cradled his shoulders and took the edge off. He rubbed the back of his neck, realizing he had truly lost touch with his grooming these past few days. "As you requested, the 'arse' is in place."

"You've been living in La-La Land long enough I'm sure your memory has been clouded over with half-truths or replaced with stinging feelings."

"Now you sound like Lucy," Gus groused, grabbing a throw pillow, dropping it on his lap, and squeezing it. Down feathers poked through the tapestry. "Need a hit of Lust?"

"Don't forget, I was Lucy's first client." He pulled a plaid handkerchief from his pants pocket and wiped off his fingers. "I like working with metal more than ice. Maybe messier but a lot warmer."

Gus chuckled. "I didn't know men carried hankies around these days."

"Shows what you know. It's a kerchief from my buddy Colin Hanks. You're not the only one who has *ties* in Hollywood."

Gus was mortified and humbled, now realizing he'd missed his eccentric and broody brother. "Okay, I'm ready. What's the big reveal?" He shook his head, growing wary.

"Not big news, just life-altering. Our mum didn't want Dad around at all. Her priority was her hooch, and he knew it. He tried being part of her life right up until the day she died. It's why, I'm sure you forgot, every neighbor in this small town kept an eye on you and Rob. As well as Uncle Graham. Even though he was closer to Rob, he checked in on you two every other day."

Gus closed his eyes and let the memories float in and out. He'd remembered only the best and the worst of his mum, but he'd forgotten those times, the many times. When Maddie and her mother, Elsie Logerquist, took him away from the house and took him on a boat trip or a nature hike. And Michael, after Gus had returned from school, they kicked the soccer ball around until way after dark. Gus often made it home when his mum was fast asleep or completely passed out.

"Is it coming back to you?" Sinjin asked quietly. "Dad was

always there for you, for the three of us. He kept it on the QT. Did you hear, or do you remember what Lucy said in the courthouse?"

All he'd been able to focus on was Lucy and her desperate expressions. He barely recalled what she'd said while on the witness stand. Gus shook his head. "My mind was running in different directions that day."

"It was from a letter he'd written to Lucy. Dude, it's no coincidence Dad wanted Lucy to stay here to help with Julie. Take it from me, Julie Maxwell is brilliant, a talented sculptress, but she needed help. She was locked in alcohol's grip, and our father wanted to help. Especially...especially since he'd failed Mum."

"What did Lucy read?" Gus stared at the set of pokers on the hearth.

"Something about second chances and how addiction can keep you tethered to a bottle."

Gus stood and stretched out his arms. He eyed the hearth suspiciously, then inspected the fieldstones. They were an assortment of cream, pink, and green. Not one was red. His breathing slowed down. He closed his eyes, opened them up, and noticed only a fireplace, a wood floor, and a thick green-and-blue throw rug. "How's Dad doing these days?"

"Playing a lot of golf. Even now. He's been spending these cold days at the Swing Shop in Kohler." Sinjin's phone pinged. "Oy. Time to get going. I still have to make the final cuts on the ice sculpture. All right?"

"Yeah, yeah. Go. I'll catch up with you later. Wanna check on Lucy's shop. Your lighthouse made of ice will be in front of it?"

"Yes, mate." Sinjin wrestled him into a bear hug. "Later, Ace."

Gus sucked in a deep breath after his brother took off. He smelled a lot of different scents and made sure not to hyperventilate. Walking through the great room and the kitchen, he let his nose lead him around. Every scent was sweet or savory, and not one smell reminded him of blood.

He checked his phone. Lucy had texted him.

Be back in time for the bed race. Stay warm.

Gus jogged upstairs and started the shower. He would not get in it until it was steaming, so he texted his dad while waiting for the water to heat up. **Can we connect?**

Chapter 33

While waiting in the queue to get his hot chocolate, Gus impatiently glanced around for Lucy. Because of the Fest, they'd missed each other this morning. He rubbed his gloved hands and pumped his arms over his head to warm up for the sleigh bed race. The second full day of the festival and the temperature had dipped down to ten degrees. To his relief, the crowds were thinner. The few folks in line politely ignored him, too busy trying to keep warm.

He snapped pictures for Instagram: the hot cocoa bar on the deck of the Coyote Roadhouse, Maddie ladling out the hot chocolate, the firepit, and the field of red dogwood.

"Morning." Maddie handed him a mug. "It's cold."

He slipped his phone back in his pocket and wrapped his fingers around the hot mug. The aroma of chocolate sent his taste buds into a tizzy. "No kidding, but it'll warm up later. It's peaceful today...at least for me."

"Make sure to tag your Fest pictures to @Baileys and #BWF," she said, pointing to her red baseball cap. It sported a snowflake emblem for the Fest. "Where's your darn hat?"

"Sorry, forgot. I was in a rush this morning." He'd practically run out of the guest house in just his underwear to catch up with Lucy. She had driven in, unloaded her lavender in the greenhouse, and then driven off. It still rattled him.

"Nice placement in yesterday's 5K," Maddie said.

"Ta. Coming in dead last gave extra time for posting fans." He squinted at the bare ice of Kangaroo Lake glittering in the afternoon sun. Twenty or so orange traffic cones were winding around to shape a figure-eight racetrack. "How were things at the lighthouse last night?"

An icy gust of wind almost blew the red-and-white striped awning off its tracks.

"The evening was a hit. We had over fifty people come to the lighthouse and light up their own lanterns. After folks let them loose, they floated over the lake. I took a lot of photos for social media. It was beautiful." Maddie nodded toward the firepit. "You're holding up the line. Get going, and good luck in the race."

Behind a plume of smoke from a tall flame, Lucy was stirring the contents of a copper pot. He kept one eye on her as he strolled along the cocoa bar and filled his mug with toppings—marshmallows and sprinkles. He squirted on whipped cream and took a sip. Before he could wipe off his mouth and get to Lucy, a phone clicked near him.

"This pic will make your fans want to lick every bit of whipped cream off your beautiful face," Sara said. "Ready for the pre-race photo session?"

"In a bit," he said through chattering teeth. "Taking a break before I get on the ice."

"I'm racing with the guys in the light crew. The Harbor B&B sponsored our bed. See you out there. I'll be with those incredible-looking men holding brooms and wearing kilts."

"It's the curling club, and they'll be sweeping the ice to help the beds move easier." He pivoted around Sara and stepped onto a brick path embedded in the snow to get to the firepit. "The race starts in an hour. See you for pics in twenty."

Gus took in and released a deep, cleansing breath of burning wood. Sara had been behaving frighteningly civil since their blowup. Brushing snowflakes off a table, his suspicions about his soon-to-be ex-publicist kept bothering him. He chastised himself. Nick Parker was a fictitious character, and Gus Reid was an actor, not a detective. Come V-Day, she'd be on the West Coast.

"Need a refill?" Lucy asked, interrupting his *Nick Parker* moment.

"Yes, more, please." He stepped back to take in her honey-colored eyes. "When did you get home?"

"This morning." She refilled his mug with hot chocolate.

"Did you have a good time on Washington Island? Get lots of lavender?"

"It was fantastic. I have a bounty of dried lavender. And the bonus...I didn't throw up on the ferry." She chuckled. "You must have had it rough yesterday, coming in last in the run."

"Ha, ha. I placed last to get alone time. Not complaining, but the crowds can be overwhelming. I'm glad you're back. For a second, I worried you would stay on the island." Gus couldn't seem to wipe off the dopey grin planted on his face. "How's it going with your cocoa mixture?"

"Moving along. This is my tenth batch." She set a copper pitcher and her mug on the picnic table. "With my last-minute touch of lavender, it's been a hit. Then again, the event turns into a win anywhere you show. Have to say, the island trip was relaxing."

"FYI, your Madly in Love candles sold out at the lighthouse. Maddie turned the sad-looking souvenir shop into what she called the *Lavender Lounge.*"

"So sweet of Maddie. And today, Sinjin and Claire are hovering around my pit of despair. I was able to film their love testimony earlier at the Harbor. They'll be handing out soap samples in exchange for emails. Good thing tomorrow's the last day of the festival."

"Ah, yes. My favorite day." He winced and rubbed his stomach protectively. "The chili cook-off."

"I'll make sure to brew cardamom tea for you later. It'll ease your gut and help with the mix of chili beans you'll be tasting."

She pulled her lower lip between her teeth, and Gus's blood pumped faster. He wanted to kiss her—a delicious hot chocolate kiss.

He couldn't concentrate. All he thought about was slipping into a private and warm place to make out with Lucy. He'd missed her fiercely.

A freezing blast of wind slapped his face. A sign from Frosty?

Gus leaned close, tangled his fingers in her hair, and kissed her. Her lips tasted of lavender.

She swirled her tongue around his and nipped his lower lip. Her warmth smoothed his cold edges.

"I missed you," he said, mourning the break from her lips. "Are you ready to slide around on the ice in a cold bed?"

"I can handle it." Lucy poked her gloved finger into his chest. "I made it on the ferry, not once queasy. I'm in it to win it."

A horn blared, and people began gathering under an inflated red arch with the snowflake-shaped Winterfest logo.

"Our bed is beautiful." She grabbed the pitcher of hot cocoa and mugs. "Have to get these back to the bar. Should I meet you over there in two?" She pointed to the starting area for the race.

Gus crossed his legs and made sure his jacket covered the bulge forming under his jeans. "Make it ten."

* * *

On the iced edge of Kangaroo Lake, Lucy kicked the tips of her boots to keep the circulation going down to her toes. A few yards off, the sleigh beds congregated around the designated starting point, a swaying inflatable arch. It flapped in the breeze and reminded her of a bizarre used car dealership.

The sight of the Wicks sleigh bed dazzled her. The wrought iron frame, painted gold, shimmered in the sunlight. Attached to the headboard were gold window boxes with tall, waving branches of purple-topped lavender sprouting out. A purple sheet spattered with gold embossed fleur-de-lis cut-outs covered the mattress. On the side, purple chiffon was draped and flowing off the edge of the bed. Gold letters were strung over the chiffon, spelling out Wicks & Balms.

Around her magnificent sleigh bed, Gus posed with Alexandra as Sara snapped pictures with a long-lens camera.

Lucy groaned.

"These pics will be perfect for *Variety*," Sara yelled, slipping and sliding on the ice. "Gus, you're doing it again. Relax and smile. Your ginger beard looks incredible against the purple scarf. Skip the vacant stare. And Alex, tilt your gold beret."

Sara dogged them with demands for over fifteen minutes—as if she were Annie Leibovitz.

Clutching onto the end of the bed, Gus sucked in his cheeks, puckered his lips, and glared at *Annie's* telephoto lens. From a short distance, Lucy witnessed his painful expression. He looked miserable. Nothing about these pictures would highlight Gus and Alexandra's Emmy-worthy scene in *Raven House*.

Lucy stepped onto the ice and made her way to the bed. Even with her ice fishing cleats, it was treacherous. The bed looked even grander up close. The fake white candles had been painted purple and twinkled in gold lanterns.

"Hey," Lucy said, "I'd love to take a few pics with Gus for my shop."

"Sounds good." Gus rotated his shoulders and stretched his neck. "The shots will do double duty and work for our social media."

"This isn't about your shop," Sara said, grimacing. "It's in ruins and closed."

All because of you.

Lucy forced out a laugh. "Thanks for noticing."

Shaking his head, Gus turned and gruffly whispered, "One effing day left."

"Twenty-four hours of hell." Lucy inhaled his not-so-subtle scent of Lust while tugging her phone from her ski jacket. "Can I get a selfie with you? *Nick*?"

"How can I resist my number one superfan?" He dropped his arm over her shoulders.

"Cheese." She tapped the phone to take a burst of shots of the two of them mugging for the camera: smiling, sticking out their tongues, and frowning.

"Angus, this isn't good for your character," Sara said indignantly. "Or—"

"It's Gus. Call me Gus," he cut her off. "Going forward, the one person who can call me Angus is my father. Focus. We have a lot to do in Baileys, and Wicks is in dire condition."

Lucy half expected and half wanted Gus to go after the truth and call Sara out. He didn't. It wasn't the right time, but dang, how she wanted this woman to pay.

"This is about your career. We have to finish this season with a big bang. Think about your nomination." Sara's usual red glossy lips had turned dark blue as she pouted.

Ignoring the publicist from Hades, Lucy glanced at her pics and liked how her red jacket looked with Gus's deep purple scarf. The shots with them smiling were genuine. "All right if I post and tag you? With #W&B and #MadlyinLove?"

Gus licked his lips, a hint too slowly. "Be my guest."

She was dressed in layers of winter gear and still shivered from his look.

Alexandra pulled out her phone. "Pic of the three of us?"

"Of course," Lucy said.

The three of them laughed for the pictures.

"Send it, bitches," Alexandra said, then slid away on the ice. "Ciao. I'm going inside and getting a hot cocktail."

Lucy wanted to follow Alexandra instead of being with a maniacal woman in the freezing cold. "Have a hot toddy for me."

"This is revolting, Angus." Sara dismantled her camera and shoved it into the bag. "Your reputation is on the line. It was bad enough when you went AWOL on me. Skipped town and ended up in Lake Bluff with...her." Sara pointed her chin toward Lucy and scowled.

Gus's PR expert looked diabolical yet pathetic. Her forehead was set in wrinkles, and her lipstick had smudged onto her teeth. Lucy wasn't sure what to think about this entire situation.

"Dial it back. I told you it was a necessary family trip."

A series of long beeps sounded from Sara's bag. She retrieved her phone and shoved it into their faces.

"Another picture of you and her," Sara sneered. "As if it wasn't hard enough to find you pictured at a courthouse. It took me the entire day to explain to your fans that you weren't in any legal trouble."

"WTF. We're done with this. You don't have to worry about my fans." Gus's eyes glittered arsenic green. "Fucking 'ell. You are stalking me."

"No, I'm not. I mean, I wasn't." Sara tossed her camera bag over her shoulder. "It's my job to know where you are at all times."

Lucy sucked in arctic air to slow her rapidly aching stomach. Déjà vu was playing out in front of her. An intense and toxic one-way relationship like the one between her mom and dad. He'd run away from Julie and...*Lulu*. She rubbed her stomach to quell the panic. Relationships of any kind were so problematic. Why did she believe she could connect people and enhance happiness? Or solve their broken hearts? Toxic mismatches were a dime a dozen. Being alone seemed simpler.

More bed frames lined up for the start of the race, and participants skated around, clinging onto kitchen brooms. A voice boomed from a loudspeaker. "T-minus two minutes and counting!"

"Sara," Gus ordered, "please, take off."

"Screw that," she yelled. "If you think for one second I'm going to disappear so you can shag this trailer trash with a mother living in a cell block, you have another thing coming. I'll meet you at the finish line for pics. In two weeks, this location shoot will be over, and we'll be back in Malibu together."

A haze came over Lucy, and she broke out into a cold sweat. The venom Sara spewed stung. She tried to contain and organize her emotions, but her heart would not allow her brain to take over. Lucy was at a loss.

"Contestants," the loudspeaker blared, "get ready. One minute."

Sara, slipping on the ice, made her way to another bed. Lucy had never hated anyone in her life until now. This person had destroyed her livelihood and, without a second thought, attacked her family.

"Are you okay?" Gus held on to her hand.

"No."

"Can you do this race? We can talk tonight. If you want to skip it, we can. Sara doesn't know what she's talking about. Don't let her slurs get to you."

"I have to race for the sake of my shop. Destroyed by Sara. How the hell did she know about my mom?" She grabbed hold of the bed frame to stay steady. "I'm furious and confused."

"Ten, nine..." the crowd started chanting along with the countdown to start the race.

"It's in public records. Or she talked to someone. I don't know." He wrapped his arms around her. "I'm sorry."

"Of course." Public knowledge about Julie's trauma and suffering. Her stomach tightened as she considered how her private and painful relationship with her mom was going to be dissected on social media. The tabloids and *TMZ* would have a field day with the crazy love nudger with love potions and her drunk mother. Gus, in the center of the media circus, would come across as the hero who saved the day for the "trailer trash." What an amazing public relations feat. This had to be Gus's endgame and why he'd paid for the addict's treatment.

"Eight, seven..." Gus's fans shouted.

She collapsed on the bed. A flood of emotions raced through her. Such a dang fool! One second, she wanted to hit something; a second later, she wanted to cry, and then finally, she was trying to bite back every curse word she longed to hurl at Gus.

"Six, five..."

Gus seemed unfazed by the toxic conversation. Was this another trick of his trade? Like thinking about dead puppies? The one he'd used to drum up tears?

"We might have a chance to win this thing." Gus put on his balaclava. "Get your broom ready."

"Four, three..."

Lucy knelt on the layers of purple bedding. With one hand, she gripped the bed frame, and with the other, she jabbed the sharpened handle of the broom into the ice. Repeatedly.

Gus whistled.

"Two, one!"

Finally. Lucy couldn't wait for the race to start...to beat up the ice and purge her anger.

The flare exploded and lit up the icy-blue sky. Gus thrust the bed, and it jolted ahead. Lucy concentrated on the ice below. She frantically jabbed the end of the broom into the slippery surface to propel the bed forward and purge the venomous thoughts spreading in her brain.

Trailer trash. Chip. *Jail.* Crack. *Malibu.* Smash.

As they approached the kilted curlers, the brawny men swept the ice like mad Scots.

She kept her sight on the finish line.

When Michael's voice rose above the din of the cheering fans, she looked to either side and realized they were in the lead. No other beds were nearby. She wiped the sweat from her brow, and her arms ached. Yet she hadn't expelled the anger and frustration. There was still too much bottled up within her.

"You rock," Gus yelled as he circled the bed around the second and last bend in the figure eight.

She dropped the broom and crashed down on the bed when they crossed the finish line. "Oh. My. God."

"We're the winners," Gus shouted with way too much enthusiasm. "You were brilliant."

Her lungs, still full of cold air, burned. She clutched her stomach to keep from getting sick, and her teeth wouldn't stop chattering. Winning the race was the last thing on her mind.

Her heart pounded so hard it hurt. She was exposed and realized Gus had betrayed her.

In one month, he'd be gone. Her shop would still be an empty shell. It was as if her bright and shiny new life in Baileys had burned out before it barely began.

She hobbled off the ice on unsteady legs and waved goodbye. Gus didn't see her. He was surrounded by a crowd of fans. Which was fine. There were too many thoughts and emotions stirring inside of her. She needed to retreat and sort them out one at a time.

Domain, Kingdom, Phylum, Class, Order, Family, Genus, Species.

Chapter 34

Lucy was stopped by dozens of people congratulating her on the stupid bed race before she could get into her truck. Her acting skills became proficient, and the short drive from the Coyote Roadhouse was excruciating.

The chills had set deep into her bones by the time she got home. She threw her backpack on the floor and toed off her boots. Shivering, she tossed a couple of logs in the fireplace and arranged them with a poker. When the flame blazed, she inhaled the best smell of all time, toasted campfire. She crashed on the sofa and let the heat sink into her body. Her mind kept spinning.

Sara was a bad person, and she was obsessed with Gus, which was bad, but worse, Gus had used Lucy's traumatic relationship with her mom as social media fodder.

She made a pot of chamomile tea for herself in an attempt to calm down.

The time ticked close to ten, yet Gus hadn't returned home. She kept looking out at the darkened guest cabin; the lack of light gave off a foreboding feeling. They needed to talk this out. At least she wanted to talk. Did Gus? Did he care? After all, he would return to LA and leave Baileys in a few weeks.

She checked her phone for messages, and nothing. Heading back into the kitchen, she tried to concentrate on brewing a blend of cardamom, honey, and ginger tea for Gus to drink after tomorrow's chili competition. Sniffing the first pot, she groaned. Too much honey. Setting the pot aside, Lucy brewed another batch. This time she added more ground cardamom and let it steep longer, but it was too strong. The third and fourth pots were too weak, so she found some cinnamon sticks on the Reid's ancient spice rack and added them. She grew anxious, removed the tea bags and gave up. All the open jars of spices were taunting her and her nose was getting stuffed up. Tears and emotions weren't conducive to tea making. She left the pots of tea on the counter and was grateful Rosamunde Reid had owned an assortment of Indian spices and many British teapots.

When her phone buzzed, she retrieved it.

Finally, a message from Gus.

Rob just came into town. Need to talk. I'll be home soon.

Her heart sank.

She understood Gus still needed to connect with Rob, but her tired thoughts started to ramble. With the poker, she stabbed at a log in the fireplace.

As embers floated out, she kept jabbing at the logs to keep her mood from spiraling downward. She gripped the poker so tight her palm began to sweat. Then, the awful feeling of anxiousness shortened her breath.

Everything about Angus Reid had to be about his image. The man manipulated two sides of himself—on-screen and off-screen—with scientific precision. Getting little recognition while in Baileys must have diminished his popularity with his female fans, and he tipped the scale back in his favor by using the Maxwell women.

With her hand still locked onto the poker, she went to the kitchen table to retrieve her phone, read Gus's text again, and checked his Instagram account. The new posts from the Fest could easily include her or, worse, her and her mom. Then, she started scrolling through tweets from the *Raven House* account. Lucy scanned the FB fan group for the show and checked for any reels from this afternoon's sleigh bed race.

What is wrong with me?

When one of the fiery embers stung her hand, she stuck the poker back into the stand next to the hearth.

Get a grip, girlfriend.

She plugged in her phone facedown on the counter and went upstairs for a bath. A soak in a tub full of her latest version of Serenity might give her clarity. *Focus on work.* She needed to stay out of the black hole of misery that threatened to swallow her up. Dang, she was a matchmaker, so there was no way she could ever admit to being lovelorn.

Except her mind kept racing, and questions popped in and out of her head. When and why did Gus seep into her psyche? Was it when they were ice fishing? And where was ground zero for this relationship?

The trial.

When Gus showed up in the courtroom, that was it...the tipping point. Lucy scrubbed her feet with a pumice stone. She wished Gus hadn't been so rock steady for her during the trial. Then celebrating and calling her his hero. Dang. Why did Gus have to go all Dave Grohl on her?

She shuddered, thinking about the *wanting*. Lucy wanted Gus more than Gus wanted her. It was a gluttonous feeling of emptiness.

Her mother had waited every day for her father to come home like a desperate housewife in a repeat episode of a soap opera. The longing in their house had been palpable. Julie never whined for her husband, but she'd had a husband, and then he was gone.

No wonder she had become an empty vessel constantly needing to be filled up. Her father had squeezed the life and love out of her. They weren't partners; they weren't even friends. He was a bloodsucking thief who robbed Julie of her spirit and forgot about Lulu.

She kicked her feet on the bottom of the tub so forcefully water splashed over the side. Like Emma Woodhouse, she wanted others to get together, but not her—Lucy Maxwell. This feeling of *emptiness* made it way too risky. *Simpler to be alone.*

Too long in the bath left her with pruned fingers and pruned toes. She searched the bedroom for a sweatshirt and found Gus's Tupac hoodie. Dressed in panties and a bra, she wrapped the empty arms of the sweatshirt around her neck. She inhaled every bit of Gus's scent of Lust.

Catching a glimpse of her image in the mirror, she didn't recognize herself. Her eyes were wild, and her hair an unruly mess of squirrel nests. The cherry and bergamot were as addictive as crack. As was Gus.

Lucy tossed the sweatshirt on the floor, got dressed, and ran back downstairs for her phone. A wicked sensation brewed deep down, and it terrified her. Gus was an actor who needed daily exaltation, and she had no intention of giving it to him.

It was for her own sanity to stay away from him, and she needed closure. After unfollowing him on every one of his social media links, she shoved her phone in her backpack and headed out the door. She needed to go to the shop and find a way to purge Gus from her soul, salvage her own image, and regain her strength to thrive in Baileys. She did not want to run away again or start over. Once was enough.

Chapter 35

Later that day and after his last race, this one on a snowmobile, Gus didn't have a chance to find or talk to Lucy. At the finish line, he was greeted and congratulated by Michael, Sinjin, and...Rob. The three men proceeded to kidnap him and drive him to Wicks. Even though he was frustrated, having lost track of Lucy, he wanted to kiss them all—even Rob—for not contacting her first.

"Sinjin," Michael asked, "are you positive a person was inside here this afternoon? For Lucy's sake, I planned to keep the doors locked tight because too many people were milling around during the festival."

Sinjin stamped his feet and blew on his hands in the quiet of the cold shop. "I'm freezing from standing outside that front door. The street quieted down when the sleigh bed race started at the Coyote." Sinjin pointed toward Lucy's office. "In there was a beam of light. It came from the back of the building, and I caught it in the corner of my eye."

"Are you sure it wasn't a glint coming from the end of your chainsaw?" Rob asked.

Gus eyed the barren shop and tried like hell to shake off the feeling of doom surrounding him. All the stock, shelves, and furniture had been removed. There were no smoke smears on the walls. Instead, the drywall had been removed in jagged chunks for the electricians to replace Lucy's wiring. The stench of bleach hung in the air.

Gus crossed his arms over his chest. "Sara did this, and I want to find out who helped her."

When Rob aimed a flashlight at the open wall closest to him and began inspecting the exposed wires, Gus recognized that he'd been given a second chance. His younger brother had shown up, which meant another opportunity to make amends.

"Does Sara have keys to the shop?" Michael asked, aiming his flashlight toward the lock on the front door. "We never switched any of the locks, and it's the same key for the front and back. It's me, you, and Lucy who have keys to get in and out."

"Sara probably had keys made at Stan's," Gus said. "I wouldn't be surprised if she'd nicked mine while we were filming."

"Yeah, but," Sinjin said, "wasn't Sara with you this afternoon at the sleigh bed race? I know someone was in the back room around then."

"At the Coyote." *Belittling Lucy.* Gus stared into a cutout in the plaster wall. "Un-fucking-fortunately."

"Let's take another look in the utility closet. The wiring looked normal initially. Nothing was amiss, but now that the plaster's been removed," Michael said, "the cameras and equipment may have blown the surge protectors with excessive amounts of voltage. You never know."

"Shouldn't we get Lucy here?" Sinjin asked.

"No, not yet," Gus shouted. "She just got back from a trip to Washington Island, and her online sales are moving along...and..." He kicked and stomped to get the snow off his boots. "This is such a clusterfuck."

Michael slapped him on the back. "Don't blame yourself."

Sinjin gave Michael a cheeky grin.

"What?" Gus growled. "Is this your way of being supportive and big-brotherly?"

Sinjin wrestled him into a headlock. "Bro, you are whipped. Lucy's got you wrapped around every one of her dainty little fingers. You have officially been *Emma-ed*!"

Michael bellowed out a laugh. "Wise words, Sinjin. You speak the truth."

Rob grunted and continued assessing the insides of the open walls.

Gus wanted to wrestle the three of them down to the ground, but instead, he managed a disapproving head shake. The truth of the matter sank into his dimly lit brain. "As much as I want to consider your poppycock theory, I don't stand a chance with Lucy since my jealous publicist destroyed her livelihood and is getting away with it. I have to prove Sara did it and make sure she pays for every bit of catastrophic damage."

"And for insurance," Michael added.

"Well, we need to find proof," Rob stated in his typical lawyerly fashion. He shined his flashlight on Gus's face. "For sure, this wasn't a one-woman job."

"Told you so!" Sinjin jogged toward the office. "Come on. I know the light came from the back, I bet from the accomplice. Rob and Michael, go check out the electric panel."

Once lined with ornate shelving units and wicker baskets, Lucy's office felt desolate. Gus's chest caved. The room looked miserable. The desk was gone, and a dozen or so shoeboxes sat on the floor in the corner as if they'd been punished.

"Whoever did this sent a loud message," Michael observed. "Sara's the one who's shouting at you right now, Gus."

"Oh, I hear her. Loud and clear." Gus sent Lucy another text.

Still with Rob at Beacon. See you soon.

A pang of guilt stabbed Gus.

Lying to Lucy was evil. In this case, it was a necessary evil, but still atrocious. He urgently needed to keep Lucy away from this situation. He wanted to protect her. If his ex-publicist could do this to the shop, who knew what else she could do to Lucy.

Gus stopped his train of thought before it crashed over the bridge of sanity.

"This is interesting," Michael said, dangling a string with a nob hanging off it. "It's a timer."

"Explain please." Sinjin stared at the timer.

"For the sprinklers," Rob said. "I've seen this in a case in Chicago. It's a typical device used to set off sprinklers. Normally, these things go off when the temperature around the sprinkler is hot enough. Not sure what happened here, as there wasn't much of a fire to create heat. There was smoke detected, but—"

Michael interrupted, "If the alarm is tampered with, anything will set off the sprinklers. And a timer can be set so they'll go off without any reason."

"Why wasn't this caught right off the bat?" Gus asked.

"Hidden behind a piece of broken plaster and not a reason to suspect anything," Michael said. "It did what it was supposed to do. In this old building, even if the heat element isn't hot enough, the system reacts. It's glitchy, but better a hair earlier and continuing longer than necessary to save the place. We can safely surmise that whoever came in here today was nervous. They returned to check and make sure it stayed hidden."

"Is it enough proof, Rob?" Gus asked.

Rob shook his head. "No, whoever did it probably wore gloves, so no prints. This person, though, knew the wiring was older and about the ins and outs of a standard electrical panel. They relied on how little it would take to make the wires spark and smoke. It's like when a pizza burns in the oven. The alarm goes off, but no sprinkler. This thing was regulated to set off the waterworks for an uncooked crust."

"Could be anyone on the crew," Gus added, then smiled at Rob. "Thanks. For coming...and volunteering your expertise."

Rob nodded.

It was now or never. Gus had to make amends the proper way. Although the timing couldn't be worse, with Michael and Sinjin as his audience, he was confident enough and capable of being—not playing—an authentic role model. He shoved his hands in his pockets. "At the courthouse, I didn't mean to put you on the spot."

"Sure." Rob sounded dubious.

Michael and Sinjin started to leave the utility closet.

"Please stay," Rob commanded. "I'm not sure I want to be alone with Gus."

Gus ignored the jab. "I deserve that. I'm here to admit how despicable I was toward you, Rob. Give me a second chance. Let's rebuild our relationship on your terms."

His younger brother appeared to give his offer some thought, but as a lawyer, Rob was terrific at modulating his facial expressions. Gus wasn't the only actor in the family.

"It's been a long time. How about we go ice fishing?"

Rob glanced down at his smartwatch.

"The equipment is ready and waiting at the house on Kangaroo Lake." Gus had more to say and stayed steady. He could wait for Rob as long as needed. It had taken over a decade to rip apart their bond, so what was another ten years to glue it back together?

"I have to get going." Rob offered. "Ice fishing? I'll consider it. Sure you want to be out on the ice and water with me, bro?"

Rob lifted his muscular arms, showing off his award-winning wrestling physique. The guy's arms could crush anything venturing too close to them. Gus combed through his hair, appreciating the solidity of his head.

"One hundred percent sure," Gus responded, keeping his childlike joy contained. "I'm in town for the month, so whenever your schedule allows, I'll be at your beck and call."

Michael shoved the timer and wires in a bag and then into his pocket. "I'll get another special investigator from out of town to come here tomorrow. I'll show him around the shop. I'm sorry I didn't do it earlier, but we don't get many crimes like this on the peninsula."

"Usually, Baileys Harbor is a quiet, safe, and trusting town," Gus mocked. "Will the inspector work on Sunday?"

"He'll work when I need him to work," Michael declared. "Besides, tomorrow is the chili cook-off."

"Don't remind me." Gus checked his phone, and there was no response from Lucy. "If you guys don't mind, can we head out?"

Rob zipped up his parka and gave Sinjin a fist bump. "I'm staying at the Harbor B&B."

"Ditto." Sinjin wiggled his finger and smacked Rob's forehead —an ancient symbol from their bro code called a *whammy*.

Gus remained hopeful he'd someday be able to give both his brothers a whammy.

"You guys head out. I'll lock up." Gus let them out the front door. His amends to Rob weren't going to be easy, but he'd made progress. A little progress each day had strengthened Gus and gotten him this far. Why did life seem so easy in Baileys?

He jogged toward the back door, and it opened, framing Lucy.

She stepped back. Had she seen a ghost?

"Hey...hi. Hon. What are you doing here?"

Chapter 36

"It's my shop." Lucy's mind and heart bickered, fear and frustration duking it out inside her. "What are *you* doing here?"

"It's a long story. Let me explain it to you when we get home," he said. "You look wiped out. Can I brew you some tea?"

"No. Thank you, I've had enough tea for one day. I have to figure something out, and this is where I need to think." She went into her office and stared at its minimal remains. Her shoulders slumped. "This isn't worth it."

"Don't go there," he said, trying to hug her.

Lucy pushed him away and wiped her nose with the back of her hand. "Did you know this is because of stupid hotel soaps?"

"No, it's Sara's fault," he protested in a gruff whisper.

"Don't even say her name." She shot him a narrow-eyed look before turning back to the boxes in the corner. "There they are. Of course they don't get destroyed. Like a nightmare. Ghosts who stick around to haunt my life."

After dragging the shoeboxes into the middle of the room, she sat next to them on the floor and crossed her legs. She tossed off the lid from the top box.

"Not one is damaged," she muttered.

"Little paper bars? Oh, soaps. Bars of soap. The old kind from hotels and motels," he said, sitting on the floor across from her. "They're in perfect shape."

"Dang it to hell," she said. "So how am I going to destroy them?"

"Why?" He picked one up and sniffed it. "This still smells flowery. And they're how old?"

She glared at him. "Why do you care?"

"Because they're important to you."

"They *were* important. Past tense." She tossed one of the bars at him. "This one's from the Excel Inn in Madison."

He caught the soap. "This wrapping's crepe paper. What a really old motel."

"Yes, and it's where my dad spent most of his time after ditching me and my mom." She pitched another bar toward him. "This one's from the Hilton."

Lucy was shattered, and the more she tried to get a grip on her emotions, the faster they spun around and out of control.

Gus grabbed the box lid. "Babe, let's put these tiny soaps away and go home."

"These soaps are not *tiny*. They are what my mother had to hold on to as she waited for my dad to come home. Julie wasn't in love with my dad—she was obsessed. After he left, she'd spend hours sorting and resorting these stupid little things."

Lucy clutched onto a soap and flung it at him. It hit his shoulder and fell to the floor. Before he could retrieve it, she'd thrown another one at him. It struck his chest and landed on the lid sitting on his lap. Nailing him with the soap was immensely satisfying.

"Please, let's go," he implored. "This is crazy."

"Don't call me crazy. That's my mother's claim to fame." She scooped up a handful of soaps and lobbed all of them at him. "Oh, wait, do you want to take a video of me falling apart? I bet the number of your devoted fans will increase. Or do you need to haul the *trash* from Green Bay?"

He stood before the bars hit him, and they scattered across the wood floor. Gus softly tapped the box away from her with his foot. "I don't understand...and I didn't call *you* crazy. You are Lucy, and Julie is your mother. She is currently getting help and not 'trash.' If throwing bars of soap at me helps, go for it. But fair warning, it won't change anything in the past."

"Maybe not," she whispered. "Or maybe *I* do need help like my mother."

"You are two different people. Individuals."

She dug out more soaps and threw them at him, one at a time.

"Aim the smelly bars at me." The grave concern in his voice was thick. "Take your time."

Each one she pitched hit his jacket and fell to the ground.

"If you need to exorcise your demons by flinging bars of soap at me, do it." He opened his arms as an invitation. "Get them out so we can talk later."

When she'd emptied the box of the soaps, Lucy collapsed to the floor and started sobbing.

Gus lifted her up and held her tight.

"This is your fault," she gurgled, "for being so...so...you. How could you use me? And my mother? We're not a pity project for you to get more fame and glory. We're trying to survive."

"I'm here for you, Lucy. And your mum. Blame me if you want, but—" Each of his words was riddled with emotion. "I'm genuinely sorry for this afternoon's tragedy, and I would never abuse your privacy or take advantage of your pain."

"I need time to find something," she said, sniffling. "Dignity or independence? Either way, I really want to go to Kat's."

When Gus nodded, Lucy saw the worry stretch across his forehead.

She stayed close against his chest as they left her destroyed shop.

Stumbling over one another, they walked down the deserted street. The ice sculptures, covered with a light dusting of snow, glittered under the streetlights. Under the awning of the Beacon's entrance, he combed through her hair with his fingers and kissed her forehead.

"See you tomorrow?" His voice was hoarse.

She had little to no energy left inside her body and soul. Nodding, she gave him the keys to her truck. "Good night, Gus."

Chapter 37

A wet tongue brushed Lucy's cheek as the stench of cumin invaded her nostrils. She lay on the sofa in Kat's living room with Lewis on the floor next to her. Scratching behind the dog's ear, Lucy sat up and eyeballed her roomie cooking in the kitchen.

"Watch the cumin," she warned. "When there's a high quantity, it can stay in the pores and starts smelling. The unmistakable scent of sweaty feet."

"Good morning, sunshine," Kat called, waving a wooden spoon at her from across the kitchen island. "It's almost six. I'm making three types of chili, so anytime you feel like getting your ass off the couch, your help will be most appreciated. Lewis is zero help. And no armchair chefs allowed."

Lucy groaned. "Can I have another hour to recover? After a night of emotional purging, I have a hangover."

"Wish I could help you, honey, but since you refused to tell me, I am in the dark and can't give you any of my sage wisdom."

"How come you're cooking here instead of downstairs at the restaurant?"

"I don't want anyone accusing me of having an unfair advantage. This is my Russian grandma's traditional chili recipe, handed down to me from the family." Kat tied on her apron. "It's called home cooking for a reason."

"Speaking of sage, add a dash of sage instead of the cumin. It gives beef an earthy flavor." She attempted combing through her hair, but her fingers were restrained by the knotted clumps. "How the hell did I end up feeling and looking so miserable?" she grumbled to herself.

"Next one up is the veggie chili." Kat stirred the pot and pushed it onto the stove's back burner. "Get up and help with the chopping. Can I trust you with a sharp knife?"

"Knives are fine." Lucy pushed off the comforter and stretched the kinks out of her neck. "It's tiny bars of soaps I'm not so confident about. Is Michael in the bedroom? I hope I haven't disturbed you two by barging in and sleeping over."

"And let the competition know my trade secrets? Hell, no. Michael is in his own kitchen cooking his...*mediocre* chili. I'm babysitting Lewis for him."

Seeing her phone on the coffee table, her heart sank at the messages from Gus. "About last night. I'm sorry I didn't explain. It's...it's..."

"All about Gus?" Kat tossed her a roll of paper toweling. "I'm out of tissues."

"Not going to cry anymore," she said, catching the roll. "I'm sure I'm cried out."

"Perhaps, but in case the onions set you off, I want you to be prepared." Kat set a red onion on the counter. "What's going on? Gus is whipped over you, according to Michael. And I agree. I've never seen a man so head over heels. Aren't you feeling the love?"

"Yes, and it terrifies me. He's going to leave, right? I mean, he lives in Hollywood...Los Angeles. Home to the beautiful people. Malibu Beach, where it's all about surfing. And then there's his obsessed publicist who outed my mother and me yesterday. Called us trailer trash. It's a perfect setup for one of Gus's social media performances. He's an *actor*. And..."

"He's a talented *professional* actor and your *friend* who wouldn't take advantage of you. Sara is a control freak who will be on the next plane to LA after the Fest. Baileys isn't her jam. And the 'beautiful people'? It's a bunch of hogwash. And the LA smog can't be good for anyone's skin."

Lucy folded the comforter and piled it with the pillows on the red velvet couch. "Totally bizarre—La-La Land. I love it and hate it."

"I'm not sure, but I would guess Gus feels the same way." Kat scraped chopped onion bits off the cutting board and into the pan on the stovetop. "Los Angeles isn't any threat to you, and Gus is a good guy. He may make a living in the limelight, but he's as down-to-earth as you and me."

The scent of onion drifted over to Lucy. She covered her mouth and nose with her hands to avoid a session of tears. They were a waste of time. "In my heart, I understand. What scares me is this...longing or yearning. Yesterday, my feelings and thoughts were free-falling out of the sky and on a wild and out-of-control ride. It scared me silly. Worse, it reminded me of my mother. She obsessed over my father, and look where she is now? In a halfway house, trying to free herself from Bacchus's demons."

Kat wiped her hands on her apron. "I know more about cooking from the heart than affairs of the heart. I do recall, though, that it was *you* who talked *me* into recognizing my feelings for Michael. They were stuffed down deeper than a Thanksgiving turkey. Once they came out, it was great, and it terrified me. It occurred to me Michael might not feel the same way or *any* way about me."

"I threw my childhood collection of hotel soaps at Gus."

"Soaps?" Kat tilted her head. "You attacked him with bars of soap?"

"It was horrible. I had an adult tantrum and used him like a punching bag."

"Were any of them Irish Spring?" Kat retrieved green peppers from the refrigerator. "If so, Gus must be the freshest-smelling target in the woods."

Despite Lucy locking her lips, a smile escaped. "If Gus hadn't thought I was nuts already, today he's sure to think I'm cuckoo."

"You know you've been so busy playing matchmaker and unbelievably successful at it. How about tending to your own heart. Could you give it a chance?"

"But it's so risky."

"Your feelings are scattered in the wind, and you're not sure if Gus wants to catch hold of them. It's terrifying. But if we don't take chances, then what? *Nothing ventured, nothing gained* isn't a cliché for nothing. And no one said love is easy."

"Yeah, but..."

In schoolmarm fashion, Kat pointed the spoon at her. "No. No, *yeah-butting.* You have to trust yourself. So, you really want Gus. You have probably been *wanting* him every day since you met him, and it all rushed out at once. An overload of emotion scared you. You didn't want to scare him."

"You are a wise woman," Lucy said, staring at the skull-and-crossbones design on her apron. "And a badass, too."

"Sage. I need to add it to the chili. Instead of cumin."

"My thoughts exactly." Lucy set the paper towel roll on the counter and squeezed Kat in a bear hug. "I'm so glad I moved here. You're such a fantastic friend. Hand me a knife and something green to cut into pieces."

"Don't you want to call Gus?"

"Not yet. I need time to process this all. Is it okay if I stay here for a bit?"

"No problem. What about the chili cook-off," Kat said. "Wanna skip it?"

"Yeah, it might be best if Gus mixes up his own drinks with ginger ale or cardamom tea."

"Oh, right, the man who can't solve the case of a good chili bean," Kat said, handing her a knife.

Lucy carefully set it down, plopped all the tomatoes into a colander, and gave them a good wash.

"And your scent?" Kat asked.

"What do you mean?"

"Which one of Ms. Emma's concoctions do you and Gus use to *heat* things up in the bedroom?"

Since their passionate hookup had been in a posh hotel after a delicious dinner, chocolate cake was the only scent popping into her mind. She lined the tomatoes on the cutting board and diced up the first one. "We were in Kohler, and my inventory was packed in the truck. I even forgot about the vial of Lust stashed in my purse."

"Ms. Emma doesn't need any of her own concoctions." Kat gathered the chopped tomato and stirred it into the pot of chili. "How funny!"

Her phone pinged with another text from Gus.

Please open Kat's door.

She dropped the knife. "Dang, he's here."

"Finally," Kat declared. "Gus got smart and decided to crash our party. I bet this is his grand gesture?"

"That idea is a little over-the-top, don't you think?" Her heart started racing, so she went to the sink and splashed water on her face. "I hope not. I'm a train wreck. Can I borrow your apron?"

"Hell, yes. This baby is tougher than Captain America's shield." Kat slipped the apron off and handed it to her. "You two can go into my bedroom. I promise I won't listen to a word. Have to get this chili done."

Lucy smoothed the apron down, patted the skull-and-cross-bones image, and opened the door. A lump caught in her throat. Gus's ginger beard looked scruffy against his colorless cheeks. She was sure no makeup existed to cover the dark gray shadows under his eyes. How could she come out looking better after acting like such an imbecile? How ludicrous.

Chapter 38

"Hey," Gus said, trying to keep it together. He only wanted to bury his face in Lucy's wild, unbraided hair. "You all right?"

"Yeah," she whispered. "I'm okay. Last night, I was a complete idiot. You didn't deserve to be pelted with soaps. I'm sorry."

"Don't apologize." Less than ten hours since he'd last seen her, and he'd never been so fucking raw. "Throwing the soaps...I needed it. Knocked a bit of sense into me."

He was lucky she had even bothered to throw the soaps at him. After the shop was in ruins and her livelihood destroyed, Gus was guilty. He'd been a dolt and almost missed her crisis. Up the entire night, sorting through his ravaged emotions, one thought became clear: if he fucked up again, he'd lose Lucy for sure.

Determined to get closer, he stepped inside the apartment and closed the door. "I'm sorry."

"Um, no offense," she said, covering her mouth and nose, "but you stink."

"I know." He modulated his voice to stifle his desperation, but panic started to set in. "I'm a bastard for not going home last night. And I lied. I wanted to figure out the details and get to the truth about how and who sabotaged your shop. I'm concerned, I'm fucking worried—"

"You lied? Wait, I'm not angry. You just smell bad, literally." She took hold of his hand and caressed it. "What have you eaten?"

Her genuine concern stirred him.

"Nothing. I've been so...I've been sticking to water." His stress level dropped down a notch as she gazed up at him. He planted his feet apart to be eye-to-eye with her and sniffed his Nick Parker tweed jacket. "And tea. There were several pots on the kitchen counter."

"Hiya, Gus." Kat waved a spoon in their direction. "No chili cheating. Go into the bedroom, you two. I need to finish this recipe."

"Hey." As if things couldn't get any worse, he was reminded that he still had to eat chili this afternoon. However, if Lucy agreed to his plan and became his plus-one for the day, he'd find this last event a lot more palatable. "Looking forward to trying your chili, Kat."

He let go of Lucy's hand and leaned over the back of the couch to scratch Lewis's head.

"I made you cardamom tea last night for your stomach," Lucy said, wrinkling her nose, "but you smell like cumin. Uh-oh, there were several jars of old spices labeled with a *C*. I think I mixed up cumin and cardamom. My bad. You have an earthy stench, babe. I'm imagining one of those creatures that comes out of the ground in *Lord of the Rings*."

"Which one?" he asked, feeling strangely better.

"I don't know. Seriously? You're a living example of how cumin turns to sweat."

"Don't feel bad, Gus. I, too, just learned about how cumin can take a turn for the worse," Kat said. "Have a shower. You'll find everything you need in the bathroom, and I have plenty of Lucy's fancy soaps."

In the bedroom, Gus smelled his jacket again. "Definitely Orcs."

Lucy lay on the bed in Kat's bedroom and closed her eyes.

Even if he smelled like a creature from Middle Earth, his mood was closer to Bilbo Baggins. He gave Lucy a mischievous grin. "Can I ask you..."

"No, I'm not getting in the shower with you," she said, lifting her eyebrow. "I want my man smelling human, so no Orcs allowed in my bed. Thank you very much."

"Not the shower. It's a bigger ask. But since you called me your man—"

"Colleague." Her cheeks turned bright pink. "My business friend. Whatever you want me to call you. Except no *LOTR* characters."

"I want to reassure you that neither you nor your mum have been mentioned or pictured on social media." He kicked off the spats and pulled off the tweed jacket. Being in the bedroom with Lucy made his heart pound. Even with Kat in the other room, he couldn't have cared less. They were together.

"Thank you, and I know you'd never stoop so low. My emotions were really taking me for a ride yesterday."

"I'm wondering about your plans for the day." He had to tamp down his excited-teen voice. "I mean, I'd love for you to be my co-star for the day. I'm stopping at different spots around the peninsula. A Door County photo op with yours truly, as *Nick Parker*. Then, we come back here for the chili contest."

"Isn't that Alexandra's job?" she asked suspiciously. "Or what's her name?"

His Hail Mary wasn't going exactly how he had pictured it in his head, but he plodded on. "I'm using a new publicity team who organized this event."

"If this is your grand gesture," she said, "it's falling flat."

"It's only because I'm not a romantic lead. I play a hard-boiled detective. In my role, the grand gesture is getting the culprit and solving the case." He started unbuttoning his shirt and untucked it.

"I didn't get any sleep last night," she said, rubbing her eyes. "What does this new publicity team of yours want me to do?"

"Alexandra, Kayla, and Maddie are on call. As soon as you say okay, they'll be here. You'll need to dress up in Hollywood fashion, hop in the limo, and have fun. You can do what you want and talk about Lust at each stop. There will be three or four stops."

"What's the catch?"

"The last stop will be here at the Beacon for the chili cook-off. The production team will be rolling, and I need your help. You sniffed out Sara and my cumin. Now I need you to root out her henchman because I'm positive she didn't act alone. I trust your nose, Lucy."

"That is the nicest compliment I've ever heard," she said.

Gus snapped his suspenders to solidify his Nick Parker character, then flexed his pecs. "Think about it while I shower."

"Get going. You'll be seeing a lot of fans today, and there's no way you'll want to get up close to them with that horrible Orc aroma."

"Right, thanks." He pulled his phone out of his pants pocket and tossed it on the bed. "Call Maddie or Alexandra or Kayla if you have questions. I promise you'll have a great time. The plan is to stop at shops or historical buildings in Sister Bay, Egg Harbor, Fish Creek, and Ephraim. Maddie cooked the whole thing up. She'll know."

"A road trip around Door County. This grand gesture thing is looking better," she said with a lovely smile.

Last night, after Lucy had bolted to Kat's place, he needed reinforcements. Calling Maddie had been a godsend. "Great."

When Lucy grabbed his phone, a sense of relief flooded him.

"What's your password?"

Gus sighed. "N-I-C-K."

"Okay, N, I, C, K," she said while tapping his phone. "I'm down with solving a good mystery with you."

Gus nearly stumbled into the bathroom, thrilled with Lucy's decision. He only had to stay focused and pay attention to make sure he never again missed any amazing part of Lucy Maxwell.

* * *

Maddie's hug nearly knocked Lucy over when she opened the door.

"This is fantastic." Maddie strode in and waved at Kat. "Happy chili day. A nice long line will be out in front of the Beacon later. Where's Gus?"

"In the shower," Lucy said, pinching her nose. "He had an accident with a pot of tea."

"Shit, is his costume ruined?" Alexandra asked, entering behind Maddie. "I brought dresses for you."

Kayla came in next, rolling her makeup case behind her. "Morning bitches. Better be coffee around."

Lucy's eyes nearly bugged out of her head as the three women swarmed around and looked her up and down.

"Ready to go all Gatsby?" Maddie asked.

"Whoa! Really?" Lucy's jaw dropped. "Okay, I'm officially awake."

"Putting on a fresh pot of java," Kat called, "and make yourselves at home. Anything you need, take it."

Lucy plopped on the couch next to Lewis and petted his thick coat. "Tell me the plan."

As the two other women entered the kitchen and hung around the island, Maddie explained, "Since your shop was trashed, we want to make it up to you. And want you to know we have your back in Baileys, your new hometown. *Raven House* and, of course, Gus wanted to help since..."

"Sara's an evil bitch," Alexandra called out. "She almost got me fired."

Lucy agreed with Alexandra and concentrated on unknotting the hair nests to keep her animosity from escaping. "What all did you bring over, Alexandra?"

"Dresses with a lot of beads, fringe, and chiffon. Strings of pearls. Or, if you want, you could do an Amelia Earhart look—a leather coat with matching knee-high riding boots."

"I probably have a pair of goggles in my makeup case," Kayla offered. "I know Gus has had to wear them in a scene or two."

Lucy was so grateful to the women around her she could hardly contain her elation. "I can't decide. I'm too nervous. I do know if I'm getting in and out of a limo, I want to be warm. The practicality of Amelia's leather coat is the best choice."

"Okay," Kayla said, unpacking her makeup and arranging it on the kitchen island. "First stop, come here and wash your face and hair in the kitchen sink. I need a clean palette."

She followed directions, wondering if Gus experienced this when he went to work—free from minute decisions and stifled by directions.

"Look out for the chili, my friend," Kat said.

Lucy laughed. "Of course."

As Kayla styled her hair and made up her face, Lucy listened to Maddie's plan and looked at Alexandra's selection of Prohibition-era costumes. The day would be fun, no doubt. Stopping into various establishments with Gus where he'd be signing autographs, and she could talk about Wicks & Balms and hand out swag.

She gasped when Alexandra held up a short, sleeveless cream dress with layers of chiffon, beaded fringe, and a beaded inset on the chest. It was perfect. "Love it, but it's cold out."

Kayla arched an eyebrow. "An addition of a leather jacket for when you're outside, and when you're inside the Escalade, you'll have Gus."

All the women broke out into devilish laughter.

As if on cue, Gus came out of the bedroom, handsome as ever with his ginger hair still damp. Lucy couldn't stop her mind from wandering. She slipped off the kitchen stool, went to him, and kissed a drop of water off his earlobe. "You look gorgeous. Now it's my turn."

"Go on. *Your man* will be waiting here," he said, sliding his hand over her butt and squeezing. "Get in the bedroom with your entourage."

The women gathered in Kat's bedroom. Lucy felt like royalty as her newly formed entourage coached her on how to act in front of the cameras. Alexandra stuck gaffer tape around her boobs to make sure they wouldn't move and nothing would fall out of the extremely low-cut dress. Then, she suggested to Lucy how to arrange her facial expressions so people wouldn't see her true feelings or thoughts.

"Am I really an open book?" Lucy slipped on a pair of gold heels.

"Yes," the three women chimed in together.

"And your toughest part will be disguising your feelings for Gus. It's written all over your face. Try not to give the tabloids any fodder, or you'll regret it. The paparazzi knows how to twist a good thing into bad juju," Kayla warned. "I know for a fact."

She was about to ask Kayla about her boo when Gus knocked on the door. "Limo's here. Ready?"

Lucy wasn't sure if she was ready, but thanks to her posse of new friends, she was prepared.

Kayla filled Lucy's backpack with makeup, wipes, and bandages.

In case anything ripped, Alexandra added in several unmentionables: bras, panties, and lace stockings.

"How..." Lucy asked.

"Trust me." Alexandra chuckled.

Maddie handed her yet another binder. The color of bright cherries. "This one stays in the limo."

When she returned to the living room, Lucy smelled Kat's delicious cooking. This time, Gus was the one who looked starstruck.

Alexandra gave him the leather coat to hold. "Take care of her, dude."

Nodding, Gus took hold of Lucy's palm. "Here, you may need it."

Lucy grasped the vial of Lust and slipped it into the pocket of her silky dress.

She hugged her fangirls goodbye and swallowed down tears. Holding tight to Gus's hand, they strolled down the stairs and outside the building. There was a red carpet at the entrance of the Beacon. Lucy wanted to gasp, then remembered her training. *Keep your mouth closed. And when in shock, smile with your lips closed.* And Lucy was in shock. The entire street had been taken over by the media. A camera or photographer was everywhere she looked. She smiled, keeping her mouth closed.

Gus waved. "Hey, all. We're taking a tour of Door County, so feel free to follow us. You'll get to know a great part of Wisconsin."

Johnny from *TMZ* ran up to her. "Lucy Maxwell, you look amazing. How do you feel?"

"Good," she said, squeezing Gus's hand. *Great.*

Chapter 39

In a twisted rock 'n' roll way, the final stop on the Lucy and Gus tour was inside a historic church located in Ephraim. She brushed an imaginary speck of dust from Gus's tweed jacket and whispered, "How are you?"

"Okay." He smiled mechanically as people filed past them. "I'm actually starting to look forward to the chili contest. I'm glad we're almost done."

She smiled at the people and nodded graciously. Truer words were never spoken. Lucy's feet had started aching the moment she'd put on the costume heels. They were gorgeous, probably Italian, and definitely not made for actual human feet.

It had crossed her mind to toss them out the window on the way to Ephraim. Instead, she decided to apply to her toes every bandage that her entourage had stuffed in her backpack.

"Hey, folks, we have to head back to Baileys," Gus announced. "Text the Beacon if you're interested in joining or donating to the chili cook-off. The proceeds will go to Feed America."

"On your postcard," Lucy added, "there's a code. Follow the link to get another teaser of season four's opener. And check out *Raven House* updates on Instagram."

"And if you enjoy the postcard scent, go to Wicks & Balms online. You'll love it." Gus then gave the crowd one of his dazzling Hollywood smiles.

After Peter escorted the last of the fans out of the historical Moravian Church, Gus pocketed the few remaining postcards Lucy had dabbed with Lust.

"It's a wrap," Peter said when the small chapel was empty. "You two together are better than Tony Stark and Pepper Potts."

"Fantastic, you're my Iron Man," Lucy replied, relishing the moment as she slipped off the sling-backed heels. "Would you mind giving me a lift to the limo, Gus? My dogs are barking."

"Sure." Gus helped her put on the butter-soft leather jacket. Lucy hoped she'd be able to buy the Amelia Earhart–style coat. She tucked loose hairs under the headband studded with pearls and beads. "Any chance I can take a quick nap in the limo?"

"Possibly." He licked his lips, took a sip from his water bottle, and shared it with her. "It's a half-hour drive."

While taking a sip, she couldn't drag her eyes off his luscious mouth.

Because of Gus, last night's nightmare had turned into a dream. Lucy wasn't planning on changing her career and turning into a wannabe Hollywood star; her feet couldn't take it. But seeing how hard Gus worked was inspiring. And he had worked harder for Lucy than his other fans today.

He catered to her at every stop and ensured she was a bigger star than him. Even when she was exhausted and all of last night's soap-throwing moments crowded in and shouted in her mind, he had taken the makeup, reapplied it to her teary eyes, and then given her his Ray-Bans.

"Trick of the trade," he'd simply said.

Not one iota of judgment or criticism. As foolish as she felt, Gus wouldn't let her free-fall into embarrassment.

"Absolutely thrilled to get to the Beacon," he said, lifting and cradling her. "It's chili time."

"Never thought I'd hear you say that." She wrapped her arms around him and nuzzled against his chest. Exhaling slowly, she made sure her warm breath tickled his neck.

It was quiet when he carried her outside the church. The paparazzi had left to get to the Beacon and the chili cook-off. A fresh coat of snow covered the ground, and the historic white church with its towering steeple was picture-perfect against the blue sky.

They slid into the Escalade. As warm air surrounded them, the tinted windows relaxed her with a sense of privacy. She placed the Hollywood heels into a soft cotton drawstring bag. "Sweet peace."

Gus took off his tweed jacket and knocked on the divider. "Take the slow route, Jimmy," he said as the privacy screen opened and then closed shut again. "Ta."

"It's wonderful not to be your driver," she said, propping her stockinged feet onto his lap. "Thanks."

"You never were a chauffeur. Discretion was impossible with your bright red truck, and there isn't a back seat." He stroked her leg. "How are you doing? Ready to go catch a thief?"

"Oh, yeah," she said, sitting up. "I know your publicist is responsible. I'm sure paying for the damages will make her reflect on her evil actions."

"Not sure she's capable of such high-level thinking. I'll hope for it."

Lucy took hold of his hand and traced an infinity loop on his palm. "Thanks for this incredible day."

He slid his other hand under the fringed hem of her dress. "It's not over yet. I know you wanted to take a quick nap, but I have a better way to give you a little break."

A rush of heat spread below her navel and tingled around her core.

"How are these stockings staying in place?" His voice was a raspy whisper.

Lounging back, she let one leg drop off the seat. He leaned over and kissed her thigh.

"Oh. I see. This lacy thong has to go." He dragged kisses across her thighs, making sure to linger in the middle.

"Mmm," she moaned softly when he pushed her dress above her hip.

As he dragged his tongue in and out of her and then kissed her folds, she combed the fingers of one ungloved hand through his hair. He moved his lips slow and fast to keep pace with the drive and the vibrations from the road.

The heat intensified, and she wanted to gasp or let out a moan, but she bit her lip. Grasping onto Gus's shoulders, Lucy writhed under his expert handling without one sound exiting her mouth.

When she was sure she was about to burn into pieces, he came up, pressed his chest into hers, and blew soft breaths against her neck. He slipped his fingers inside and stroked until she couldn't hold back, and a long, low growl escaped her lips. The pleasure released, and she collapsed against the car door, completely relaxed.

Gus kissed her cheek. "Better than a nap, hey?"

"Ah, yeah."

He handed her the kerchief from his breast pocket. "Love these handy old-time costume bits."

She dabbed the beads of sweat off her forehead and glanced out the window. "Dang, we're almost back in Baileys."

He arched his eyebrow. "Want another round?"

She shook her head. "No, it's your turn. Not fair. Besides, I want to be skin-to-skin. None of these crazy costumes between us. Way too many contraptions."

"There's a certain charm to the old ways." Gus laughed, held her hand, and started to peel off her remaining elbow-high satin gloves. He kissed her forearm each time he revealed more skin.

"Oh my," she moaned. "We aren't going to be able to get out of this car."

Gus's phone pinged. "To be continued," he said before answering the call.

After rearranging her costume, she touched up her makeup, found the extra pair of black lace thongs in her purse, and slipped them on. The other pair were no longer useful. She put the excruciating heels back on.

As the Escalade turned on Main Street, the entire street had been infested again with the paparazzi. "Now, I am one hundred percent certain I don't have any extra teeth in my mouth. Thanks."

"That was Maddie. They're ready for us." Gus held her hand. "Show off your smile all you want. It's perfect."

Lucy slid out of the truck, smiled, and faced the cameras. The questions and lights blurred, and they didn't bother her. Her feet, though, still ached. Gus hopped out of the truck and waved.

"Hold on." Gus kissed her cheek, lifted her up, and cradled her. "The encore."

The photographers whistled and shouted out compliments.

He carried her into the Beacon, where no one noticed their arrival. The chili contest was in full swing. When Gus set her down, she sighed. They were surrounded by good and real friends, so there was no need for a dramatic entrance.

* * *

Gus scanned the crowd at the chili cook-off with Lucy's hand tucked safely in his. There were tables along the restaurant's perimeter. Each one was covered with white linen and pots of chili.

"There's Kat." Lucy pointed one of her gloved fingers. "She's with Michael at the table by the kitchen entrance."

He shivered. Moments ago in the limo, he had pulled off the long silk glove and kissed the length of her arm.

"Look at those two lovebirds," she said. "You can thank me later. *Emma* strikes again."

People were lined up in front of Kat for her chili, and the line for Michael's dish was significantly shorter. He nodded toward the couple. "And me? Don't I get a little cred?"

"A smidge," she said, "but don't let it go to your head."

"This is going to be a challenge. I'm dreading it. Thankfully, I only have to taste six kinds of chili."

"I'll make you the good tea—with *cardamom*—tonight, Mr. Sidekick."

"Hey, you two." Johnny from *TMZ* punched his arm. "Thanks for letting me in the door."

"You have special honors," Gus said. "I wanted you to get the inside story for this season. You're the only one who knows about the Emmys, so you can be the first to roll with any red-carpet gossip. Now, though, can you interview the fans and the extras? Hopefully, you'll feature Baileys and this fundraiser."

"I'm down for it all," Johnny said, giving him a fist bump. "The only paparazzi invited in. This is sick. Can I start with a pic of you two?"

Gus adjusted his tweed jacket and put his newsboy cap on. Lucy patted down the layers of beads and pearls on her ornate dress.

"Ready?" Gus took hold of her gloved hand again. "Say cheese."

Johnny snapped pictures. "Thanks, guys. Should I post on Instagram?"

"Absolutely. Later, you can take more shots," Gus offered. "As many in the bowling alley as you want."

"Thanks, Johnny," she said as he jogged away. "Isn't that Sara's job? I'm confused."

"Not anymore. It's Johnny's." Gus looked around to find the crew. "She's done. Peter agreed and gave her the news this morning. Still, she's not off the hook. Whoever helped her is probably here today. Ready to be Nick Parker's assistant?"

"Sure. My nose is on it." She scrunched it up. "Detecting and sniffing out the crook. Who do you suspect?"

He brought out his notepad to look through his notes. He could barely read his late-night scrawls.

"It's probably the guy in the flannel shirt," Lucy said.

He glanced around the bowling alley. "That would be almost all of the men in here."

She threw her head back and laughed. "Not all. Stan and Bob are wearing their costumes: knickers with suspenders. Such a strange fashion combo."

Gus spotted Sara surrounded by a few of the crew members. They were seated at a corner table. He wanted this to be finished and done. History. He pulled his phone out and scrolled through the pictures he'd copied of his entire team. Although he recognized faces, names had evaded him.

One guy draped his arm over Sara's shoulders.

Gus took hold of Lucy's hand. "Let's take a *Gatsby* stroll over to their table."

"I'm ready when you are." She kissed his cheek.

A familiar warmth shot through him. He had to get this grand gesture out of the way. For Lucy as well as himself.

"Cheers, all. You mates having a good time?" He hauled out his classic British accent to throw the whole table off.

"Great." A man wearing a blue flannel shirt said. "I'm Kenny, the head electrician."

"Of course," Gus said, "I remember."

"Hi, guys. Hey, Sara," Lucy said, twisting one of her long pearl necklaces around her fingers. "Have you tried any of the chilis yet?"

"No." Sara sneered. "Did you two have fun on the magic tour bus?"

He tightened his grip on Lucy's hand.

"It was an adventure." Lucy widened her eyes. "I have a new appreciation for the publicity elements in La-La Land. It's dang rigorous."

"It's a lot of work," Sara said, giving Gus a strange look. He couldn't tell if she was about to attack or retreat so he squeezed Lucy's hand tighter.

An unfamiliar crew member came up to him with his hand extended. "Hi," said Gus. "Have we met?"

"Hey, just wanted to introduce myself. I'm Jack, the new key grip."

"Thanks, Jack-the-key-grip." Gus couldn't recall this guy's face from his research last night, but his flannel shirt looked the same as Kenny's.

"Second group for final scenes," Jack said. "Key grip on the new set crew."

Another dude said, "I'm Cody."

Gus waved. Was he an idiot to think he could scheme and find out who helped Sara? It would be easier if she confessed and ran back to Malibu. "Tell me. You boys stoked to start shooting the scenes here in the alleys?"

Kenny nodded. "This place is outstanding. We looked around the back. It's like an antique shop behind those pins. It still smells of leather. These scenes will be better than the..." He stopped short and stared at Lucy. "So sorry. About Wicks."

"It's okay," Lucy said, staring at Kenny. "It's not your fault."

Had Lucy's nose picked up a scent?

Sara twisted the cap off a bottle of Perrier and took a swig. "I'm ready to bowl if you guys are."

Gus wanted a script handed to him. It would give him the directions to solve the crime. So simple for Nick Parker and a pain in the ass for Gus Reid. *Think.*

He spotted four glasses on the table. He'd bet one of them belonged to her accomplice. Prohibition era be damned. DNA, baby.

"Have a great game," Gus said, nearly running toward Michael with Lucy in tow.

"Slow down," she complained. "Otherwise, I will need to ditch these dang shoes. Where are you going?"

"To the lovebirds. I need help from Michael. Did you get a *scent* about her adoring crew?"

"Not really. It's hard because her perfume is so strong it masks any other scent I may be able to sniff out. I couldn't even tell if any of those guys wore aftershave."

"Once we prove it, she'll have to pay for the damage at your shop." Scratching his jaw, he wasn't sure of his next step but knew with certainty that it was the last. "Lucy, I love being your hero."

Chapter 40

"Yo, Michael," Gus said, grabbing his elbow. "What's up with the other inspector and the timer?"

"Timer?" Lucy asked.

"It was left at the shop, and we found it last night. It's the reason I didn't make it back to you."

She responded by nodding calmly.

"Not yet," Michael said. "I'll call him."

Gus's mind raced. He wanted a confession before the end of the chili fest. After being patiently tutored by him in math years ago, Gus had learned Michael worked at his own dogged, determined pace. Hell, it took him a decade to realize he loved Kat.

Michael ended the call. "The timer won't be assessed until tonight. He's coming to the Beacon later."

"Any way to get DNA off it?" Gus asked. "I mean Sara and the crew. There are glasses on the table."

Michael let out a gut-busting laugh. "Do you remember you're an actor and not a detective?" He groaned, sucked in a deep breath, and started laughing until tears rolled down his face.

"I bet it's Jack. Aren't key grips always the bad boys?" Lucy showed off her dimple.

"Yeah, but Kenny," Gus replied, "he's an electrician. Tall, lanky, and *wiry*."

"DNA. As if." Michael snorted between loud bursts of laughter. "Haven't you ever watched *Dateline*?"

Keep it simple, stupid.

"Michael, do you know how much the timer is worth?" Gus asked while googling timers on his phone.

"It's high-tech, sophisticated, and worth a pretty penny."

"But it says on the web that they're only anywhere from two hundred bucks to five hundred bucks." Gus's frustration escalated. "Oh, poppycock."

Michael shook his head. "Hell, no. You're looking at house timers. The one in Lucy's shop was commercial grade. I'd say closer to a grand, if not more."

"A pretty expensive timer," Lucy added. "I'm sure it wasn't egg-shaped."

Money. Gus wasn't a detective, but he understood money. Wanting it, needing it, and living without it. The timer cost enough for its owner to want it back and was worth breaking into the destroyed shop.

"Can you get it from the inspector and bring it here?" Gus hated the desperation in his voice, but this business with Sara had to end. Full stop.

"I don't know, man. It's evidence, and—"

"Not yet. We don't even know if a crime has been committed." Gus clenched his teeth.

"All right, it's in my truck for the inspector," Michael said. "This chili contest has taken hold of my brain. I'll get it if you serve my chili for me."

"Go ahead. Your freaking chili will be fine."

"What are you planning?" Lucy asked after hugging Kat, who had to leave and deal with a kitchen crisis. "I want to help."

"Not sure yet." Gus stood behind the table and started ladling chili into bowls held out in front of him. He wanted to pinch his nose. The smell was ghastly.

The line in front of him grew. Gus knew the people weren't in line for chili. They only wanted to get a closer look at him. He smiled and looked appreciative, even though he wanted to gag at the smell of cumin. When the pot was nearly empty, Kat ran up and gave him another one. This chili smelled better. Kat and Lucy chuckled at his groan of relief.

"Here's the timer." Michael handed him a Ziploc storage bag.

"I think this needs to go back to its rightful owner." Gus had no idea where he was going with this scene.

"So, this is the bad guy." Lucy touched the bag. "Since one of those dicks left it in my shop, should I be the one to return it to him? Or her?"

Gus loved a lot about Lucy, especially the way she thought.

She opened the bag and sniffed.

Michael covered his mouth to muffle another one of his loud laughs. "Are you part German shepherd?"

Lucy jutted out her chin. "More of a badass beagle."

"Did you get a scent?" Gus asked eagerly. "This is it. All you have to do is sniff out the owner of the timer."

Lucy made a face. "I'm good, but not that good. How 'bout I hand it to Jack because he looks the most suspicious. Then we can see how it plays out."

Michael agreed, and Kat returned. "Hey, clue me in."

"Come on, let's go watch the fireworks. They're going to be set off in the bowling alley, and I want to get a front-row seat," Michael said.

A sense of finality ripped through Gus as he approached Sara. Had he been too complacent or fat-headed to comprehend what was going on with his publicist? For one second, he regretted not doing something different, but he couldn't figure out which actions he might have taken to change the situation. Sara wasn't operating in reality. She'd caused real-life shock waves with irrevocable damage. Especially for Lucy.

Lucy kissed his cheek and walked ahead of him with the bagged timer swinging in her satin-gloved hand. He'd never forget the sway of her hips and how the beaded fringe of her flapper dress swung back and forth against her gorgeous legs.

Kat and Michael sat at one of the antique score tables in the bowling alley as he followed her. She could go it alone, however, he wasn't about to let her do his dirty work for him.

"Hey, guys." He crossed his arms over his chest. Trying to look tough in a tweed jacket was a challenge. "How was the game?"

"This is a great bowling alley." Jack offered a high five. "Filming the last scenes in here will be kick-ass."

Gus obliged Jack with a hard hand slap.

"Listen, guys," Lucy said, holding out her gloved hand and swinging the bag. "Those of you who were part of the film crew working in Wicks & Balms, I know you were all professional. Despite the damage, I don't have any hard feelings. Oh, and I found this in the utility room the other day. Wondering if it belongs to any of you?"

Gus held his breath as Jack reached over and took the bag from Lucy.

Gotcha.

"Way too easy," Lucy murmured, turning to Gus with a thumbs-up.

"Hey, sorry. Isn't this yours?" Jack dropped the bag onto Kenny's lap, who sat snug against Sara. "Weren't you looking for it?"

As Kenny stared at the bag, Sara opened her mouth. No words exited.

"The lighting expert." Gus glared at him. "The timer's worth a few dollars, isn't it?"

"It doesn't belong to Kenny." Sara's voice cracked. "What the fuck is it anyway?"

Kenny untangled himself from Sara, stood, and thrust it at her. "I'm tired of your games. I won't be your boy toy anymore."

Sweat beaded on Sara's upper lip, glistening under the bright lights. She handed the timer to Gus. "I have no idea what this little scene is about."

"You. It's about the villain getting caught red-handed." Nick Parker stepped onstage. "Why did you destroy Lucy's shop?"

Sara jutted her chin toward Kenny. "Ask him. He's the electrician."

Gus shook the bag with the timer in front of Sara's face. The woman had no remorse, no regret, no conscience. "You're lying."

He sensed the cameras multiplying around them. Instinctually, he started to resort to his "Poppycock" trick to look calm on the outside, but that was Angus's ruse. He was Gus now and could be himself—angry.

Lucy sidled up, gently lowered his arm, and took hold of the timer.

"You will figure it out eventually, Sara," Lucy stated. "In the meantime, here is what's going to happen. You're going to go over to Michael and confess. And then he will arrest you."

Sara cackled. "A fireman. Sure."

"Yes, firemen can arrest criminals." Lucy handed the bag to Kenny. "And Kenny here will be telling Michael every sordid detail of how you ruined Wicks. And then, Michael will put handcuffs on you."

Gus waved at Michael to join them.

"You three don't scare me." Sara scowled.

"Okay, then." Gus clutched onto Lucy's hand. "We'll go find your brother and tell him everything." At the mention of Peter, he saw a hint of fear. "As the director and executive producer of the show, he knows the total cost of the reparations being made at Wicks, and he can take it out of your paycheck. Or he won't bother and just give you the boot."

"Haven't you gained enough attention, Sara?" Lucy

demanded, waving her gloved hand at the circle of people gathered to watch the fireworks. "Here's your chance to be the star. Does this make you feel good?"

Sara glanced at all the people surrounding her, and every one of them glared at her with pure hatred. Gus's longtime friends were standing up for him and Lucy.

"As soon as we came here, you didn't need me." Sara glowered at Lucy. "And it was pretty obvious using Lucy was the only way I could get you back."

"You need help," Gus said. Her face was a contorted expression of confusion and pain.

"Enough." Michael pulled a pair of handcuffs from his belt, dangled them in front of Sara, and slapped them on her wrists. "Time to take you to the police station."

"I despise you all," Sara said.

Michael escorted Sara and Kenny out of the Beacon and were met by Peter at the entrance.

Lucy hugged Gus. "Nice work, Detective Parker."

They collapsed into one another, completely relieved.

"Seems as if you've got a swell assistant," George said, slapping him on the back.

Gus whipped around to find his father grinning ear to ear. "Dad? What are you doing here?"

"It's a rare occasion when all my boys are in one place. I wanted to know how things are going." George turned and gave Lucy a brief hug. "I'm pleased as punch that all will be tickety-boo with your mum."

"Thanks for your solid support, George. I couldn't have started over or done this...alone." Lucy kissed Gus on the cheek and hurried over to Maddie where she was gathering the first round of chili votes.

He impulsively gave his dad another hug. "I'd expected you at the courthouse."

"I didn't go because I'd learned you showed up in Lake Bluff at Sinjin's and planned to be in court."

A wallowing sense of self-pity and disappointment threatened to pummel Gus into the ground. "Oh."

His father grabbed his hand and grasped it. "Son, no. I meant when I heard you were in court for Lucy, I knew I didn't have to be there because *you* came for her. Knowing she had you in her corner, I sussed out that something had changed. You showed up, sober as the judge, for Lucy. I might add, you're better-looking than me."

The stale air in the bowling alley dissipated, and the crowd in the Beacon had relocated to the bar in anticipation of the chili cook-off. Gus pulled his father toward him and wrapped him in a bear hug. He noticed his aftershave scent remained the same after so many years—Old Spice. Freed from his past resentments, Gus remembered.

"Hold on, I have something for you." Gus jogged behind the table where he'd doled out chili for Michael. The Crock-Pots were empty, and the white tablecloth was spotted with chili-colored remnants. From under the table, he retrieved his bag. After finding what he was looking for, he strode back to his father to make his amends.

"I followed your instructions." Gus handed him the blueprints-for-sex book. "I'm thinking about the endgame...daily. Since Mum passed away, my vision has been cloudy, and most, if not all, of my fucking booze-laden decisions were bad. Constantly, I turned the simplest of choices into a torrential storm and avoided accountability. Blaming those closest to me and playing the victim was an easy role for me to take on. I'm sorry for the pain I've caused you."

Clutching the book with both hands, George let out a long breath. "I suffered with frustration—unable to help you—not pain. Every day is a new chance though, and I never gave up hope. You're smart, a bit of an arse, and I love ya." He wiggled his middle finger and slapped Gus's forehead with a whammy. "Don't let this go to your big Hollywood head."

Rubbing his forehead, Gus shook his head. "It's good to be home, Dad."

"So will it be ice fishing or golfing?"

"Golfing in spring. I've committed my ice fishing time to others." Gus glanced at Lucy as she and Maddie, with a clipboard in hand, came up to them.

"I'm done tallying the first-round votes. Where did Peter go? And where the hell is Stan?" Maddie gave his dad a quick hug. "Hey, George."

"Peter's gone." Gus scanned the room, relieved that most everyone had lost interest in him. "But Stan is by the step-and-repeat with the other extras."

"Is Peter coming back? I'll need him to do the final judging pretty soon." Maddie's organized calm grew into panic.

"How about I take over for Peter?" Lucy took hold of his hand. "Would that be cool? I'll sit between the two gents." Lucy did a two-step Charleston dance move and swung her leg out. "It will be peachy to get out of these kickers."

"A good photo op." Maddie rearranged her clipboard. "Since the three of you are in costumes, sure, but don't play favorites."

His father patted his back. "Oy, you've been through a lot worse. This is nothing."

Gus briefly closed his eyes and took in short, deep breaths. There was no way out of it; it was time to face the inevitable and eat chili. They went to the bar, where Stan met him, and Lucy sat in the middle.

Maddie handed the three of them a clipboard listing the flavors of the six finalists. Gus read the ingredients and stuffed down a gag. "This is going to be tough."

"Don't be a wanker." Maddie grabbed hold of Kat's microphone. "Ladies and gents, the finalists have been determined. We won't divulge the chefs' names until after the top three winners are picked by our esteemed panel of judges: Stan Reeves, owner of Stan's Hardware; Lucy Maxwell, proprietor of Wicks & Balms; and our hometown hero, Angus Reid, the star of *Raven House*, and for many of us in Baileys, a trusted and true friend. Gus, as friends call him, possesses a rare quality: integrity."

The standing-room-only crowd gathered around the bar and dining area, applauding and letting out whoops and hollers. People patted his back and wished him well. Never had he imagined that he'd be eating chili while surrounded by good friends and longtime alliances. A sense of belonging embraced him.

Gus lifted his glass of water. "Thank you, Maddie. Your work in Baileys amazes me. Your kind words thrill me. And I reckon I can speak for the lot of us, when it's twenty below in town, thanks to you, we are always bundled up in warmth and love."

"Hear, hear, bro," Rob yelled, standing beside his father. "Good luck!"

"Glad you could make it." Gus tipped his glass toward his brother. Another amends would be made soon. "Truly, I am."

"Enough of this woo-woo chatter." Maddie rang a copper cowbell. "Let the games begin!"

With about a gallon of water and the promise of one of Lucy's concoctions to soothe his stomach, Gus survived the chili tasting. It had to be one of the best performances of his life.

Chapter 41

Lucy pulled out the book from the shelf to reveal the Snake Pit's secret entrance. She rolled in her carrying case of Lust and Serenity products. Extras to sell at her pop-up during the Valentine's Day party. She checked her phone for any updates from Gus.

"There you are!" Kat took the suitcase from her hands. "This is your night, so you need to schmooze. Dinner's in an hour. Where's Gus?"

"He'll be here later. He had to go to the airport with Peter. They're dropping off Sara."

"Hallelujah." Kat pumped her fists in the air. "Ding dong, the witch is dead."

Lucy smiled and glanced around the speakeasy. The tables were covered with red linens, each topped with a Tiffany lamp. Strings of heart-shaped fairy lights floated above. And the licorice chandelier, Lucy's pride and joy, sparkled above the bar. She'd been able to take it to Julie for repairs when they met for the first time in Green Bay without any bars or security.

"This is beautiful. Have I told you how much I love you for doing this for me? I have to make it up to you. Organizing a proxy opening and pop-up is an ace idea."

"Girl, you've thanked me daily. There will be a time when I have to call in a favor," Kat joked menacingly. "The speakeasy chef planned a prix fixe dinner tonight, so the food won't detract from your scents."

"No onion soup, I take it?" Lucy raced to keep up with Kat without tripping on her heels. The black pumps were more comfortable than her last heels, although she'd always prefer her garden clogs. Her new black sheath dress was light as a feather compared to wearing the hot, over-beaded Gatsby dress the other day. "Where's Michael?"

"In the kitchen cooking. He's making his winning curry chili." Kat shook her head, disgusted. "My g'ma's recipe did not deserve third place. I swear, you three judges played favorites."

"Your chili made it into *my* top three. Gus has a special interest in the curry."

"Still smarts, girl," Kat said.

"Hey, Bob." Lucy set her pink handbag on the bar and scanned the few people who had begun to gather. "Thanks for volunteering tonight."

"Wouldn't miss it for the world. Stan is around—he's talking to your friend who designed the sleigh bed. They had to take it apart to get it in here, so he's giving her a hand putting it back together."

"Check this out." Kat handed her a menu engraved on linen paper. "The appetizer is a beet, goat cheese, and asparagus salad. The entrée is lemongrass risotto. They're delicious dishes with or without using your nose, and they will satisfy the foodies in the crowd."

Lucy couldn't concentrate on the food choices. She kept wondering about Gus and had an uneasy feeling. Would he fly home to Malibu for a run on the beach?

Settle down. Her nerves were messing with her head. *Or was it the chakra?*

"Maddie called Rob, so he'll be here with his bigwig lawyer

friends. Claire and Sinjin are putting the finishing touches on the sleigh bed." Kat pointed to the TVs behind the bar. "Later, we'll start the videos of your love testimonials."

"I have them cued up," Bob said. "I'm your AV guy, so just give me the go-ahead."

"Will do, thanks." Lucy forced her mind to stay in the present.

"There's a group of people," Kat said, "not sure who, coming in from Kohler. From Sweet Tomato or the Immigrant Room? I don't know how many, but the manager arranged several tables to accommodate."

"Look who's arrived." Michael came up to her. "Ms. Emma. Is it okay if Lewis is here? He's in the kitchen. I want to make sure four-legged friends are welcome."

"Dang, yes. I can't wait to pet my fishing compadre."

"How did it go with the electrician today?" Michael gave Kat a quick hug.

"The guy was like a *wire-whisperer.* He evaluated the damage and focused on the utility room. It will take a couple of weeks to fix it. I think—" Lucy crossed her fingers. "—I'll be able to open my doors by my birthday. Not a bad gift."

"Fantastic." Michael gave her a high five.

The dimly lit speakeasy was the perfect spot for lovers to rendezvous, speak in hushed tones, and whisper lusty ideas into each other's ears. "I wish I'd had time to make more Lust."

"Don't worry about your quantities. Not needed," Kat said. "Maddie created a list of pics with your products and QR codes, laminated them in the usual Maddie fashion, and set one on every table. All people need to do is take a picture with their phone and order. Can you handle it?"

"Hells, yes. Thankfully, I hired an intern."

"And I'll be passing these out with every drink." Bob set down a coaster embossed with the Wicks logo. "Aren't they sweet?"

"This is fantastic," Lucy said, swallowing down a swell of tears. "I feel so blessed to have another family. Baileys is my home."

A man dressed in a pinstriped black suit came up to her. "Ms. Maxwell?"

"Yes, is something wrong?"

"No, miss. I'm on security detail for several guests. He opened his suit coat and showed off a pinstripe vest and gold pocket watch. "All right if I dressed for the occasion?"

"Not a problem. Who are you guarding?"

"Can't say." He flipped the watch open. "In thirty minutes, my partner will be escorting them inside. I need to check where they'll be seated."

"I can show you," Kat offered, leaving with the G-man.

"This is a star-studded event," Michael said. "Any other celebrities coming?"

"Quite a few. Kayla, the makeup artist, is coming with her boo. I found out he's one of the Chrises."

"Huh?" Michael asked Bob for a soda. "What's a Chris?"

"Either Chris Pine, Evans, Hemsworth, or Pratt."

"Hemsworth? Thor?" Michael furrowed his brow, then smiled. "Oh, I get it."

"Since you're a hero already," Lucy said, "and a fireman, you should know about all the Hollywood heroes."

"Which one is coming with Kayla?"

"She wouldn't tell me." Lucy sipped her drink. "Then the other co-stars on *Raven House* will be coming since it's a break from filming, and it's Valentine's Day, so they're coming with their significant others. Alexandra is bringing a plus-one. Her name is Emily, I believe."

"Who is going to be your date?"

"What? Who?" Lucy stammered. "I don't have a…"

"Gus? Where is the FHW?" Michael laughed. "Can't tell me the Hollywood star doesn't have it bad for you."

"He's at the airport and will show up eventually. Probably got caught in traffic, or paparazzi stopped him."

Michael grabbed his soda. "Did our testimonial look okay?"

"Yes, you and Kat did a great job. Thank you for sharing your love story. I enjoyed your bit about giving up beer for her."

"Worth it." He lifted his glass. "Now, I'm going to find Kat."

Her nerves quivered as more guests started to arrive. Originally, she'd wanted to make a speech and then decided to let the testimonials do the talking for her. Love stories were more compelling.

Her heart skipped when she caught sight of a ginger-headed man coming around the corner, then realized it was Sinjin with Claire.

"People are oohing and aahing over the sleigh bed." Claire gave her a hug. "They're taking pics and posting it with #serenityrules and #purplevibes."

All three of their jaws dropped as Kayla approached them with her Chris.

"Go," Claire said, shoving an elbow into her ribcage.

Lucy swallowed down her sheer awe at the beauty of the Hollywood couple and led them to a corner of the speakeasy. While she arranged her phone on her tripod, the two love bunnies giggled and wrapped their arms around each other on the leather sofa.

"Ready?" Lucy asked.

They both nodded, looking completely smitten.

"One question. What was the moment you fell in love?"

While listening to their story, Lucy kept smiling. She felt like a cheeky cupid. "Perfect, you two. I'm going to send this to the AV guy. Thank you. Go eat, have a drink, and be merry." She gathered her belongings and rushed off to get this latest testimonial finished. At the corner of the bar, she went to work and made sure the video looked and sounded okay, and then she sent it to Bob.

The bland and basic question produced the best results. Lucy was always tickled when couples figured it out and confessed that one moment. It was usually less than a second before their hearts melted into one another's.

As the crowd filled the Snake Pit, Lucy took a quick break to the ladies' room. She adjusted her dress and made sure her makeup hadn't faded. A lot of pictures were going to be taken tonight. A message from Gus popped up on her phone, and her heart started pounding.

Finally.

Where are you?

When she strode out of the bathroom, two adorable dogs were sitting with their person in the hallway, one corgi and the other a golden-haired retriever.

"Meet Humphrey and Bogart." Gus tugged on their leashes, and then the three approached her. Neither dog barked nor whined.

"Is this why you were at the airport all day?" She crouched down to pet them. "For a second, I thought you had hopped on a plane and jetted back to Malibu for a run on the beach."

"No way. It was these two. Their flight was late." Gus caressed her back, then nuzzled and kissed her neck. "I'm loving Baileys, and running along the shore of Lake Michigan is on my to-do list."

"To-do list?" Firefly feelies sizzled inside her.

He scratched the corgi's neck. "I hope you're okay with a few more flatmates because I bought the house from George."

"On Kangaroo Lake?" Her heart pounded so hard she didn't trust her hearing. "And the greenhouse?"

He took her hand and pressed it against his chest. "You can rip up your rental lease. I now own the house. We can live in it together with Humphrey and Bogart. Only if you want, of course. I would still like to take you to Malibu for your birthday, though."

She inhaled his magnetic scent of cherries and bergamot and relished the joy flooding through her. "Sure, yeah. After my opening though, and we go by train."

"Absolutely. Happy Saint Valentine's Day," he whispered and slid his hand across her waist. "I promise I won't let the dogs eat any of your pivotal ingredients."

Gus tangled his hand with hers, and little sparks of joy heated her up.

"One thing." Lucy nervously tapped one toe behind her other heel. "I filmed Kayla and Chris's love testimonial."

"He's here? Fantastic."

She shook her head. "Yes, but what I'm trying to ask you... what was the moment for you? This is strictly for Wicks & Balms. When did you, I mean...if you have..."

"Fall in love with you?" Gus smiled.

"Well?"

"The lighthouse."

"I did apply a lot of layers of Serenity on your neck. You were stressed, though, and needed to relax."

"No, not that time." He held her hand. "When we were bombarded by the paparazzi, and you caught the cheese hat. I remember perfectly how relieved I was when you caught it. It took me a while to realize it wasn't about the hat but all about my heart."

She pulled him in for a kiss, and Gus held up his hand. "Don't tempt me. It's your turn."

"Last October," she said immediately.

He frowned. "But I hadn't even arrived?"

"Oh, I thought you meant Baileys. I know I fell in love the moment I walked down Main Street."

"Ha, ha. Everyone who stops by falls for this town." He bumped against her shoulder. "Fess up."

"Okay." She closed her eyes. The moment most definitely or might have been when they had first met. But love at first sight was unrealistic and not good for her business. And her head had to catch up with her heart.

"When I asked you about the rose sachet in front of everyone. You listened to the question intensely and answered it with complete sincerity. Not a smirk to be seen. That was the moment.

You took me seriously and believed in me. I knew in my heart I could trust you."

Lucy took hold of a leash and twined her other fingers with Gus's. They strolled back into the speakeasy. As soon as the cameras started clicking and flashing, the dogs ran around, tying their legs together with the leashes.

Laughing, Lucy and Gus fell against one another and kissed. They made it a leisurely kiss to satisfy the paparazzi, and then it heated up fast. It didn't matter. Time to let everyone know the blissful truth. They were a match made in heaven...Baileys.

Lucy & Gus in Summer

Taking a day off from the shop to enjoy the July heat, Lucy rubbed a lavender leaf on her temple and checked her phone. Gus had sent his acceptance speech. He'd written it out in a matter of hours right after his Emmy nomination was announced: **Gus Reid, Lead Actor in a Mini Drama—Raven House.**

The Universe had Gus's back, so composing his list of thanks early wasn't premature. She smelled victory at the Emmy Awards come September. And she couldn't wait to be seated beside him at the ceremony in LA.

Lucy plucked another flower off one of the new lavender plants in the backyard. Out on the lake, Gus and Michael were fishing. Only their baseball caps hovered over the edge of the aluminum rowboat. She wondered if they were sleeping. Except Lewis barked, and then Humphry and Bogart, and the two men popped their heads up for a look.

Kat, *woman-ing* the barbeque, shook her head. "They better bring in a couple of fresh fish to go with my grilled corn. These cobs are going to be tasty with my paprika dressing."

Lucy read the speech.

Walk on Stage

Gus Reid

Thank you to the Academy for this esteemed award. I want to take a moment to say cheers to my dad, George. And my mum. (Pump statue skyward)

And brothers Sinjin and Rob. Thank you, Peter Boden, for directing me to reach for higher standards unknown to me. And casting me in a role without any hooch. (Tap chip)
To my good friends in Baileys Harbor — I'll always be here for you.
This can be an ugly, painful business, but the stories we tell make people laugh, cry, and think. And think we must. Our minds and mental health leave ratings in the dust. We must take time to listen. People operate smoothly while living in pain and fear. We must make strides to care for ourselves and thrive. Under your chairs, find my gift to you all. There's a vial of oil. Lust. It works better than a mood ring. It'll give you hope.
(Look at camera) I love you, Lucy.
Fade Out.

"Look! I caught one!" Gus hollered, swinging a fish off the line.

"Congrats!" she shouted, then went back to work filling the basket with as many lavender roots as it would hold. Her mom would appreciate the new plantings. Lucy had taught the women in the rehab facility how to make essential oil, so their garden had to have a hearty supply.

She'd gone to Green Bay every Sunday. Occasionally, SJ joined, and the three of them worked in the garden. And Julie always rubbed Lucy's nose in the fact that she'd been right. Lucy and Gus were meant to be together.

Her decision to expand the shop had paid off. The renovation money was more than adequate to cover reconstruction costs, so she added a greenhouse on the back patio to grow hard-to-find ingredients. Growing blood oranges had been a fun challenge.

When Wicks opened in March, all her scents had sold like hotcakes. The latest neroli scent, Lush, started selling as much as Lust. Lucy's stock of Madly in Love and Serenity constantly competed for second and third place.

She had earned her *Emma* reputation in Baileys and beyond. New matches were always coming her way. Because of Gus, friends, and family, Lucy had the joyful job of following her nose and mixing up new love concoctions.

The End

$Love$

"Love has nothing to do with what you are expecting to get–only
with what you are expecting to give–which is everything."
– Katharine Hepburn

Acknowledgments

To Sense a Passion started as *Scent of a Kiss,* turned into *When Lucy Met Gus,* and then for a short time was titled *Love Concoctions.* Each name has a brief history which resonates within the pages. In truth, I chose *To Sense a Passion* because the rhythm of the words echoed *To Catch a Thief.* A movie that has been ever-present in my mind and where my love for romantic capers sprouted.

To get this book into the hands of readers, it took a treacherous winding path that almost led off a cliff. There were times I wanted to chuck it into Lake Michigan. However, with each stumble and reset, the story became better.

My steadfast critique partner Carla Luna Cullen kept me focused and her spice expertise is truly appreciated. Carla's endless words of encouragement picked me up at the lowest points.

Jennifer Rupp aka Jennifer Trethewey was a superfan of my work before I even knew what a superfan meant.

To my friends/sisters/groupies: Kathy, Jill, Rachael, Swati, Kristen, Lisa, Sheila, and Bryn. Thanks for making me feel like a rock star.

All of the members, past and present, of Red Oak Writing and our fearless leader Kim Suhr. Every round table meeting has developed my stories and strengthened my craft.

When my friend Lesley took a chance and edited my roughest of drafts, I knew this story had a life. Then the lovely agent Ann Leslie Tuttle gushed over the manuscript. With her editorial assistance, Gus and Lucy's story blossomed.

To the whole Penske family with your stash of Avon lotions

and deodorants. You know who you are. I'm so lucky to be part of this loving and amazing family.

My kids and husband have always had my back and made it impossible to fall.

Love you all to the moon and back!

About the Author

Audrey Lynden writes contemporary romances and sets them in her beautiful home state of Wisconsin. There are always fun happenings, interesting histories and quirky traditions that occur in the many charming towns across the state. They happily find their way into her stories.

As a one-time journalist, she's inclined to keep up with the news, but dives deep into celebrity gossip to escape. She has a love for magazine subscriptions because they drop in the mailbox like Christmas gifts. Flipping through the pages, she always finds nuggets for her novels.

Every winter she binges all seasons of *Brooklyn Nine-Nine*.

For sneak peeks and giveaways, sign up for Audrey Lynden's newsletter:
www.audreylynden.com

www.ingramcontent.com/pod-product-compliance
Lightning Source LLC
Chambersburg PA
CBHW030937120726
47906CB00002B/604